List, Ye Landsmen
A Romance

William Clark Russell

Cease, rude Boreas, blustering railer!
　List, ye landsmen all, to me;
Messmates, hear a brother sailor
　Sing the dangers of the sea.

From *The Storm* by
George Alexander Stevens (1710–80)

Publisher's Note

This book contains words that are offensive. The book was first published in 1892 when such language was not thought of as being unacceptable. However, rather than censor or bowdlerize the book we have reproduced it in full.

© Typographical arrangement and "About the Author" section are copyright of Solis Press

First published in 1892; released as an ebook in 2012

All rights reserved. No part of this publication may be reproduced, stored in a retrieval system, or transmitted, in any form or by any means, electronic, mechanical, photocopying, recording or otherwise, except as permitted by the UK Copyright, Designs and Patents Act 1988, without the prior permission of the publisher.

ISBN: 978-1-907947-53-7

Published by Solis Press, PO Box 482, Tunbridge Wells TN2 9QT, Kent, England

Web: http://www.solispress.com

Twitter: @SolisPress

Contents

	Publisher's Note	2
Chapter I	Arrive in the Downs	5
Chapter II	I Visit my Uncle at Deal	13
Chapter III	The Gibbet	21
Chapter IV	I Escape from the Press	29
Chapter V	Captain Michael Greaves of the *Black Watch*	36
Chapter VI	I View the Brig	44
Chapter VII	A Strange Story	53
Chapter VIII	A Startling Proposal	62
Chapter IX	I Fight Van Laar	70
Chapter X	We Tranship Van Laar	80
Chapter XI	The *Rebecca*	92
Chapter XII	The Round Robin	106
Chapter XIII	A Midnight Scare	118
Chapter XIV	I Send My Letter	130
Chapter XV	The White Water	140
Chapter XVI	Greaves' Island	151
Chapter XVII	The Ship in the Cave	161
Chapter XVIII	We Tranship the Dollars	172
Chapter XIX	Off the Island	185
Chapter XX	We Start For Home	199
Chapter XXI	A Fight	211

Chapter XXII	Greaves Sickens	225
Chapter XXIII	The Whaler	237
Chapter XXIV	A Sailor's Will	248
Chapter XXV	Aurora Entertains Us	264
Chapter XXVI	A Tragic Shift of Course	277
Chapter XXVII	Bol's Ruse	291
Chapter XXVIII	I Scheme	305
Chapter XXIX	Amsterdam Island	318
Chapter XXX	My Scheme	329
Chapter XXXI	A Quaker Skipper	343
Chapter XXXII	Mynheer Tulp	359
About the Author		375
Contemporary Reviews of *List, Ye Landsmen!*		378
Also Available from Solis Press		380

Chapter I.
I Arrive in the Downs

SAILORS visit many fine countries; but there is none – not the very finest – that delights them more than the coast of their own native land when they sight it after a long voyage. The flattest piece of treeless English shore – such a melancholy, sandy, muddy waste, say, as that which the River Stour winds greasily and slimily through past Sandwich, into the salt, green, sparkling waters of the Small Downs – the English sailor will look at with a thirstier and sharper pleasure than ever could be excited in him by the most majestic and splendid scenery abroad.

Thus in effect thought I, as I stood upon the quarter-deck of the *Royal Brunswicker*, viewing the noble elevation of the white South Foreland off which the ship was then leisurely rolling as she flapped her way to the Downs with her yards squared to the weak westerly breeze; for – to take you into my confidence at once – this part of the coast of old England I had the best of all reasons for loving. First of all, I was born at Folkestone; next, on losing my parents, I was taken charge of by a maternal uncle, Captain Joseph Round, whose house stood on the road between Sandwich and Deal; and then, when I first went to sea, I was bound apprentice to a master sailing out of Dover Harbour; so that this range of coast had peculiar associations for me. Consider. It comprised the sum of my boyish, and of most, therefore, of my happiest, memories; indeed, I could not gaze long at those terraces of chalk, with their green slopes of down on top, and with clusters of houses between sparkling like frost, and many a lozenge-shaped window glancing back the light of the sun with the clear, sharp gleam of the diamond, without recollection stealing in a moisture into my eyes.

The ship was the *Royal Brunswicker*. I was her first mate. The name of her master was Spalding; mine William Fielding. Captain Spalding had married a relative of my mother's. He was a north-countryman, and had sailed for many years from the Tyne and from the Wear; but two years before the date of this story – that is to say, in the middle of the year 1812 – he had been offered the command of the *Royal Brunswicker*, a small, cosy, lubberly, full-rigged ship of 490 tons, belonging to the Port of London. I was stopping at Deal with my uncle at that time, and heard that Captain Spalding – but I forget how the news of such a thing reached me at Deal – was in want of a second mate. I applied for the post, and, on the merits of my relationship with the captain's wife, to say no more, I obtained the appointment.

We sailed away in the beginning of September 1812, bound to the east coast of South America. Before we were up with the Line the mate – a sober, grey-haired, God-fearing Scotsman – died, and I took his post and served as mate during the rest of the voyage. We called at several ports, receiving and discharging cargo, and then headed for Kingston, Jamaica, whence, having filled up flush to the hatches, we proceeded to England in a fleet of forty sail, convoyed by a two-decker, a couple of frigates, and some smaller ships of the King. But in latitude twenty degrees north a hurricane of wind broke us up. Every ship looked to herself. We, with top-gallant masts on deck, squared away under bare poles, and drove for three days bow under in foam, the seas meeting in slinging sheets of living green upon the forecastle. We prayed to God not to lose sight of us, and kept the chain-pumps going, and every hour a dram of red rum was served out to the hearts; and there was nothing to do but to steer, and pump, and swear, and hope.

Well, the gale broke, and the amazing rush of the wings of seas sank into a filthy, staggering sloppiness of broken, rugged surge, amidst which we tumbled with hideous discomfort for another two days, so straining that we would look over the side thinking to behold the water full of tree-nails and planks of bottom sheathing. But the *Royal Brunswicker* was built to swim. All the honesty of the slow, patient, laborious shipwright of her time lived in every fibre of her as a noble conscience in a good man. When the weather at last enabled us to make sail and proceed from a meridian of longitude many degrees west of the point where we had parted company with the convoy, we found the ship staunch as she had been at the hour of her birth.

All the water she had taken in had tumbled into her from above. What say ye to this, ye sailors of the paddle and the screw? We made the rest of the passage alone, cracking on with the old bucket to recover lost time, and keeping a bright lookout for anything that might betoken an enemy's ship.

And now on the afternoon of 19 September, in the year of God 1814, the *Royal Brunswicker* was off the South Foreland, languidly flapping with square yards before a light westerly breeze into the Downs that lay broad under her bows, crowded with shipping.

The hour was about three. A small trickle of tide was working eastward, and upon that we floated along, more helped by the fast failing run of the stream than by the wind; but there would be dead water very soon, and then a fast gathering and presently a rushing set to the westward, and I heard Captain Spalding whistle low as he stood on the starboard quarter, sending his gaze aloft over the canvas, and looking at the slipping which had opened upon us as the South Foreland drew away, seeking with his slow, cold blue north-country eye for a comfortable spot in which to bring up.

The coast of France lay, for all its whiteness, in a pale orange streak upon the edge of the sea, where it seemed to hover as though it were some sunny exhalation in process of being drawn up and absorbed by the sun that was shining with September brightness in the southwest sky. But over that smudge of orange-coloured land slept a roll of massive white clouds, the thunder-fashioned heads of them a few degrees high, and clouds of a like kind rested in vast shapeless bulks of tufted heaped-up vapour – very cordilleras of clouds – on the ice-smooth edge of the water in the northeast. The sea streamed in thin ripples out of the west; and upon the light movement running through it the smaller of the vessels at anchor in the Downs were lazily flourishing their naked spars. Captain Spalding called to me.

"I shall bring up, Bill," said he; for Bill was the familiar name he gave me when we were alone, though it was always "Mr. Fielding" in the hearing of the men. "I shall bring up, Bill," said he. "I don't quite make out yet what the weather's going to prove. See those clouds? Who's to tell what such appearances signify in these waters? But the westerly wind's failing. There's nothing coming out astern that's going to help us," and he looked at the horizon that way, "I shall bring up."

I was mighty pleased to hear this, though indeed I had expected it: for now might I hope to get leave to pay my uncle, Captain Joseph Round, a visit for a few hours. I believe Spalding saw what was passing in my mind; he gazed at the land and then round upon the sea, and fell a-whistling again in a small note, shaking his head. I reckoned that I could not do better than ask leave at once, and said:

"As you intend to bring up, I hope you'll allow me to go ashore for a few hours to see how Uncle Joe does. He'd not forgive me for failing to visit him should he hear that the *Royal Brunswicker* had anchored almost abreast of his dwelling-place, and that I had missed your consent simply for not seeking it."

He sniffed and looked suspiciously about him awhile, and answered:

"Don't ask me for leave until the anchor's down and the ship's snug, and the weather's put on some such a face as a man may read."

"Ay, ay, sir," said I.

"Bill," said he, "go forward now and see all clear for bringing up. There's a good berth some cables' length past that frigate yonder – betwixt her and the pink there."

As I was walking forward a man came clumsily sprawling over the side on to the deck. His face was purple; he wore a hair cap, a red shawl round his throat, and a jersey. I peered over the rail and saw a small Deal galley hooked alongside, with two men in her.

"Going to bring-up, sir?" said the man.

"Yes," I answered.

"Where are ye bound to?"

"To London."

"Want a pilot?"

"You'll find the captain aft there," said I. "You are from Deal, I suppose?"

"Whoy, yes."

"Have you ever heard of Captain Joseph Round?"

"Ever heard of Cap'n Joseph Round?" echoed the man. "Whoy, ye might as well ask me if I've ever heard o' Deal beach."

"Is he living?"

"There's ne'er a fish a-swimming under this here keel that's more living."

"And he's well, I hope?"

"It's going to be a bad job when old Cap'n Round falls ill. Old Cap'n Round's one of them gents as never knows what it is to have so much as a spasm; though when the likes of them *are* took bad, it's common-loy good-noight," said he with an emphatic nod.

"I don't reckon your services will be required," said I; "but I may be wanting to go ashore after we've brought up, and you can keep your eye upon this ship if you like."

"Thank ye, sir. Loike to see a paper, sir?" and here the man thrust his hand under his jersey and pulled down a tattered newspaper a few weeks old, gloomy with beer stains and thumb marks; but news, even a few weeks old, must needs be very fresh news to me after an absence of two years, during which I had caught but a few idle and ancient whispers of what was happening at home. I thanked the man, put the newspaper in my pocket, meaning to look at it when I should have leisure, and stepped on to the forecastle, where I stood staring about me awaiting orders from the captain.

The scene on the water was very grand. There were, probably, two hundred sail of wind-bound ships at anchor. Every kind of rig, I think, was there, from the tall spars of the British frigate down to the little, squab, apple-bowed, wallowing hoy. I am writing this in the year 1849. A great change in shipping has happened since 1814. You have men-of-war now with funnels and paddle-wheels; steam has shortened the passage to India from four months to two months and a half, which is truly wonderful. Nay, the Atlantic has been crossed in three weeks, and I may yet live to see the day when the run from Liverpool to New York shall not exceed a fortnight. But the change since 1814 is not in steam only. Many are the structural alterations. Ships I will not deny have gained in speed and convenience; but they have lost in beauty. They are no longer romantic, and picturesque, and quaint. No; ships are no longer the gay, the shining, the castellated, the spacious-winged fabrics of my young days.

Could you possess the memory of the scene of Downs, as it showed on that September afternoon from the forecastle of the *Royal Brunswicker*, you would share in the affectionate enthusiasm, the delight and the regret with which I recur to it. How am I to express the light, the life, the colour of the picture; the fiery flashing of glossy, low, black, wet sides, softly stooping upon the silken heave of the sea; the gleam of storied windows in tall sterns; the radiance of giltwork on the quarter galleries of big West and East Indiamen, straining motionless at their hempen cable and lifting star-like trucks to the altitude of the mastheads of a line-of-battle ship! I see again the long, low, piratic-looking schooner. Her brand-new metal sheathing rises like a strong light, flowing upward out of the water on which she rests to within a strake or two of her covering board. I see the handsome brig with a rake of her lower masts aft and topgallant masts stayed into a scarce perceptible curve forward. There is a short grin of guns along the waist and a brilliant brass-piece pivoted on her forecastle; she is a trader bound to the west coast of Africa. She will be making the Middle Passage anon; but she will take care to furnish no warrant for suspicion while she flies the peaceful commercial flag on this side the Guinea parallels. And I see also the snug old snow, of a beam expanded into the proportions of a Dutchman's stern, huge pieces of fresh beef slung over the taffrail, a boat triced up to the forestay, and a tiny boy swinging, knife in hand, at the mast.

But what I most clearly see is the fine English frigate motionless in the heart of the forest of shipping that stretches away to right and left of her. With what exquisite precision are her yards braced! How admirably furled is every sail, and how finely managed each cone-shaped bunt! There is no superfluous rigging to thicken her gear. Whatever is not wanted is removed. Her long pennant floats languidly down the topgallant mast, and at her gaff-end ripples the flag of Great Britain – the fighting flag of the State; the flag that, by the victory at Trafalgar but a few years since, was hauled to the very masthead of the world, with such stout hearts still left, in this year of God 1814, to guard the hilliards, that one cannot recall their names without a glow of pride coming into the cheek and a deeper beat entering every pulse.

Ah! thought I, as I gazed at the fine frigate, delighting with appreciative nautical eye in the hundred points of exquisite equipment which express the perfect discipline of the sea; admiring the white line of hammocks which crowned the grim, silent, muzzled tier of ordnance, the spot of red that denoted a marine, the agility of some fellows in her forerigging – Heavens! how different from the slow and cumbersome sprawling of the heavily-breeched merchant Jack! Ah! thought I, while I kept my eyes bent in admiration upon the frigate, who would not rather be the first lieutenant of such a craft as that than the first mate of such an old wagon as this? And yet I don't know, thought I, keeping my eyes fastened upon the frigate. It is good to be a sailor to begin with – best sailor, best man, spite of uniforms and titles and the colour of the flag he serves under. And which service produces the best sailor, I wonder? And here I told over to myself a number of names of seamen who had risen to great, and some of them to glorious, eminence in the Royal Navy, all of whom had served in the beginning of their years in the merchant service; and then I also thought to myself, who sees most of the real work – the hard, heavy, perilous work of the ocean – the man-of-warsman or the merchantman? And I could not but smile as I looked from that trim and lovely frigate to our own sea-beaten hooker, and from the few lively hearties of the man-of-war visible upon her decks, to the weather-stained, round-backed men of our crew, who were hanging about waiting for the captain to sing out orders. No, I could not help smiling.

But while I smiled a volley of orders was suddenly fired off by Captain Spalding from the quarter-deck, and in an instant I was singing out too, and the crew were hauling upon the ropes, shortening sail.

We floated to the spot that Spalding had singled out with his eye, the Deal boat towing alongside, with the fellow that had boarded us inside of her, for the captain had promptly motioned him overboard on his stepping aft, and then the anchor was let go, and the sails rolled up. It was just then sunset. The frigate fired a gun; down fluttered her ensign, and a sort of tremble of colour seemed to run through the forests of masts as every vessel, big and little, in response to the sullen clap of thunder from the frigate's side, hauled down her flag. A stark calm had fallen, heavy masses of electric cloud were lifting slowly east and south, but they were to my mind a summer countenance. Methought I had used the sea long enough to know wind by my sight and smell without hearing or feeling it; and I was cocksure that those clouds signified nothing more than a storm or two – as landsmen would call it – a small local matter of lightning and thunder, with no air to notice, and a silent night of stars to follow.

When I had attended to all that required being seen to by me acting as the mate of the ship, I went aft to Captain Spalding, who was walking the deck alone, smoking a pipe, and said to him, "It's going to be a fine night."

"I believe you are right," said he, gazing into the dusk of the evening, amid which the near shipping looked pale, and the more distant craft dark and swollen.

"Are you going ashore?" said I.

"No," he answered. "There's nothing at Deal to call me ashore. I know Deal and I don't love it. Bill."

"I should like to shake Uncle Joe by the hand," said I.

"So you shall," said he. "But see here, my lad, you must keep a bright lookout on the weather. If ever you're to keep your weather eye lifting 'tis whilst you are visiting Uncle Joe, for should there come a slant of wind, I'm off! there'll be no stopping to send ashore to let you know that I'm going."

"Right you are," cried I heartily, "a bright lookout shall be kept. But there'll be no slant of wind this night – a little thunder, but no wind," said I, catching as I spoke the dim sheen of distant lightning coming and going in a winking sort of way upon the mass of stuff that overhung the coast of France.

I stepped below into my cabin to change my clothes. It will not be supposed that my slender wardrobe showed very handsomely after two years of hard wear. I put on the best garments I had, a shaggy pilot coat, with large horn buttons, and a velvet waistcoat, and on my head I seated a round hat with a small quantity of ribbon floating down abaft it, so that on the whole my appearance was rather that of a respectable forecastle hand than that of the chief mate of a ship.

Here whilst I am brushing my hair before a bit of broken looking glass in my cabin let me give you in a few sentences a description of myself. And first of all, having been born in the year 1790, I was aged twenty-four, but looked a man of thirty, owing to the many years I had passed at sea and the rough life of the calling. I was about five foot eleven in height, shouldered and chested in proportion, very strong on my legs, which were slightly curved into a kind of easy bowling, rolling air by the ceaseless slanting of decks under me; in short taking me altogether you would fairly have termed me at that age of twenty-four a fine young fellow. I was fair, with dark reddish hair and dark blue eyes, which the girls sometimes called violet; my cheeks and chin were smooth shaven, according to the practice of those times; my teeth very good, white, and even; my nose straight, shapely, and proper, but in my throat and neck I was something heavy. Such was I, William Fielding, at the age of twenty-four. I write without vanity. God knows it is too late for vanity! Suppose a ghost capable of thinking: figure it musing upon the ashes of the body it had occupied – ashes mouldering and infragrant in a clay-rotted coffin twelve foot deep.

Even as such a ghost might muse, so write I of my youth.

I pocketed the boatman's newspaper, lest the cabin servant, coming into my cabin, should espy and carry it away. And I also put in my pocket some trifles which I had purchased as curios at one or another of the ports we had visited, and then going on deck I hailed the boat that had been keeping close to us, but that was now lying alongside a brig some little distance away, and bade the fellows put me ashore.

Sheet lightning was playing round the sea, but stars in plenty were shining over our mastheads; the water was very smooth; I did not feel the lightest movement of air. Forward on our ship a man was playing on the fiddle, and a group of seamen in lounging attitudes were listening to him. I also heard the voice of a man singing on the vessel lying astern of us: but all was hushed aboard the frigate; the white lines of her stowed canvas ruled the stars in pallid streaks as though snow lay upon the yards; no light showed aboard of her; she lay grim, hushed, big in the dusk with a suggestion of expectancy in the dominating sheer of her bows and in the hearkening steeve of her bowsprit, as though steed-like she was listening with cocked ears and wide nostrils; and yet, dark as it was, you would have known her for a British man-of-war, spite of the adjacency of some East and West Indiamen which looked in the gloom to float nearly as tall as she.

"It's a quarter to eight, Bill," exclaimed Captain Spalding, going to the companion way and standing in it, while he spoke to me with one foot on the ladder. "You will remember to keep your weather eye lifting, my lad. At the first slant I get my anchor; so stand by. Ye'd better ask Uncle Joe to keep his window open, that you may smell what you can't see and hear what you can't smell. My respects to Uncle Joe. Tell him if I'm detained here tomorrow I may pay him a visit, unless he has a mind for a cut of Deal beef and a piece of ship's bread down in my cabin. Anyhow, my respects to him," and he vanished.

I dropped into the mizzen chains, got into the galley, and was rowed ashore.

Chapter II.
I Visit my Uncle at Deal

THE boat was swept to the beach, and I sprang on the shingle. I paid the men their charges, and paused a moment to realize the thrilling, inscrutable, memorable sensation which visits a man who, after a long absence, treads his native soil for the first time.

After the chocolate faces of the West, and the yellow faces of the East, and the copper-coloured faces of the South; after two years of mosquitoes, of cathedral-like forests, of spacious roasting bays, of sharks and alligators, and league-broad rivers, and songless birds angelically plumed, and endless miles of ocean; after – but I should need a volume to catalogue all that follows this *after* – after the *Royal Brunswicker*, in a word, how exquisite was my happiness on feeling the Deal shingle under my foot; how rejoiced was I to be in a land of white men and women, who spoke my own native tongue with its jolly, hearty, round, old Kentish accent, and who lived in a kingdom of roast beef and Welsh mutton and the best ales which were ever brewed in this world!

While I paused, full of happy thought, the men who had brought me ashore dragged their boat up the shingle. Two or three others joined them, and the little company rushed the boat up in thunder. They then went rolling silently into Beach Street and disappeared. I was struck by the absence of animation fore and aft the beach. Many luggers and galley-punts lay high and dry, but only here and there did I observe the figure of a man, and, as well as I could make out in the evening dusk, the figure was commonly that of an old man. Here and there also a few children were playing, and here and there at an open door stood a woman gossiping with another. But though I saw lights in the public houses, no sounds of singing, of voices growling in argument, of maudlin calls, such as had been familiar to my ear in old times, issued from the doors or windows. I was surprised by this apparent lifelessness. A fleet of two hundred sail in the Downs should have filled the little town with bustle and business, with riotous sailors and clamorous wenches, and a coming and going of boats.

There were two ways by which my uncle's house was to be reached – the one by the road, the other by the sand hills, a desolate waste of hummocky sand, stretching for some miles from the north end of Deal toward the town of Sandwich and the River Stour. I chose the road because I wanted to taste the country air, to sniff the aromas of the fields and the hedges as I marched along, and because I wished to put as much distance as the highway permitted between me and the sea. The sky overhead was clear; there was no moon as yet, but the stars shone in a showering of light, and there was much lightning, which glanced to the zenith and fell upon the white road I was stepping along; and now and again I caught a low hum of thunder – an odd, vibratory note, like the sound of an organ played in a church and heard at a distance on a still evening. The atmosphere was breathless, and I was mighty thankful; but sometimes I would catch myself whistling for an easterly wind, for I knew not from what quarter a breeze might come on such a still night, and if the first of it moved out of the south or west, then, even though my hands should be upon the knocker of my uncle's door, I must make a bolt of it to the beach or lose my ship.

My Uncle Joe's house was a sturdy, tidy structure of flint, massively roofed and fitted to outweather a century of hurricanes. He had designed and built it himself. It stood at about two miles from Deal, withdrawn from the road, snug, among a number of trees, elm and oak. Rooks cawed in those trees, and their black nests hung in them; and in winter the Channel gales, hoary with snow, shrieked through the hissing skeleton branches with a furious noise of tempest, that reminded Uncle Joe of being hove-to off the Horn.

He had been a sailor. Uncle Joe had been more than a sailor – he had been pilot and smuggler. He had commanded ships of eight hundred tons burthen, full of East Indian commodities, and he had commanded luggers of twenty tons burthen, deep with contraband goods, gunwale flush with teas, brandies, laces, tobacco and hollands. Uncle Joe had been a good friend to me when I was a lad and an orphan. He and his wife were as father and mother to me, and I loved them both with all the love that was in my heart. It was Uncle Joe who had educated me, who had bred me to the sea, who saw when I started on a voyage that I embarked with plenty of clothes in my chest and plenty of money in my pocket; and to Uncle Joe's influence it was that I looked for a valuable East or West Indian command in the next or the following year.

I pulled the house-bell and hammered with the knocker. It was dark among the trees; the house stood black, with a dim red square of window, where some crimson curtains shut out the lamplight. Until the door was opened I listened to the weather. All was hushed save the thunder. I could hear the faint, remote beat of the surf upon the shingle, that was all. Not a leaf rustled overhead; but though there was not more lightning, the thunder was more frequent down in the south, as though the clouds over France were blazing bravely.

A middle-aged man, clad somewhat after the manner of the longshoremen of those days – clearly a decayed or retired mariner – pulled open the door, and, as this was done, I heard my uncle call out:

"Is it Bill?"

"It is," said I, delighted to hear his voice; and I pushed past the sailor who held open the door.

My uncle came out of the parlour into the passage, looked up and down me a moment or two, and extending his hand, greeted me thus:

"Well, I'm junked!"

He then shook my hand at least a minute, and bidding me fling my cap on to a hall chair, he dragged me into the parlour – the snuggest room in world, as I have often thought; full of good paintings of ships and the sea, of valuable curiosities, and fine oak furniture.

Every age has faces of its own, countenances which exactly fit the civilization of the particular time they belong to. It is no question of the fashion of the beard or the wearing of the hair. There was a type of face in my young day which I rarely behold now, and I dare say the type which I am every day seeing will be as extinct fifty years hence as is the type that I recollect when I was a young man. How is this, and why is this? It matters not. It may be due to frequent new infusions of blood; to the modifications – do not call it the progress – of intellect; it may be due – but to whatever it may be due it is true; and equally true it is that my Uncle Joe had one of those faces – I may indeed say one of those heads – which as peculiarly belong to their time as the fashions of garments belong to theirs.

He was clean shaven; his temples were overshot; they set his little black eyes back deep, and his baldness, co-operating with these thatched and overhanging eaves, provided him with so broad a surface of forehead that he might have sat for the portrait of a great wit. My uncle had a wide and firm mouth; the lips were slightly blue: but this colour was not due to the use of ardent spirits – oh, no! A teetotaller he was *not*, but never would the mugs *he* emptied have changed the colour of his lips. They were blue because his heart was not strong, and the few who remember him know that he died of heart disease.

He was the jolliest, heartiest figure of a man that a convivial soul could yearn to embrace; a shape moulded by the ocean, as the Deal beach pebble is moulded by the ceaseless heave of the breakers. He thrust me into a capacious armchair and stood on rounded shanks, staring at me with his face flushed and working with pleasure.

"And how are you, uncle?"

"Well."

"And Aunt Elizabeth?"

"Well."

"And Bessie?"

"Well."

"Where are they?"

"Coming downstairs."

And this was true; a moment later my aunt and cousin entered – my aunt a grave, pale gentlewoman in a black gown, black being her only wear for these twenty years past, ever since the death of her only son at the age of four; my cousin a handsome, well-shaped girl of seventeen with cherry-ripe lips and large flashing black eyes, and abundance of dark hair with a tinge of rusty red upon it – they entered, I say, and they had fifty questions to ask, as I had. But in half an hour's time the greetings were over, and I was sitting at a most hospitably laden supper table, having satisfied myself, by going out of doors, that the night was quiet, that there was still no stir of wind, and that nothing more was happening roundabout than a vivid play of violet lightning low down in the sky, with frequent cracklings and groanings of distant thunder.

I was not surprised that Uncle Joe and his family had not heard of the arrival of the *Royal Brunswicker* in the Downs; though I had been somewhat astonished by his guessing it was I, when I knocked.

"So you're chief mate of the ship?" he exclaimed.

"I am."

"How has Spalding used ye, Bill?"

"Handsomely. As a father. I shall love Spalding till the end of my days, and until I get command I shall never wish to go afloat with another man."

"Well," said my uncle, "it is not every skipper, as you know, that would allow his first mate a run ashore, himself waiting aboard the while for a slant of wind to get his anchor. No. Don't let us forget the weather. Bess, my daisy, there's no call for Bill to keep all on looking out o' doors; get ye forth now and again and report any sigh of wind you may hear. I'll find out its quarter, and Bill shall not fail his captain."

"What's the news?" said I.

"News enough," he said; and I sat and listened to news, much of which was extraordinary.

I heard of the Yankees thrashing us by land and sea, of fierce and desperate fighting on the Canadian lakes, of the landing of the Prince of Orange in Holland, and of his being proclaimed King of the United Netherlands, of Murat proving a renegade and suing for peace with this country, of gallant seafights down Toulon way and in the Adriatic and elsewhere, of the investment of Bayonne by the British army, of the entry of the Allies into Paris, of peace between England and France, of Louis XVIII in the room of Bonaparte, and – which almost took my breath away – of Bonaparte himself at Elba, dethroned, his talons pared, his teeth drawn, but with his head still on his shoulders, and in full possession of his bloody reason.

"And so he was quietly shipped to Porto Ferraro," said I, "in a comfortable thirty-eight gun British frigate, instead of being hanged at the yardarm of that same craft."

"He is too splendid a character to hang," said my aunt mildly.

"Junked if I wouldn't make dog's meat of him," cried Uncle Joe.

"They should have hanged him," said I.

"They have hanged a better man instead," exclaimed my cousin Bess.

"A king?"

"No, Bill, he was not a king," said my uncle, "he was the master of a ship and part owner, a young chap, too – a mighty pity. They had him up at Sandwich on a charge of casting the vessel away. He was found guilty and hanged, and he's hanging now."

"Where does he hang?" said I.

"Down on the Sandhills."

"A time will come, I hope," said I, "when this beastly trick of beaconing the sea-coast, and the river's bank, and the highways with gibbets will have been mended. Spalding was telling me that up in his part of the country travelling has grown twice as far as it used to be, by the gibbets forcing people to go out of their way to avoid the sight of them."

"I am sorry for the hanged man," said my uncle, "but wilfully casting a ship away, Bill, is a fearful thing – so fearful that the gibbet at which I'd dangle the fellow that did it should be as high as the royal mast head of the craft he foundered! What d'ye think of that drop of rum?"

"Is that wind?" said my aunt.

"Thunder," said Uncle Joe.

Bess went to the house door: I followed. We stood listening; the noise was thunder; there was not a breath of air, but all the stars were gone. A sort of film of storm had drawn over them, and I guessed I was in for a drenching walk to the beach. But Lord! rain to a man whose lifetime is spent in the eye of the weather!

"Bess," said I, "you've grown a fine girl, d'ye know."

"No compliments, William, dear. I am going to be married."

"If I had known that before!" said I, kissing her now for the first time, for congratulation.

This was fresh news, and we talked about the coming son-in-law, who, to be sure, must be in the seafaring line too, for once inject salt water into the veins of a family, and it takes a power of posterity to flush the pipes clear.

"What's wrong with Deal town?" said I. "Is it the neighbourhood of the gibbet that damps the spirits of the place?"

"What d'ye mean, Bill?"

"Why, there's nothing stirring along the beach. There are some two hundred craft off the town and the beach is as though it were in mourning;

your luggers lie grim as a row of coffins, nothing moving amongst them but some shadow of old age – like old Jimmy Files, for example."

"It'll be the press," said my aunt,

"Ho!" said I. "Is the king short-handed once more?"

"There's not only what's called deficiency, but what's termed disaffection," said my uncle. "The vote this year was for a hundred and forty thousand Johnnys and Joeys. They vote, and Jack says be d—d to ye."

"Any men nabbed out of Deal?" said I.

"Five boatmen last month," answered Uncle Joe. "I should think they'd be glad to set them ashore wherever they be. Put a pressed Deal man into your forecastle and then fire your magazine."

"I'm a mate; they'll not take me," said I.

"There's been no press for some days that I've heard of," said my uncle, "but you'd better get to the beach by way of the sand hills. The Johnnys don't hunt rabbits. They beat the alleys out of Beach Street, and you hear of them Walmer way and down by the Dockyard."

He sat deep in an armchair, smoking a long clay pipe. His face shone, his little shining eyes followed the smoke that rose from his lips. His posture, his appearance as he sat with a stout leg across his knee and a shining silver buckle on his square-toed shoe, seemed to say: "What I've got is mine, and what I've got is enough. The Lord is good; and good too is this house and all that's in it." A small fire burnt briskly in the grate, and on the hob was a bright copper kettle with steam shooting from its split lip. The dance of the fire-flames ran feeble shadows through the steady radiance of the oil lamp, and the colours of the room were made warmer and richer by the delicate twinkling. My aunt knitted, and cousin Bess, with her chin in her hand, listened to the conversation. Upon the table was a large silver tray with glasses, decanters of rum and brandy, and silver bowl and ladle for the brewing of punch.

These things supplied a completing and satisfying detail of liberal and handsome comfort. What happiness, thought I, to settle down ashore in such a house as this, with as many thousands as would keep me going just as Uncle Joe is kept going! When are those fine times coming for me? thought I; and there now happening a pause in the talk, whilst my uncle, lifting the kettle off the hob, brewed with skilful hand a small quantity of rum punch – the most fragrant and supporting of hot drinks, and loved a great deal too well in my time by skippers and mates whose conscience blushed only in their noses – I pulled from my pocket the boatman's newspaper, and turned the sheet about, not reckoning, however, upon *now* coming across anything fresh.

"What have you there, William?" said Bess.

"A north country rag," said I, "some weeks old. The gift of a Geordie, no doubt, to the waterman who gave it to me."

Such news as it contained related largely to shipping. There was a column of items of maritime intelligence. My eye naturally dwelt upon this column, and I read some passages aloud. At last I came to this paragraph:

> A correspondent informs us that the brig *Black Watch*, 295 tons, built in 1806, by Mr. W. Dixon, of Sunderland, is fitting out in the Thames presumably for a privateering cruise. She is said to have been purchased by a gentleman of Amsterdam, but the person who goes in command of her is Captain Michael Greaves, who belongs to this town. If the owner be a Dutchman, as rumour asserts, it is not to be supposed that letters of marque will be issued.

"What do *you* say, uncle?" said I.

"I cannot tell. I know nothing about letters of marque, Bill. If she's furrin'-owned her capers can't be countenanced by our State, can 'ey?"

"No," said I.

I looked again at the paragraph.

"Michael Greaves – Michael Greaves." I seemed to know the name. I pondered, found I could get nothing out of memory, and turned my eye upon another part of the paper.

"Here is an account of the casting away of the *William and Jane*."

"That's the ship for whose murder her skipper is swinging on the sand hills," said my uncle.

I read the story – an old-world story, not infrequently repeated since. Do not we know it, Jack? A ship mysteriously leaks; the carpenter sounds the well, and his eyes are damned by the captain for hinting at a started butt; all hands sweat at the pumps; the water gains; the mate thinks the leak is in the fore-peak, and the master, who is intoxicated, stutters with blasphemies that the mischief is in the after-hold; the people leave in the boats: the derelict washes ashore, and is found with four auger holes in her bottom; the master is collared and charged. At the trial the carpenter states that the master borrowed an auger from him and forgot to return it. Master is damned by the evidence of the mate and a number of seamen; is condemned to be hanged by the neck, and is turned off on the Deal sand hills protesting his innocence.

"Why the Deal sand hills?" said I.

"As a warning to the coast," answered my uncle.

"And look again at the newspaper. The scuttling job was managed right abreast of these parts, behind the Good'ns. Oh, it's justice – it's justice!" and he handed me a glass of punch.

"Is it wind or rain?" exclaimed my aunt, lifting her forefinger.

"Rain," said my uncle – "a thunder squall. Ha!"

A sharp boom of thunder came from the direction of the sea. 'Twas like a ship testing her distance by throwing a shot. You found yourself hearkening for the broadside to follow. I looked at the clock and again went to the house door. The earth was sobbing and smoking under a fall of rain that came down straight like harp strings; the lightning touched each liquid line into blue crystal; the trees hissed to the deluge, and I stood listening for wind, but there was none.

"I'll wait till this shower thins," said I, "and then be off."

"It'll be a wet walk, William, I fear," said my aunt.

"It's a wet life all round, with us sailors," said I, extending my tumbler for another ladleful of punch, in obedience to an eloquent gesture on the part of my uncle.

It was midnight before they would let me go, and still there was no wind. I was well primed with grog, and felt light and jolly; had accepted an invitation to spend a month of my stay ashore down here at Sandwich; had listened with a countenance lighted up with smiles to Uncle Joe's "I'll warrant ye it shall go hard if I don't help you into command next year, my lad," pronounced with one eye closed, the other eye humid, and his face awork with punch and benevolence; then came some hearty hand-shaking, some still heartier "God-bless-ye's," and there being a pause outside, forth I walked, stepping high and something dancingly, the collar of my pea-coat to my ears, the round brim of my hat turned down to clear the scuppers for the next downpour.

Chapter III.
The Gibbet

THERE was plenty of lightning, some of the flashes near, and the sky overhead was soot. But the thunder was not constant. It growled at intervals afar, now and again burst at the distance of a mile, but without tropic noise. It seemed to me that the electric mess was silting away north, and that there would come a clear sky in the south presently, with a breeze from that quarter.

This being my notion, I stepped out vigorously, with a punch-inspired lift of my feet, as I made for the sand hills, singing a jolly sailor's song as I marched, but not thinking of the words I sang. No, nothing while I marched and sang aloud could I think of but the snug and fragrant parlour I had quitted and Uncle Joe's hearty reception and his promises.

When I was got upon the sand hills I wished I had stuck to the road. It was the hills, not the sand, that bothered me. I soared and sank as I went, and presently my legs took a feeling of twist in them, as though they had been corkscrews; but I pushed on stoutly, making a straight course for the sea, where the lightning would give me a frequent sight of the scene of Downs; where I should be able to taste the first of the air that blew and hit its quarter to a point; and where, best of all, the sand hardened into beach.

But oh, my God, now, as I walked along! think! it flung out of the darkness within pistol shot, clear in the wild blue of a flash of lightning. It stood right in front of me. I was walking straight for it; I should have seen it, without the help of lighting, in a few more strides; the sand went away in a billowy glimmer to the wash of the black water, and a kind of light of its own came up out of it, in which the thing would have shown, had I advanced a few paces.

It was a gibbet with a man hanging at the end of the beam, his head coming, according to the picture printed upon my vision by that flash of lightning, within a hand breadth of the piece of timber he dangled at, whence I guessed, with the velocity of thought, that he had been cut down and then tucked up afresh in irons or chains.

I came to a stand as though I had been shot, waiting for another glance of lightning to reveal the ghastly object afresh. I had forgotten all about this gibbet. Had a thought of the horror entered my head – that head which had been too full of the fumes of rum punch to yield space for any but the cheeriest, airiest imaginations – I should have given these sand hills the widest berth which the main road provided. I was no coward; but Lord! to witness such a sight by a stroke of lightning! I say it was as unexpected a thing to my mood, at that moment of its revelation by lightning, as though not a word had been said about it at my uncle's, and as though I had entered the sand hills absolutely ignorant that a man hung in chains on a gibbet, within shy of a stone from the water.

This ignorance it was that dyed the memorable rencounter to a complexion of darkest horror to every faculty that I could collect. While I paused, breathing very short, hearing no sound but the thunder and the pitting of the rain on the sand, and the whisper of the surf along the beach, a vivid stroke of lightning flashed up the gibbet; there was an explosion aloft; rain fell with a sudden fury, and the hail so drummed upon my hat that I lost the noise of the surf in the sound. A number of flashes followed in quick succession, and by the dazzle I beheld the gibbet and its ghastly burden as clearly as though the sun was in the sky.

The figure hung in chains; the bight of the chain passed under the fork betwixt the thighs, and a link on either hand led through an iron collar, which clasped the neck of the body, the head lolling over and looking sideways down, and the two ends of the chain met in a ring, held by a hook, secured by a nut on top of the timber projection. But what was that at the foot of the gibbet? I believed, at first, that it was a strengthening piece, a big block or pile of wood designed to join and secure the bare, black, horrible post from which the beam pointed like some frightful spirit finger, seaward, as though death's skeleton arm held up a dead man to the storm.

This was my belief. I was now fascinated and stood gazing, watching the fearful thing as it came and went with the lightning.

Do you know those Deal sand hills? A desolate, dreary waste they are, on the brightest of summer mornings, when the lark's song falls like an echo from the sky, when the pale and furry shadows of rabbits blend with the sand, till they look mere eyes against what they watch you from, when the flavour of seaweed is shrewd in the smell of the warm and fragrant country. But visit them at midnight, stand alone in the heart of the solitude of them and realize then – but, no, not even *then* could you realize – the unutterably tragic significance imported into those dim heaps of faintness, dying out at a short distance in the blackness, by such a gibbet and such a corpse as I had lighted upon, as I now stood watching by the flash and play of near and distant lightning.

But what was that at the foot of the gibbet? I took a few steps, and the object that I had supposed to be a balk of timber, serving as a base-piece, arose. It was a woman. I was near enough now to see her without the help of the lightning. The glimmering sand yielded sufficient light, so close had I approached the gibbet. She was a tall woman, dressed in black, and her face in the black frame of her bonnet, that was thickened by a wet veil, showed as white as though the light of the moon lay upon it. I say again that I am no coward, but I own that when that balk of timber, as I had supposed the thing to be, arose and fashioned itself, hard by the figure of the hanging dead man, into the shape of a tall woman, ghastly white of face, nothing but horror and consternation prevented me from bolting at full speed. I was too terrified to run. My knees seemed to give way under me. All the good of the rum punch was gone out of my head.

The woman approached me slowly, and halted at a little distance. There might have been two yards between us and five between me and the gibbet.

"What have you come to do?" she exclaimed in a voice that sounded raw – I can find no other word to express the noise of her speech – with famine, fatigue, fever; for these things I heard in her voice.

"I have come to do nothing; I am going to Deal," I answered, and I made a step.

"Stop! I am the mother of that dead man. Show me how to take him down. I cannot reach his feet with my hands. You are tall, and strong and hearty, and can unhook him. For God's sake, take him down and give him to me, sir."

"His mother!" cried I, finding spirit, on a sudden, in the woman's speech and dreadful avowal; "God help thee! But it is not a thing for me to meddle with."

"He was my son, he was innocent and he has been murdered. He must not be left up there, sir. Take him down, and give him to me who am his mother, and who will bury him."

"It is not a thing for me to meddle with," I repeated, looking at the body, and all this time it was lightning sharply, and the thunder was frequent and heavy, and it rained pitilessly. "It would need a ladder to unhook him, and suppose you had him, what then? Where is his grave? Would you dig it here? And with what would you dig it? And if you buried him here, they would have him up again and hook him up again."

"Oh, sir, take him down, give him to me," she cried in a voice that would have been a shriek but for her weakness.

"How long have you been here?" said I, moving so as to enable me to confront her, and yet have my back on the gibbet, for the end of my tongue seemed to stick like a point of steel into the roof of my mouth, every time the lightning flashed up the swinging figure and I saw it.

"I was here before it fell dark," she answered.

"Where do you come from?"

"From Harwich."

"You have not walked from Harwich?"

"I came by water to Margate, and have walked from Margate. Oh, take him down – oh, take him down!" she cried, stretching her arms up at the body. "Think of him helpless there! Jimmy, my Jimmy! He is innocent – he is a murdered man!" she sobbed; and then continued, speaking swiftly, and drawing closer to me: "He was my only son. His wife does not come to him. Oh, my Jim, mother is with thee, thy poor old mother is with thee, and will not leave thee. Oh, kind, dear Christian sir" – and she extended her hand and put it upon the sleeve of my coat – "take him down and help me to bury him, and the God of Heaven, the friend of the widow, shall bless thee, and I will watch, but at a distance from his grave, until there shall be no fear of his body being found."

"I can do nothing," said I. "If I had the will, I have not the means. I should need a ladder, and we should need a spade, and we have neither. Come you along with me to Deal; come you away out of this wet and from this sight. You have little strength. If you linger here, you'll die. I will get you housed for the night, and," cried I, raising my voice, that she might hear me above a sudden roll of thunder, "if my ship does not sail out of the Downs tomorrow, I may so work it for you as to get your son's body unhooked, and removed, and buried, where it will not be found. Come away from this," and I grasped her soaking sleeve.

Now at this instant, there happened that which makes this experience the most awful and astonishing of any that I have encountered, in a life that, Heaven knows, has not been wanting in adventure. I am not a believer in latter-day miracles; I am not a fool – not that I would quarrel with a man for believing in latter-day miracles. We are all locked up in a dark room, and I blame no man for believing that he – and perhaps he only – knows the way out. I do not believe in latter-day miracles; but I believe in the finger of God. I believe that often He will answer the cry of the broken heart. This is what now happened, and you may credit my relation or not, as you please.

I have said that I grasped the woman's soaking sleeve, intending to draw her away from the gibbet; and it was at that moment that the body and the gibbet were struck by lightning; they were clothed with a flash of sunbright flame. In the same instant of the flash, there was a burst and shock of thunder, the most deafening and frightful explosion I have ever heard. The motionless atmosphere was thick, sickening, choking with the smell of sulphur. I was hurled backward, but not so as to fall; it was as though I had been struck by the wind of a cannon-ball. For some time the blackness stood like a wall against my vision; more lightning there was at that time, one or two of the flashes tolerably vivid, but the play on my balls of sight, temporarily blinded, glanced dim as sheet lightning when it winks palely past the rim of the sea.

Presently I could see. I looked for the woman, scarce knowing whether I might behold her dead in a heap on the sand. No; she stood at a little distance from me. Like me, she was unable to get her sight. She stood with her white face turned toward Sandwich – that is to say, away from the gibbet; but even as I regained my vision so hers returned to her. She looked around, uttered an extraordinary cry, and, in a moment, was under the gibbet, kneeling, fondling, clasping, hugging, wildly talking to the chained and lifeless figure, whose metal fastening had been sheared through by the burning edge of the terrific scythe of fire!

Yes; the eye or the hook by which the corpse had hung had been melted, and there lay the body, ghastly in its chains, but how much ghastlier had there been light to yield a full revelation of feature and of such injury as the stroke of flame may have dealt it! There it lay in its mother's arms! She held its head with the iron collar about its neck to her breast; she rocked it; she talked to it; she blessed God for giving her son to her.

The rain ceased, and over the sea the black dye of tempest thinned, a sure sign of approaching wind, driving the heavy, loose wings of vapour before it. In another minute I felt a draught of air. It was out of the south. Standing on those sand hills, a familiar haunt of mine, indeed, in the olden times, I could as readily hit the quarter of the wind – yea, to the eighth of a point – as though I took its bearings with the compass before me. I might be very sure that this was a breeze to freshen rapidly, and that even now the boatswain of the *Royal Brunswicker* was thumping with a handspike upon the fore-scuttle, bidding all hands tumble up to man the windlass. Spalding must not be suffered to stare over the side in search of me while he went on giving orders to make sail. It was very late. How late, I knew not. I had heard no clock. Maybe it was one in the morning.

Now, what was I to do? I must certainly miss the ship if I hung about the woman and the body of her son. Even though I should set off at full speed for Deal beach, I might not immediately find a boatman. Yet hurry I must. I went up to the woman, almost loathing the humanity that forced me closer to the body, and exclaimed:

"Come away with me to Deal. You shall be housed if I can manage it; but you must rise and come with me at once, for I cannot stay."

She was seated on the sand under the arm of the gibbet, and half of the body lay across her, with its head against her breast. One of her arms was around it. She caressed its face and, as I spoke, she put her lips to its forehead. There was no cap over the face. Doubtless a cap had been drawn over the unhappy wretch when he was first turned off, but when they hung a man in irons they removed his cap and sheathed the body in pitch to render it weatherproof. Pirates, however, and such seafaring sinners as this man, were mainly strung up in irons in their clothes; and this body was dressed, but he was without a hat.

The woman looked round and up at me, and cried very piteously:

"Dear Christian gentleman, whoever you maybe, help me to seek some place where I may hide my child's body, that his murderers shall not be able to find him. O Jim, God hath given thee to thy mother. Sir, for the sake of thine own mother, stay with me and help me."

"I cannot stay," I cried, breaking in. "If you will not come I must go."

She talked to the body.

On this, seeing how it must be and hoping to be of some use to the poor creature before embarking, I said not another word, but started for Deal beach, walking like one in a dream, full of horror and pity and astonishment, but always sensible that it was growing lighter and yet lighter to windward, and that the wind was freshening in my face as I walked. Indeed, before I had measured half the distance to Deal, large spaces of clear sky had opened among the clouds, with stars sliding athwart them; and low down southeast was a corner of red moon creeping along a ragged black edge of vapour.

When I came to the north end of the town, where Beach Street began and ended in those days, I paused, abreast of a tall capstan used for heaving up boats, and looked about me, I had thought, at odd moments as I walked along, of how my uncle had explained the silence that lay upon Deal by speaking of the press-gang; but, first, I had no fear for myself, for I was mate of a ship, and, as mate, I was not to be taken; and next, putting this consideration apart, the press-gang was scarcely likely to be at work at such an hour – at least at Deal, the habits of whose seafaring people would be well known to the officers of His Majesty's ships stationed in the Downs or cruising in the Channel. But the general alarm might render it difficult for me to find a man to take me off to the ship, and more difficult still to find anyone willing to adventure a lonely walk by moonlight out on to the sand hills to help the woman I had left there.

I stood looking about me. A number of vessels were getting their anchors in the Downs. The delicate distant noise of the clinking of revolving pawls came along in the wind, with dim cries and faint chorusings, and under the moon I spied two or three vessels under weigh standing up Channel. This sight filled me with an agony of impatience, and I got upon the shingle and crunched, sweating along, staring eagerly ahead.

A great number of boats lay upon the beach, some of them big luggers, and in the dusk they loomed up to twice their real size. Nothing living stirred. This was truly astonishing. About half a mile along the shingle, toward Walmer, lay a boat close to the wash of the water; I could not tell at that distance, and by that light, whether there was a man in her or near her, but I supposed she might be a galley-punt, ready to "go off," as the local term is and I walked toward her. A minute later I came to a small, black wooden structure, one of several little buildings used by the Deal boatmen for keeping a lookout in. I saw a light shining upon a bit of a glazed window that faced me, and stepping to this window, I peered through and beheld an old man seated on a bench, with an odd sort of three-cornered hat on his head, and dressed in grey worsted stockings and a long frieze coat. An inch of sooty pipe forked out from his mouth, and I guessed that he was awake by seeing smoke issuing from his lips, though his head was hung, his arms folded, his eyes apparently closed. I stepped round to the door, beat upon it, and looked in.

"I am mate of the *Royal Brunswicker*" said I. "She's getting her anchor in the Downs, and I want to get aboard before she's off and away. Where shall I find a couple of men to put me aboard?"

He lifted up his head after the leisurely manner of old age, took his pipe out of his mouth with a trembling hand, and surveyed me steadfastly, as though he was nearly blind.

"Where are ye from?" said he.

"From the house of my uncle. Captain Joseph Round."

"Captain Joseph Round, is it?" exclaimed the old fellow suspiciously. "I can remember Joe Round – Joey Round was the name he was known by – man and boy fifty-eight year. He'll be drawing on to sixty-five, I allow. What might be yower name?"

By this time I had recollected the old fellow, and his name had come to me with my memory of him.

"Martin – Tom Martin," said I, "you are going blind, old man, or you would know me. My name is William Fielding – Bill Fielding sometimes along the beach here, among such of you drunken, smuggling swabs as I chose to be familiar with. Now, see here, I must get aboard my ship at once, and there'll be another job wants doing also, for the which I shall be willing to pay a guinea. Tell me instantly, Tom, of three men – two to row me aboard, and one to send on a guinea's worth of errand."

"Gi's your hand, Mr. Fielding. Bless me, how you're changed! But ain't that because my sight ain't what it was? You want three men? Two to put ye aboard, and – "

"And one to send on a guinea's worth of errand – on a job I needn't explain to you here. Now bear a hand, or I shall lose my ship."

On this, he blew out the rushlight by which he had been sitting, shut the door of the old cabin, and moved slowly and somewhat staggeringly over the shingle up into Beach Street, along which we walked for, I daresay, fifty yards. He then turned into a sort of alley, and pausing before the door of a little house, lifted his arm as though in search of the knocker, then bade me knock for myself, and knock loud.

I knocked heartily, but all remained silent for some minutes. I continued to knock, and then a window just over the doorway was thrown up, and a woman put her head out. A crazy old lamp, burning a dull flame of oil, stood at the corner of the alley or side street and enabled me to obtain a view of the woman.

"Who are ye?" said she, in a voice of alarm, "and what d'ye want?"

"Is Dick in?" quavered old Martin, looking up at her,

"Why, it's old Tom!" exclaimed the woman. "Who's that along with ye?"

"Capt'n Round's nevvy. Master Billy Fielding, as we used to call him. His ship's in the Downs, there's a slant o' air out of the south, and he wants to be set aboard. Is Dick in, I ask ye?"

"What's that to do with you?" answered the woman, drawing her head in with a movement of misgiving, and putting her hands upon the window as though to bring it down. "No, he ain't in, so there; neither him nor Tom, so there. You go on. I don't like the looks of your friend Mr. Billy Fielding; a merchantman with hepaulets, is it? And what's an old man like you a-doing out of his bed at this hour? Garn home, Tom, garn home;" and down went the window.

"Is that woman mad?" cried I. "What does she take me to be? And does she suppose that you, whom she must have known all her life – I'll tell you what, Tom Martin, I'm not going to lose my ship for the want of a boat. If I can't find a waterman soon I shall seize the first small punt I can launch with mine own hands. Hark!"

I heard footsteps; a sound of the tread of feet came from Beach Street. I walked up the alley to the entrance of it, not for a moment doubting that the fellows coming along were Deal boatmen, fresh from doing business out at sea. Old Tom Martin called after me; I did not catch what he said; in fact I had no chance to hear; for when I reached the entrance of the alley, a body of ten or twelve men came right upon me, and in a breath I was collared, to a deep roaring cry of "Here's a good sailor!"

Chapter IV.
I Escape from the Press

I STRUGGLED and was savagely gripped by the arm. I stood grasped by two huge brawny men, one of whom called out, "No caper-cutting, my lad. No need to show your paces here."

"I am first mate of the *Royal Brunswicker*," I exclaimed.

"You looks like a first mate – the chap that cooks the mate. You shall have mates enough, old ship – shipmates and messmates."

"Let me go. You cannot take me; you know it. I am first mate of the *Royal Brunswicker* – the ship astern of the frigate – ."

"Heave ahead, lads," exclaimed a voice that was not wanting in refinement, though it sounded as if the person who owned it was rather tipsy.

At the moment of seizing me the company of fellows had halted within the sheen of the lamp at the corner of the street. They were a wonderfully fine body of men, magnificent examples of the British sailor of a period when triumphant successes and a long victorious activity had worked the British naval seaman up to the highest pitch of perfection that he ever had attained, a pitch that it must be impossible for him under the utterly changed conditions of the sea life to ever again attain. They were armed with cutlasses, and some of them carried truncheons and wore round hats and round jackets and heavy belts. Two of the mob were pressed men.

"Heave ahead, lads," cried the refined dram-thickened voice.

I looked in the direction of the voice, and observed a young fellow clad in a pea-coat, with some sort of head-gear on his head that might have been designed to disguise him.

"Sir," cried I, "are you the officer in command here?"

"Never you mind! Heave ahead, lads; steer a straight course for the boat."

In a moment the whole body of us were in motion. A seaman on either hand grasped me by the arm, and immediately behind were the other two pressed men.

"Tom Martin," I roared out, hoping that the old fellow might yet be within hearing; "you see what has happened. For God's sake report to Captain Round."

"Who's that bawling?" angrily and huskily shouted the young officer in the pea-coat.

I marched for a few paces in silence, mad and degraded; bewildered, too; nay, I may say confounded almost to distraction by the hurry of the astonishing experiences which I had encountered within the last hour.

"What ship do you belong to?" I presently said, addressing a big bull-faced man who guarded me on the left.

"The frigate out yonder," he answered in a deep, wary voice; "keep a civil tongue in your head and give no trouble, and what's wrong will be righted, if wrong there be," and he looked at me by the light of a second lamp that the company of us was tramping past.

"I am mate of the *Royal Brunswicker*, now probably getting her anchor astern of your frigate," said I. "Cannot I make your officer believe me, for then he might set me aboard?"

The fellow on my right rumbled with laughter as though he would choke. We trudged onward, making for that part of the beach upon which King Street opens. Presently one of the pressed men in my wake began to curse; he used horrible language. With frightful imprecations he demanded to know why he should be obliged to fight for a king whose throat he thirsted to cut; why he should be obliged to fight for a nation which he didn't belong to, whose people he hated; why he was to be converted into a bloody piratical man-of-war's man, instead of being left to follow the lawful, respectable calling of a merchant seaman – .

A mighty thump on the back, that sounded like the blow of a handspike upon a hatch-cover, knocked his hideous speech into a single half-choked growl, and the young gentleman with the refined but husky voice called out:

"If that beast doesn't belay his jaw, stuff his mouth full of shingle and gag him."

I guessed that this gang were satisfied with picking up three men that night, for they looked neither to right nor left for more, and headed on a straight course for their boat. After the ruffian astern of me had been thumped into silence scarce a word was uttered. The sailors seemed weary, as though they had had a long bout of it, and the officer, perhaps, was too sensible of being under the influence of drink to venture to define his state by more words than were absolutely needful. I had heard much of the brutality of the press-gang, of taunts and kicks, of maddening ironic promises of prize money and glory to the miserable wretches torn from their homes or from their ships, of pitiless usage, raw heads, and broken bones. All this I had heard of, but I witnessed nothing of the sort among the men into whose hands I had fallen. In silence we marched along, and the tramp of our feet was returned in a hollow echo from the houses we passed, and the noise of our tread ran through the length of the feebly lighted street, which the presence of the King's seamen had desolated as utterly as though the plague had been brought to Deal out of the East, and as though the buildings held nothing but the dead.

By the time we had arrived at that part of the beach where lay the boat – a large cutter, watched by a couple of seamen armed with cutlasses and pistols – my mind had in some measure calmed down. The degradation of being collared and manhandled was indeed maddening and heart-subduing; but then I was beginning to think this – that first of all it was very probable I must have lost my ship, press-gang or no press-gang, seeing that I could not get a boat to put me aboard her; next, that my being kidnapped, as I call it, would find me such a reason for my absence as Captain Spalding and the owners of the vessel must certainly allow to be unanswerable. Then, again, I was perfectly sure of being released and sent ashore when I had represented my condition to the captain or lieutenant of the frigate; and I might also calculate upon old Tom Martin communicating with my uncle, who would, early in the day, come off to the frigate and confirm my story.

These reflections, I say, calmed me considerably, though my mind continued very much troubled and all awork within me, for I could not forget the horrible picture of the gibbet and the prodigious flash of fire which had delivered the dead hanging son to his wretched mother; and I was likewise much haunted and worried by the thought of the poor woman sitting upon the sand under the gibbet, fondling the loathsome body and whispering to it, and often looking over the billowy waste of glimmering sand, that would now be whitened by the moon, in the direction I had taken, expecting, perhaps, that I should return or send some human soul to help her bury the corpse, that it might not be hooked up again.

The Downs were now full of life. There was a pleasant fresh breeze blowing from the southward, and the water came whitening and feathering in strong ripples to the shingle. The moon was riding over the sea south of the southernmost limit of the Goodwin Sands. She was making some light in the air, though but a piece of moon, and a short length of her silver greenish reflection trembled under her. Almost all the vessels had got under weigh and were standing in groups of dark smudges east or west. It was impossible to tell which might be the *Royal Brunswicker*, but I could see no craft answering to her size in that part near the frigate where she had brought up.

When we were come to the cutter we three pressed men were ordered to get into her. I quietly entered, and so did one of the other two, but the third – the man who had cursed and raged as he had walked along – flung himself down upon the shingle.

"What you can't carry you may drag," he exclaimed, and he swore horribly at the men.

"In with the scoundrel!" said the lieutenant.

And now I saw what sort of tenderness was to be expected from press-gangs when their kindness was not deserved, for three stout seamen, catching hold of the blaspheming fellow, one by the throat, as it seemed, another by the arm, and a third by the breech flung him over the gunwale as if he were some dead carcass of a sheep, and he fell with a crash upon the thwarts and rolled, bloody with a wound in the head and half stunned, into the bottom of the boat.

The lieutenant sat ready to ship the rudder, others of the men got into the boat, and the rest, grasping the line of her gunwale on either hand, rushed her roaring down the incline of shingle into the soft white wash of the breakers, themselves tumbling inward with admirable alertness as she was waterborne. Then six long oars gave way, and the boat sheared through the ripples. The breeze was almost dead on and the tide was the stream of flood, the set of it already strong, as you saw by the manner in which the in-bound shadows of ships in the eastward shrank and melted, while those standing to the westward, their yards braced well forward or their fore and aft booms pretty nigh amidships, sat square to the eye abreast, scarcely holding their own. The frigate lay in a space of clear water at a distance of about a mile and three-quarters. Though the corner of moon looked askant at her, she hung shapeless upon the dark surface, a mere heap of intricate shadow, with the gleam of a lantern at her stern and a light on the stay over the spritsail yard.

The man who had been thrown into the boat sat up. He passed his wrist and the back of his hand over his brow, turned his knuckles to the moon to look at them, and broke out:

"You murdering blackguards! I'll punish ye for this. If I handle your blasted powder it'll be to blow you and your – ."

"Silence that villain!" cried the lieutenant.

"A villain yourself, you drunken ruffian! You are just the figure of the baste I've been draming all my life I was swung for. Oh, you rogue, how sorry I am for you! Better had ye given yourself up long ago for the crimes you've committed than have impressed me. The hangman's work would have been over, but my knife – ."

"Gag him!" cried the lieutenant.

The fellow sprang to his feet, and in another instant would have been overboard. He was caught by his jacket, felled inward by a swinging, cruel blow, and lay kicking, fighting, biting, and blaspheming at the bottom of the boat. In consequence of the struggle four of the oarsmen could not row, and the other two lay upon their oars. The lieutenant, in a voice fiery with rage and liquor, roared out to his men to pinion the scoundrel, to gag the villain, to knock the blasphemous ruffian over the head. All sorts of wild, drunken, savage orders he continued to roar out; and I was almost deafened by his cries of rage, by the howling and shouting of the man in the bottom of the boat, by the curses and growlings of the fellows who were man-handling him.

On a sudden a man yelled: "For God's sake, sir, look out!" and, lifting my eyes from the struggling figure in the bottom of the boat, I perceived the huge bows of a vessel of some three hundred or four hundred tons looming high, close aboard of us. She had canvas spread to her royal mastheads, and leaned from the breeze with the water breaking white from her stem, and in the pause that followed the loud, hoarse cry of "For God's sake, sir, look out!" one could hear the hiss and ripple of the broken waters along her bends.

"Ship ahoy!" shouted one of the seamen.

The man in the bottom of the boat began to scream afresh, struggling and fighting like a madman, and hopelessly confusing the whole company of sailors in that supreme moment. The boat swayed as though she would capsize; the lieutenant, standing high in the stern sheets, shrieked to the starboard bow oar to "pull like hell!" others roared to the approaching ship to port her helm; but, in another minute, before anything could be done, the towering bow had struck the boat! A cry went up, and, in the beat of a pulse, I was under water with a thunder as of Niagara in my ear.

I felt myself sucked down, but I preserved my senses, and seemed to understand that I was passing under the body of the ship, clear of her, as though swept to and steadied at some depth below her keel by the weight of water her passage drove in downward recoil. I rose, bursting with the holding of my breath, and floated right upon an oar, which I grasped with a drowning grip, though I was a tolerable swimmer; and after drawing several breaths – and oh, the ecstasy of that respiration! and oh, the sweetness of the air with which I filled my lungs! – my wits being still perfectly sound, I struck out with my legs, with no other thought in me *then* than to drive clear of the drowning scramble which I guessed was happening hard by.

The oar was under my arms, and my ears hoisted well above the surface of the water. I heard a man steadily shouting – he was at some distance from me, and was probably holding, as I was, to something that floated him – but no other cries than that lonely shouting reached me; no bubbling noises of the strangling; nothing to intimate that anything lived.

I turned my head and looked in the direction of the ship. Her people may or may not have known that they had run down a boat. Certainly she had not shifted her helm; she was standing straight on, a leaning shadow with the bit of moon hanging over her mastheads.

In a few moments the fellow that was shouting at some little distance from me fell silent; but whatever his plight might have been, I could not have helped him, for the tide was setting me at the rate of some two or three miles in the hour into the northeast, and, to come at him, he being astern of me as regards the direction of the tide, I should have been obliged to head in the direction whence his voice had proceeded and seek for him; and so, as I say, I could not have helped him.

We had pulled a full mile, and perhaps more than a mile, from the shore when we were run down. The low land of Deal looked five times as far as a mile across the rippling black surface on which I floated. Yet I knew that the distance could not exceed a mile, and I set my face toward the lights of the beach and struck out with my legs; but I moved feebly. I had swallowed plentifully of salt water when I sank, and the brine filled me with weakness, and I was heavy and sick with it. Then, again, my strength had been shrunk by the sudden dreadful shock of the collision and by my having been under water, breathless and bursting, while, as I might take it, the whole length of the ship was passing over me. I knew that I should never reach the land by hanging over an oar and striking out with my legs. The oar was long and heavy; there was no virtue in the kick of my weakened heels to propel the great blade and loom of ash held athwart as I was obliged to hold it. And all this time the tide was setting me away northeast, with an arching trend to the sheerer east, owing to the conformation of the land thereabouts; so that though for some time I kept my face turned upon Deal, languidly, almost lifelessly, moving my legs in the direction of the lights of that town, in reality the stream was striking me into the wider water; and after a bit I was able to calculate – and I have no doubt accurately – that if I abandoned myself to my oar and floated only (and in sober truth that was all I could do, and pretty much all that I had been doing), I should double the North Foreland at about two miles from that point of coast, and strand, a corpse, upon some shoal off Margate or higher up.

I looked about me for a ship. Therein lay hope. I looked, not for a ship at anchor, unless she hove in view right on end of the course my oar was taking, but for a vessel in motion to hail as she came by; but I reckoned she must come by soon, for on testing my lungs when I thought of the shout I would raise if a ship came by, I discovered that she would have to pass very close if she was to hear me. Indeed, what I had undergone that night, from the moment of lighting upon the gibbet down to this moment of finding myself floating on one oar, had proved too much for my strength, extraordinarily robust as I was in those days: and then, again, the water was bitterly cold – cold, too, was the wind as it brushed me, with a constant feathering of ripples that kept my head and face wet for the wind to blow the colder upon.

The light was feeble, the moon shed but scant illumination, and whenever she was shadowed by a cloud, deep darkness closed over the sea. There were vessels near and vessels afar, but none to be of use. A large cutter was heading eastward about half a mile abreast of me; I shouted and continued to shout, but a drowning sigh would have been as audible to her people. She glided on, and when the moon went behind a cloud the loom of the cutter blended with the darkness, and when the moon came out again, and I looked for the vessel, I could not see her.

I afterward learned that I passed five hours in this dreadful situation. How long I had spent hanging over the oar when my senses left me I know not; I believe that dawn was not then far off; I seem to recollect a faintness of grey stealing up off the distant rim of the sea like a smoke into the sky, the horizon standing firm and dark against the dimness as though the water were of thick black paint; and by that time I guess I had been carried by the tide to a part of the Channel that lies abreast of the cliffs between the town of Ramsgate and the little bay into which the Stour empties itself.

Chapter V.
Captain Michael Greaves of the *Black Watch*

I FOUND myself in the cabin of a ship. I lay in a hammock, and when I opened my eyes I looked straight up at a beam running across the upper deck. I stared at this beam for some time, wondering what it was and wondering where I was; I then turned my head from side to side, and perceived that I was in a hammock, and that I lay in my shirt under some blankets.

How came I here, thought I? If this be the *Royal Brunswicker* they've shifted my berth, or have I blundered into another man's bed! I lifted my head to look over the edge of the hammock, for the canvas walls came somewhat high, the bolster was small and my head lay low, and I was startled to find that I had not the power to straighten my spine into an upright posture. Thrice did I essay to sit up and thrice did I fail, but by putting my hand on the edge of the hammock and incurving the flexible canvas to about the level of my nose, I contrived to obtain a view of the interior in which I swung; and found it to consist of a little berth or cabin, the walls and bulkheads of a gloomy snuff colour, lighted by a small scuttle or circular port-hole of the diameter of a saucer, filled with a heavy block of glass, which, as I watched it, darkened into a deep green, then flashed out into snowy whiteness, then darkened again, and so on with regular alternations: and by this I guessed that I was not only on board a ship, but that the ship I was on board of was rolling heavily and plunging sharply, and rushing through the seas as though driving before a whole gale of wind.

There was no snuff-coloured cabin, with a scuttle of the diameter of a saucer, to be found on board the *Royal Brunswicker*; this ship therefore could not be the vessel that I was mate of. I was hugely puzzled, and my wits whirred in my brain like the works of a watch when the spring breaks, and I continued to peer over the edge of the hammock that I held pressed down, vainly seeking enlightenment in a plain black locker that stood under the scuttle and in what I must call a washstand in the corner of the berth facing the door, and in a small lamp, resembling a cheap tin coffee-pot, standing upon a metal bracket nailed to the bulkhead.

As nothing came to me out of these things I let go the edge of the hammock and gazed at the beam again overhead, and sunk my sensations into the motions of the ship, insomuch that I could feel every roll and toss of her, every dive, pause, and staggering rush forward as though it were a pulse, and I said to myself, "It blows hard, and a tall sea is running, and I am on board a smaller ship than the *Royal Brunswicker*, and our speed cannot be less than twelve knots an hour through the water."

I now grew conscious that I was hungry and thirsty, and as thirst is pain even in its very earliest promptings – unlike hunger, which when first felt is by no means a disagreeable sensation – I endeavoured to sit up, intending in that posture to call out, but found myself, as before, helpless. Then I thought I would call out without sitting up, and I opened my mouth, but my lungs would deliver nothing better than a most ridiculous groan. However, after some ten minutes had passed, the top of a man's head showed over the rim of the hammock. The sight of his eyes and his large cap of fur or hair startled me; I had not heard him enter.

"Have you your consciousness?" said he.

I answered "Yes."

"I am no doctor," said he, "and don't know what I am to do now that your senses have come to you."

"I should like something to drink," said I.

"You shall have it," he answered, "give the drink a name? Brandy-and-water?"

"Anything," I exclaimed. "I am very thirsty."

"Can you eat?"

"I believe I shall be able to eat," I replied, "when I have drunk."

The head disappeared. Memory now returned. I exactly recollected all that had befallen me down to the moment when, as I have already said, I fancied I beheld the faint colour of the dawn lifting like smoke off the black edge of the sea. I gathered by the light in the cabin that it was morning and not yet noon, and conceiving that I might have been taken out of the water some half-hour after I had lost consciousness, I calculated that I had been insensible for nearly five hours. This scared me. A man does not like to feel that he has been as dead to all intents and purposes as a corpse for five hours, not sleeping, but mindless and, for all he knows, soulless.

I now heard a voice. "Give me the glass, Jim." The man whose head had before appeared showed his face again over the edge of the hammock. "Drink this," said he, holding up a glass of brandy-and-water.

I eagerly made to seize the glass, but could not lift my head, nor even advance my hands the required distance.

"Go and bring me the low stool out of my cabin, and bear a hand," said the man, and a minute later he rose till his head was stooping under the upper deck. He was now able to command the hammock in which I lay, and lifting my head with his arm he put the tumbler to my lips, and I drank with feverish greediness. He then put a plate of sandwiches formed of while loaf bread and thin slices of beef upon the blankets and bade me eat. This I contrived to do unaided. While I ate he dismounted from the stool, gave certain instructions which I did not catch to his companion who, as he did not reach to the height at which the hammock swung, I was unable to see, and then came to the edge of the hammock, and stood viewing me while I slowly munched.

I gazed at him intently and sometimes I thought I had seen his face before, and sometimes I believed that he was a perfect stranger to me. He had dark eyes and dark shaggy eyebrows, was smooth shaven and looked about thirty-four years of age, but his fur cap was concealing wear; the hair of it mingled with his own hair and fringed his brow, contracting what had else been visible of the forehead, and it was only when the hammock swung to a heavier roll than usual that I caught a sight of the whole of his face. The brandy-and-water did me a great deal of good. It made me feel as if I could talk.

"You're beginning to look somewhat lifelike now," said he; "Can you bear being questioned?"

"Ay, and to ask questions."

These words I pronounced with some strength of voice.

"Well, you'll forgive me for beginning?" said he, gazing at me fixedly and very gravely. "I want to know what sort of a man I've picked up. Were you ever hanged?"

The sandwich which I was about to bring to my mouth was arrested midway, as though my arm had been withered.

"Half-hanged call it," said he, continuing to eye me sternly, and yet with a singular expression of curiosity too. "Gibbeted, I mean – triced up – cut down, and then suffered to cut stick on its being discovered that you weren't choked?"

Weak as I was I turned of a deep red; I felt the blood hot and tingling in my cheeks.

"You'll not ask me that question when I have my strength," said I.

"You have been delirious, and nearly all your intelligible talk has been about a gibbet and hanging in chains."

"Ha!" said I.

"I had learnt off Margate that a man had been hanged at Deal."

I said "Yes," and went on eating the sandwich I held.

"We picked you up off Ramsgate, floating on an oar belonging to a boat of one of His Majesty's ships. Now, should I have found anything suspicious in that? Not at all. Your dress told me you were not a navy Johnny. There was a story, and I was willing to wait and hear it; but when, being housed in this hammock, you turned to and jawed about a gibbet and about hanging in irons; when I'd listen to you singing out for help to unhook the body, to stand clear of the lightning – 'Now is your time,' you'd sing out; 'by the legs and up with it,' "'Tis for a poor mother's sake,' a poor mother's sake – I say, when I'd stand by hearkening to what the great dramatist would call the perilous stuff which your soul or your conscience, or whatever it might have been that was working in you, was throwing up as water is thrown up by a ship's pump, why – ."

The colour of temper had left my face. I eyed him, slightly smiling, munching my sandwich quietly.

"Captain Michael Greaves," said I, "I am no half-hanged man."

On hearing the name I gave him he started violently; then, catching hold of the edge of the hammock, so tilted it as to nearly capsize me, while he thrust his face close to mine.

"What was that you said?" cried he.

"I am no hanged man."

"You pronounced my name," he cried, continuing to hold by the hammock and swinging with it as the ship rolled.

"I know your name," I replied. "Have you ever sailed with me?"

"No."

"How does it happen that you know me?"

"Is not this a brig called the *Black Watch*" said I, "and are not you, Captain Michael Greaves, in command of her?"

"Chaw! I see how it is," he exclaimed, the wonder going out of his face while he let go of my hammock. "You have had what they call lucid intervals, during which you have picked up my name and the name of my vessel – though who the deuce has visited you saving me and the lad? and neither of us, I swear, has ever once found you conscious until just now."

"Will you give me some more brandy-and-water? I am still very thirsty. A second draught may enable me to converse. I feel very weak, but I do not think I am as weak as I was a little while ago;" and I lifted my head to test my strength, and found that I was able to look over the edge of the hammock.

In doing this I got a view of Captain Michael Greaves' figure. He was a square, tall, well-built man – as tall as I, but more nobly framed; his face, his shape, his air expressed great decision and resolution of character. He wore a pea-coat that fell to his knees, and this coat and a pair of immense sea-boots and a fur cap formed his visible apparel. He stepped out of the berth, and in a minute after returned with a glass of brandy-and-water. This I took down almost as greedily as I had emptied the contents of the first glass. I thanked him, handed him the tumbler, and said:

"You were chief mate of a ship called the *Raja*?"

"That is so."

"In the month of November, 1809, you were lying in Table Bay?"

He reflected, and then repeated:

"That is so."

"There was a ship," I continued, "called the *Rainbow*, that lay astern of you by some ten ships'-lengths."

He gazed at me very earnestly, and looked as though he guessed what was coming.

"One morning," said I, "a boat put off from the *Raja*. She hoisted sail and went away toward Cape Town. A burst of wind came down the mountain and capsized her, whereupon a boat belonging to the *Rainbow* made for the drowning people, picked them up, and put them aboard their own ship."

He thrust his arm into the hammock and grasped my hand.

"You are Mr. Fielding. You were the second mate of the *Rainbow*. You it was who saved my life and the lives of the others. Strange that it should fall to my lot to save yours; and for me to suppose that you had been hanged! By Isten! but this is a little world. It is not astonishing that I should not have known you. You are something changed in the face; likewise you have been very nearly drowned. We shall be able to find out how many hours you lay washing about in the Channel. And add to this a very long spell of emaciating insensibility."

"I was never hanged," said I.

"No, no," he said, "but all your babble was about gibbets and chains."

"If it had not been for a gibbet and a man dangling from it in chains, in all human probability I should not now be here. I was delayed by an object of horrible misery, and the period of my humane loitering tallied to a second with the movements of a press-gang, or I should be on board my own ship, the *Royal Brunswicker* of which vessel I am mate. Where will she be now?" I considered awhile. "Say she got under weigh at two o'clock this morning – how is the wind, Captain Greaves?"

"It blows fresh, and is dead foul for the *Royal Brunswick*er if she be inward bound."

"Then," said I, "she may have brought up in the Downs again. I hope she has. I may be able to rejoin her before the wind shifts. In what part of the Channel are you?"

"Out of it, clear of the Scillies."

"*Out of the Channel?*" I cried, "Do you sail by witchcraft? What time is it, pray?"

"A few minutes after eleven."

"You were off Margate this morning at daybreak," said I, "and now, at a few minutes after eleven o'clock, you are out of the Channel?"

"I was off Margate three days ago at daybreak," he answered.

"Have I been insensible three days? It is news to strike the breath out of a man. Three days! Of course the *Royal Brunswicker* has arrived in the Thames and – out of the Channel, do you say? How am I to get ashore?"

"We will talk about that presently."

I lay speechless, with my eyes fastened upon the beam above the hammock.

"You have talked enough," said Captain Greaves; "yet there is one question I should like to ask, if you have breath enough to answer it with: How came you to hear that this brig's name is the *Black Watch*?"

"I read of the brig in an old newspaper that I was hunting over for news at my uncle's house last evening."

"Not last evening," said he, smiling.

"And have I been three days unconscious?"

"I suppose my name was given as the commander of this brig?"

"Yes; fitting out for a privateering cruise."

"Did the newspaper say so?"

"I think it did."

"There is no lie like the newspaper lie," said he. "I have no doubt that Ananias conducted a provincial journal somewhere in those parts where he was struck dead. But we have talked enough. Get now some sleep, if you can. A dish of soup shall be got ready for you by and by, and there is some very fine old Madeira aboard."

He went out, but returned to put a stick into my hammock, bidding me knock on the bulkhead should I need anything, as the lad, Jimmy Vinten, would be in and out of the cabin all day, and would hear me if he (Greaves) did not. I lay lost in thought, for I was not so weak but that I was able to think with energy, even passion, though I was without the power to continue much longer in conversation with Captain Greaves. I was mightily shocked and scared to think that I had been insensible for three days, babbling of gibbets and hanged men, and the angels know what besides; yet why I should have been shocked and scared I can't imagine, unless it was that I awoke to the knowledge of my past condition in a very low, weak, miserable, nervous state. Here was I clear of the Channel in an outward-bound brig, whose destination I had yet to learn, making another voyage ere the long one I was fresh from could be said, so far as I was concerned at all events, to be over. But this was not a consideration to trouble me greatly. First of all, my life had been miraculously preserved, and for that I clasped my hands and whispered thanks. Next, the brig was bound to speedily fall in with some ship heading for England, and I might be sure that Greaves would take the first opportunity that offered to tranship me. It was very important to me that I should get to England quickly. There was a balance of about a hundred and fifty pounds due to me for wages, and all my possessions – trifling enough, indeed – were in my cabin aboard the *Royal Brunswicker*. If my uncle did not procure me command next voyage Spalding would take me as his mate; but I must make haste to report myself, for I might count upon old Tom Martin telling Captain Round that I had been taken by a press-gang, and then of course all England would have heard, or in time would hear, that a press-boat, with pressed men aboard, had been run down in the Downs with loss of most of her people, as I did not doubt, and Spalding, believing me drowned, would appoint another in my place as mate.

Well, in this way ran my thoughts, and then I fell asleep, and when I awoke the afternoon was far advanced, as I saw by the colour of the light upon the scuttle. I grasped the stick that lay in my hammock, and was rejoiced to find that the long spell of deep refreshing slumber had returned me much of my strength. I beat upon the bulkhead with the stick, and in two or three moments a voice, proceeding from somebody standing near the hammock, asked me what I wanted.

It was a youth of about seventeen years of age, lean, knock-kneed, sandy, and freckled, and of a "moony" expression of countenance that plainly said "lodgings to let." I never saw a more expressionless face. It made you think of a wall-eyed dab – of the flattest of flat fish. Yet what was wanting in mind seemed to be supplied in muscle. In fact he had the hand of a giant, and his whole conformation suggested sinew gnarled, twisted, and tautly screwed into human shape.

"I am awake. You can see that," said I.

"I see that," answered the youth.

"I am hungry and thirsty, and wish for something to eat and something to drink."

"There's bin pork and madeery ready agin your arousin'. Shall I get 'em?" said the youth.

I was astonished to hear him speak of pork, but nevertheless made answer, "If you please."

He returned with a tray and handed up to me a basin of excellent broth and a slice of bread, a wineglass, and a small decanter of Madeira. I looked at the broth and then looked at the youth and said, "Do you call this pork?"

He upturned his flat face and gazed at me vacantly. "Where is the pork?" said I.

"There ain't none, master."

"Poor idiot!" I thought to myself. I now discovered that I could sit up; so I sat up and ate and drank. The Madeira was a noble wine; the like of it I have never since tasted. That meal, coming on top of my long sleep, went far to make a new man of me, and I felt as though I should be able to dress myself and go on deck, but on throwing my legs over the edge of the hammock I discovered that I was not quite so strong as I had imagined; I trembled considerably, and I was unable to hold my back straight; so I lay down again, well satisfied with my progress, and very sure I should have strength to rise in the morning.

The youth stayed in the berth while I ate and drank, and I asked him some questions.

"Where is Captain Greaves?"

"On deck, master. We have been chased, but ain't we dropping her nicely, though! Ah! She's *that* size on the sea now," said he, holding up his hand, "and at two o'clock we could count her guns."

"This is a fast brig then?"

"She's all legs, master."

"What are you?"

"I'm the capt'n's servant and cabin boy."

"What's the name of your mate?"

"Yawcob van Laar."

"A Dutchman?" said I; and then I remembered having read in the paper that this brig had been purchased or chartered by a Dutch merchant of Amsterdam, so that it was likely enough she would carry some Dutch folk among her crew.

"Are you all Dutch?"

"No, master. There be Wirtz, Galen, Hals, and Bol; them four, they be Dutch. And there be Friend, Street, Meehan, Travers, Teach, Call, and me; Irish and English, master."

I was struck by the fellow's memory. His face made no promise of that faculty.

"Eleven men," said I aloud, but thinking rather than talking; "and a mate and a captain, thirteen; and the ship's burden, if I recollect aright, falls short by a trifle of three hundred tons. Her Dutch owner appears to have manned her frugally for such times as these. Most assuredly," said I, still thinking aloud, gazing at the flat face of the youth who was looking up at me with a slightly gaping mouth, "the *Black Watch* is no privateer. Where are you bound to?"

"Dunno, master."

"You don't know! But when you shipped you shipped for a destination, didn't you?"

"I shipped for that there cabin," said the youth, pointing backward over his shoulder with an immense thumb.

I finished the wine, handed down the decanter and bowl, and asked the youth to procure me a pipe of tobacco. This he did, and I lay smoking and musing upon the object of the voyage of the *Black Watch*. The vessel was being thrashed through the water. It was blowing fresh, and she hummed in every plank as she swept through the sea. The foam roared like a cataract past the scuttle, but her heel was moderate; the wind was evidently abaft the beam, the sea was deep and regular in its swing, and the heave and hurl of the brig as rhythmic in pulse as the melody of a waltz.

Chapter VI.
I View the Brig

PRESENTLY it fell dark; but hardly had the last of the red, wet light faded off the scuttle when the youth Jim re-entered the berth and lighted the coffee-pot-shaped lamp, and as he went out Captain Greaves came in.

He asked me how I felt. I told him that I was almost well, that I hoped to be quite well by the morning, in which case I would beg him to transfer me to the first homeward bound craft that passed, though she should be no bigger than a ship's longboat. He viewed me, I thought, somewhat strangely, smiled slightly, was silent long enough to render silence somewhat significant, and then said: "A beast of a frigate showing no colours has kept me anxious this afternoon. We have run her hull down, but she has only just thought proper to shift her helm. Possibly an Englishman who took us for a Yankee." Saying this he pulled off his fur cap and exhibited a fine head with a quantity of thick, black hair curling upon it; he next produced and filled a pipe of tobacco and, removing his pea-coat, he lighted his pipe at the lamp and seated himself on the locker in the attitude of a seaman who intends to enjoy a yarn and a smoke.

I was strong enough to hold my head over the edge of the hammock; thus we kept each other in view.

"D'ye feel able to talk, Mr. Fielding?" said Greaves.

"Very able, indeed," I answered. "Your Madeira has made a new man of me."

"How happened it," said he, "that you should be washing about on the oar of a man-of-war's boat off Ramsgate, the other morning, when we fell in with you?"

I begged him to put a pinch of tobacco into the bowl of my pipe and to hold the lamp to me, and when I had lighted my pipe and he had resumed his seat I began my story; and I told him everything that had befallen me from the time of my arrival in the Downs in the ship *Royal Brunswicker* down to the hour when I found myself afloat on an oar, heading a straight course east by north with the stream of the tide. He listened with earnest attention, smoking very hard at some parts of my narrative, and emitting several dense clouds, which almost obscured him when I told him how the lightning had liberated the corpse and how, as it might seem, the fiery hand of God himself had delivered the body of the malefactor to the weeping, praying mother.

"It was an evil moment for me when I fell in with that gibbet," said I. "I had not the heart to leave the wretched mother, though my first instinct on catching sight of her was to run for my life. But I thank God for my wonderful preservation; I thank Him first and you next, Captain Greaves."

"No more of that. We're quits."

"It is clear that you keep a bright lookout aboard this brig."

"Had your life depended upon the eyes of my men, the perishable part of you would have been by this time concocted into cod and crab. I'll introduce you to the individual to whom you owe your life."

He opened the door of the cabin and putting a silver whistle to his lips blew, and in a moment a fine retriever bounded in.

"Galloon, Mr. Fielding; Mr. Fielding, Galloon."

The dog wagged his tail and looked up at me.

"Did he go overboard after me?" said I.

"You shall hear. It was break of day, the water quiet, the brig under all plain sail, the speed some five knots. I was walking the quarter-deck, and there was a man on the forecastle keeping a lookout. Suddenly that chap Galloon there" – here the "chap" wagged his tail and looked up at me again as though perfectly sensible that we were talking about him – "sprang on to the taffrail and barked loudly. I ran aft and looked over, but not having a dog's eye saw nothing. 'What is it, Galloon?' said I. He barked again, and then with a short but most piercing and lamentable howl he sprang overboard. I love that dog as I love the light of day, Mr. Fielding, much better than I love dollars, and better than I love many ladies with whom I am acquainted. The brig was brought to the wind, a boat lowered, and the people found Galloon with his teeth in the jacket of a man who was laying over an oar."

"The noble fellow!" said I, looking down at the dog.

Greaves picked him up and put his head over the edge of the hammock, and I kissed the creature's nose, receiving in return a caressing lick of the tongue that swept my face.

"Why do you call him Galloon?" said I.

"I have been dreaming of galleons all my life," he answered.

He relighted his pipe and resumed his seat, and the dog lay at his feet, gazing up at me.

"I took the liberty," said I, "of asking the youth called Jimmy to tell me what port this brig was bound to. He answered that he did not know."

"He does not know," said Captain Greaves. "No man on board the *Black Watch*, saving myself, knows where we are bound to."

"I recollect reading in that newspaper paragraph I have spoken of that the brig is owned by a merchant of Amsterdam. I recollect this the better because it led me to ask my uncle, Captain Round, whether a British letter of marque would be issued to a foreigner despite his sending his ship a-privateering under English colours."

"We are not a letter of marque. It is perfectly true that this brig is owned by an Amsterdam merchant. His name is Bartholomew Tulp, and he is my stepfather."

I asked no more questions. I would not seem curious, though there was something in Captain Greaves' reserve, and something in the enigmatic character of this ocean errand, which made me very thirsty to hear all that he might be willing to tell. Never had I heard of a ship manned by a crew who knew not whither they were going. I speak of the merchant service. As to the Royal Navy, the obligation of sealed orders must always exist; but when a man enters as a sailor aboard a merchantman, the first and most natural inquiry he wishes his captain to answer is, "Where are you bound to?"

Greaves sat watching me, as did his dog. The captain smoked, with a countenance of abstraction and an air of deep musing, whilst he lightly stroked his dog's back with his foot.

"My mate is a devil of a fool!" he exclaimed, breaking the silence that had lasted some minutes. "He is a Dutchman, and his name is van Laar. He speaks English very well, but he is no sailor. The wind headed us after leaving Amsterdam, and, having my doubts of van Laar, I told him to put the brig about, and she missed stays in his hands. Worse – when she was in irons, he did not know what to do with her. I abominate the rogue who misses stays; but can villainy in a sailor go much further than not knowing what to do when a ship has missed stays?"

"I have met," said I, "with some fine seamen among Dutchmen."

"Van Laar is not one of them," he answered. "Van Laar is no more to be trusted with a ship than he is with a bottle of Hollands. He does not scruple to own that he hates the English, and I do not like to sail in company with a man who hates my countrymen. I took him on Mynheer Tulp's recommendation. I was opposed to shipping a Dutchman in the capacity of mate, but I could not very well object to a man as a Dutchman," said he, laughing, "to Mynheer Tulp."

"Does the mate know where the brig is bound to?" I inquired.

"No."

"How very extraordinary!"

He looked at me gravely; his face then relaxed. Finding his pipe out, he arose, put on his coat and cap, and said:

"I will leave you for the night. What do you fancy for your supper – what, I mean, that you, as a sailor, will suppose my brig's larder can supply?"

I answered that a basin of broth with a glass of brandy-and-water would make me an abundant supper.

"But before you leave me," said I, "will you tell me where my clothes are? I must hope to be transhipped tomorrow, and to step ashore with nothing on but a blanket – ."

"Your clothes have been dried and are in the cabin," said he. "When Jimmy brings your supper ask him for your clothes. And now good-night, and pleasant dreams to you, Mr. Fielding, when it shall please you to fall asleep."

The dog sprang through the door, and I lay with my eyes fixed upon the flame of the lamp, diverting myself with inventing schemes of a voyage, one of which should fit this expedition of the *Black Watch*.

Early next morning I awoke after a sound, refreshing night of rest, and, dropping out of my hammock, found that I was pretty nigh as hearty as ever I had been in my life. Greatly rejoiced by this discovery, I attired myself in my clothes, which had been thoroughly dried. A razor, a brush, and one or two other conveniences were in the cabin. I was struck by Greaves' kindness. I seemed to find in it something more than an expression of charitable attention and grateful memory. Now being dressed, and now testing myself on my legs, and finding all ship-shape aboard, from the loftiest flying pennant of hair down to the soles of my shoes, I opened the door of the berth and stood awhile looking in upon the cabin. It was a small snug sea-interior, well lighted, and breezy just now with the cordial gushing of wind down the companion-hatch. A table and a few seats comprised the furniture; those things, and a lamp, and a stand of small-arms, and some cutlasses.

While I viewed this interior I heard Greaves' voice in a cabin on the starboard side forward.

"Not coffee, but cocoa!" on which another voice, which I recognized as the lad Jimmy's, shouted out, to the accompaniment of the howling of a dog:

"Not coffee, but cocoa!"

"Again," said the voice of Captain Greaves.

"Not coffee, but cocoa," yelled the lad, and again the dog delivered a long howl.

"For the third time, if you please."

"Not coffee, but cocoa!" shrieked the lad, and the accompanying howl of the dog rose to the key in which the boy pitched his voice, as though in excessive sympathy with the shouter.

A door forward was then opened, and the youth Jimmy came out. He stopped on seeing me, and cried out, " 'Ere's Mr. Fielding," and then went on deck. Galloon bounded up to me, and while I caressed him Greaves, with his shirt sleeves turned up, and holding a hair-brush, looked out of his door, saw me, approached, and shook me heartily by the hand. I answered a few kind questions, and asked if there was anything in sight from the deck.

"Yes," said he, "but nothing to be of any use to you. You can feel the heave. It blows fresh."

"It is a very buoyant heave," said I; "I should imagine you are at sea with a swept hold."

He continued to brush his hair.

"Excuse me, is your lad Jimmy an idiot?"

"Not at all. Perhaps I know why you ask. You heard me and Galloon giving him a lesson just now. Jimmy Vinten is no idiot, but he wants a faculty, and Galloon and I are endeavouring to create it. He cannot distinguish dishes. He will put a bit of beef on the table and call it pudding. He'll knock on my door and sing out, 'The pork's sarved,' when he means pease soup. His memory is remarkable in other ways. Wait a minute, and we'll go on deck together."

I sat upon a locker to talk to Galloon, to kiss the beast's cold snout, and with his paw in my hand, while his tail swayed like the naked mast of an oysterman in a quick sea, I thanked him with many loving words for having saved my life. His eye languished up at me. Oh! if ever there was an expression of serene and heartfelt satisfaction in the eye of a dog that for some noble action is being thanked with caresses, it shone in Galloon's eyes while he seemed to listen to me. After a few minutes Greaves joined me, equipped in his pea-coat, fur cap, and top boots – a massive privateering figure of a man, handsome, determined of gaze, yet with something of softness in his looks, and intimations of gentleness in the motions of his lips and in his occasional smile. He led the way up the companion steps, and I stood upon the deck of the brig looking about me.

Seasoned as I was to the life which the ocean puts into the shipwright's plank, I should not have suspected, from the motion of the vessel only, that so considerable a sea was running. The wind was two or three points abaft the beam; it was blowing half a gale – a clear gale. The clouds were flying in bales and rags of wool toward the pouring southern verge of the ocean; the dark blue brine, sparkling with the flying eastern sunshine, swelled in hills to the brig's counter, and the foam swept in sheets backward from each rushing head. The brig was under whole topsails and a topgallant sail, but abreast, to leeward, was another brig heading north, stripped to a single band of main topsail and a double-reefed forecourse – ay, Jack, the square foresail and mainsail in my time carried two and sometimes three reefs – and the beat of the head seas obscured her in frequent snowstorms as she struggled wildly aslant amid the dark blue billows. *We* were roaring through the water at ten or eleven knots. To every stoop of the bows the foam rose boiling above the catheads, with a mighty, thunderous bursting away of the parted seas on either hand. Ships in those times made a great noise when they went through the water. They were all bow and beam, and anything that was over took the form of stern, immensely square, and as clamorous when in motion as any other part of the ship. The *Black Watch* would be laughed at as a cask in these days, but as vessels then went she was a clipper. Her lines were tolerably fine at the entry; then her bulk rolled whale-like aft, with the copper showing two feet above the water-line, and then she narrowed into a clipper run to the deadwood and the sternpost. Her sheer forward gave her a bold bow. I watched her for a few minutes as she rolled over the seas – and I was sensible that Captain Greaves' eye was upon me as I watched – and I thought her a very smart, handsome, powerful vessel, the sort of ship a freebooter would instantly fall in love with, and furiously determine to possess himself of, yea, though a pennant shook at her masthead.

She was armed on the forecastle with a long brass eighteen-pounder, pivoted; on the main deck with four nine-pound carronades, two of a side; and aft with a second long brass eighteen-pounder, likewise pivoted. She carried three boats – one stowed in another abaft the caboose, and a big boat chocked and lashed abreast of the other two boats. Her decks were very white; the brass pieces flashed, and there was a sparkle of glass over the cabin, and a frosty brilliancy of brine all about her planks as you see in white sand with sunshine upon it. Her sails soared square with a great hoist of topsail, and the cloths might have been stitched for a man-of-war, so perfect was the sit and spread of the heads, the fit of the clews to the yardarms.

I took notice of the men; half the crew were on deck cleaning paint-work, coiling down, differently occupied. They were big, burly fellows for the most part, variously attired, and as I watched, one of them, a vast, square, carroty man, called out to another in a deep, roaring voice; I did not know Dutch, but what that man said sounded very much like Dutch, and the other man answered him in the same tongue.

And now, having looked at the sea, and at the brig, and at such of the crew as were visible forward, I directed my eyes at the figure of an individual who was walking to and fro in the gangway. He was the mate, van Laar; as burly as the burliest of the figures forward, his eyes small, black, and fierce, his face a mass of flesh, in the midst of which was set an aquiline nose, whose outline in profile was hidden by the swell of the cheek as you lose sight of the line of a ship's sail past some knoll of brine. He had not the least appearance of a sailor: was not even dressed as a sailor; looked as though he had just arrived out of the country in a cart to buy or sell eggs and butter in Amsterdam market.

I observed that his behaviour grew uneasy while I gazed about me, Greaves at my side receiving from me from moment to moment with a countenance of complacency some morsel of appreciative criticism. That Dutch mate, van Laar, I say grew uneasy. He darted glances of suspicion at me. I never would have supposed that any human eyes set in so much fat should have possessed the monkey-like nimbleness of that man's. At the same time I noticed that he seemed to pull himself together after the captain had stepped on deck. He shook the laziness out of his step, directed frequent looks aloft, eyed the men as though to make sure there was no skulking, and in several ways discovered a little life. But his heart was not in it; his business was not *here*.

The captain and I paced the deck. Even as we started to walk, the boatswain, one of the burliest of the Dutchmen, piped the hands to breakfast. The silver notes rang cheerily through the little ship and wonderfully heightened to the fancy the airy, saucy, free-born look of the timber witch as she thundered along with foam to her figure-head; her white pinions beat time to the organ melodies of the ocean wind; smoke hospitably blew from the chimney of her little caboose; Dutch and English sailors entered and departed from that sea kitchen, carrying cans of steaming tea with them into their forecastle; there was a pleasant noise of the chuckling of hens; the sun shone brightly among the wool-white clouds; splendid was the spacious scene of sea rolling in sparkling deeply-blue heights, and every surge, as it ran, magnificently draped itself in a flashing veil of froth.

"I like your little ship, Captain Greaves," said I.

"I have been watching you, and I see that you like her," he answered.

"You carry two formidable pieces in those brass guns."

"We may pick up something worth defending."

He then asked me how long I had been at sea, and put many questions which at the time of his asking them struck me as entirely conversational: that is to say, he led me to talk about myself, and the impression produced was that we chatted as a couple of men would who talked to kill time; but, afterward, in thinking of this conversation, I found that it had been adroitly, but absolutely inquisitional – on his part. In fact, I not only related the simple story of my career; I acquainted him with other matters, such as my attainments as a navigator, my ignorance as a linguist, my qualifications as a seaman – and all, forsooth, as though, instead of killing the time till breakfast with idle chat, I was very earnestly submitting my claims to him for some post aboard his brig.

While we walked and talked I remarked that he kept the Dutch mate in the corner of his eye, but he never addressed him. Once he found the brig half a point, perhaps more than half a point, off her course. He spoke strongly and sternly to the man at the helm, but never a word did he say to van Laar, whom to be sure he should have reprimanded for not conning the brig. I thought this silence very significant.

Presently the lad Jimmy – I called him a lad; his age was about seventeen – this lad came out of the caboose with the cabin breakfast. His knock-kneed legs seemed to have been created for the carriage of a tray full of crockery and eatables along a sharply heaving deck. Galloon trotted out of the caboose at the youth's heels, and they descended into the cabin together. Presently Jimmy arrived to announce breakfast, and with him was Galloon.

"What is there for breakfast?" inquired Captain Greaves.

"There's sausage and 'am and tea," answered the lad.

"Nothing of the sort," said Greaves. "There is no sausage aboard this ship, and I ordered neither " 'am,' as you call it, nor tea. Say eggs and bacon and coffee."

The lad put himself in the position of a soldier at attention.

"Say eggs and bacon and coffee," he shouted; and the dog howled in company with the youth.

"Again, if you please."

"Say eggs and bacon and coffee," roared the lad; and the dog increased its volume of howl as though to encourage the youth to support this trial.

"A third time, if you please."

The dog began before the lad and howled horribly while Jimmy yelled, "Say eggs and bacon and coffee."

The four of us then entered the cabin, where I found an excellent breakfast prepared. Galloon sat upon a chair opposite me, and he was waited upon by Jimmy as the captain and I were.

"You are treating me very hospitably. Captain Greaves," said I.

"I am happy to have found a companion," he answered. "After van Laar" – he stopped with a look at the skylight – "Dern Mynheer Tulp, though he *is* my stepfather and the one merchant adventurer in this undertaking. How sullen and obstinate is the Dutch intellect! Yet who but Dutchmen could have reclaimed a bog from the sea, dried it, settled it, and flourished on it?"

"I hope this weather will soon moderate," said I. "I am anxious to get to England."

"Of course you are. And so shall I be anxious presently."

"Where do you touch, captain?"

"Nowhere. An empty ship has plenty of stowage room, and there are provisions enough aboard to last such a crew as my people number as long a time as would make two or three of Anson's voyages."

"Ah!" thought I with a short laugh, with the velocity of thought founding a fancy of his errand upon his mention of the name of Anson, and upon my recollection of his saying that he had been all his life dreaming of galleons.

"What amuses you?" said he.

"Galloon there," said I, laughing again and looking at the dog.

Chapter VII.
A Strange Story

WHEN we had breakfasted Captain Greaves said: "Will you smoke a pipe with me in my cabin?"

"With much pleasure," I answered.

"First, let me go on deck," said he, "to take a look around. It is Yan Bol's watch and I cannot trust van Laar to see that the deck is relieved even when it is his own turn to come below. Bol is my carpenter, bo'sun, and sailmaker. He stands a watch; but that sort of men who live in the forecastle and eat and drink with the sailors are seldom useful on the quarter-deck. Yet here am I talking gravely on such matters to a man who knows more about the sea than I do."

With that he stepped on deck. I kept my chair and talked with Galloon until Greaves returned. He then conducted me to his cabin. It was a large cabin, at least three times the size of the berth I had occupied during the night. It was on the starboard quarter, well lighted and cosily furnished. Here was to be felt at its fullest the heave of the brig as she swept pitching over the high seas. Whenever she stooped her stern the roaring waters outside foamed about our ears. The kick of the rudder thrilled in small shocks through this part of the fabric, and you heard the hard grind of the straining wheel ropes in their leading blocks as the steersman put his helm up or down.

Captain Greaves took a canister of tobacco from a shelf and handed me a pipe. We filled and smoked. He bade me lay upon a locker and himself sat in his sleeping shelf or bunk, which, being without a top and standing at the height of a knee from the deck, provided a comfortable seat. We discoursed awhile on divers matters relating to the profession of the sea. He asked me to examine his quadrant, his chronometer (which he said was the work of the maker who had manufactured the watch that Captain Cook had taken with him on his last voyage), his charts, of which he had about a score in a canvas bag, and certain volumes on navigation. These things I examined with considerable professional interest. While I looked his eye was never off me. He appeared to be deeply ruminating, and he smoked with an odd motion of his jaw as though he talked to himself. When I was once more seated upon the locker he said:

"I shall cease to call you mister. What need is there for formality between two men who have saved each other's life?"

"No need whatever."

"Fielding," said he, looking and speaking very gravely, "you have greatly occupied my thoughts since you returned to consciousness yesterday, and since I discovered that you were not a half-hanged pirate or smuggler, but a gentleman and an English sailor after my own heart. I mean to tell you a very curious story, and when I have told you that story I intend to make a proposal to you. You shall hear what errand this brig is bound on. You shall learn to what part of the world I am carrying her, and I believe you will say that you have never heard of a more romantic nor of a more promising undertaking."

He opened the door of his berth and looked out. Van Laar was seated at the table, eating his breakfast. Greaves closed the door and seated himself on his bed.

"Last year," said he, "I was in command of a small vessel named the *Hero*. It matters not how it happened that I came to be at the Philippines. There I took in a small lading for Guayaquil. When about sixty leagues to the south'ard of the Galapagos Islands we made land, and hove into view an island of which no mention was made in any of the charts of those seas which I possessed. There was nothing in *that*. There is much land yet to be discovered in that ocean. I have no faith in any of the charts of the Western American seaboard, and trust to nothing but a good lookout. We hove this island into view, and I steered for it with a leadsman in the chains on either hand. I hoped to be of some humble service to the navigator by obtaining the correct bearings of the island; but I had no mind to delay my voyage by sounding, saving only for the security of my own ship.

"We sighted the island soon after sunrise, and at noon were abreast of it. It was a very remarkable heap of rock, much after the pattern of the Galapagos, gloomy with black lava, and the land consisted of masses of broken lava, compacted into cliffs and small conical hills, that reminded me somewhat of the Island of Ascension. I examined it very carefully with a telescope and beheld trees and vegetation in one place, but no signs of human life – no signs of any sort of life, if it were not for a number of turtle or tortoises crawling upon the beach and looking like ladybirds in the distance. But, as we slowly drew past the island, we opened a sort of natural harbour formed by two long lines of reef, one of them incurving as though it was a pier and the handiwork of man. The front of cliff that overlooked this natural harbour was very lofty, and in the middle of it was a tremendous fissure – a colossal cave – the shape of the mouth like the sides of a roughly-drawn letter A. Inside this cave 'twas as dark as evening; yet I seemed with my glass to obscurely behold something within. I looked and looked, and then handed the telescope to the mate, who said there was something inside the cave. It resembled to his fancy the scaffolding of a building, but what it exactly was neither of us could make out.

"The weather was very quiet; the breeze off the island, as its bearings then were at this time of sighting the cave, and the water within the natural harbour was as sheet-calm as polished steel. I said to the mate:

"'We must find time to examine what is inside that cave. Call away four hands and get the boat over. Keep a bright lookout as you approach. There is nothing living that is visible outside, but who knows what may be astir within the darkness of that tremendous yawn? At the first hint of danger pull like the devil for the ship, and I will take care to cover your retreat.'

"To tell you the truth. Fielding, the sight of that extraordinary cave and the obscure thing within it, along with the natural harbour, as I call it, had put a notion into my head fit, to be sure, to be laughed at only; but the notion was in my head, and it governed me. It was this: suppose that huge cave, I thought to myself, should prove to be a secret dock used by picaroons for repairing their vessels or for concealing their ships under certain conditions of hot search? Because, you see, it was a cave vast enough to comfortably berth a number of small craft, and their people would keep a lookout; and who under the skies would suspect a piratic settlement in a heap of cinders? – So I, as a good, easy, ambling merchantman – a type of scores – come sliding close in to have a look, and then out spring the sea wolves from their lair, storming down upon their quarry to the impulse of sweeps three times as long as that oar upon which Galloon saw you floating."

He paused to draw breath. I smiled at his high-flown language.

"Do you find anything absurd in the notion that entered my head?" said he.

"Nothing absurd whatever. You sight a big cave. There is something inside which you can't make out. Why should not that cave be a pirates' lair of the fine old, but almost extinct, type, capable of vomiting cutthroats at an instant's notice, just as any volcanic cone of your island might heave up smoke and redden a league or so of land to the beach with lava?"

"Good. Fill your pipe. There is plenty of tobacco in this brig. I brought my ship to the wind and stopped her without touching a brace, that I might have her under instant command, and the boat, with my mate and four men, pulled to the island. While she was on the road we put ourselves into a posture of defence. I watched the boat approach the entrance to the lines of reef. She hung on her oars, warily advanced, halted, and again advanced; and then I lost sight of her. She was a long while gone – a long while to my impatience. She was gone in all about half an hour; and I was in the act of ordering one of the men to fire a musket as a signal of recall, when she appeared in that part of the natural harbour that was visible from the deck. The mate came over the side; his face was purple with heat and all a-twitch with astonishment.

"'The most wonderful thing, sir!' he cried.

"'What is it?' said I.

"'There's a ship of seven hundred tons at the very least, hard and fast in that big hole, everything standing but the topgallant masts, which look to me as if they'd been crushed away by the roof of the cave. Her jib boom is gone and the end of her bowsprit is about three fathoms distant inside from the entrance.'

"'Anybody aboard?' I asked.

"'I heard and saw nothing, sir,' said he.

"'Did you sing out?'

"'I sang out loudly. I hailed her five times. All hands of us hailed, and nothing but our own voices answered us.'

"'How the deuce comes a ship of seven hundred tons burthen to be lying in that hole?' said I.

"My mate was a Yorkshireman. His head fell on one side and he answered me not.

"'Are her anchors down?' I asked.

"'Her anchors have been let go,' he answered. 'The starboard cable appears to have parted inboard. I saw nothing of it in the hawse-pipe. There are a few feet of her larboard cable hanging up and down.'

"'Swing your topsail,' said I. 'She will lie quiet. There is nothing to be afraid of upon that island.'

"I then got into the boat, and my men pulled me to the mouth of the piers of reef.

"I was greatly impressed by the appearance of these reefs on approaching them. They looked like admirably wrought breakwaters, which had fallen into decay but were still extraordinarily strong, very rugged, imposing, and serviceable. The width of the entrance was about five hundred feet. The water was smooth as glass, clear as crystal, and when I looked over the side I could see here and there the cloudy sheen of the bottom, whether coral or not I do not know – I should say not. And now, right in front of me, was the great face of gloomy-looking cliff, and in the centre the mighty rift, shaped like that," said he, bringing the points of his two forefingers together and then separating his hands to the extent of the width of his two thumbs. "No doubt the wonderful cave was a volcanic rupture. The height of the entrance was, I reckoned, about two hundred feet, and the breadth of it at its base about fifty. It stood at the third of a mile from the mouth of the natural harbour. I could see but little of the ship until I was close to, so gloomy was the interior; but as the men rowed, features of the extraordinarily housed craft stole out, and presently we were lying upon our oars and I was viewing her, the whole picture clear to my gaze as an oil painting set in the frame of the cavern entrance.

"She was a lump of a vessel painted yellow, with a snakelike curl of cutwater at the head of the stem, and a great deal of gilt work about her headboards and figurehead. I knew her for a Spaniard the instant I had her fair. She had heavy channels and a wide spread of lower rigging. Her yards were across, but pointed as though she had ridden to a gale, and the canvas was clumsily furled as if rolled up hurriedly and in a time of confusion. But I need not tease you with a minute description of her," said he. "It was easy to guess how it happened that she was in this amazing situation. Perfectly clear it was to me that she had sighted this island at night, or in dirty weather, when the land was too close aboard for a shift of the helm to send her clear. Once in the harbour her commander, in the teeth of a dead inshore wind, could not get out. What, then, was to be done? Here was a place of shelter in which he might ride until a shift of wind permitted him to proceed on his voyage. So, as I make the story run to my own satisfaction, he let go his anchor; but scarcely was this done when it came on to blow, the canvas was hastily furled to save the strain, but she dragged nevertheless. A second anchor was let go, and still she dragged – and why? Because, as a cast of the lead would have told the Spanish captain, the ground was as hard as rock and as smooth as marble, and there was nothing for the anchors to grip. Dragging with her head to sea and her stern at the cliff's huge front, the ship floats foot by foot toward the cave, threading it with mathematical precision. The roof of the cave slants rearward, and as she drifts into the big hole her royal-mastheads graze and take the roof; the masts are crushed away at the crosstrees, otherwise all is well with the ship. She strands gently, and is steadied by her topmast heads pressing against the roof. Thus is she held in a vice of her own manufacture, and so she lies snug as live calipee and callipash in their top and bottom armour. That must be the solution, Fielding."

"Did the water shoal rapidly in the cave?" said I.

"Yes; the ship lies cradled to her midship section; forward she may be afloat. But there she lies hard and fast for all that, motionless as the mass of rock in whose heart she sleeps."

"You boarded her, I suppose?"

"Certainly I boarded her," continued Greaves. "It is by no means so dusky inside the cave as it appeared to be when viewed from the outside. I left a hand to attend the boat and took three men aboard. I believe I should not have had the spirit to enter that ship alone. By Isten! but she did show very ghastly in that gloom – very ghastly and cold and silent, with the appalling silence of entombment. No noise – I mean that faint, thunderous noise of distant surf – no noise of breakers penetrated. Well, to be sure, by listening you might now and again catch a drowning, bubbling, gasping sound, stealthily washing through the black-water in the cave along the sides of the ship; but I tell you that I found the stillness inside that cave heart-shaking. I went right aft and looked over the stern, and *there* it was like gazing into a tunnel. How far did the cavern extend abaft? There would be one and an easy way of finding that out – by rowing into the blackness and burning a flare in the boat. This I thought I would do if I could make time.

"The ship was a broad, handsome vessel, her scantling that of a second-rate; she mounted a few carronades and swivels: clearly a merchantman, and, as I supposed, a plate-ship. She had a large roundhouse, and steered by a very beautifully and curiously wrought wheel, situated a little forward of the entrance to the roundhouse. It did not occur to me that she might be a rich ship until I looked into the roundhouse; *then* I found myself in a marine palace in its way. Enough of that. The sight of the furniture determined me upon attempting a brief search of her hold. The impulse was idle curiosity – I should have believed it so anyway. I had not a fancy in my head of any sort beyond a swift glance of curiosity at what might be under hatches. Yet, somehow, before I had fairly made up my mind to look into the hold, a singular hope, a singular resolution had formed, flushing me from head to foot as though I had drained a bottle of wine. 'Look if that lamp be trimmed,' said I to a man, pointing to one of a row of small, wonderfully handsome brass lamps, hanging from the upper deck of the roundhouse. No, it was not trimmed. The rest of them were untrimmed. We searched about for oil, for wicks, for candles, for anything that would show a light. Then said I to two of the men, 'Jump into the boat and fetch me a lantern and candle. Tell the mate that I am stopping to overhaul this ship for her papers, to get her story.'

"While the boat was gone I walked about the decks of the vessel, hardly knowing what I might stumble on in the shape of human remains, but there was nothing in that way. The boats were gone, the people had long ago cleared out. Small blame to them. Good thunder!" cried he, shuddering or counterfeiting a shudder; "who would willingly pass a night in such a cave as that? The boat came alongside with the lantern. We then lifted the hatches, and I went below. Life there was here, a hideous sort of life, too. Lean rats bigger than kittens, living skeletons horrible with famine. They shrieked, they squeaked, they fled in big shadows. There was not much cargo in the main hold, but cargo there was. I will tell you exactly the contents of the main hold of *La Perfecta Casada*," he exclaimed, coming out of his bed, opening a drawer, and taking out a small book clasped by an elastic band. He read aloud, "Five thousand serons of cocoa – "

"A minute," said I. "Do I understand you to mean that you counted five thousand serons of cocoa while you looked into the hold of that ship, the hour being about two o'clock – I have been following you critically – and your own ship hove to close in with the land?"

"Patience," said he; "it is a reasonable objection, but as a rule I do not like to be interrupted when I am telling a story. Five thousand serons of cocoa – " he repeated.

"Pray," said I, forgetting that he did not like to be interrupted, "what is a seron?"

"A seron is a crate."

"Well, sir?"

"Sixty arobes of alpaca wool – ."

"What is an arobe?"

"An arobe is twenty-five pounds." He continued to read: "One thousand quintals of tin at one hundred pounds per quintal; four casks of tortoiseshell, eight thousand hides in the hair, four thousand tanned hides, and a quantity of cedar planks."

He now looked at me as though he expected me to speak. I addressed him as follows: "What I am listening to is a very interesting story. It is an adventure, and I love adventures. It is said that the charm of the sailor's life lies in its being made up of adventures. That is a lie. Men pass many years at sea and meet with no adventures worth speaking of. A sailor's life is a very mechanical, monotonous routine."

"What do you think of the cargo of *La Perfecta Casada*?"

"*La Perfecta Casada* is the name of the ship in the cave?"

"Yes," he answered.

"It is a very good cargo so far as it goes, but there is very little of it."

"There is enough," said he, with a gesture of his hand. "I should be very pleased to be able to pay the value of that cargo into my banking account."

I made no remark, and he proceeded: "When I had taken a peep into the main hold I caused the after hatch under the roundhouse to be raised, and here I found a number of cases. They were stowed one on top of another, with pieces of timber betwixt them and the ship's lining – an awkward looking job of stevedoring, but good enough, no doubt, to satisfy a Spanish sailor. I left my men above, and descended alone into this part of the hold, and stood looking for a short time around me, roughly calculating the number of these cases, the contents of which I could not be perfectly sure of, though one of two things I knew those contents must consist of. I called up through the hatch to the men to hunt about the ship and find me a chopper or saw, and presently one of them handed me down an axe. I put down the lantern, and letting fly at the first of the cases, with much trouble split open a part of the lid. I would not satisfy myself that all those cases were full until I had split the lids of five as tests or samples of the lot. Then finding that those five cases were full, I concluded that the rest were full. To make sure, however, I beat upon many of them, and the sound returned satisfied me that the cases were heavily full."

"Of what?" said I.

"My men," he continued, taking no notice of my interruption, "were, no doubt, considerably astonished to observe me hacking at the cargo with a heavy axe, as though I had fallen mad, and splintering and smashing up what I saw through sheer lunatic wantonness. I did not care what they thought so long as they did not form correct conclusions. I regained the deck, and bid the fellows put the hatches on while I explored the cabins for the ship's papers. There was a number of cabins under the roundhouse, and in one of them, which had, undoubtedly, been occupied by the captain, I found a stout tin box, locked; but I had a bunch of keys in my pocket, and, strangely enough, the key of a tin box in which I kept my own papers on board the *Hero* fitted this box. I opened it, and seeing at once that the contents were the ship's papers, I put them into my pocket and called to my men to bring the boat alongside. But I had not yet completed my explorations. I threw the axe into the boat, entered her, and pulled into the harbour to look at the weather and to see where the *Hero* was. The *Hero* lay at the distance of a mile, hove-to. The weather was wonderfully fine and calm. We pulled into the cave again to the bows of the ship, and cut off a short length of the hemp cable that was hanging up and down from the hawse-pipe, having parted at about two feet above the edge of the water. The cable was perfectly dry. We unlaid the strands and worked them up into torches and set fire to three of them – that is to say, I and two of the men held aloft these blazing torches, while the other two pulled us slowly into the cave past the ship. There was not much to see after all. The cavern ended abruptly at about a hundred yards astern of the ship. The roof sloped, as I had supposed, almost to the wash of the water, it and the walls working into the shape of a wedge. I had thought to see some fine formations – stalactites, natural columns, extraordinary incrustations, and so forth. There was nothing of the sort. The cave was as like the tunnelling of a coal mine as anything I can think of to compare it with; but how gigantic, to comfortably house a vessel of at least seven hundred tons, finding room for her aloft to the height of her topmast head! It was more like a nightmare than a reality, to look from the black extremity of the cave toward the entrance, and see there the dim green of the day – for the light showed in a faint green – with the upright fabric of the ship black as ink against that veil of green faintness. The water brimmed with a gleam as of black oil to the black walls. One of my men said:

"'Suppose it was to come on to blow hard, dead inshore how would it fare with that ship, sir?'

"'What could happen to hurt her?' I answered. 'Never could a great sea run within the barriers of reefs, and no swell to stir the ship can come out of that sheltered space of water, and keep its weight inside.'

"In truth, I talked to satisfy myself, and satisfied I was. Not the worst hurricane that sweeps those seas can stir or imperil that vessel as she lies. She is as safe as a live toad in a rock, and will perish only from decay."

"But do her people mean to leave her there?" said I.

"We may assume so," he answered, "seeing that she was encaved, as far as I can reckon from the dates of her papers, in or about the month of August, 1810."

Chapter VIII.
A Startling Proposal

Captain Greaves, having pronounced the words with which the last chapter concludes, came out of his bed-place and opened the cabin door. Galloon entered. The captain stood looking. Mr. van Laar was still at breakfast. Captain Greaves and I had been closeted for a very considerable time, yet van Laar still continued to eat at table, and even as I looked at him through the door which the captain held open, I observed that he raised a large mouthful of meat to his lips. Captain Greaves exclaimed, "I am going on deck to look after the brig, I shall be back in a few minutes." He then closed the door, and I occupied the time during which he was absent in patting Galloon and thinking over my companion's narrative.

As yet I failed to see the object of his voyage. Could it be that that object was to warp the Spanish ship out of the cave and navigate her home? I might have supposed this to be his intention had his brig been full of men; but Greaves' crew were below the brig's complement as the average ran in those days of teeming 'tween-decks and crowded forecastles, and they were much too few to do anything with a ship of seven hundred tons ashore in a cave; unless, indeed, Greaves meant to ship a number of hands when on the Western American seaboard.

He returned after an absence of a quarter of an hour.

"I have stripped her of the main topgallant sail," said he; "Yan Bol has the watch. I will tell you what I like about Yan Bol – he has the throat of a cannon; he does not shout, he explodes. He sends an order like a twenty-four-pound ball slinging aloft. The wind of his cry night beat down a sheep."

"Van Laar enjoys his food," said I.

"Van Laar is a gorging baboon," he exclaimed; "but he shall not long be a gorging baboon in my cabin or even on board my ship."

He resumed his seat in his bed, and, pulling from his pocket the little book from which he had read the particulars of the cargo in the main hold of *La Perfecta Casada*, he fastened his eyes upon a page of it, mused a while, and proceeded thus:

"We left the Spanish ship, pulled clear of the reef, and got aboard the *Hero*. I called my mate to me, told him that the island was uncharted, and that it behoved us to clearly ascertain its situation in order to correctly report its whereabouts. Together we went to work to determine its position; our calculations fairly tallied, and I was satisfied. I then ordered sail to be trimmed, and we proceeded on our voyage. When the ship had fairly started afresh I went into my cabin and examined the papers I had brought off the *Casada*. Those papers were, of course, written in Spanish. Though I speak Spanish very imperfectly, almost unintelligibly, I can make tolerable headway, with the help of a dictionary, when I read it. I possessed an English-Spanish dictionary, and I sat down to translate the *Casada*'s papers. Then it was that I discovered there were five thousand serons of cocoa among the cargo, I did not count those serons when I was on board."

"I understand."

"The particulars I have here," said he, slapping the book, "were in the manifest; but there was more than cocoa and wool and tin in that ship – very much more. The cases in the after-hold were full of silver – I had hoped for *gold* when I sang out to my men to seek an axe; but silver it proved to be, and the papers I examined in my cabin told me that those cases contained in all five hundred and fifty thousand milled Spanish dollars of the value, in our money, of four shillings and ninepence apiece, though I am willing to reduce that quotation and call the sum, in English money, ninety-eight thousand pounds."

I opened my eyes wide. "Ha!" said I, "now I think you need tell me no more. This brig is going to fetch the money."

"That is the object of the voyage."

"Your men as yet don't know where they are bound to?"

"Not as yet. I do not intend that they shall know for some time. I want to see what sort of men they are going to prove. They shipped on the understanding that I sailed under secret orders from the brig's owner, and that those orders would not be revealed until we had crossed the equator."

"Van Laar knows nothing, then?"

"No more than the lad Jimmy. If he did – but the cormorant *shan't* know."

"Ninety-eight thousand pounds!" quoth I, opening my eyes again.

"There are several fortunes in ninety-eight thousand pounds," said he, smiling.

"You spoke of a gentleman named Tulp."

"Bartholomew Tulp, my stepfather. I will finish my story. I had plenty of time for reflection, for my voyage home was long. I made up my mind to get those dollars. I was satisfied that the money would remain as safely for years, ay, for centuries if you like, where it lay as if it had been snugged away in some secret part of the solid island itself. There was, indeed, the risk of others sighting the island, landing, discovering the ship, exploring, and then looting her. That risk remains the single element of speculation in this adventure. But what, commercially, is not speculative in the Change Alley meaning of the term? You buy Consols at seventy; next day the city is pale with news which sinks the funds to fifty. Spanish dollars to the value of ninety-eight thousand pounds lie in the hold of a ship encaved in an island south of the Galapagos. Is fortune going to suffer them to stay there till we arrive? I say 'yes.' You, as a seafaring man, will say 'yes.' You know that vessels sighting that island will, seeing that it is not down on the charts, or else most incorrectly noted – for no land where that island is do I find marked upon the Pacific charts which I have consulted – I say you will know that vessels sighting that island will give it a wide berth for fear of the soundings. You will suppose that if a vessel should find herself unexpectedly close in with that land her people will see nothing in a mountainous mass of cinder to court them ashore. You will hold that even supposing a thousand ships should pass the island within the date of my proceeding on my voyage from it in the *Hero* and the date of my arrival off the island in this brig *Black Watch*, there are ninety-nine chances against every one of those thousand ships so opening the land as to catch a sight of the vessel in the cave. The cave itself looks at a distance like a vast shadow or smudge upon the front of the cliff. You must enter the natural harbour, and pull close to the mouth of the cavern, to behold the ship. Yes, it is true that the telescope will at a distance resolve the darkness of the cave into a something that is indeterminable, but that is more than mere shadow. But that this may be done a ship must be in the exact situation the *Hero* was in when I happened to point the glass at the cave, and I say there are ninety-nine chances against any one of a thousand ships being in the exact situation. The money in the *Casada*'s hold is there now, has been there since 1810, and but for me, might be there until the ship falls to pieces with decay. What do you say?"

"Those waters are but little navigated," said I. "All the chances you name are against a vessel sighting your *Casada* as she lies in her shell according to your description. I am of your opinion. The money is there and will remain there. The mere circumstances of those dollars having been a secret of the island for four years is warrant enough to satisfy any man that the island will continue to keep what is now your secret."

He looked extremely gratified, and continued:

"How was I to proceed in the adventure that I was determined to embark on? I am a sailor, which means, of course, that I am a poor man."

"Just so," said I.

"My mother has been dead eight years. Of late I had seen and heard but little of my stepfather. I was aware, however, that he was doing a very good trade as a merchant in Amsterdam. It occurred to me to propose the adventure to him, and when I had finished my business with the *Hero* in the Thames I went across to Amsterdam, with the *Casada*'s papers in my bag, and passed a week with Mynheer Bartholomew Tulp. I needed a week, and a week of seven long days, to bring the old man into my way of thinking. Tulp has Jewish blood in him, and the blood of the Jew is as thick as glue. A Tulp, four generations ago, married a Jewess. The descendants have ever since been marrying Christians, but it will take many generations to extinguish in the Tulps the Mosaic beak, the Aaronic eye, the Solomon leer, the Abrahamic wariness which entered into the Tulps, four generations ago, with honest Rachael Sweers. First Tulp wanted to know how I proposed to get the money. By hiring a small vessel and sailing to the island. How much was he to have? He must make his own terms. How much would I expect? I was in his hands. Supposing, when the money was on board, the crew rose and cut my throat? That was a peril of the sea. He could protect his outlay by insurance, the cost of which he was welcome to deduct from my share of the dollars should I bring the spoil home in safety.

"He was so full of objections that on the morning of the sixth day of my stay at his house I flung from him in a rage. 'I know what you *want*,' I told him: 'you want the silver and you don't want to pay for it. I will see you – ' and I damned him in the names of Abraham, Isaac, and Jacob. He is a little man: he arose from a velvet armchair, and following me on tiptoe as I was leaving the room, he put his hand upon my shoulder and said in a soft voice, 'Michael, how much?' To cut this long yarn short, he commissioned me to seek a vessel, and when I had found the sort of ship I wanted I was to enter into a calculation of the cost of the adventure and let him know the amount I should need within as few guilders as possible. That is the story."

"It is a very remarkable story. I am flattered by your confiding this secret to me."

"It was necessary," he answered.

I did not see *that*, but I let the remark pass. "Where did you meet with this brig?"

"She is owned by a friend of mine who lives at Shadwell. I was thinking all the way home of the *Black Watch* as the ship for my purpose, and strangely enough, among the vessels lying near me in the Pool when I brought up was this brig. In London I shipped the English sailors we have on board and sailed for Amsterdam at the request of Tulp, who desired to victual and equip the ship himself. He put van Laar upon me, on some friend's recommendation, and the remainder of the hands – much too few, but the spirit of Rachael Sweers sweats like a demon in Tulp when there is a stiver to be saved – I shipped at Amsterdam."

"But will not this be strictly what the longshoremen would term a salvage job?"

"I do not intend that it shall be a salvage job. What? Deliver up the dollars to the Dutch or British government and be put off with an award that would scarce do more than pay wages?"

"You mean to run the stuff?"

He nodded. "There is time enough to talk over that," said he; "and yet perhaps it's right I should tell you that Tulp and I have arranged for the running of the dollars so that we shall forfeit not one farthing."

"Well, I heartily wish you joy of your discovery," said I. "This voyage will be your last, no doubt, if the dollars are still where you saw them."

I looked at a little clock that was ticking over a table; it was a quarter after eleven. I then looked at the small scuttle or window which swung with regular oscillations out of the flash of the flying foam into the light of the blowing morning. I then looked at Galloon, and wondered quietly within myself how long it would take me to get home; for the speeding of the brig was continuous; the heave of the sea that rushed her forward was full of the weight of a sort of weather that my experience assured me was not going to fail us on a sudden. When, then, was I going to get home? and while I kept my eyes fastened upon Galloon, I mused with the velocity of thought upon my uncle Captain Round; upon my adventure with the press-gang; upon the *Royal Brunswicker*, and her arrival in the Thames: upon my little property in the cabin I had occupied aboard her, and on the wages which Captain Spalding owed me.

Greaves glanced at the clock at which I had looked. He then said, "Will you be interested to know how Mynheer Tulp proposes to divide the money?"

I begged him to acquaint me with Tulp's proposal.

"There are five hundred and fifty thousand dollars," said Greaves. "Of this money the ship takes half. For ship read Tulp; Tulp's share, therefore, is two hundred and seventy thousand dollars or fifty-five thousand pounds."

"These are big figures," said I. "They slide glibly from the tongue. I suppose a man could behold another fellow's fifty-five thousand pounds without feeling faint; but call a poor sailor into a room and show him fifty-five thousand pounds in gold and tell him it is his, and I believe you would find a large dose of rum the next thing to be done with him."

"The ship gets half," continued Greaves, "I as commander get two-thirds of the remainder."

"How much is that?"

"Thirty-six thousand pounds."

I whistled low and long.

"The mate," proceeded he, "not van Laar, but the mate – " he paused and looked at me with an expression of significant attention; "the mate gets one-third of the remainder – thirty thousand five hundred and fifty-six dollars, or six thousand one hundred and eleven pounds." He read these figures from his little book.

"A good haul for the mate," said I.

"The balance of sixty-one odd thousand dollars," he went on, "goes to the men according to their rating. This they will receive over and above their wages, which average from three to six pounds a month."

"I think Mr. Tulp's division into shares very fair," said I.

"Now," said he, "why do I tell you all this? Why am I revealing to you what not a living soul on board knows or even suspects?"

I regarded him in silence.

"Cannot you anticipate the proposal I intend to make? Will you take van Laar's place on board my brig, and act as my mate?"

I started from my chair. Not for an instant had I suspected that his motive in telling me his story was to enable him to make this offer. I started with so much vehemence that Galloon growled, stirred, and elevated his ears.

"It is a magnificent proposal," said I. "It is an offer of six thousand pounds."

"More," he interrupted. "Your wages will be ten pounds a month."

"I do not like the idea," said I after a pause, "of taking van Laar's place."

"From him, do you mean?"

"From him, of course. The post is another thing."

"It is I," said he, "not you, who take it from him. Now, pray, distinctly understand this. Fielding, that, whether you accept or not, van Laar will shortly cease to be my mate. If you refuse then Yan Bol comes aft, and Laar either takes his place or goes home in the first ship we meet."

He spoke with a hard face and some severity of voice. It was quite clear that his mind was resolved, so far as van Laar's relations with the brig was concerned.

"It is a fine offer," said I.

"You will give me time to think it over, I hope?"

"What time do you require?"

I again looked at the little clock.

"I shall be able to see my way in a few hours, I hope."

"That is not sailor fashion," said he, stepping to a quadrant case and taking the instrument up out of it. "A sailor jumps; he never deliberates."

"I have no clothes save what I am wearing," said I.

"We are well stocked with slops," he exclaimed. "Dutch-made, to be sure, but they are good togs."

"I am without nautical instruments," said I, looking at the quadrant which he held.

"I have three of these," he answered, "and one is at your service."

I rose and took a turn, full of thought, wishing to say "Yes" but wishing to consider, too.

"Even were van Laar," said he, "as good and trustworthy a seaman as ever stepped a deck, I would rather have a fellow-countryman for a mate than a Dutchman, though the Dutchman were the better man. In this case it is wholly the other way about. Here are you, fresh from a long voyage, with the experiences of the sea green upon you. You are young; you are English. I owe you my life; and what a debt is that! Together we can make this voyage not only a rich but a jolly jaunt. On the other hand, is van Laar – no, plague on him, he is not on the other hand, he is out of it. Well, I must now go on deck to take sights. Let me have your answer soon."

He extended his hand, received mine, pressed it cordially, and quitted the cabin.

I followed with Galloon, and, entering the stateroom, paced the deck of it and turned Greaves' proposal over. While I paced, van Laar, with a quadrant in his hand, came out of a cabin abreast of the captain's. He stared me full and insolently in the face, and said in a tone of irony:

"Veil, how vhas it mit you? Do you feel like going home now?"

"The sun will have crossed his meridian if you don't hurry up," said I.

"Vot der doyvel vhas der sun to you, sir?"

I turned my back upon him and continued to pace the deck, not choosing that he should fasten a quarrel upon me – as yet, at all events.

His insolence, however, helped me in my reflections by extinguishing him as a condition to be borne in mind. I had been influenced by compunction; now I had none. I watched the fat beast climb the companion ladder, and after him, and then over the side into the seething water to lie drowned forever, went all compunction. How could Greaves work with such a man? How could he live in a ship with such a man? So, opening the door of my mind, I kicked Mate van Laar headlong out of my contemplation, and resolution did not then seem very hard to form.

I sat down, and said to Galloon:

"What shall I do?"

Galloon stood upon his hind legs, and, resting his fore feet upon my knees, looked up at me with eyes which beamed with cordial invitation and affectionate solicitude.

"What shall I do, Galloon?" said I. "Six thousand pounds is a large sum of money for a man of my degree. Can I doubt that the dollars are in the ship inside the cave? If Tulp is to be convinced, I should. There was the Spanish manifest; there were the cases beheld by Greaves' own eyes. Why should Greaves invent this yarn? I will stake my life, Galloon, upon its being true. Six thousand pounds! And d'ye know, my noble dog, that there is more money in six thousand pounds than your master's reckoning of the Spanish dollar swells the amount to? In Jamaica the Spanish dollar passes for six-and-eightpence; in parts of North America for eight shillings; and in the Windward Islands for nine shillings;" and then I told Galloon what I should do when I received the six thousand pounds: how I would buy me a little house at Deal and a boat, live like a gentleman on the interest of what was left, and spend the time merrily in flashing and sailing.

The dog listened with attention. At times I seemed to catch a slight inclination of the head, as though he nodded approvingly. I counted upon my fingers all the advantages which must attend my acceptance of Greaves' offer. First, the post of mate at ten pounds a mouth, with a voyage before me of at least twelve months; then my association with a man whose company was exceedingly agreeable to me, between whom and me there must always be such a bond of sympathy as nothing but the prodigious and pathetic services we had done each other could establish; then the possibility – nay, the more than possibility, of my receiving six thousand pounds as my dividend of the adventure. These and the like considerations I summed up. What was the *per contra*? The forfeiture of a few weeks of holiday ashore! Spalding's debt to me stood good, and would be paid whenever I turned up to receive the money. My being seized by the press-gang, the boat being stove, and my being picked up insensible and carried away into the ocean – all this was no fault of mine. Therefore Spalding would pay me the money.

"Galloon, I will accept," said I, and jumped up; and the dog fell to cutting capers about me, springing here and there, like a dog in front of a trotting horse, and barking joyously.

Chapter IX.
I Fight Van Laar

About the hour of four, that same afternoon, I followed Greaves out of his berth into the state cabin and living room. We had been closeted for an hour, and during that hour our discourse had related wholly to the voyage. I followed him into the cabin. There had been no change in the weather since the morning. The brig was rushing through the swollen seas under whole topsails and some fore-and-aft canvas, to keep her head straight, for now and again she would yaw widely with the swing of the surge, and, indeed, it needed two stout fellows at the wheel to keep the sheet of rushing wake astern of her a fairly straight line.

We had not entered the cabin five minutes when van Laar descended the companion steps. It was four o'clock. Yan Bol had come on to the quarter-deck to relieve the mate until the hour of six, and van Laar, descending the ladder, was rolling in a thrusting and sprawling walk to his berth, without taking the least notice of the captain and me, when Greaves stopped him.

"Van Laar, sit down. I have something to say to you."

The Dutch mate rounded suddenly. The insipid and meaningless layers of fat which formed his face were quickened by an expression of surprise. He had pulled his cloth cap off on entering, and now worried it between his hands as he stared at Greaves. His mind worked slowly. Presently he gathered from the looks of Greaves that he was to expect something unpleasant, on which he said:

"I do not wish to sit down. Vy der doyvil should I sit down? Vot hov you to say, Captain Greaves?"

"You are already aware that I am dissatisfied with you," said Greaves.

"'Ow vhas dot?"

"I desire no words. Enough if I tell you *simply* that you do not suit me."

"Vy der doyvil did you engage me, den?"

"I was misled by Mynheer Tulp, who was misled by Mynheer somebody else," answered Greaves, admirably controlling his voice, but nevertheless sternly surveying the man whom he addressed. "I was told that you knew your duty as a seaman and as a mate, but you are so ignorant of your duty that I will no longer trust you on my quarter-deck."

"Vy der doyvil did you ask me to schip? If I do not know my duty, vhas dere a half-drown man ash we drag on boardt dot can teach her to me?"

"I do not choose to go into that," exclaimed Captain Greaves calmly. "I presume you are not so ignorant of the sea but that you know what my powers as a commander are?"

"Hey! you speaks too vast for me."

The captain slowly and deliberately repeated his remark.

"Oh, yes," exclaimed van Laar, with a slow sideways motion of the head. "I need not to be instrocted as to dere powers of a commander, nor do I need to be instrocted as to dere rights of dose who sail oonder her. I vhas your mate; what hov you to say against dot?"

"Which will you do," said Greaves, with a note of impatience in his voice, "will you take the place of second mate, in the room of Yan Bol, who will be glad to be relieved of that trust, or will you go home by the first ship that'll receive you?"

Van Laar looked from Greaves to me, and from me to Greaves, and putting his cap upon the table, and thrusting his immensely fat hands into his immensely deep trousers' pockets, he exclaimed, with a succession of nods:

"Dis vhas a consbiracy."

"Conspiracy or no conspiracy," said Greaves, scarcely concealing a smile, "you will give me your answer at once, if you please. My mind is made up."

"Dis vhas your doing," said van Laar, looking at me; and he pulled his right hand out of his pocket and held it clenched.

"Make no reference to that gentleman," cried Greaves, "I am the captain of this ship, and all that is done is of my doing, I await your answer."

"Vy der doyvil," said van Laar deliberately, with his eyes fastened upon my face, "vhas not you drown? Shall I tell you? Because you vhas reserve for anoder sort of end," and here he bestowed a very significant nod upon me.

I felt the blood in my cheeks. I could have whipped him up the steps and overboard for talking to me like that, I looked at Greaves, met his glance, bit my lip, and held my peace.

"Which will you do, Mr. van Laar?" said Captain Greaves. "If you do not answer for yourself I will find an answer for you."

"Gott, but I hov brought my hogs, as you English say, to a pretty market, I am dere servant of Mynheer Bartholomew Tulp."

"I am master of this ship and you are my mate. I can break you and send you forward. I can have you triced up and your broad breech ribbanded. I can swing you at the yardarm till your neck is as long as an emu's. Why do I tell you this? Because you are ignorant of the sea and must learn that my powers are not to be disputed by any man under me, from you down, or, as I would rather say, from you up," he added, with a sarcastic sneer.

"Vhat vhas your offer?" said the mate.

There was a perversity in this man's stupidity that was very irritating. The captain quietly named again the alternative.

"Vat vhas dis voyage about?" inquired the mate.

"That is my affair."

The Dutchman stood gazing at one or the other of us. He then put on his cap and saying, "I vill schmoke a pipe in my bed und tink him out," he made a step toward his berth.

"I must have your answer by six o'clock," said the captain.

The mate, taking no notice of Greaves' remark, entered his berth and closed the door.

Greaves and I were silent upon the man's behaviour; he was so absolutely and helplessly in the power of his captain that the sense of fair play would not suffer us to speak of him.

"I will tell Jimmy," said Greaves, "to get the slop chest up, and you can overhaul it for the clothes you require. You will want a chest; *that* can be managed. What else will you require? Your bedroom needs furnishing. I can lend you a razor and give you a hairbrush. Linen and boots you will find among the slops. As to wages – we will àrrange it thus: I shall give a written undertaking to each of the crew, on announcing to them the purpose of this voyage. In my undertaking to you, in which I shall state your share, I can name the wages agreed upon – ten pounds a month, starting from today, which of course, I will make a note of in my log book. Does this meet your views?"

"Handsomely," I answered.

He left his seat.

"With your leave, captain," said I, "it is *captain* now; it shall be *sir* anon."

"No, no," he interrupted, "not the least need; not as between you and me, Fielding. In the presence of the crew and in the interests of discipline, why, perhaps it had better be an occasional sir for me, you know, and a *mister* for you, d'ye see? But the words may be uttered with our tongues in our cheeks. What were you going to say?"

"That with your leave, I will at once write a letter to my uncle Captain Joseph Round, relating my adventures, telling him where I am, but not where I am bound to, and requesting him to communicate with Captain Spalding, that my wages may be sent to my uncle at Deal. We may fall in with a ship in any hour and I will have a letter ready."

"Right," he exclaimed, "you will find pen and ink and paper in my cabin;" and he sprang up the hatch, whistling cheerily, as though his mind were extraordinarily relieved, not indeed through my agreeing to serve under him – oh no, I am not such a coxcomb as to believe *that* – but because he had as good as cleared van Laar off his quarter-deck.

I entered his berth, and finding the materials I required for producing a letter, I returned to the cabin, seated myself at the table, and began a letter to my uncle Joseph. The chair I occupied was at the forward end of the table, and when I raised my eyes from the paper, I commanded both the captain's and the mate's berths. It was about half-past four. There was plenty of daylight; the windy westering sunshine came and went upon the cabin skylight with the sweep of the large masses of vapour across the luminary. The roar of frothing waters alongside penetrated dully. The lift of the brig was finely buoyant and rhythmic, insomuch that you might almost have made time out of the swing of a tray over the table, as you make time out of the oscillations of a pendulum.

I had nearly completed my letter when, happening to lift my head to search the skylight for a thought, or perhaps for the spelling of a word, I beheld the fat countenance of van Laar surveying me from his doorway. On my looking at him he withdrew his head, with a manner of indecision. I went on writing. The lad Jimmy came into the cabin, followed by Galloon. The boy, as I call him, busied himself, and I went on with my letter, the dog jumping on to the chair which he occupied at meals, and watching me. Presently, looking up, I again perceived van Laar's head in his doorway. Once more he withdrew, but at the instant of signing my letter, I heard a strange noise close beside me; I seemed to smell spirits; I raised my eyes. Van Laar stood at the table, leaning upon it, and breathing very heavily; his breathing, indeed, sounded like a saw cutting through timber; his little eyes were uncommonly fierce and fiery, and the flesh of his face of a dull red. The moment my gaze met his, he exclaimed:

"You vhas a broodelbig!"

His accent was so much broader than the spelling which I have endeavoured to convey it in that I did not understand him. I believed he had applied some injurious Dutch word to me.

"What do you say?" I exclaimed.

"I should like to know," said he, fingering the cuffs of his coat as though he meant to turn them up, "vhat sort of a man you vhas. Who vhas you? 'Ow vhas it you vhas half drown? 'Ow comes you into dere water? Vhas you chooked overboart? Maype you vhas a pirate? I should like to know some more about you. Vhat schip vhas yours? Have you a farder? Vere vhas you porn?"

"Return to your cabin and finish your pipe and bottle," said I. "Do not meddle with me, I beg you."

"Meddle! Vhat vhas dot? Meddle; I must hov satisfaction of my questions. My master is Mynheer Tulp. Am I to give oop my place to a half-drown man, vhen I hov agree for der voyage mit Mynheer Tulp's consent?" He swelled his breast and roared – "No beast of an Englishman shall take dere place of van Laar in a schip dot vhas own by Mynheer Tulp." He then smote the table furiously with his fist, and, putting his face close to mine, he thundered out – "You are a broodelbig!" *Now* I understood him to mean "a brutal pig," my ear having, perhaps, been educated by his previous speech.

"Jimmy," I exclaimed, "hold the dog!" and, with the back of my hand, I slapped the Dutchman heavily on the nose.

The dog growled. Jimmy sprang and clasped the creature round the neck, holding him in a vice, and grinning with every fang in his head between the dog's ears. A fight to an English lad, himself clasping a growling dog to his heart! Match him such another joy if you can!

Having struck van Laar, I stood up and immediately pulled off my coat and waistcoat. Van Laar also undressed himself, and, while he did so, he bawled out:

"I vhas sorry for you. Better for you had you never been porn. If I vhas you, I like some more to be drown or hang dan to be you."

He stripped himself to his flesh, keeping nothing but his trousers on, and stood before me like a vast mass of yellow soap. He was drenched with perspiration. Galloon barked hoarsely at him. I was almost disposed to regard this exhibition of himself as an appeal to my sensibility. He was shaped like a dugong – after the pattern, indeed, of one of the most corpulent of those interesting marine epicenes. He opposed to me a ton of infuriate flesh. How could I strike it, or rather *where*? It would be like plunging my fist into a full slush-pot.

"Dere better der man dere better der mate!" he roared, call upon Cott, if you belief in Him, to help you. Dere better der man dere better der mate! Goom on!"

Poising his immense fists close against his face, he approached me, and then, hoping perhaps to end the business at a *coup*, he rushed upon me, whirling both his arms with the velocity of a windmill in a strong breeze. I took a step and planted a blow, but not without compunction, for I saw that the poor devil had no science. I say I planted a blow in his right eye, which instantly took a singular expression of leering. I backed and he followed, still swinging his arms; and certainly, had I permitted one of those rotary fists to descend upon my head, I must have gone down as though to the blow of a handspike. But alas! for poor van Laar. He knew nothing of boxing, and I was well versed in that art. I dodged him for a while, hoping that, by winding him, I should be able to bring the battle to a bloodless close. But the fellow had very remarkable staying powers; he seemed unnaturally strong in the wind considering his tonnage. He continued to thrash the air, seeking to rush upon me, while he thundered:

"Dere better der man, dere better der mate!"

So, to end the business, I knocked him down. He fell flat and heavily upon his back. Jimmy roared with laughter, and Galloon barked furiously at the yellow heap on the deck, straining in the lad's arms to get at it. Greaves came into the cabin. He stopped when in the companion way, and stared at the motionless figure of van Laar.

"Is the man killed?" cried he.

"Oh, dear, no," I answered. "He's only resting."

"What is all this about?" he demanded.

I told him how it had come about, but when I repeated the insulting expression which had been twice made use of, van Laar sat up and said:

"It vhas true, but I will fight no more mit you. I allow dot you are der better man. I said, 'Dere better der man, dere better der mate,' and dat shall be as Cott pleases."

"Go to your cabin, sir!" cried Greaves, looking at him with disgust; but, on van Laar turning his face, the captain's countenance relaxed. The Dutchman's eye was closed, and it painted upon his countenance the fixed expression of a wink; otherwise he was not hurt. I had known how to fell him without greatly injuring him or drawing blood, and the worst of the knockdown blow I had administered lay in the shock of the fall of his own weight.

"Go to your cabin, sir," repeated the captain, "and keep to it. Consider yourself under arrest. Your brutal conduct now determines me to clear the ship of you, and you shall be sent home by the first vessel that I can speak."

"You vhas in a hurry," said van Laar, getting on to his legs, and beginning to pick up his clothes: "had you vaited you would have foundt me first. It vhas me," he roared, striking his fat chest, "who tell you, and not you who tell me, dot I leave for goot dis footy hooker. But stop," cried he, wagging his fat forefinger at the captain, "till I see Mynheer Tulp. Den I vhas sorry for you," and thus speaking he went to his cabin, bearing his clothes with him.

I put on my coat and waistcoat, and exclaimed, "I am truly grieved that this should have happened. Yonder lad Jimmy witnessed the fellow's treatment of me."

"There is nothing to regret," said Greaves. "Yes, I regret that you did not punish him more severely. He knows that you have been insensible for three days, and the coward, no doubt, counted upon finding you weak after your illness."

"It is well for him," said I, "that he should have made up his mind at once that I am the better man. I felt a sort of pity for the shapeless bulk when I saw it rushing upon me, with its arms whirring like the flails of a thresher upon a whale. A fellow apprentice of mine, in the third voyage I made, was the son of a prize-fighter. He had learnt the art from his father, and claimed to have his science. Many a stand-up affair happened between this youth and me, during our watches below. He showed me every trick at last, though the education cost my face some new skins."

"If van Laar shows himself on deck, or indeed, if he leaves his berth, I'll clap him in irons," said Greaves. "Meanwhile, Fielding, you will enter upon your duties at once, providing you feel strong enough."

"Perfectly strong enough," said I.

"Very well," said he, "you will relieve Yan Bol at four bells, and I will call the crew aft and tell them that you are mate of the *Black Watch*."

So here now was I chief mate of a smart brig, with ten pounds a month for wages, not to mention the six thousand pounds I was to take up if we brought our cargo of dollars home in safety. Truthfully had I told Greaves that my adventures at sea had been few, but surely now life was making atonement for her past beggarly provision of strange, surprising experiences, by the creation of incidents incomparably romantic and memorable, as I will maintain before the whole world, was that incident of the gibbet, on the sand hills near Deal.

When I reached the deck I found a noble, flying, inspiring scene of swelling and cleaving and foaming brigand ocean curling southward. Through the lustre of an angry, glorious sunset, the froth flew in flakes of blood, and every burst of white water from the courtesying bows was crimson with sparkles as of rubies. I wondered, when I looked at the see-saw sloping of the deck, how on earth the Dutchman and I had managed to keep our pins while we fought. Yet, why did I wonder? I found myself standing beside the captain, no more sensible than he of a swing and sway that when it came to a roll was roof-steep often, gazing forward with him at the crew, who were assembling in response to the boatswain's summons, preparatory to laying aft.

This was a small business and promptly dispatched. Two men were at the wheel, and eight men, leaving Jim Vinten out, came to the mainmast to hear what the captain had to say. He said no more than this: "Yan Bol, and you men: Mr. van Laar is under arrest in his cabin, and Mr. William Fielding here is and will be the mate of the *Black Watch*. He is a much better man than van Laar. You would split your throats with huzzas did you know how very much smarter Mr. Fielding is than van Laar. We want nothing but sharp and able men aboard the *Black Watch*. You'll know why anon – you'll know why anon. I have my eye upon ye, lads, and so far, I'm very well satisfied. You seem a willing crew; keep so. A man, after he has heard our errand, would sooner have cut his throat than fail me. Heed me well, hearts, for this is to be a big cruise. Here's your mate, Mr. William Fielding," and he put his hand upon my shoulder.

The fellows stared very hard. They were strangers to me as yet, and I knew not which were Dutch and which were English; but some exchanged looks with a half-suppressed grin, and those I guessed were English. Yan Bol stood forward – Yan we called him, though he spelt his name with a J. He was, as you have heard, boatswain, carpenter, and sailmaker, a stern, bearded, beetle-browed man, heavily clothed with hair – leonine – indeed, in the matter of hair.

"I beg pardon, captain," said he, "does Herr van Laar goom forward?"

"No," answered the captain," he goes over the side presently, when there's a ship to pick him up."

"I vhas to be second mate still?"

"Yaw, it is so, Yan. We want no better man."

But the compliment was not relished. Methought Yan Bol, as he fronted the stormy western light, looked sterner and more beetle-browed, hairier, and more bearded than before, when he understood that he was to remain second mate.

"There are three Dutchmen aboard not counting you, Bol," said the captain, "and seven Englishmen. I want such a distribution of watches, as will put the three Dutchmen under you, Yan. Wirtz, you and Hals will come out of the starboard into the larboard watch, and Meehan and Travers will take their place. That's all I've got to say, excepting this – pipe for grog, Bol, to drink the health of the new mate."

This dismissed them chuckling. Bol sounded this whistle, and Jimmy presently came out of the cabin and went forward with a can of black rum swinging in his hand.

"I am lumping the Dutchmen together under one head," said Greaves, as we paced the deck, "to give their characters a chance of developing, before they learn the motive of this voyage. Not that I have more or less faith in Dutchmen than in Englishmen; but sailors of a nationality do not distrust one another, therefore whatever is bad will quickly ripen: but mix them with others and you arrest rapid development by misgiving; and a difficulty, that might come to a head quickly, is delayed until a remedy becomes difficult or impracticable."

"I understand you, sir." He smiled on my giving him the *sir* for the first time. "You want to get at the character of your crew as promptly as may be."

"That I may clear my forecastle of whatever is doubtful. A cargo of five hundred and fifty thousand dollars makes a rich ship, and a rich ship is a wicked temptation to wicked men. It is a pity we could not manage with fewer hands; but death, sickness, many disabling causes are to be considered; the voyage is a long one there is the Horn; we could not have done with less men."

"I wonder what notion of this voyage the men have in their heads," said I. "I watched them while you talked. I could not see that they made sign by grin, or stare, or look."

"They would not be sailors if they were not careless of the future," said Greaves. "What's for dinner today? *That's* it, you know. Is there a shot in the locker? Is there a drop of rum in the puncheon? Is there a fiddle aboard? and if the answer be yea, marry, a clear, strong, manly bass voice sings out, 'All's well.' Those men don't care, because they don't think. Can't you hear them talk, Fielding? – 'Where the blazes are we bound to, I wonder? – Hand us that pipe along for a draw and a spit, matey.' – 'I'm for the land o' shoe-shine arter this job, bullies' – 'Der bork in dis schip vhas goodt,' says a Dutchman. Then grunt goes another, and snore goes a third, and the rest is snorting. Don't it run so. Fielding? *You* know sailors as well as I. But I'll tell you what; it'll put gunpowder into the heels of their imaginations, to learn that we're going to load dollars out of a derelict. They shan't know yet a bit. Well it is that van Laar doesn't know either. Tulp was for having me explain the nature of our errand to him. 'No, by Isten,' said I – which I believe is Hungarian – 'no, by Isten,' I exclaimed, 'no man shall know what business we're upon till I have gained some knowledge of the character of the company of fellows who are under me.'"

"All this makes me feel your confidence in me the more flattering, sir." said I.

"Don't *over* sir me. I must replace a guzzling and gorging baboon of a Dutch mate – a worthless mass of unprofessional fat – I must replace this hogshead of lard by a *man*, and Galloon finds me the man I need lying half-drowned off Ramsgate. I want him very earnestly, very imperatively. I must have a mate – a smart, English seaman. Here he is; but how am I to keep him? He is not going to be detained by vague talk of a voyage whose issue I decline to say anything about, whose motive is mysterious – criminal, for all he is to know – imperilling the professional reputation of those concerned in it, with such a gibbet as that which stands upon the sand hills at the end of it all. No; to keep you I must be candid, or you wouldn't have stayed."

"That is true."

"See to the brig, Fielding. She's a fine boat, don't you think? If she didn't drag so much water – look at that lump of sea on either quarter – she'd be a comet in speed. "Why the deuce don't the shipwrights ease off when they come aft, instead of holding on with the square run of the butter-box to the very lap of the taffrail?"

He looked aloft; he looked around the sea; he walked to the binnacle and watched the motion of the card; he then went below.

It was nearly dark. The red was gone out of the west, but the dying sheen of it seemed to linger in the south and east, whither the shapeless masses of shadow were flying across the pale and windy stars, piling themselves down there with a look of boiling-up, as though the rush of vapour smote the hindmost of the clouds into steam.

Why, thought I, it was but a day or two ago that I, mate of the *Royal Brunswicker*, was conning that ship, with her head pointing t'other way, in these same waters; and then I was thinking of Uncle Joe, and of some capers ashore, and of the relief of a month or two's rest from the derned hurl of the restless billow, as the poets call it, with plenty of country to smell and fields to walk in, and a draught of new milk whenever I had a mind. Only a day or two ago – it seems no longer. Insensibility takes no count of time. In fact, whether I knew it or not, I went to sea again on this voyage on the same day on which I arrived in the Downs, after two years of furrin-going. How will it end? I shall become a fish. But six thousand pounds, thought I, to be picked up, invested, safely secured betwixt this and next May, I dare say! Oh, it's good enough – it's good enough; and I whistled through my teeth, with a young man's light heart, as I walked, watching the brig closely, nevertheless, and observing that the fellows at the helm kept her before it, as though her keel was sweeping over metal rails.

Chapter X.
We Tranship Van Laar

It blew fresh all that night and all next day. I was for carrying on, and shook a reef out of the forecourse and set the topgallant sail; and when Greaves came on deck he looked up, and that was all. He would not trust the brig with too much sail on her in a staggering breeze when van Laar had charge of the deck; but he trusted her now, and trusted her afterward to Yan Bol when he came to relieve me; and hour after hour the *Black Watch* stormed along, bowing her spritsail yard at the bowsprit's end into the foam of her own hurling till it was buried, and every shroud and backstay was as taut as wire, and sang, swelling into such a concert as you must sail the stormy ocean to hear, with a noise of drums rolling through it out of the hollow of the sails, and no lack of bugle notes and trumpeting as each sea swept the brig to its summit.

On the third day the weather was quiet. It was shortly before the hour of noon. A light swell was flowing out of the north, but the breeze was about northwest, and the brig was pushing through it under studding-sails. The men were preparing to get their dinner, one of the Dutch seamen at the wheel, and Greaves and I standing side by side, each with a quadrant in his hand.

"I wish," exclaimed the captain, "that something would come along – something to receive van Laar! The fancy of that fellow confined in his berth is not very agreeable to me. Jimmy tells me that he smokes all day; that he removes the pipe from his mouth merely to eat. Then, indeed, the pipe is for some time out of his mouth."

"Sail ho!" I exclaimed at that instant; for, while he addressed me, my gaze was upon the sea over the lee bow, and there, like a hovering feather, hung a sail.

Greaves looked at her, and exclaimed:

"I hope she is coming this way, I hope she is homeward bound, and that she will receive van Laar."

We applied our eyes to our quadrants, made eight bells, and, leaving Yan Bol to keep a lookout, went below.

"How am I to foist van Laar upon a ship's captain?" said he, as we entered his berth to work out the latitude. "Is he a passenger? Then he must pay. But van Laar is not a man to pay, and not one doit shall I be willing to pay for him. Is he a distressed mariner whom we have picked up? No. What is he but an inefficient officer, full of mutiny beef, tobacco, and schnapps? I may find difficulty in persuading a captain to take him.

I hope it may not come to it, but I fear I shall be forced to throw him overboard."

We worked out the latitude and entered the cabin. Galloon sat upon his chair at the table, watching Jimmy lay the cloth for dinner.

"What are you going to give us to eat, Jimmy?" said the captain.

"Oh, I know, master," replied the lad with his foolish smile; and here I observed that Galloon looked at him. "It's roast beef today, master."

"There is no fresh beef in the ship; therefore we are not going to have roast beef for dinner. Corned beef it is, not roast beef. Say corned beef, not roast beef."

The boy, stiffening himself into the posture of a private soldier at sight of his officer, cried in a groaning voice:

"Say corned beef, not roast beef!" and Galloon howled in sympathy.

"Again, if you please."

"Say corned beef, not roast beef!" bawled the youth; and Galloon's howl rose high in suffering.

"Once more."

The boy bellowed, and the dog's accompaniment made a horrible duet.

Scarcely had the noise ceased when van Laar opening his door, put his head out, and cried:

"Vhas dere cornedt beef ready?"

"You will give that man ship's bread for his dinner," said Greaves calmly. "If he shows his nose again I will have a hammock slung for him in the lazarette – the lazarette or the fore-peak – he may take his choice; but the hatch will be kept on."

These words had no sooner left the captain's lips than van Laar came out of his berth.

"You debrive me of my liberty," he shouted in his deepest tones, "and I vhas content till ve meets mit a schip to take me out of dis beesly hooker. But, by Cott! mine dinner vhas to be someding more dan schip's bread, or I vhas sorry for you, Dis is Mynheer Tulp's schip. I oxpects my full rations. If not, I goes to der law vhen I gets home, and I takes der bedt from oonder you und your vife. A pretty consbiracy – first against mine liberty and now against mine appetite. I have brought my hogs, as you Englishmen say, to a nice market indeedt."

"Mr. Fielding," said Captain Greaves quietly, "step on deck, if you please, and send Yan Bol to me with the bilboes. You will keep the deck till Yan Bol returns."

I hastened up the ladder, and found Yan Bol tramping to and fro. I repeated the captain's instructions to him.

Who vhas der bilboes for?" said he, in a voice that trembled upon the ear with the power of its volume.

"Van Laar," said I.

He looked not in the least surprised.

"For Herr van Laar. I shall hov to pick out der biggest;" and he went forward to fetch the bilboes, as the irons in which sailors' legs were imprisoned were in those days termed.

We had considerably risen the sail that I had made out shortly before eight bells, and I took the telescope from the companion way to look at her. She was apparently a small brig, smaller than the *Black Watch*, visible as yet above the horizon to the line of her bulwark rails only. I found something singular in the trim of her canvas, but she was too far off at present to make sure of in any direction of character, tonnage, or aspect, and I returned the glass to its brackets, satisfied at all events to have discovered that she was heading to cross our hawse, and would be within easy speaking distance anon.

Bol came aft with the bilboes and descended into the cabin, whence very soon afterward there arose through the open skylight a great noise of voices. Van Laar was giving trouble. He declined to sit quietly while Yan Bol fitted him. His deep voice roared out Dutch oaths, intermingled with insults in English levelled at Captain Greaves.

Galloon barked furiously, and Yan Bol's deeper notes rolled upward like the sound of thunder above the explosions of artillery. Presently I heard a noise of wrestling; then van Laar called out:

"All right, all right! Let me go! Put her on! I vhas quiet now, but after dis, if I vhas you, I vould hang myself."

His voice was then muffled, as though he had been dragged or carried into his cabin, and a few minutes later Yan Bol came on deck, lifting his hair with one hand and wiping the sweat from under it with the other.

"He gifs too much trouble," said he, with a massive shake of his head, "it vhas not right. He vhas a badt sailor, too. I could have told Captain Greaves dot before we sailed from Amsterdam. Van Laar put a ship ashore two years ago. He vhas too fat and lazy for der sea. He vhas ignorant, and has not a sailor's heart in him."

"I do not know what sort of a sailor he is," said I, "but a more insulting son of a swab I never met in my life."

"Dere's a ship dot may take him," said Bol, levelling a hand as big as a shovel at the sea.

"Mr. Bol, please to keep your eye upon her while I am below," said I; "one needs to be wary in these waters."

"Let me look at her," said he, and he fetched the glass. "Dere vhas noting for dis brig to be afraid of in *her*" said he, after a slow Dutch gaze and ruminating pause; "it vhas not all right, I belief, but vhat vhas wrong mit her vhas right for us."

Jimmy passed with the cabin dinner from the galley. A minute later he arrived to report it served. I went below, and was about to sit down when I suddenly exclaimed:

"Hark, what is that?"

"Van Laar singing," said Greaves.

He took his seat, looking very severely, but on a sudden his face collapsed, and he burst into a fit of laughter.

"Ye Gods, what a voice!" he cried. "He is improvising, and pretty cleverly too. He is asking in Dutch for his dinner, *rhyming* as he goes along and shouting his fancies to a Dutch air. Yet shall he get no beef, though he should sing till his windpipe splits. I am getting mighty sick of this business. What of the sail?"

"We are rising her fairly fast and she's heading our way. The wind is taking off and I don't think we shall be abreast much before another hour."

Van Laar ceased to sing.

"Is Jimmy an idiot?" said I, when the lad's back was turned.

"Not at all. He is a very honest lad, with the strength of two mules in his limbs. He has sailed with me before. I have carried him on this voyage because of his foolishness. I did not want too much forecastle intelligence to be dodging about my table."

"Hark!" said I, "van Laar is calling."

"Captain," roared the voice of the Dutchman, in syllables perfectly distinct, though dulled by the bulkhead which his lungs had to penetrate, "vhas I to hov any dinner? Dis vhas Mynheer Tulp's ship. I vhas sorry for you if you starf me."

Jimmy returned.

"When did Mr. van Laar breakfast?" said Greaves to him.

The youth looked up at the clock in the skylight, and answered instantly:

"At one bell, master," meaning half-past eight.

"What did he have?"

"A trayful, master," and I noticed that the boy talked with his eyes fixed on Galloon, while the dog looked up at him as though ready to howl presently.

"But what did he have?"

"He had coffee, mutton chops, sights of biscuits, a tin of preserved pork, more biscuit, master, ay, and fried bacon – twice he sent me to the galley for fried bacon, and he was eating from one bell till hard upon fower."

"There are no mutton chops on board this ship," said Greaves, "and as to tins of preserved pork – but you will guess," said he, looking at me, "that the hog's trough was liberally brimmed; and still the beast grunts. Listen!"

Van Laar was now singing again. Presently he ceased and talked loudly to himself. He then fell silent; but by this time Greaves and I had dined and we went on deck.

The brig, that had seemingly shifted her course, as though to stand across our hawse, was lying hove-to off the weather bow. There was a colour at the peak. I brought the glass to bear and made out the English ensign, union down. She had a very weedy and worn look as she lay rolling and pitching somewhat heavily upon the light swell. Her sails beat the masts with dislocating thumps, and in imagination I could hear the twang of her rigging to the buckling of her spars. She was timber laden; the timber rose above her rails.

"What on earth is she towing?" exclaimed Greaves, looking at her through the glass.

I could not make the object out; something black, resembling a small capsized jolly-boat, rose and fell close astern of her. It jumped with a wet flash, then disappeared past the brow of a swell, jumped again and vanished as though hoisted and sunk by human agency. We ran the ensign aloft and bore slowly down, and when we were within speaking distance hove to.

Presently we made out the queer flashful object astern of the dirty, woebegone little brig to be nothing more nor less than a large cask, suspended at the end of the trysail gaff; the line was rove through a big block up there and led forward, but into what part of the ship I could not then perceive. Three men were squatted on the timber that was built round about the galley chimney; their hands clasped their knees, they eyed us with their chins on their breasts. The melancholy appeal of the inverted ensign was not a little accentuated by the distressful posture of those three squatting men. A fourth man stood aft. He was clad in a long yellow coat, and wore a red shawl round his neck, and a hat like a Quaker's. When we were within speaking distance, and silence had followed the operation of bringing the brig to a stand, the man in the yellow coat called in a wild, melancholy voice across the water:

"Brig ahoy!"

"Hallo!"

"Will you send a boat?"

"What is wrong with you?"

"Anan?"

"What is wrong with you?" roared Greaves.

"There's nothen' that's right with us," was the answer.

"What ship is that?"

"The *Commodore Nelson*."

"Where are you from, and where are you bound to?"

"From Quebec to the Clyde."

"The Clyde!" exclaimed Greaves, looking at me. "Where does he make the Clyde to flow? But he's homeward bound, and you shall induce him to take van Laar. Go over to him, Fielding, and see what is wrong;" and he called across the water to the man in the yellow coat, "I will send a boat."

A boat was lowered; four men and myself entered her. We pulled alongside the wallowing little brig, and I clambered aboard. It was like hearkening to the sound of a swaying cradle. She creaked in every pore, creaked from masthead to jib boom end, from the eyes to the taffrail. She was full of wood and rolled with deadly lunges. The three men continued to sit upon the timber that was piled round about the galley chimney. They turned their eyes upon me when I stepped on board, but seemed incapable of taking more exercise than that.

I made my way over the deck cargo to where the man in the yellow coat was standing, and as I went I observed that the end of the line which was rove through the block attached to the gaff led through another block, secured near one of the pumps and fastened – that is to say, the end of the line was fastened – to the brake or handle of the pump, which was frequently and violently jerked, causing water to gush forth, but intermittently and spasmodically.

"What is wrong with you?" said I, approaching the man who awaited me instead of advancing to receive me, as though he had some particular reason in desiring to converse with me aft.

"Everything is wrong," he answered, in a patient, melancholy voice. "First of all, will ye tell me what's today?"

"Do you mean the day of the week or the day of the month?"

"Both," he answered.

Not a little astonished by this question, I supplied him with the information he desired.

"Thought as much," said he, mildly jerking his fist. "Two days wrong. Yesterday was my birthday and a' never knew it."

"Did you say that you are bound to the Clyde?"

"That's where this cargo's consigned to," he answered, "and of course us men go along with it."

"What are you doing down in these latitudes?"

He gazed round the sea with a lost-my-way expression of eye, and replied:

"I don't know where we are."

"The Canary Islands bear about thirty leagues east-southeast," said I.

He stared at the horizon as though, by looking hard, he would see the Canary Islands.

"Pray, what are you?" said I, looking at him and then glancing at his little ship and the three men who sat disconsolately clasping their knees on top of the deck-load.

"I am the second mate and carpenter."

"Where's your captain?"

"Gone blind and mad," he answered.

"And your mate?"

"Gone dead," he replied, "it's been an uncomfortable voyage so far," he continued, speaking with patient melancholy and with an odd expression of expectation in his eyes. "We left Quebec, and the mate he takes on and dies. He couldn't help it, poor chap, but t'other – " He gazed at the deck as though to direct my imagination below. "It was drink, drink all around the clock with him; no sharing – a up-in-the-corner job; cuddling a bottle all day long and the blinds drawed. Then he goes mad. That ain't enough. Then he goes blind. *That* ain't enough. What must he do but break a leg! And there he lies," said he, pointing straight down with a forefinger pale as though boiled, like a laundress's hand. "The navigation was left to me – 'deed, then, it had been left to me for some time – but *I* never shipped to know navigation. No fear. Me, indeed!" he exclaimed, laughing dully. "I'm a carpenter by trade. However, here I was; so I hove the log and steered east, and here I am!" he exclaimed with another patient, forlorn look around the ocean.

"You have lost your way," said I. "You are not the first sailor who has lost his way. But have you never sighted anything with a skipper to give you the latitude and the longitude and a true course for the Clyde?"

"Plenty have we sighted, but nothing that would speak us. The only thing that showed a willingness to speak us turned out a privateer, and night drawing down," he exclaimed, slightly deepening his voice, "saved our throats."

"That cask astern of you," said I, "is a novel dodge for keeping your ship pumped out."

A little life came into his melancholy eye.

"The men took ill," said he. "Five of them were down, and still are down, and the nursing of 'em all, including of the captain, blind and mad, and the cook unable to stand with dropsy, is beginning to tell upon my spirits."

"That I can believe."

"There was but four men left. There sits three of 'em. Who was to do the pumping? The swinging of a yard's pretty nigh as much as we can manage. I didn't want to get waterlogged: I wish to get home. My wife'll be wondering what's become of me. So, after thinking a bit, I rigs up this here pumping apparatus, as ye see, and if the weather holds fine, and the drag of the cask don't jump the pump out, I think it'll answer."

"Well," said I, "what can we do for you?"

"I should like to be put in the way of getting home, sir," he answered. "We don't want for food and water. There ain't no purser like sickness," he exclaimed with a melancholy smile. "When I fell in with your brig I was a-steering east, with the hope of making the land and coming across some village or town where I might larn what the day of the month was, and how to head. It's one thing not to know what's o'clock, but I tell ye it makes a man feel weak in the mind to lose reckoning of the day of the week and not know what the date of the month is."

"What is your name?"

"Tarbrick, sir."

"Well, Mr. Tarbrick, we shall be able to be of service to you, I believe. We have a Dutchman on board who wants to get home. He and the captain have fallen out, and the Dutchman desires to return by the first passing ship. You may guess that he speaks English, and that he is a navigator, when I tell you he was mate of that vessel. Will you receive him?"

"Will I?" he cried, his face lighting up. "Why, he's just the man we want."

"Is there nothing else we can do for you?"

"No, sir; and I never reckoned on getting so much," he answered mildly and sadly. "I reckoned only on larning the day of the week and the date of the month, and getting the course for a straight steer home."

"Keep all fast as you are," said I, "and I will return to you." I dropped into the boat and was rowed aboard the brig. Greaves was impatiently walking the deck. He came to that part of the rail over which I climbed, and said:

"Will the brig take van Laar?"

I answered, "Yes."

His face instantly cleared. I gave him the story of the *Commodore Nelson*, as it had been related to me by Mr. Tarbrick, and explained the object of the cask under the stern and the lines rove from it to the pump handle. He laughed, but there was a note of admiration in his laughter.

"That Tarbrick is no fool, spite of his thinking the Clyde lies down this way. I have heard of worse notions than that of making a ship pump herself out. The cask is half full of water, I suppose?"

"It would not be heavy enough for the down-drag unless it were half full of water," said I.

"And it is guyed to either quarter, of course," he continued, "otherwise, when the brig moves, it must be towed directly from the gaff-end, which would never do. A clever notion. Bol!"

The boatswain, who was standing forward looking at the brig, immediately came aft.

"Come below with me," said the captain, "and free van Laar. That brig will receive him. Keep your boat over the side, Mr. Fielding, and stand by to receive van Laar and his clothes."

They entered the cabin. In a few minutes I heard a confused noise of voices. Van Laar's tones were distinguishable, but I could not collect what he said. Bol came under the skylight and asked me to send down a couple of hands to bring up van Laar's chest. Presently van Laar cried out, "Disvhas Mynheer Tulp's schip, and you vhas kicking me out of her."

"You leave at your own request," I heard Greaves say.

"Dot vhas valse," shouted the Dutchman. "But you are a whole ship's gompany to von man. Yet vill I have der bed from oonder you und your vife."

"Now step on deck, if you please."

"Dere law – " but the rest was lost to my ear by the Dutchman getting into the companion way. He emerged, looking very pale, greasy, even fatter than he had before shown; scowled when he met my glance, stared around him with the bewilderment of a newly-released man, and called out, "Vere is der schip?" He saw her as he spoke, shaded his eyes while he looked at her, and, falling back a step, exclaimed, "I vhas not going home in dot schip."

"That is the ship, and you are going home in her," said Greaves. "The boat is alongside, and Mr. Fielding waits for you to jump in."

"You vhas sorry for dis by an' by. Do you inten' dot I should drown by your sending me to dot footy hooker? Who has been on boardt her?" he shouted, looking around him with a frown; "you, sir?" cried he to me. "Vot vhos dot oonder her taffrail? I must know vot dot vhas before I stir!"

"It's nothing that will hurt you," answered Greaves, who, as I might see, dared not meet my gaze for fear of laughing.

"Vhat vhas it, I ask? I hov a right to know;" and here the poor fat fellow, for whom I was beginning to feel a sort of pity, made spectacles of his thumbs and forefingers, and put them to his eyes to stare at the cask and repeated, "Vhat vhas it? Sir, oblige me by handing me dere glass."

"Mr. van Laar," said Greaves, "I should regret to use force, but if you don't instantly get into that boat I shall have you lifted over the side and dropped into her."

"Who vhas it dot has been on boardt? Vhas it you, sir?" cried the Dutchman, again addressing me. "Dos she leak? Vot vhis her cargo? Vot are her stores? I have had no dinner, and you are sending me to a schip dot may be stone proke."

All this while the crew of the brig, saving those in the boat, had been standing in the fore-part, looking on. I thought to find some signs of sympathy with van Laar among the Dutch seamen, but if sympathy were felt, it found no expression in their faces or bearing. The grinning had been broad and continuous, but now I caught a murmur or two of impatience that might have signified disgust.

"Will you enter the boat?" cried Greaves. Van Laar began to protest. "Aft here, some of you," exclaimed Greaves, "and help Mr. van Laar over the side."

The Dutchman immediately went to the rail, crawled over it, breathing heavily, then pausing when he was outside, while he still grasped the rim, and while nothing was visible of him but his fat face above the rail, he roared out:

"Down mit dot beastly country, England! Hurrah for der law! Hurrah for der right! Ach, boot I vhas sorry for you by an' by."

He then dropped into the boat, I followed, and we shoved off. Galloon barked at the Dutchman as we rowed away. Van Laar talked aloud to himself, constantly wiping his face. His speech was Dutch, and I did not understand what he said. Presently he broke out in English:

"Yaw; a timber cargo. Dot vhas my fear. Dere you vhas, and dot's to be my home, and vot oonder der sky is dot cask oonder der taffrail? Der schip's provisions? Very like, very like. She hov a starved look. And who vhas dose dree men sitting up dere? Vhas dot der captain in dere yellow coat? He hov der look of a man who lives on rats. An' I ask vhat dos a timber schip do down here? By Gott! I do not like the look of her."

I paid no attention to his words, and put on a frowning face to preserve my gravity, which was severely taxed, not more by van Laar's talk and appearance than by the grins of the men who were rowing the boat. We approached the brig, and Mr. Tarbrick came to the main rigging, as though he would have me steer the boat alongside under the main chains.

"Brick, ahoy!" shouted van Laar, standing up, and setting his thick legs apart to balance himself; for the boat swayed with some liveliness upon the swell that was running.

"Hallo!" responded Tarbrick, with a flourish of his hand.

"Vhat vhas dot cask oonder your shtern?"

"It keeps the pump a-going," cried Tarbrick.

"Goot anchells!" cried van Laar, "do I understand that you hov not a schip's gompany strong enough to keep der pumps manned?"

"We are four well men and myself," shouted Tarbrick; "the rest are sick."

"I do not go home in dot schip," said van Laar, sitting down.

"Oars!" I cried, as we swept alongside. "Mr. van Laar, I beg you will step on board. Pray give us no trouble. You *must* go, you know, though it should come to my having to send for fresh hands to *whip* you aboard," by which word whip he perfectly well understood me to mean a tackle made fast to the yardarm, used for hoisting. "Mr. Tarbrick, call those three fellows of yours aft to get this chest over the side."

The three men rose in a lifeless way from the top of the timber, shambled to abreast of the boat in a lifeless way, and in a lifeless way still dragged up van Laar's sea-chest, to the grummet handle of which a rope had been attached.

"On deck dere," called van Laar, getting up again and planting his legs apart, "how moch do you leak in der hour?"

I winked at Tarbrick, who was leaning over the rail, but the man was either a fool or did not catch my wink, for he answered, in his melancholy voice:

"It's a-drainin' in very unpleasantly. I han't sounded the well since this morning, but," he added, as though to encourage van Laar, "we're full of timber and can't sink."

Down sat the Dutchman again, with a weight of fall upon the thwart that made the boat throw a couple of little seas away from her quarters.

"Here I sthop," he said, doggedly folding his arms.

"You will force me to row back to the brig, obtain fresh hands, and whip you aboard, Mr. van Laar."

"You vhas a big," he said, without looking at me.

"Men," he exclaimed, addressing the seamen in the boat, "dere *Black Vatch* belongs to Mynheer Tulp, I vhas mate of her by Mynheer Tulp's consent. Vill you allow your lawful mate to be put into dis beast of a schip, to starf, to drown, to miserably perish?"

"You had better jump on board," said one of the men.

"Cast off!" I exclaimed. "I must return to Captain Greaves for further instructions."

"Shtop!" shouted the Dutchman. "On deck dere, how vhas you off for provisions?"

"Very well off," answered Tarbrick. "There's plenty to eat aboard this here brig."

"And how vhas you off for drink?"

"Come and judge for yourself, sir. There's been too much drink. It's been the ruin of us," exclaimed Tarbrick.

On this van Laar, putting his hands upon the lanyards of the main rigging, got into the chains. We instantly shoved off and were at some lengths from him while he was still heavily clambering on to the deck.

"Blowed if his weight don't make the little craft heel again," exclaimed one of the men. "See what a list to larboard she's took."

I regained the *Black Watch* mightily rejoiced that the Dutchman was off my hands. So vast a mass of flesh had made the transferring of it a very formidable undertaking. He was an elephant of a man; it needed but an impassioned gambol or two on his part to capsize a boat three times larger than anything the *Black Watch* carried. Besides, van Laar was not the sort of man that one would care to sacrifice one's life for. As we pulled away I looked over my shoulder, and now the Dutchman had cleared the rail and was wiping his face, with Tarbrick in the act of approaching him. When he saw that I looked he shook his first and roared. His words fell short; his tones alone came along like the low of a cow. My men burst into a laugh, and a minute later we were alongside the *Black Watch*.

The moment the boat was hoisted we trimmed sail and were presently pushing through the quiet glide of the dark blue swell, and very soon the magic of distance was dealing with the poor little craft in our wake. The afternoon was advanced, the light in the heavens and upon the water was soft and red and still. In the south clouds were terraced upon the horizon, every towering layer of radiant vapour defined with an edging of gilt. There was wind enough to keep the water sparkling wherever the light smote it; our sails soared like breasts of yellow silk breathing without noise to the courtesying of the craft.

A rich ocean afternoon it was, and the beauty of it entered the little vessel which we were leaving astern of us even as a spirit might, vitalizing her with colours and with a radiance not her own, converting her into a gem-like detail for the embellishment of the wide, bare breast of sea. Greaves and I stood looking at her; but the instant I levelled the telescope the enchantment vanished, for then she showed as a crazy old brig once more, a cask in tow of her, her sails ill-set, and the bulky figure of van Laar striding here and there, with many marks of agitation in his motions.

"The captain mad and blind in the cabin," said Greaves; "five men sick in the forecastle and the others crushed in spirits, forecastle fare for cabin fare, and bad at that; the water draining into the hold; and the vessel fearfully to the southward of her destination. I do not envy van Laar."

However, long before we ran the little vessel out of sight, they had got her head pointed in a direction that was right for the British Channel, if not the Clyde. The breeze had freshened, she was leaning over, and the cask astern had been cut adrift.

Chapter XI.
The *Rebecca*

Now, when van Laar was gone all hands of us seemed to settle down very comfortably to the rough, hard, simple discipline of the sea-life. The more I saw of Greaves, the more I saw of the brig, the better I liked both. Over and over again I congratulated myself upon my good fortune. I seemed to trace it all to that gibbet on the sand hills. I know not why. What more ghastly, what more hideously ominous, you might say, could the mind of man imagine than a gibbet and a dead felon hanging from it in irons, and a mother receiving the horrible burthen of the beam from the fire-bright hand of the storm, and nursing the fearful object as though it were once again the babe that she had suckled? What more hideously ominous than such things could man ask of Heaven to initiate his career with, to inaugurate a new departure with? But that gibbet it was which kept me waiting when by walking I must have missed the press-gang and, for all I can now tell, have safely got me aboard the *Royal Brunswicker*.

Be this as it will. I liked Greaves; I liked his little ship; I liked my position on board of her; and I could find no fault with the crew. The people of my watch ran about without murmurs. Yan Bol seemed to have the whole company well in hand. The spun-yarn winch was often a-going; we were a very clean ship; the complicated machinery aloft was carefully looked to; the long guns were kept bright. I had overhauled the slop-chest and taken what I wanted, and there lay, in a big sea-box which Greaves had somewhere fished out for me, as comfortable a stock of clothes as ever I could wish to sail out of port with.

I did not imagine, however, that the crew would long content themselves with what, while Greaves remained dumb, must be to them no more nor less than an aimless sailing over the breast of the ocean. Sailors do not love to be long at sea without making a voyage. Our crew might look at the compass and note that the course was a straight one for cutting the equator; but what imaginations were they to build up on the letters S.S.W.? We were not a king's ship. There was no obligation of *passivity*. The sailors were merchant seamen, claiming all the old traditional rights of their calling; of exercising those rights, at all events, whenever convenient: the rights of grumbling, cursing, laying aft in a body and expostulating, holding forward in a body and turning deaf ears to the boatswain's music. "Surely," I would sometimes think, while I paced the deck, eyeing the fellows of my watch at work, "those men will not wait till we are south of the line to hear what the errand of this brig is!"

It came to pass that, a few days after we had got rid of Van Laar, I went on deck at midnight to take charge of the brig until four in the morning. The noble wind of the northeast trade was full in our canvas – a small, fresh, quartering gale – the sky lively with the sliding of stars amid the steam-tinctured heap of the trade-cloud swarming away southwest. Studdingsails were out and the brig hummed through it, shouldering the seas off both bows into snowstorms. The burly figure of Yan Bol stood to windward, abreast of the little skylight. He waited for me to relieve him, and, while he waited, he sang to himself in a deep voice, like the drumming of the wind as it flashed into the hollow of the trysail and fled to leeward in a hollow roar under the boom.

"Is that you, Bol?"

"Yaw, it vhas her himself," he answered.

"This will do," said I, stepping up to him.

"Yaw, dis vhas a nice little draught," he replied.

I made a few quarter-deck inquiries relating to the business of the brig during his charge of the deck since eight o'clock, and was then going aft to look at the binnacle, but stayed on finding that he lingered.

"Do you know," said he, "I vhas not very gladt to be second mate."

"Why not?"

"Veil, I believe dot der men vouldt hov more respect for me if I vhas one of demselves."

"But you are bo'sun, anyway, and your rating, therefore, is higher than that of the others."

"Dot may be," he replied, "but a bo'sun in der merchant service vhas no better dan vhat you call in your language a common sailor. He blows a whistle; dot, and a dollar or two more money, and dere you hov der difference."

"Who else could be second mate?" said I. "As bo'sun of this vessel it would not please you to be ordered about by an able seaman."

He was silent. It was too dark to see anything of the man save the shapeless lump of shadow which he made against the stars over the sea. "Mr. Fielding," said he, "can you tell me vhere dis brig vhas boun' to?"

"I know where she is bound to," I answered.

"Ho, *you* know, sir!" he exclaimed, with a tone of surprise trembling through his deep voice; "Ve all tink dot she vhas der captain's secret."

"If you all did think that," said I, "why do you ask me where the brig is bound to."

"It vhas about time dot ve knew where ve vhas boun' to," said Bol. "Dis vhas a larsh verld. Dere vhas many places in him. Some of dose places I have visited and vish never to see again. Derefore I likes to know where ve vhas boun' to."

"It is for the captain, not for me, to tell you that," said I.

"Vhen shall he speak?" said Bol.

"In good time, I warrant you."

"I vhas villing to agree dot vhere we sailed to should be der captain's secret for a leedle time; but now ve hov been siomevhiles at sea, und still she vhas a secret, und I belief dot der men did not suppose dot she vouldt be a secret so long. Dere vhas no cargo. Nothing vhas consigned. Derefore, if ve vhas boun' anywhere it vhas to a port to call for orders. Und after – ."

"The captain will not keep the crew in ignorance much longer," said I.

"But you can tell us, Mr. Fielding, vhere ve vhas boun' to? "

"I know where we are bound to."

"Dot vhas strange! You come on board as a shipwreckt man, vhich vhas quite right; und you take Heer Van Laar's place, vhich vhas also quite right; and of all der crew, excepting der captain, you alone know vhere der brig vhas boun' to! Mr. Fielding, oxcuse me, I mean no offense, but I say again dot vhas dom'd strange."

There was jealousy here which I witnessed, understood, and, to a degree, sympathized with. Here was I, a stranger to the brig – a stranger, I mean, in the sense of not having formed one of her company when she sailed from Amsterdam; here was I, not only installed in the room of van Laar, and, for all I knew, regarded by the crew as the cause of that man's expulsion from the ship, but in possession of knowledge withheld from all hands. This might excite a feeling against me among the men, which would be unfortunate. The voyage had opened with so much promise that I had resolved to spare no effort to make a jolly jaunt of it to the uttermost end of the traverse, whether that end was to be called the Downs, or Amsterdam. Preserving my temper, and speaking in the kindliest voice I could command, I said to the big figure alongside of me:

"Yan Bol, I do not wonder you are surprised that I should know what is hidden from you. You are an officer of this ship as well as I."

"Nine, nine!" he exclaimed in a voice as deep as a trombone.

"But why am I entrusted," I continued, "with the secret of this voyage a little while before it is communicated to the crew? I will tell you. Captain Greaves wanted a mate in the room of van Laar. It was not to be supposed that I would accept the offer of the post of mate unless I knew where I was bound to. Therefore, to secure my services, Captain Greaves explained the nature of this expedition. With the others of you it was different. You agreed to sail in this brig, and you were willing, when you agreed to sail, to be kept in ignorance of the brig's destination. Had I been at Amsterdam when a crew was wanted for the *Black Watch*, and had I been invited to join her as able seaman, boatswain, chief mate, what you will, I should have answered: 'Tell me first where you are bound to, for I will not join your ship until I know where she is going and what her business is?'"

"Veil, dot vhas right," he exclaimed, half smothering a huge yawn. "I hov noting to say against dot. But you hov der ear of your captain. You vhas his countryman: you vhas old friendts, I hov heard. You vill make us men tankful to you if you vill ask him to let us know vhere ve vhas boun' as conveniently soon as may pe."

"I will speak to him as you wish," said I.

He bade me good-night very civilly, and his great shape rolled forward and vanished in the blackness that lay upon the fore part of the brig.

I paced the deck, musing over this conversation. It seemed to me to justify Greaves' resolution to withhold all knowledge of the ship's errand from the men until their characters lay somewhat plain to his gaze; but on the other hand, I conceived that it would be a mistake to irritate them by keeping silence too long. They had a right to know where they were going. Then the provocation of silence might lead to murmurs and difficulties, and what would *that* mean.

I was again on deck at eight o'clock in the morning. One of the most comfortless conditions of the sea-life is this ceaseless turning in and turning out. It is called watch and watch. The ladies will want to know what watch and watch means. Ladies, watch and watch means this: Snob is chief mate. He takes charge of the ship from midnight until four o'clock in the morning. Nob, who is the second mate, is then roused up, comes on deck, and looks after the ship until eight o'clock in the morning. At this hour Snob's turn has come round. He arrives, and takes over the ship until noon. Another four hours brings the time to four o'clock, when the ordinary watch is split in halves, and each half, called a dog-watch, lasts two hours. This provides change and change about, so that Snob, who last night had charge from twelve to four, will tonight be in bed during those hours, weather permitting.

When I stepped on deck at eight o'clock I found a brilliant morning all about, but a softer sea, a lighter wind than I had left, a languider courtesying of the brig, even a dull flap at times forward when the cloths of the heavy forecourse hollowed into the stoop of the bows as a child's cheek dimples when it sucks in its breath. The trade-wind was not taking off. Not at all. The heavens were gay with the flight of the trade-cloud, as gay as ever the sky could be made by a dance of sea-fowl on the wing; and while that vapour flew, one knew that the wind was constant. Only we had happened just now to have washed with foam rising in thunder to each cathead into a pause or interval of the inspiring commercial gale of the North Atlantic; the strong, glad rush of air which had hoarily veiled every deep blue hollow with white brine, torn flashing from each curling head, had sunk for a little into a tropic fanning, and the swell of the sea was small and each surge no more than a giant ripple, with scarce weight enough in its run to ridge into foam.

But, bless me, had a week of stark calm descended upon our heads we should still have done uncommonly well. Our average progress, since the day on which I had recovered consciousness on board the *Black Watch*, had come very near to steam as steam is in these days in which I am writing, though to what velocities the boiler may hereafter attain I am not here to predict.

Greaves stood abreast of the wheel. He was looking through a telescope at some object that lay about three points on the weather bow. He continued to gaze with a degree of steadfastness that rendered him insensible of my presence. I looked and seemed to see some small vessel upon the edge of the sea; but I could not be sure. She was above a league distant, and the morning light was confusing that way with the blending of the shadowy lift of the swell, the violet shadows of the clouds, and the hazy splendour of the early morning distances. My caressing and speaking to Galloon, who lay near his master, caused Greaves to bring his eye away from the glass.

"Good-morning, Fielding. The breeze has fallen slack. I am trying to make out the meaning of that little schooner down there;" and he pointed over the bow with his telescope. "Look for yourself."

I levelled the glass, and beheld a schooner of about a hundred tons, rolling broadside to the sea, abandoned, or, if not abandoned, then helpless. Her jib boom was gone; so, too, was her fore topmast; otherwise she seemed sound enough, saving that for canvas she had nothing set but her gaff foresail, though, as I seemed to find, when I strained my gaze through the glass, her mainsail was not furled, but lay heaped upon the boom, as though the halliards had been let go and nothing more done.

"She'll be worse off than the craft that van Laar's gone home in," said I, returning the telescope to Greaves.

"Do you believe in dreams?" said he. "No," I answered. "Do not be in too great a hurry with your 'noes,' " he exclaimed. "I like a man to reflect when he is asked a question in metaphysics."

"I know nothing about metaphysics," said I, "and I do not believe in dreams."

"I believe in the unseen," said he, putting down the glass, and folding his arms and leaning back against the rail, as though settling himself down for a talk or an argument. "The materialist tells you not to put your faith in anything you can't see, or handle, or smell, that you can't bring some organ or function of sense to bear upon, in short. Throw yourself down upon your back, and look straight up into the sky. What do you see? Hey? But do you see it? Yes. Do you understand it? No. It is visible, and yet it is the unseen; for at what does a man look when he gazes straight up into the sky?"

"There are few things worth going mad for," said I, "and two things I am resolved shall never send me to Bedlam."

"What are they?"

"One of them's that," said I, pointing straight up.

"What do you make of yonder schooner?," said he.

I described such features as I had observed.

"She has a black hull, and a thin line of painted ports," said he.

"She has."

"She has lost her fore topmast and jib boom."

"That's so."

"It is very extraordinary!" he exclaimed. "I dreamt last night, or in one of this morning watches, that I sighted that schooner. I saw her in my dream as I have been seeing her in that glass there. She was wrecked forward, she lay in the trough, she showed no canvas but her gaff foresail. There it all is!" he said, pointing; "and yet how quick you are with your 'No' when I asked if you believed in dreams!" He smiled and continued, "But my dream carried me further than I intend to go in these waking hours; for, in my dream, I launched a boat, where from I can't tell ye, and went aboard that schooner. I looked about me, her decks were lifeless. I stepped below into her little cabin, and what d'ye think I saw? The figure of Death seated in an armchair at the table with a pack of cards in one skeleton hand. He pointed to a chair and began to deal. I awoke, and wasn't sorry to wake. There lies the schooner. How very extraordinary! Is old Death below, waiting for a partner? You shall find out, Fielding. I'll lay you aboard. By thunder, rather than go myself I would forfeit all the money I hope to take up at the end of this run."

Many lies are told of us sailors by landsmen, but when they call us a superstitious clan they speak the truth. Superstitious, indeed, are sailors. I am talking of the Jacks of my time; I understand that the mariner is more enlightened in these days. I looked at the little schooner anxiously. I felt no reluctance to board her; but, though I had told Greaves that I did not believe in dreams, I discovered, nevertheless, that this dream had communicated a particular significance to the little craft. I had meant to talk to him about my chat with Yan Bol at midnight, and the subject went out of my head while I looked at the schooner and thought of Greaves' dream.

"I will board her," said I, "and enter her cabin."

"Oh, yes," said he, "I shall want you to do that. My dream was so vivid that I shall ask you to take notice of the fittings of that cabin for the sake of corroboration, and let me be first with you – ."

He shut his eyes as one seeking strongly to realize his own imaginations, and said: "It is a square cabin with a square table directly under an oblong skylight. There is a chair at the head of the table. In that chair sat the skeleton, not answering to Milton's magnificent fancy:

> What seemed his head
> The likeness of a kingly crown had on.

No, the thing was uncrowned. It was a skeleton, but it lived, and made as though it would deal the cards it held. Opposite is another chair; on either hand are lockers. There are sleeping berths at the foot of the companion ladder, and that's all that I can remember," said he, opening his eyes.

Jimmy announced breakfast. Yan Bol came aft to take charge while I went below. The burly Dutchman looked at me meaningly, and then I recollected my talk with him; but I resolved to say nothing to the captain this side my excursion to the schooner.

Before we sat down Jimmy received one of his lessons. There was a ham upon the table, and he called it a leg of mutton. I had long ago discovered that the boy was honestly wanting in the power to distinguish between articles of food. Sometimes I supposed he blundered on purpose to divert his master, who appeared to enjoy the concert that was part of the lesson, but I was now convinced that though he had the names of many varieties of meats, and even dishes, at his tongue's end, he was utterly unable to correctly apply them. His confidence in his own indications was the extraordinary part of his misapplications. He spoke, for instance, of the ham as a leg of mutton as though quite sure; then to the first syllable of correction that fell from Greaves, and to a faint, uneasy groan which the dog always gave when Greaves spoke on these occasions – as though the noble beast knew that the boy had blundered and that the duet was inevitable – Jimmy stiffened himself into a soldier-like posture, nose in the air, hands up and down like a pump handle, and the dog looking at him ready to howl. The lesson ended, we sat down and fell to.

"Your teaching does not seem to make the lad see the difference between meats," said I.

"I have hopes of him," he answered, "and Galloon's face is good on these occasions."

He then talked of the schooner, of his dream, and his discourse ran in such a strain that I discovered that secretly he was not only of a serious and religious cast of mind, but superstitious beyond any man I had ever sailed with. Thought has the speed of the lightning stroke, and I remember as I sat listening to him, saying very little myself – for I had but the shallowest understanding of the subject he had got upon; I say that I remember thinking: Suppose this voyage should be the consequence of a dream? Suppose this Pacific quest for hard Spanish milled dollars should be an effect of superstitious fancy? Suppose the whole scheme should be as unsubstantial in fact as the actors in the revels in the 'Tempest'? But the image of Mynheer Tulp swept as an inspiration of support into my mind. I had entertained myself by figuring that man. In thinking over this voyage I had depicted its promoter, and my fancy gave me the likeness of a little withered Dutchman in a velvet cap, with a nose of Hebraic proportions, a keen black eye, a wary, sarcastic smile, and a mind whose horizon was the circumference of a guilder. I seemed to see the little creature looking over Greaves' shoulder at me as I mused upon my companion's somewhat foggy talk, and I said unto myself, "Tulp believing, all's well."

When we went on deck the schooner was within musket shot. She had seemingly been in collision with another vessel, though her hull looked perfectly sound; nor did she sit upon the sea, nor rise with the slope of the swell, as if she had more water in her than was good for buoyancy. Nothing alive was visible aboard.

I know not a more forlorn object, the wide world over, than an abandoned vessel encountered deep in the heart of an ocean solitude. She sucks in the desolation of the sea and grows grey, lean, and haggard with the melancholy that sometimes raves and sometimes sleeps, but that forever dwells upon the bosom of the deep. There is no fancy in this. Many ways are there in which loneliness may be personified or illustrated: the widow weeping upon the tomb of her only child, a blind man in a crowd, a prostrate figure on some wide spread of midnight moor, over whose vague and distant edge a red eye of moon is glancing under a lid of black cloud. In many ways may loneliness be represented, but there is no expression of it that equals, to my mind, the abandoned ship. Is it because the movement of the sea communicates a fancy of life to the vessel? She looks to be sentient as she sways, to be sensible that she is the only object for leagues upon the prodigious liquid waste over which the boundless heavens are spread. Some unfurled canvas flaps; the wheel revolves, or the tiller shears through the air to the blows of the seas upon the rudder: there may be the ends of gear snaking overboard; they move, they writhe like serpents; they seem to *pour* as though they were the life blood of the vessel draining from her heart. And terrible is the silence of the decks. It is not the silence of the empty house that was yesterday full and clamorous with merry voices. It is such a silence as you meet with nowhere else, deepened to the meditative mind by sounds which would vex and break in upon and destroy all other silence. Yes, to my mind the abandoned ship at sea is the most perfect expression of human and inanimate loneliness.

This I thought as I gazed at that little schooner. Greaves watched her with a look of uneasiness. He came to my side and said, in a low voice:

"Take a boat, will ye Fielding, and explore that craft? She's been abandoned for weeks; I am sure of that. You'll find nothing alive, and if it wasn't for that dream of mine last night I'd pass on. But I *must* find out whether the cabin furniture is as I beheld it in my sleep."

A boat was lowered; three men jumped in. I followed, and gained the side of the schooner. We pulled under her stern to see her name, and read in big white letters on the slope of her counter the word *Rebecca*. I fastened a superstitious eye upon the two little starboard portholes, which, as I might guess, illuminated her cabin. What was inside?

"Two of you," said I to the men, "come aboard with me. You, Travers, remain in charge of the boat."

The men who scrambled over the side were Friend and Meehan. We stood gazing and listening. The foresail occasionally flapped as the little vessel heaved to the swell, but the water washed along the bends noiseless as quicksilver. Saving the wreckage forward, I could see nothing wrong with the schooner. There were signs of confusion, as though she had been abandoned in a hurry: the sails had come down with a run, and lay unfurled; the decks were littered with ropes' ends. But all deck fixtures were in their place; nay, there was even a small boat chocked under the starboard gangway forward, but the bigger boat, which such a craft as this would carry, was missing.

My eye went to the skylight, and I started. It was oblong. "What more of the dream remains to. be verified?" thought I. The skylight was closed, the frames secured within, the glass filthy. I peered and peered to no purpose. On this I stepped to the companion, while the two seamen moved forward to look down the hatches in obedience to my orders; but I paused when I was in the companion way. I seemed to smell a damp odour as of a vault. "Good God!" thought I, "if there *should* be anything horrible at the head of the table, with a pack of – Chut! ye fool!" I said to myself, "say a prayer and shove on, and be hanged to you!" and down I went.

Well, there was no skeleton; there was nothing horrible to be seen. If the grim Feature had ever occupied the head of that table, he had found a companion; he had played his trump card: he had won of a surety, and he and his opponent were gone. But had I veritably beheld a living skeleton seated at the table and motioning as though it would deal, I could not have been more scared – no; let me say I could not have been more impressed than I was – by the sight of the furniture of the cabin. It was precisely as Greaves had described it. It was the plainest sea interior in the world – nothing whatever worth looking at, nothing in it to detain the attention for an instant; yet it was all exactly as Greaves described it. I was revisited by the misgiving of an earlier hour. "The man is an extraordinary dreamer," I said to myself. "He may be a little mad. A few people dream as this man has dreamt, and those few, I suspect, will be found somewhat mad at root. Has he dreamt of the ship in the island cave? Did he, that he might justify to *himself* his faith in his extraordinary vision by sailing on this quest – did he *forge* that manifest which, backed by his eloquent advocacy, no doubt, induced old Bartholomew Tulp to put his hand in his pocket?"

I stood thus thinking when I heard my name called.

"Hallo!" I exclaimed.

"There's somebody alive forrad!" cried one of the men.

I ran on deck.

"What is it?"

"This way, sir," shouted Meehan.

I followed the fellow to the forecastle – that is to say, to the hatch by which the forecastle was entered and quitted.

"There's somebody knocking," cried Friend.

"Thump back and sing out," I cried.

The man did so, and we heard a faint voice, feeble as a sweep's call-down from the height of a tall chimney.

"Don't you see what has happened?" cried I. "Why, look! This vessel has been in collision – struck some vessel on end. Her bowsprit has been run in by the blow, and *the heel of it has closed the slide of the hatch over the people who are below here!*"

I thumped and sang out. A voice dimly responded. I thumped again, and roared at the top of my lungs:

"We'll have you out of this, but you must wait a bit. Do you hear me?" and there was a note in the faint, inarticulate response that made me know I was heard.

I looked about, but my eye sought in vain for such machinery of tackles as I required to free the men below. I did not choose to waste time by hunting, and told Meehan to jump into the boat and pull, with Travers, over to the brig. By this time the two vessels had so closed to each other as to be within easy speaking distance. I hailed the *Black Watch*, and Greaves stood up and made answer.

"There are two men locked up in this schooner's fo'c'sle, and the heel of the bowsprit – " and I explained how it happened that the hatch was closed and immovably secured. He flourished his arm. I then requested him to send me the necessary gear for clearing the hatch by running out the bowsprit; I likewise asked him for a couple more men. Again he flourished his arm. By this time the boat was alongside the brig.

"What have you found aft in the cabin?" shouted Greaves.

"Nothing but ordinary furniture," I answered.

"I see," he cried, "that the skylight is oblong. Is the table square?"

"It is, sir."

"A chair at the head and foot?"

"Ay, sir, and lockers on either hand."

His figure hardened into a posture of astonishment. He stood mute. I could readily imagine an expression of superstitious dismay on his face; or rather, let me say, that I *hoped* this, for methought it would be ominous for our faith in those distant South Pacific dollars if he should accept the startling realization of this dream with the tranquillity of a man who dreams much, and who believes in his dreams, and whose actions are governed by them.

The boat returned with the additional assistance I required, and with the necessary gear for freeing the forecastle hatch. The business was somewhat tedious. It was a case of what sailors know as *jam*. It involved luff upon luff, much sweating and swearing, much hard straining and hoarse chorusing at the little forecastle capstan. At last we started the bowsprit, the heel ran clear of the hatch, and two of the men, grasping the hatch cover, swept it through its grooves.

The moment the hatch was open a figure rose up out of the darkness below; another followed at his heels. I looked for more, but there were but two, and those two stood blinking and rubbing their eyes, and turning their heads about as though their motions were produced by clockwork. One of them was the strangest looking man I had ever seen. Did you ever read the story of Peter Serrano? If so, then figure Serrano with his beard cropped, his hairy body clothed in a sleeved waistcoat and a pair of short pilot breeches, the hair of his head still long, and rings in his ears, the whole man still preserving a good deal of that oyster-like expression of face and sandy grittiness of complexion which Peter got from a long residence upon a shoal.

This man might have been Peter Serrano after he had been trimmed, washed, and cared for ashore. His eyes were small and fiery, the edges of the lids a raw red. He was about five feet tall, with the smallest feet that ever capered at the extremities of a sailor's trousers. His companion was of the ordinary type of merchant seamen, red-haired, of a heavy cast of countenance; the complexion of this man was of the hue of sailors' duff – which you must go to sea to understand, for there is no word in the English language to express the colour of it. They had risen through the hatch with activity; as they stood they seemed fairly strong on their pins. But the light confounded them, and they continued to rub and to weep and to mechanically rotate their heads for some few minutes after I had begun to talk to them.

"Well, my lads," said I, "this is a stroke of fortune for you. Talk of rats in a hole! How came ye into this mess? But, first, are ye English?"

"English both," said the little man.

"How come ye to be locked up after this fashion?"

The little chap looked round at us with streaming eyes and said, in just the sort of harsh, salt, gritty voice that my imagination had fitted him with before he opened his lips – a voice that was extraordinary with its suggestion of sand, the seething of surf, and the spasmodic shriek of the gull: "Tell us the time, will yer?"

I looked at my watch and gave him the hour. He lugged out a great silver turnip from his breeches' band; the dial plate of that watch was about the size of a shilling, and the back of it came nearly to the circumference of a saucer.

"What does he say?" he exclaimed, holding up the watch. "This here blaze is like striking of a man blind."

"The time by your watch," said I, looking at it, "is seven o'clock."

"Is he right?" asked the little man eagerly. "Not by nearly four hours," said I. "If he ain't furder out it's all one," exclaimed the other sailor. "Me and my mate," said the little man, "has had a good many arguments about the time while we've been locked up below, but I think my tally'll come out right."

"How long have you been locked up below according to your tally?" said I.

"This here's a Wednesday, ain't it?" he inquired, once again straining the moisture out of his eyes with his knuckles, and blinking at me.

"No," said I; "it's Thursday."

"Nearer than you, Bobby, anyway!" he cried. "Your tally brought it to Saturday."

"How long have you been locked up, men?"

"Why," he exclaimed, "if this here's a Thursday" – his voice broke like that of a youth entering manhood, as he continued – "we've been locked up a fortnight when it shall ha' gone nine o'clock."

A murmur of pity and amazement escaped my men.

"And it happened like this," continued the little fellow, beginning to walk swiftly in a small circle: "Me and Bobby was in the same watch. We had come below and turned in, We was waked by a crash, and I heard the hatch cover closed. There went eight of us to a crew, but when I sings out only Bobby answers. The others who was below may have heard the capt'n or mate singing out on deck afore the collision. They was gone. Bobby and me tries to open the hatch. No fear! Eh, Bobby?" exclaimed the little fellow, who continued to walk very rapidly in a circle. "And how did it happen that that there hatch was closed? Why, I don't know *now*. How did it happen?" he yelled.

I explained. The little fellow looked at the bowsprit heel, at the hatch, and then his mate, and exclaimed:

"Wrong again, Bobby! Bobby was for having it that the hatch had been closed 'spressly to drown us by one of the sailors as him and me hated, as him and me had fought with and licked times out o' counting."

I was about to ask the fellows how they had managed to breathe in their black hole of a forecastle during their fortnight's imprisonment, when I caught sight of a stove funnel piercing the forecastle deck and rising a few feet above it. That funnel was all the answer my question needed. I inquired how they managed to obtain food and the little sore-eyed man answered that they had lifted the hatch of the forepeak and found oil for their lamps and water to drink, some barrels of bread and flour, and a piece or two of beef; for, luckily for them, the provisions in this schooner were stowed forward. There was coal in the forepeak. They lighted the forecastle stove and so dressed their victuals; but they were always forced to be in a hurry with their cooking, for the fire carried the fresh air up with it; and when they had raked the coals out they would sit with their heads close in to the stove to breathe the air as it gushed in again through the flue.

"Did you never try to break out?" said one of my men.

"Time arter time, mate. There was sights o' trying, and you see what it's comes to," exclaimed the little fiery-eyed man, starting to walk in a circle again.

At this moment I was hailed by Greaves:

"How many men have you released?"

"Two, sir; there are no more."

"Then bring them aboard, Mr. Fielding. I wish to proceed."

"Get your clothes," said I to the little man, "and come along."

He stopped in his circling walk and looked at the fellow he called Bobby; then, as if influenced by the same thought, they both cast their eyes over the schooner, first staring up at the broken topmast, then at the bowsprit, then running their gaze over the decks.

"Have you sounded the well?" cried the little man to me.

"No, I have not," I answered.

He flew to the pumps; his feet twinkled as he fled. I never witnessed such activity; it seemed impossible in a man who had been suffering from a fortnight of black hole. He pounced upon the sounding-rod, dropped the bar down the well, whipped it up, looked at it, uttered a gull-like cry, flung the iron down, and was with us in a jiffy.

"Bobby," he exclaimed, "nut dust ain't in it with her."

"Don't I know her for a corker?" responded Bobby. "Froth and pop when it blows, and a dead marine at heart."

"Bobby, what d'ye think?" said the raw-eyed little man, questioning his mate as though the suggestion had been made.

The man looked round the sea, looked up aloft, and answered:

"Agreeable."

"We'll carry the schooner home, sir," said the little fellow, addressing me.

"You two?"

"Say us four, sir. There's a two-man power for each hand a-coming out of such a salvage job as this."

I observed some of my men gaze about them thirstily and enviously and a little gloomily.

"Are you resolved?" said I, looking at the fellow, doubting my right to suffer them to embark on such an adventure after their long, weakening spell of imprisonment.

"It's two blocks, ain't it, Bobby?" said the little man.

"Ay," answered Bobby, "nothing wanting but this: First, that this kind gentleman will help us to secure the bowsprit afore he takes away his men; and, next, that he gives the course to steer for the Henglish Channel."

I was again hailed impatiently by Greaves, on which I got upon the rail and told him that the two men wished to carry their schooner home. Should I permit them to do it, considering – .

"Certainly," he shouted; "they'll pick up help as they go along."

I then called out that I would stay a little while longer, that I might secure the bowsprit and set them a course; and I then bade the little man with the fiery eyes go below and rummage the cabin that had been occupied by his captain for such charts as might be there. He was off like a hare, and returned in a few minutes with a small bag of charts, one of which represented the North Atlantic Ocean; and, while my people were busy with the bowsprit, I, with a pencil, marked upon the chart the track and courses for the red-eyed man and his mate to pursue. We then made sail on the schooner, shook hands with the two fellows, and entered the boat.

As I was about to drop over the side I overheard one of my men, in a grumbling voice, say:

"Is this here traverse of ourn going to consist of rummaging jobs, I wonder. Nothen but boarding so far, and what for?"

"Vere vhas ve boun'?" said another. "By Cott! boot I like to know by dis time vere ve vhas goin'."

Chapter XII.
The Round Robin

THERE was business to be done in getting the boat aboard and in starting the brig afresh upon her course. Nevertheless, I found moments for a look at the retreating schooner, and, while she still lay plain to the naked sight, I saw the little man with the fire-ringed eyes seize the tiller, while the other fellow who had been called Bobby clumsily sprawled aloft, and fell to hacking at the rigging of the wrecked fore topmast, which presently went overboard with its two yards.

By this time eight bells had been made by Greaves. It was Yan Bol's watch. I went below to wash and shift myself; dinner was then ready. Galloon took his seat, and Greaves occupied the head of the table with Jimmy behind him to wait upon us.

"I wish my dream had not proved so accurate," said Greaves.

"It was extraordinarily accurate," said I.

"Nothing was missing in that little cabin but the figure of Death."

"I shall grow superstitious," he exclaimed, "and little things will trouble me."

"It was a providential dream, captain," said I. "It has saved the lives of two men."

"Well, perhaps it has," he answered a little complacently. "Certainly, but for my dream, I should not have sent you aboard the schooner."

"I know but of one instance like it – at sea," said I. "The nephew of a French skipper dreamt three times in succession that some castaway wretches were lodged upon a lonely rock – where, I forget. The captain yielded to the influence of the third time of dreaming, and shifted his helm, made the rock, saw the men, and brought them off in a dying state."

We continued to talk of the schooner, of the chances for and against the two men navigating her home unless they picked up help on the road, of dreams, and such matters. Jimmy withdrew. It was my watch below, and I was in no hurry to leave the table.

"This seems a voyage of overhauling," said I. "First we board the melancholy Tarbrick, who doesn't know the day of the month; then we board the little *Rebecca*, whose two forecastle rats of sailors don't know what o'clock it is. What further in the boarding line lies between this time and our business t'other side the Horn?"

"We want nothing further in the boarding line," Greaves answered; "our port is south of the Galapagos, and we are in the North Atlantic and in a hurry."

"Has it ever occurred to you to imagine what became of the people of that locked-up ship of yours?"

"No; why should I trouble myself to imagine? She has been in that cave since 1810."

"You may be sure," said I, "that if any of her people came off with their lives they'd report her situation. The ship then would long ago have been visited, and the cargo and the half-million dollars taken out of her."

"Long ago."

"Strange that you, who have been dreaming of galleons all your life, as I remember you told me, should have lighted upon what is much the same as a galleon – not, indeed, worth Candish's or Anson's treasure ships, but all the same a very pretty little haul."

"It is quite true," said he, smiling gravely, "that I have been dreaming all my life of galleons. I read about the Spanish plate and treasure ships when I was a boy; about the cargoes of gold and silver, of precious gems, of massive and splendid commodities which the Pacific breezes used to solemnly blow over the seas, betwixt Acapulco and the Philippines. I used to read of the buccaneers and their marvellous doings on the western American seaboard, north and south of Panama, wherever there was a town to sack, a village to plunder. It was a sort of reading to fire my spirits. It sent me to sea. Yes, truly I believe I went to sea through reading about the old rovers. It is strange, as you say, that I should have lighted upon something locked up in a cave – something that comes as near to my notion of a galleon *now* as it would have been remote to me when I was a boy, had I heard of her with her half a million of silver dollars *only*; for then nothing could have satisfied me under a couple of millions in gold!"

He eyed me somewhat dreamily as he spoke. We were smoking; I chipped at my tinder-box for a light.

"What do you think of the crew?" said he suddenly.

"I can find no fault."

"D'ye think they are trustworthy?"

"Are they to be trusted on board a ship with half-a-million of dollars in her hold?"

He nodded.

"I don't see why they are not to be trusted," said I. "You must trust a crew of some sort; you can't work this brig without men. Should you doubt these fellows, what's to be done?"

"Done!" cried he, with his eyes sparkling; "you don't suppose that I would carry them to a shipload of silver if I *didn't* trust them? I'd visit port after port, ay, if it had to come to my going away for New Holland, until I had collected such a crew as I felt I *could* trust."

"It might take years."

"So it might. But how many years would it take in this beggarly calling of the sea, to amass such a fortune as lies waiting in a hole in an island to be divided betwixt Tulp and me and you and the men?"

"No years of the sea calling could compass it."

After a pause, he exclaimed:

"Yet I am struck by one remark you have made. This brig cannot be navigated without men. It must, therefore, come to my trusting the crew, and perhaps I might find no honester fellows than those on board."

"They are beginning to want to know, pretty earnestly too, I guess, where they are bound to."

"*That* I suppose," he answered; "but how do you know what's in their minds?"

I repeated the conversation I had held with Yan Bol in the night. He listened "attentively. With what sort of manner did he express himself?" he asked.

"He was respectful, sir," I answered, for now I would often *sir* my friend out of habit.

He sat for awhile in silence, thinking and drumming upon the table. Shortly afterward we went to our respective berths, and I lay reading in a book he had lent me until four o'clock. That book – what was it? It was *The Castle of Otranto*. I recollect nothing of it saving the gigantic helmet. But what a wizardry there is in names! Memories for me are imperishably wreathed round about the title of that old-fashioned, all but forgotten novel. Never do I hear the name of that book pronounced but there arises before me the picture of the interior of the brig *Black Watch*. I behold the plainly-furnished cabin, the stand of arms, the midship table upon which Greaves and I would lean, heads supported on our elbows, for an hour at the time, yarning over the past, talking about the future. There is a finer magic in names, even than in perfumes – a subtler power of evocation. I forget the story that that old book tells, but the simple utterance of the name of it will yield me a vision as sharp in detail, as brilliant in colour, as though it were the reality beheld at noontide.

The trade wind freshened again in the evening. At sundown it was blowing too strong for a topgallant studding sail. There was the promise of a gale in the windward sky, though I felt pretty sure that no gale was meant; and the mercury hung steady in the cabin. But such a sky as it was! Bronzed with the western light, and the green seas shaping out of it in dissolving heaps, and on all sides a wilderness of confused airy colouring that sobered, as the eye watched, to the stemming of the shadow out of the east. I never beheld such a wreckage of cloud. All northeast it was like the ruins of a vast continent of vapour, huge heaps of the stuff, mighty pyramids, round-backed mountains staring with copper countenances sunward, and of a milk-white softness in their skirts. I thought I spied twenty ships among them, low down, where the sea line worked against the ridged and rising and breaking stuff, and every ship was a pinion of cloud that soared into a Tenerife, then went to pieces, and sailed in rent and ragged masses over our mastheads.

I spent my dog-watch alone, and paced the deck, keeping an askant eye upon the crew, who were lounging about the galley. I admired the postures of the men. How long does a man need to follow the sea to acquire the art of leaning? The boatmen of our coasts are artists in this picturesque accomplishment; but there is no man leans with the art of the old, deep-water sailor. Not a bone in him but lounges. The very pipe in his mouth loafs.

And of the several loafing, lounging pictures upon which my eye rested the completest were the Dutchmen's. But *they* were built for it, bolstered as they were by a swell of stern that pitched their bodies into an attitude unattainable by the English Jacks, who, like all British sailors, were remarkable for flatness *there*. Yan Bol walked to and fro abreast of the row of loungers, his hands buried in his pockets, a pipe inverted betwixt his lips, his deep voice rumbling at intervals. The tones of the men – I could not hear their speech – the looks of them, one and all, hinted at a sort of dog-watch council.

'Twas a perfect ocean picture in that dying light. The brig pitched heavily as she rushed forward, and under the wide yawn of the swollen foresail you saw, as her bows came down, the streaming rush of the white waters set boiling by her steam, and sweeping up the green and freckled acclivity into whose hollow she had swept. You saw the figures of the men dimming to the deepening shadow, one clear tint of costume after another waning, the red shirt growing ashen, the blue blending with the gloom, here and there a face stealing out red against the light of a flaming knot of rope-yarns handed through the galley door for lighting a pipe.

Oh, but I felt weary of it, though! That salt hissing over the side, that sullen thunder of smiting and smitten surge, that ceaseless shrilling and piping aloft, the buoyant rise, the roaring fall – I was fresh from two years of it, and here it was all to do and to hearken to and to suffer over again, for how many months? But, courage! thought I, whistling "Tom Bowling" in time with the lift of the seas; there should be plenty of land in sight from the height of such a heap as six thousand pounds will make. Only is it a dream? is it a dream? is it a dream? and the melody of "Tom Bowling" sped through my set teeth shriller than the song of the backstay that my hand had grasped.

The night passed. Nothing of moment happened. The brig throughout my watch had averaged over eleven knots an hour, and once, on heaving the log when the wind freshened into a squall, the fore topmast studding sail being on her, the speed rose to thirteen. It was noble sailing. The race of the milk astern was so glaring white that in the darkest hour one could almost have seen to read by it as by moonlight. Let what will come along, thought I, here be your true heels for scornful defiance. What was likely to come along of a perilous sort? Well, it was impossible to say. Prior to the peace two stout French frigates had been dispatched on a six months' cruise off the African coast; they had stretched across to the Western Islands; they had picked up a Guineaman or two; but we did not know then that their fate had overtaken them in the shape of a two-decker glorified by bunting that was, is, and forever will be abhorred by the French. We did not know, I say, that the two Crapeaux had been carried away, tricolours under the Union Jack, all in correct keeping with historic teaching, to enlarge, by two fine ships, the fighting powers of Britannia. But, supposing those two frigates afloat; we were at peace with France, though, to be sure, the frigates might not have got the news of peace. What was there to be afraid of on the ocean? The Yankee – the jolly privateersman on his own hook! For those two we needed to keep a bright lookout until we should be well south of the equator. Yet could I not imagine anything afloat likely to beat, I will not say to match, the *Black Watch. That* I felt, as I counted the knots on the log line by the feeble light of a lantern, while the brig washed roaring before the trade squall, and whitened out the dark ocean till it looked sheer snow astern.

Next morning I was in my cabin after breakfast when the lad Jimmy brought me a message from Greaves. I put down my book and pipe, got out of my bunk, pulled on my coat, and went to the captain's berth. He was holding a sheet of paper before him, with an expression of amusement on his face.

"Here's a Round Robin," said he. "You may judge of the quantity of literature that freights our forecastle by observing the number of 'his marks.' It seems there are but two that can write their names."

He extended the sheet of paper. On inspecting it I found that it was formed of several sheets – spotted, fly-blown, and mouldy – seemingly blank fly leaves from two or three old volumes. These fly leaves were stuck together by glue, and the artist who had fashioned the sheet had thought proper to clothe the sailors' sentiments with crape, by ruling broad lines of tar along the margins. This strange Round Robin ran thus:

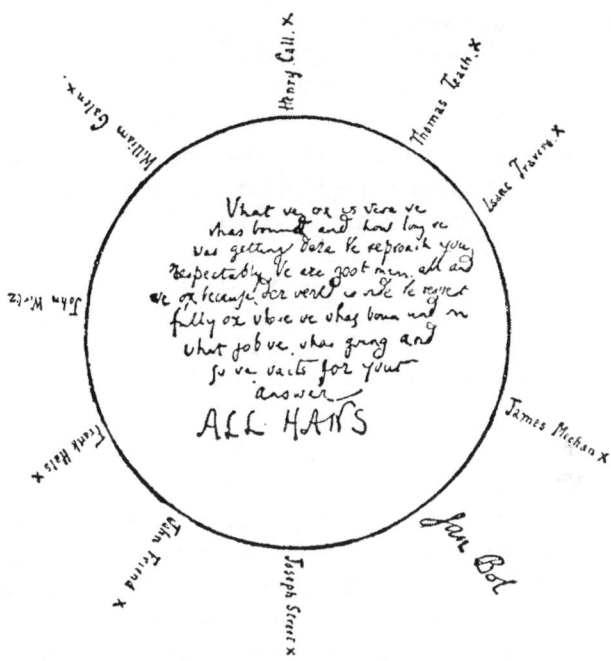

The ink with which this Round Robin was manufactured was pale, and might have been compounded of lampblack mixed with water. The handwriting was extraordinary – a Dutch scrawl, scarcely decipherable here and there. When I had read it through, and twisted the thing round so as to peruse the names, I burst into a laugh.

"It is Yan Bol's dictation," said Greaves, "and Wirtz took it down. Probably a whole book of *Paradise Lost* gave Milton less trouble than this composition of the poor devils forward."

"What shall you do, sir?" said I, putting the paper down on the table.

"Oh, the petition forces my hand. It is the whole ship's company, you see, barring Jimmy, who delivered it. I will ask you to step on deck and tell Bol that I'll communicate the business of the voyage to the men this afternoon at eight bells." I was about to leave the berth. "I'll frankly own, Fielding," he exclaimed, "that I am influenced by you in this matter. If you were in my place you would no longer withhold the secret of this errand from the crew?"

"I would not. My argument is that this brig must, under any circumstances, be navigated by a ship's company. A time must come when you will be obliged to trust your crew, and the present crew seem to me as likely and trustworthy a lot as a man must hope to meet with in the republic of the merchantman's forecastle."

"I lack decision," he exclaimed, "and why? The stake is a huge one. Well, give Yan Bol my message, will you?"

I left him, fetched my cap, and went thoughtfully on deck. I had reckoned him, when we first met, a man of strong and energetic character – a person in the first degree qualified for the control of a ship bound on such a mission as this of gathering dollars from a hole in a rock. His indecision now was a disappointment, and it puzzled me. It did not please me that my views should influence him. I wished that he should stand bolt upright under his own burden. That my views would *not* have influenced him in any other direction than this, which concerned the trustworthiness of the men, I fully believed, and my opinion weighing with him in this matter increased my suspicion of the credibility of his story of the ship imprisoned in the cave; for I felt that, if he had no doubts at all that his ship with her cargo of dollars was as matter of fact a reality as the *Black Watch* herself, his method of approaching her would be based on iron-hard resolutions; whereas, if he had *dreamt* of the ship – if his hope and faith were those of a dream only – then might there, then would there, be an element of uncertainty in his views; and such an element of uncertainty I seemed to find in his first resolution not to impart the secret of the voyage to the men until the brig was south of the equator, and in his sudden determination *now* to communicate that secret at four o'clock this afternoon.

I gained the deck. Yan Bol stumped the planks. He was clad in heavy clothes, and his figure looked more than half its usual size. In fact, the further we drew south the more clothes did Yan Bol heap upon his back. His notion was that what was good to keep out the cold was good to keep out the heat.

It was a Dutchman's notion of apparel, like to the Frenchman's idea of washing: "Why should I wash myself? I shall be dirty again."

Yan Bol came to a stand when I rose through the hatch. He wore a fur cap with flaps, which the wind shook about his ears. I did not choose to be in a hurry, though he seemed to guess my mission, and eyed me out of the flat expanse of his face with a civil, or at least unconscious, frown of expectation. I looked up at the canvas; I gazed round upon the sea; I walked very deliberately to the binnacle, and stood for some moments with my eyes upon the compass-card, observing the behaviour of the brig as she was swung along her course by the quartering seas. I then leisurely approached Bol.

"The captain," said I, "has received the men's Round Robin and has read it."

"Mr. Fielding, I like to learn vhat he tinks of her as a Roundt Robin?" exclaimed Bol.

"Wouldn't you first like to hear what his answer is?"

"Yaw, certainly. But she vhas a first-class Roundt Robin, and I likes to know vhat der captain says to him."

"At four o'clock this afternoon you will pipe the crew aft, and the captain will then tell you all what errand this brig is bound on."

"Veil, dot vhas as he should be," he exclaimed. "Ve like to know by dis time vhere ve vhas boun'. Did you read dot Roundt Robin?"

"I did."

"Vhas she goodt?"

"Good enough to make me laugh."

"She vhas serious, by Cott, Mr. Fielding. Vere could her laughter be? Dot is vhat I like to hear now."

"A Round Robin is not a thing to be criticized," said I. "No man is supposed to have had a particular share in the manufacture of it. If you want me to praise this Round Robin I shall suppose you the author of it."

"Dot vhas right, but still I ox," said he, in his deep voice, slouching his cap to scratch his head, "vere could her laughter be?"

"You have the captain's message," said I, "and you will repeat it to the men."

I then took another leisurely look round, and returned to my berth, my pipe, and my book.

At eight bells in the afternoon watch, the trade wind blowing freshly on the quarter, the sea running in dark blue heights with the frequent sparkle of silver flying fish at the coppered forefoot of the brig, and the sun sliding moist and warm and misty amid the breaks in the clouds southwest, Yan Bol, coming out of the caboose, where no doubt he had been smoking a pipe in company with the cook, who was a Dutchman, Hals by name, stood upon the forecastle, and putting his whistle to his lips blew a piercing summons, which, methought, found an echo in the very hollow of the distant little main royal itself, and then, opening his mouth, he delivered, in a voice of thunder, an order to all hands to lay aft.

The men were awaiting this command; they did not need to be urged aft. I had noticed the impatience with which they followed the chiming of the bell denoting the passage of time in ship fashion. On board the *Black Watch* we kept our little bell telling the hours and the half-hours as punctually as though we had been a ship-of-war.

The crew came swiftly and gathered abaft the mainmast, whence the quarter-deck went clear to the taffrail. Greaves had been on deck for above half-an-hour past, and I had been watching the ship since noon. No man can look so expectant as a sailor. He it is who above all men reaches to the highest possibilities of expression in the shape of expectation – that is to say, when at sea, when some weeks of shipboard are between him and the land he has left; when the full spirit of the monotony of the life possesses him, and when a very little thing becomes a very great thing merely because there is very little indeed of anything.

I had some difficulty to hold my countenance when I looked at the crew. They were going to hear a secret; it was a time of prodigious excitement, and every face was shaped by rough sensations and feelings. Greaves was smoking a long paper cigar; he flung what remained of it overboard, and with a glance behind him, as though calculating the distance of the man at the helm, that the fellow might hear what was said, he approached the sailors.

"I received the Round Robin, men," said he, "and I read it. You want to know where this brig is bound to? I don't blame ye. Mind," he added, wagging his forefinger kindly at them, "I don't blame ye. But you will remember, my lads, that when you agreed with me for the round voyage, whether at London or at Amsterdam, it was understood as a part of our compact that nothing was to be said about the destination of this brig until we were south of the equator."

"Dot vhas right enough, sir," said Yan Bol, "ve all say yaw to dot."

"We are not south of the equator yet," said Greaves.

"Dot vhas still very right," returned Bol.

"Why should you expect me to break through my understanding with you?"

"Captain, it's like this," exclaimed one of the Englishmen, named Thomas Teach. "Had the secret of this here expedition remained yourn and yourn only, we should have been willing to wait for your own time to larn where we was going to. We've got nothing to say against Mr. Fielding – quite the contrairy; he's a good mate, and I reckon as he finds us men that are under him willing and civil."

"True," said I loudly.

"But," continued Teach, Mr. Fielding wasn't one of the original ship's company. With all proper respect, sir, to him and to you, us men consider that since he knows where we're a-going to, it's but fair that we, as the original company, should likewise be told where we're a-going to without waiting to receive the news till we cross the equator."

He looked along the faces of his mates, and there was a general murmur of assent, Bol's grunt deeply accentuating the forecastle note of acquiescence.

"Enough!" cried Greaves, "I am not here to reason with you, but to keep my promise. You want to know where this brig is bound to? Now attend, and you shall have the whole secret in the wag of a dog's tail. D'ye know the Galapagos, any of you?

"I've sighted them islands," answered the seaman named Friend. The rest held their peace.

"Well," continued Greaves, "south of the Galapagos there's an island, and in that island there's a cave, and in that cave there stands, grounded, with the heads of the topmasts hard pressed against the roof of the cave, a large full-rigged ship, and in the hold of that large full-rigged ship, there lies, stowed away, a number of cases filled with Spanish dollars. Those cases we are going to fetch, and *that's* the brig's errand."

The four Dutch seamen gazed slowly at one another; the Englishmen's glance had more of life, but it was easy to see that every man marvelled greatly, each according to his powers of feeling astonished. I seemed to notice that one or two doubted their hearing, by their manner of gazing about them as though to make sure of their surroundings. After a pause Yan Bol said:

"She vhas roundt der Hoorn."

"Where else, Yan?" exclaimed Friend.

"A ship in a cave!" cried William Galen; "dot vhas funny, captain."

"Fire away with your remarks, and ask your questions," said Greaves good-naturedly, and he plunged his hands in his pockets, and walked to and fro abreast of the men.

"Ship or no ship," exclaimed Travers, "I allow that that there island's to be our port – there and home a-constitooting the voyage?"

"That's so," said Greaves; "any more questions?"

"A ship in a cave! Dot vhas strange," said Bol. "Suppose dot ship hov gone proke, und you findt der cave mit noting inside? Ve go home all der same?"

"All the same," echoed Greaves.

"And if the vessel's there, sir, *and* the dollars?" said a man named Call, in a thin voice.

"What do you want to know?" demanded Greaves.

The fellow, with some hesitation, brought out his question. "Was the job going to bring more money than the wages that was to be took up?"

"When the divisions have been made," replied Greaves, looking at Bol, "there will remain a trifle over sixty-one thousand dollars – about twelve hundred and twenty pounds – to be divided among the eleven of ye according to your ratings."

Again the sailors gazed at one another with looks of astonishment, which, in several of them, quickly made way for broad grins.

"That's a hundred pounds a man," said Call, in his thin voice.

"The divisions will be according to your ratings, I told you," exclaimed Greaves. "Bol would get more than the cabin boy. He would expect more." Bol gave a short, massive nod. "You have now heard the nature of this voyage," said Greaves, coming to a pause in his walk to and fro abreast of the men, "does any man among you find anything to object to in it? Is there any man among you," he continued, after a considerable interval of silence, during which I had observed him regard the men steadfastly one after the other, "who feels disinclined to make the voyage round the Horn to the island and home again with a small cargo of silver money?"

"She vhas a voyage to suit me," said Bol, "I likes der scheme."

Several of the men made observations to the same effect.

"May we take it, sir," said the small-voiced Call, "that we receive the wages we agreed for as well as this here hundred pound a man, to call it so?"

"You *may* take it," said Greaves shortly.

"Beg pardon, cap'n," said Hals, the cook, knuckling his forehead, and contriving a clumsy sea bow with a scrape of a spadeshaped foot, "how long might dot ship hov been in der cave?"

"How long? Since 1810."

"Who see her, cap'n," said Bol.

"I did."

"And did you see der dollars?" said Hals, again knuckling his brow and again scraping his foot.

"Yes; but you now know the motive of the voyage, and there's an end. If any man is not satisfied let him say so. We can make shift, no doubt, with fewer hands, and the fewer the crew the larger each man's share. Note that. The fewer – " and he repeated the sentence. "I have agreements in my pockets for each of you, in which Heer Bartholomew Tulp, the charterer of this brig and the promoter of this expedition, agrees to divide the sum of sixty-one thousand dollars – supposing the ship to be still in the cave and the money to be still on board of her – in which Mr Tulp, I say, agrees to divide sixty-one thousand dollars among the crew who return home in the ship, the proportions according to their ratings to be determined." He put his hand upon his breast. "But, before I hand you these documents, I must know that you are satisfied with the intention of the voyage."

"We are satisfied," was the answer delivered by a number of voices, as though one man had spoken.

On this, without saying another word, he pulled out a little bundle of papers, and, glancing at each – all being inscribed with the respective names of the men – he handed one to Yan Bol, and a second to Friend, and a third to Meehan, and so on, until every man saving the fellow at the wheel had a paper.

"Give this to Street, Mr. Fielding," said Greaves; and, taking the paper, I went to the wheel and gave it to the man who grasped the spokes.

The only two sailors who could read, Bol and Wirtz, opened the papers and looked at them. The others put theirs in their pockets.

"There is nothing more to be said," exclaimed the captain; "but should any man feel dissatisfied – whether today, after you have talked over what I have told you, or later on, when you have had plenty of leisure to think – let him come to me. He shall have his wages down to date, and be transhipped or set ashore at the first opportunity; for the fewer we are the richer we are. You can now go forward."

He turned and stepped aft, calling to me.

Chapter XIII.
A Midnight Scare

CAPTAIN GREAVES stepped aft, calling to me, as I have said, and I followed him below to his berth, after pausing to make sure that Yan Bol had taken charge of the brig; for it would be his watch till six, and mine till eight, and his again till midnight.

The captain closed the door of his berth, and exclaimed:

"I have no bond or agreement bearing Tulp's signature to offer you, because the document he signed was made out in the name of van Laar, and is, consequently, worthless; but *my* undertaking will secure you as effectually as though it bore Tulp's name; and I now propose to make out such a bond for you."

He took a sheet of foolscap from a drawer, seated himself, dipped a quill into an ink-dish, and wrote.

I have lost that paper. Years ago I mislaid it, though there were few memorials of my life that I could not have better spared. Its substance, however, I recollect, of course, and what Greaves wrote was to this effect:

That having appointed me chief mate of the brig *Black Watch*, in the room of Jacob van Laar, he agreed that the share in dollars – to wit, 30,556 – that was to have been van Laar's had he proved himself a competent mate and remained in the ship, should be paid to me – that is to say, to William Fielding; and here he entered certain particulars stating my age, place of birth, my professional antecedents; and he likewise sketched very happily in words my face and appearance, "that Tulp," said he, "shall not be able to pretend you are not the right man, and so wriggle out of what this document commits him to, in case I should not live to reach home."

More went to this document than I need trouble you with. I watched him while he wrote. There was an expression of enthusiasm in his face, as though he found a sort of joy in writing freely about thousands of dollars. "Should it prove a dream," thought I, stooping to caress Galloon, who lay at my feet, "what will the jolly Dutch and English hearts of this brig say when we arrive at the island – if such an island exists! – and find not only no ship, but not even a cave?" But the vision of Tulp came to the rescue again. A spectre, formed mainly of a leering eye, a sleek and wary grin, and a velvet cap, seemed to gaze at me from behind Greaves; and I pocketed the document with a feeling that almost rose to conviction after I had read it, at my friend's request, and thanked him very warmly for his kindness and for his friendly and particular interest in me.

We sat talking over what had passed between him and the crew.

"One point," said he, "I believe I have scored: I have made them understand that the fewer they are the richer they will be. I hope this notion may not lead to some of them chucking the others overboard. They'll all stick to the ship till the island is reached and the dollars are stowed. *Afterward* will be my anxious time. But the adventure must be gone through, and it remains also to be seen whether the brig is not to be navigated during the homeward run by fewer men than we now carry. The fewer the better. I should wish to see six men forward – no more – and three of us aft, for Jimmy is to be reckoned as a cabin hand, and, saving Bol and Wirtz, there's not a man, in my humble opinion, whose spine that knock-kneed, shambling, slobbered Cockney lad – a creature you would set down as a funeral-and-wedding idiot merely – has not the strength to snap."

Soon afterward we went to supper, for at sea the last meal is so called, and in the cabin we supped at half-past five; at six I relieved Yan Bol. The men seemed to be waiting for him to come off duty. They were smoking and talking round about their favourite haunt – the caboose. Some of them were so hairy and some of them so flat of countenance that it was impossible to gather what was in their minds from the looks of them. Bol went into the caboose, whence presently issued a quantity of tobacco smoke in a procession of puffs. I heard his voice rumbling; it was like the groaning of a distant tempest. I was too far aft to hear what he said, and there was likewise much noise of wind in the rigging, and a shrill lashing of brine alongside.

The sailors made a press at the caboose door, some in and some out, and those who were out stood in hearkening postures, their heads eagerly bent forward, the hand of the hindmost upon the shoulder of his fellow in front of him. Bol's voice rumbled. It was clear he was reading aloud, so continuous was the rumbling, and presently I found that I had guessed right when I saw the outermost man hand his paper in through the caboose door. In short, every sailor wanted his document read aloud, two men only being able to read, and of these two, Yan Bol was the more intelligible to the Englishmen.

Well, after this for some days I find nothing worth noting. A thing then happened, a trifling ocean incident some might deem it, but it left an odd strong impression upon me, and after all these years I can live through it again in memory as though now was the hour of its happening.

We had sailed out of the northeast trade wind, and had entered that zone of equatorial calms and baffling winds which is termed by sailors the doldrums. To this point we had made a fine run. Such another run down the South Atlantic must promise us a prompt arrival at the island, unless we should meet with the Dutchman van Decken's devil's luck off the Horn. Neither Bol nor I spared the men, when our forefoot smote the greasy waters of the creeping and sneaking parallels. To every breath that tarnished the white surface of the sea we braced the yards, making nothing of running a studding sail aloft, though five minutes afterward the watch might be hauling it down with all aback forward and the brig going astern. By this sort of watchfulness, and by the willingness of the men, and by the slipperiness of our coppered bends, we sneaked our keel forward, every twenty-four hours showing what sometimes rose to a "run."

It was in about one degree north, that down east at sunrise, in the heart of the dazzle there, we spied a sail, a topsail schooner, that as the morning advanced lifted toward us as though she were set our way by a current, for, often as I looked at her, I never could see that she shifted her helm to close us whenever a draught of air swept the shadows out of her canvas and held them steadily shining and gave her life for a while.

A serene cloudless day was that, the light azure of the sky whitening into a look of quicksilver where it sloped to the brim of the sea, and the sea floating thick and hushed and white, with a long and lazy heave that ran a drowsy shudder through our canvas. Greaves thought the schooner a man-of-war, something British stationed on the West African coast, well out in the Atlantic for a sniff of mid-ocean air, brought there by a chase, and now bound inward again, though subtly lifting toward us at present, attracted by the smartness of our rig, and inspired by a dream of slaves. But I did not think her a man-of-war, I did not believe her English. A Yankee I did not reckon her. In short, I seemed to know what she was not.

The morning wore away. At noon the schooner was showing to the height of her covering board, that is to say, she had risen her bulwarks above the line of the horizon, but the refraction was troublesome; she swam in the lenses of the telescope, she was blurred as though pierced with fragments of looking-glass along the risen black length of her, and sometimes I seemed to see gun-ports, and sometimes I believed them an illusion of the atmosphere.

"What do you think of her, Fielding?" said Greaves, while we stood at noon, quadrants in hand, taking the altitude of the sun.

"I don't like her looks, sir," I answered.

"Nor I. I believe now that she is a large Spanish schooner with hatches ready at a call to vomit cut-throats in scores. We'll test her."

A light breeze was then blowing off the starboard quarter. Our helm was shifted, the yards braced to the air of wind, and the brig was headed about west. We made eight bells, and grasped our quadrants, waiting and watching. For about ten minutes the schooner, that was now dead astern, held steadily on; her broad spaces of canvas then came rounding and fining down into a thin silver stroke, somewhat aslant. Greaves picked up the glass and levelled it at her.

"She is after us," he exclaimed, "and, blank her, it won't be dark for another seven hours!"

"She may yet prove an English man-of-war," said I.

"I wish I could believe it now," said he; "we must make a stern chase of it. Our heels are as smart as hers, I dare say, and this is good weather for dodging until the blackness comes, unless the beast should send boats, in which case there are thirteen of us, mostly Englishmen."

He went below to work out the sights, leaving me to put our brig into a posture of defence, and to make the most of the weak catspaws which breathed and died. Ammunition was got up, the two long brass guns loaded with round shot, the carronades with grape to slap at the first boat that should come within range. In a very little while our decks presented a somewhat formidable appearance with chests of muskets and pistols loaded with ball and slugs, round and grape shot ready for handling, a cask full of cartridges, a sheaf of boarding-pikes, cutlasses at hand to snatch, and so on, and so on.

It is old-fashioned stuff to write about! yet your grandfathers managed very handsomely with it, *somehow*, old stuff as it is. It's the city of Amsterdam that is shored up and held on end by piles; so does the constitution of this country rest on the boarding-pike. You clap a trident in the hand of your goddess of the farthing and the halfpenny. Why not a boarding-pike? *That* is Britannia's own symbol. It was not with a trident that this invincible goddess charged into the channels, and swarmed over the bristling and castellated sides of her thrice-tiered thunderous enemies, and swept all opponents under hatches and battened them down there. It was the boarding-pike that did *that* work. But a weapon, the most victorious of all in the hands of the British tar, is doomed, I fear. Its fate is sealed. The giant Steam has laid it across his knee, and waits but to fetch a breath or two to break it in twain. Be it so. But laugh at me not as an old-fashioned proser when I say that it will be an evil day for England when the boarding-pike shall have been stowed away as a weapon that can be no longer serviceable in the hands of the British Jacks.

We ran the ensign aloft; the schooner took no notice. Some breathing of air down her way enabled her to slightly gain upon us. She sneaked her hull up the sea to the strake of her water line, but she was end on, and little was to be made of her. It then fell a sheet calm, and the stranger at that hour might have been about five miles astern of us. It was a little after four in the afternoon. The heat was fierce. The planks of the deck burnt like hot furnace-bricks through the soles of the shoes, the pitch bubbled between the seams, and in the steamy vapour that rose from the brig's sides the lines of her bulwark rails snaked faking to her bows as though they were alive. The very heave of the sea fell dead; at long intervals only came a rounded slope sluggishly travelling to us, brimming to the sides of the brig, slightly swaying her, and making you think, as it rolled dark from t'other side of the vessel, of the sullen rising of some long, scaly, filthy monster out of the ooze to the greasy chocolate surface of a West African river.

"What is that?" suddenly exclaimed Greaves, who had been standing at my side looking at the schooner.

I pointed the glass.

"A boat, sir," said I. "A minute – I shall be able to count her oars. Five of a side. She is a big boat and full of men."

He took the telescope from me and levelled it in silence.

"She is a privateersman," said he. "There's nothing of the man-o'-war in the rise and fall of those blades; and if yonder oarsmen are not foreigners, my name is Bartholomew Tulp. Fielding, those scoundrels must not arrest this voyage, by Isten! There is nothing for them to plunder. They will cut our throats and fire the brig. Oh, blow, my sweet breeze! What sort of a gunner are you?

"A bad gunner," I answered.

"I'll try 'em myself. I'll try 'em with the first shot!" he cried, with his face full of blood and his eyes on fire. "There will be time to load and slap thrice at them before they're alongside, and then – ." He turned, and shouted orders to the men to arm themselves to repel boarders and to prepare for a bloody resistance. "Every man of ye will have to fight as though you were three!" he roared. "You will know what to expect if you let those beauties board you. Yan Bol – " and he shouted twenty further instructions, which left the men armed to the teeth, ready to leap to the first syllable of order that should be rendered necessary by the movements of the boat.

But at this moment I caught sight of a dim blue line on the white edge of the sea in the north. It was a breeze of wind, something more than a catspaw. The colour was sweet and deep, and it spread fast; yet not so fast but that it was odds if the boat were not alongside before our sails should have felt the first of the wind.

Greaves sighted the long brass stern-piece, lovingly smote it, and then directed it on its pivot as though it were a telescope. "Stand by to load again, men!" he cried to a couple of sailors who were at hand, and applied the match.

The explosion made a noble roar of thunder. The gun might have been a sixty-four pounder for *that* – nay, big as one of those infernal pieces which worried well-meaning Duckworth in the Dardanelles. The ball flew ricocheting for the boat, rhythmic feathers of water attending its flight, as though it chiselled chips of crystal out of the mirror it fled along. It missed the boat, but it fell close enough to flash a burst of while water that may have wetted some of the rogues; and, indeed, it was so finely aimed that our men roared out a cheer for the marksman.

That round shot achieved an unexpected result. The oars ceased to sparkle, the boat came to a stand; and this while our piece was loading afresh.

"Oh, ye saints, one and all, give it to me to smite 'em this time," prayed Greaves through his teeth.

Wink went a gun in the bows of the boat; a puff like a cloud of tobacco smoke out of Yan Bol's mouth rolled a little aside, and floated stationary and enlarging. The report came along like the single bark of a dog, but we saw nothing of the ball.

"Oh, come nearer – oh, come nearer!" groaned Greaves in his throat; and again he laid the piece, and again he applied the match, and a second volcanic burst of noise followed the fiery belch.

The final flash of water was astern of the boat this time; but Greaves' second dose, levelled with amazing precision, considering the range, coming on top of the wind, the fresh, dark blue shadow of which would now be visible to the fellows astern, satisfied them. With mightily relieved hearts we beheld them pull the boat's head round for the schooner, and, some minutes before they were got within the shadow of her side, the breeze was rounding our canvas, and the brig was wrinkling the water as she gathered way to the impulse aloft.

"Those gentry have not yet arrived at the Englishman's notion of boarding," said Greaves. "Your brass gun always speaks loudly. There was a note in the voice of this chap that deceived them. Their own schooner, probably, carried nothing so heavy."

He slapped the breech of the brass piece, sent a contemptuous look at the schooner, and fell to pacing the deck.

The breeze slightly freshened and we drove along – considerably off our course, indeed, but that could not be helped: for the blue shadow of the wind was over the schooner; she was heeling to the small, hot gush of the draught; she had picked up her boat and was in pursuit of us. We waited awhile, and then, finding that she held her own – nay, that she was very slowly closing us, indeed – we put our helm up and squared away dead before it, leaving her to follow us as best she might with nothing more that would draw than a square topsail and topgallant sail and a big squaresail.

By sunset we had run her into an orange-coloured star on the edge of the dark blue sea in the north; yet the cuss was still in chase, and, when the dusk came, we braced up on the larboard tack, with the hope of losing her, and steered southeast.

It was dark at eight o'clock, and a strange sort of darkness it was. All the wind was gone, and the sea gleamed like black oil smoking. The atmosphere had that smoky look; spiral folds of gloom seemed to stand up on the ocean, stretching tendrils of vapor athwart the stars and hiding most of them. 'Twas a mere atmospheric effect; yet all this blending of dyes, this thickening and thinning of the dusk, this heavy and stagnant intermingling of shadow around the sea produced the very effect of vapour. Sight was blinded at the distance of a pistol-shot, and the ocean lay as though suffocated under the burden of the hush of the night.

We kept all lights carefully screened, and the lookout was told to keep his ears open; but neither Greaves nor I felt uneasy. The schooner had been far astern when the evening fell, and our shift of helm, with a pretty considerable run into the southeast, could scarcely fail to throw her off the scent. But it is true, nevertheless, that vessels in stagnant weather have a human trick of turning up close together. I have been in a flat calm with a ship a long mile and a half distant from us, and in a few hours both vessels have had boats out towing, to keep the ships clear. Have vessels sexes? I believe so. It will not do to talk of the magnetic influence of *wooden* fabrics. Ships are sentient; the male ship with the nostrils of her hawse-pipes sniffs the female ship afar, and the twain, taking advantage of a breathless atmosphere, and of the helplessness of skippers – which there is no virtue in cursing to remedy – all imperceptibly float one to the other till, if permitted, they affectionately rub noses, then, lover-like, quarrel, snap jib booms, bring down topgallant masts, and behave in other ways humanly.

It was somewhere about ten o'clock that night that Greaves and I were seated on the skylight, smoking and talking, but all the while keeping an eye upon the deep shadow in whose heart the brig was sleeping, and listening for any sound upon the water. All hands were on deck. They lay about, dozing or mumbling in conversation; but they were in readiness, armed as when the boat had been approaching, and the carronades and two great guns were loaded and deck lanterns were alight below, hidden. The brig was prepared, nay, doubly prepared; for it was no man's intention to let the boats of the schooner take us unawares. Our voyage and our lives were not to be brought to a hideous and untimely end by a scoundrel picaroon.

I had seen Yan Bol that afternoon before the dusk closed in, after looking at the schooner, advance his fearful fist and writhe it into an incomparable suggestion of throttling, with such an expression of countenance as was as heartening as the accession of a dozen picked men. And this little circumstance was I relating to Greaves as we sat together on the edge of the skylight, smoking.

"He is a heavy, terrible man," said Greaves. "If the schooner's people are Spanish, as I believe, I shall reckon Yan Bol good for ten of them, at least. The other Dutchmen would be good for four apiece, and the remainder may be left to our own countrymen of the jacket."

"The Dutch fight well," said I.

"Deucedly well," he answered; "often have they proved our match. I would rather have fought the combined fleets at Trafalgar than De Winter's ships. Duncan's was a more difficult, and, therefore, a more splendid victory than our nation seems to have realized. But the truth is, little Horatio's flaming sun filled the national sky at that time with its own blazing light, and all was sunk in the splendour, though there were other suns; oh, yes, there were *other* suns!"

"Hark!" I cried, "we are hailed."

"Hailed?" he echoed in a whisper.

We listened. A figure came out of the darkness forward and said in a low voice, "There's something hard by, hailing us." Greaves and I went to either rail, and searched the thick and silent darkness, over which hovered a faint star or two, pale and dying. I strained my ears. I could hear no sound of oars, not the least noise of any kind to tell that a vessel was near us. I looked for a sparkle of phosphorus, for any blue or white gleam of sea-glow, such as the stroke of an oar, whether muffled or not, will chip out of the water in those parts. The hail was repeated. It was the same hail I had before heard. It sounded like "Ship there!" and seemed to proceed out of the blackness over the larboard bow.

Galloon barked sharply and furiously.

"Silence, you scoundrel!" hissed Greaves at the dear old brute, and the dog instantly ceased to bark. "Do you see anything. Fielding?"

"Nothing, sir," I answered, crossing the deck. "The cry seemed to me to come from off the water on the larboard bow, and if it is our friend of today or any other ship, she is *there*."

He went forward and I lost his figure in the blackness.

All hands were now wide awake. The gloom was so deep betwixt the rails that nothing was to be seen of the men, but I gathered from their voices that they were moving briskly here and there to look over the side and to peer into the smoky gloom over the bows. I went right aft, and first from one quarter and then from the other of the brig I stared and hearkened, straining my vision against the blackness till my eyeballs ached, straining my hearing against the incommunicable hush upon the ocean until I felt deaf with the sound of the beat of the pulse in my ear. Oh, it was such a night of wonderful silence that, had the full moon been overhead, the imagination might have heard the low thunder of the orb as it wheeled through space.

Greaves arrived aft.

"Is that you, Fielding?"

"Yes, sir."

"I can see nothing, and the sea is as silent as a graveyard o' night. Is that hail some piratic trick? I tell you what: the words might have been English, but they were not delivered by an English throat. I shall make no answer. There is nothing to be done but to watch for fire in the water; should it show, to hail *then*, and to let fly if the answer is not to our liking."

He called for Yan Bol. The Dutchman's deep voice responded, but even while he approached us the hail was repeated.

"There again!" cried I.

"Was it in English?" said Greaves.

"It was 'ship ahoy,' sir, very plain indeed, but thin, more distant than before, I fancy, and still off the larboard bow."

At this instant there was a great commotion forward; I heard laughter, the cackling of affrighted cocks and hens, followed by a shout in the voice of the boy Jimmy:

"Here's the chap as has been a-hailing, master."

A singular noise of the beating of wings approached us, and I discerned the figure of the boy Jimmy, as he stood before us grasping something.

"Shall I wring un's neck, master?" he cried, with a note of idiotic mirth in his voice.

"What the devil is all this about?" shouted Greaves. "What have you there?"

"The big Chaney cock with the croup, master," answered the boy.

I burst into a laugh, but a laugh that, perhaps, was not wanting in a little touch of hysteria, so poignant was the feeling of relief after the deep uneasiness of the last quarter of an hour. The men, heedless of the discipline of the vessel, had come pressing aft in the wake of the boy, and forward there continued a wild concert of cocks and hens cackling furiously.

"Fetch a lantern, one of you," bawled Greaves; "curse that poultry! Who started them all? That row's as bad as a flare if there's anything near on the lookout for us."

A lantern was brought and the glare of it disclosed the tall, muscular, knock-kneed form of the youth Jimmy, grasping by the neck a huge, long-legged, ostrich-shaped cock, of the kind known as Cochin China. The faces of the seamen crowding aft to hear and see showed past him in phantom countenances, contorted out of all resemblance to themselves by their grins and stare of expectation, and by the dim light that touched them, and by the deep darkness behind them.

"What have you got there?" cried Greaves.

"It's the big cock, master. He's croupy," answered the lad in his imbecile voice, continuing to grasp the fowl so tightly by the neck that, croup or no croup, the thing hung silent, as though dead, save that now and again it would give an uneasy, sick, protesting flap of its wings. "He wasn't well this arternoon, master. I was passing the coop, when I heard him sing out, 'Ship ahoy!' and I stopped to listen, and he sung out, 'Ship ahoy!' again. He was standing on one leg and the skin of his eyes was half drawed down, and I speaks to the cook about him, who tells me to go and be d—d."

"He gooms, captain, vhen I vhas busy mit der crew's supper; I had shcalded myself. No vender I spheaks short," exclaimed the voice of the cook among the crowd behind the lad.

"Bear a hand with your yarn, Jimmy!" cried Greaves.

"Well, master, when I hears that we was hailed, I came out of the bows, where I was lying down, and I listened, and I hears nothing; but by and by the hail comes, and I says to myself, 'Ain't I heard that woice before?' and I stands listening till it sounds again. 'It's old Chaney,' says I, and steps aft to the hen-coop, knowing in what part he lodges, and here he is, master. Shall I wring un's neck?"

"Cook," exclaimed Greaves, "take that cock from Jimmy and put it back in its coop. Go forward, men, but keep your eyes lifting till this thickness slackens. That hail *may* have come from a cock with the croup, as the lad says, but all the same, be vigilant till we can use our eyes. There may be something damnably close aboard even while I'm talking."

The men answered variously in their gruff voices, and the mob of them rolled forward and vanished in the deep obscurity. The lantern which had been brought on deck was again taken below, and all now being silent fore and aft, Greaves and I lay over the side, listening and straining our sight into the murkiness; but not a sound came off the sea. No sparkle anywhere showed the life of a lifted blade; no deeper dye of ink indicated the presence of anything betwixt us and the horizon.

For an hour Greaves and I patrolled the deck, talking over the cock with the croup, over false alarms at sea; taking about the preternatural hush and sepulchral repose of the night; and then we talked of the voyage, of the island, of the ship in the cave; and on such matters did we discourse. And while we were conversing – an hour having passed since the incident of the croupy cock – we heard afar the tinkling and musical, fountain-like rippling of water brushed by wind, and a few minutes later, a pleasant breeze was cooling our cheeks, steadying our canvas, and propelling the brig, whose wake, as it streamed from her, trailed like a riband of yellow fire, while the wire-like lines which broke from her bows shone, as though at white heat, with the beautiful glow of the sea. The wind polished the stars and cleansed the atmosphere till you could see to the gloomy line of the horizon. By midnight the moon was shining, the heavens were a deep blue, and Greaves had gone below, satisfied that the brig was the only object in sight within the whole visible compass of the deep.

Though it had been Yan Bol's watch from twelve to eight, yet, while the captain and I remained aft, he had kept forward. Now that Greaves had gone below, and my watch would be coming round shortly, Yan Bol came along to the quarter-deck.

"She vhas an oneasy time, Mr. Fielding," he exclaimed in his trembling, deep voice, that made one think of thunder heard in a vault.

"It was," said I; "but the sea is clear, and there's an end to the trouble."

"We should hov fought, by Cott," said he, "had der needt arose. Ve did not like dot dis voyage should be stopped by a bloydy pirate. It vhas strange, Mr. Fielding, dot der cock should cry out in English."

"It sounded English," said I.

"Oh, she vhas goodt English. I like," said he, broadly grinning, "dot my English vhas always as goodt. She vhas an English cock, maype, though schipped at Amsterdam. Had she been Dutch she vouldt hov spoke my language."

At this moment eight bells – midnight – were struck. I thought to see Yan Bol instantly trudge forward with the alacrity of a seaman whose watch below has come round, but he evinced a disposition to linger, as on a previous occasion.

"I likes to findt a ship in a cave full of dollars, Mr. Fielding," said he.

"There is a very great deal that one would like," said I.

"Sixty-von tousand dollar," he continued, "vhas a goodt deal of money. Dot money us men vill take oop. Und how much vill she leave, I vender?"

"Eh?" said I. "Yes, Bol, that will be a matter of counting, won't it?"

"I like to know, Mr. Fielding, vy she vhas sixty-one tousand dollar? Vy not a leedle more or a leedle less, or much more, or some tousands less? Dot'll mean," he continued after a pause, during which I remained silent, "dot dere vhas a large share ofer und aboove der sixty-one tousand dollar; but how vhas us men's share arrived at I like to know?"

"Why do you not ask the captain? Why do you ask me these questions? I am not the captain."

"No, dot vhas very right. But you hov der captain's confidence; und vy do I ox, Mr. Fielding? Because der captain's yarn is vonderful – ." He broke off, looking at me very earnestly.

"Do you distrust the story?" said I.

"Hov I said so, hov I said so, Mr. Fielding? But she vhas vonderful all der same."

I was silent. He continued to look at me for some moments in a dull Dutch way, then, seeming to check some observation he was about to make, he exclaimed:

"Veil, der coast vhas clear. I feel like sleeping. Goodnight, Mr. Fielding."

Chapter XIV.
I Send My Letter

AT SUNRISE nothing was to be seen of the schooner, though a seaman was sent on to the main royal yard with a telescope, where he swept the sea in all directions.

We crossed the equator before noon and drove into the South Atlantic, with a pleasant breeze of wind out of the east. A day or two of such sailing would send us clear of the zone of calms and catspaws, and then, with the southeast trade wind strong on the larboard bow, the yards braced forward, the blue seas breaking in foam from the sides, we might hope for a smart run southwest, with weather enough to follow to bring that wonderful island of Greaves within reach of a few days of us, instead of a few months of us, as it had been and still was.

I considered very seriously whether I should repeat to the captain my brief conversation with Yan Bol – that chat, I mean, which I have related at the end of the last chapter. For my own part I could not comfortably settle my views of Yan Bol, yet I saw nothing to object to in the man. Nothing could I recollect him saying of a kind to excite misgiving. Though he was acting as second mate, he associated with the seamen as one of them, slept and ate with them in their forecastle, and yet had their respect. This I observed and thought well of. He was a bold and hearty seaman – a practical sailor. Of navigation he knew nothing; indeed, he once owned that he could never understand how it happened that the progress of a ship altered time; the reason, he said, had been explained to him on several occasions, but it was all the same – it was a mystery "und it vhas vonderful dot any man vhas born mit brains to understand him."

And yet I could not arrive at any conclusion to satisfy me. "Am I influenced almost unconsciously against him," thought I, "by his Dutch airs and graces? Am I moved to an inward, secret dislike by a certain freedom of speech and accost, by a sort of familiarity I have noticed among Germans, and thought particularly detestable in Germans?" though I had heretofore found such Dutchmen as I had encountered too stodgy and stolid, too insipid and inexpressive, too torpid in mind and laborious in perception to be readily capable of vexing one by that kind of freedom and easiness of address and bearing which makes you thirsty to kick the beast whose burden it is. No, I could not trace my doubts of Yan Bol to my dislike of his behaviour to me. Indeed, I could not trace any doubts at all. And yet I never thought of him quite comfortably. If Greaves' dollar-ship was no vision of his slumbers, if Greaves' chests of milled silver were veritably aboard *La Perfecta Casada* in the cave he had described, then we should be a rich brig when we set sail from the island; we should need an honest crew to carry us safely home. Was Yan Bol honest? If a doubt of him arose he was the one man of the whole ship's company whom it would be Greaves' policy to get rid of as soon as possible, because he was the one man of all our little ship's company the most capable, should he take the trouble to exert himself, of obtaining an ascendancy over his mates, and of directing them for good or ill as he decided.

These being my thoughts I resolved to repeat to Greaves the questions which Bol had put to me touching the money in the island ship. He listened to me anxiously and attentively.

"I hope that man will not go wrong," said he, when I had concluded; "I like him."

"He is a good man in the forecastle-sense of the word," I answered.

"I like him," he repeated. "He controls his mates; he is the sort of man to keep them straight if he chooses, and I am almost resolved to make him choose, by promising him a handsomer share than his bond states – not at the expense of the crew, no; but by drawing on my own and the ship's share. Tulp must do what I want when I plan for the interests of all."

"That is a hammer to drive the nail home," said I, "for this has to be considered, captain; your cases of dollars will be handed over the side. The men are not fools; they will count them and roughly calculate the value of every case. As we sail home there will be much talk forward. The amount of money on board will, of course, be exaggerated. Bol will say, 'I am second mate and boatswain, and my share is to come out of sixty-one thousand dollars, eleven sharing. How much does the Englishman get, the stranger that did not sail with us from Amsterdam, who is merely a shipwrecked man, and not one of us?' He will wish to know how much, and he may breed trouble if he docs not learn how much. On the other hand, if he gets the truth and compares it with *his* share – ."

"All this has been in my head. I will confirm him in such honesty as he has by a written undertaking to pay him more dollars." He added, after thinking a little while, "I wish he had not asked you those questions. But the fellow may doubt my story. All hands may doubt it." He gazed at me significantly for a moment, and continued: "He might have hoped to get you to tell him something that he could repeat to the others, and that would hearten 'em. Should he question you again, encourage him to talk."

"Very good, sir."

"You are not to know the value of the freight of dollars."

"I will know nothing when I converse with him."

"But I shall want you to persuade him that my yarn is true," said he with a faint smile, but with a gleam in his eyes which neutralized that weak expression of good humour.

The relations between the master and the mate – between the captain and the lieutenant – instantly made themselves felt by me. I looked him in the face awaiting instruction.

"You will be able to convince him that my yarn is true," said he.

"He has all the reasons which I have for believing it."

"Do you believe it?"

"Why, yes! Mynheer Tulp's promotion of this voyage is all the proof that one wants."

He cast his eyes upon the deck, and a light smile twitched his lips. When he next spoke it was to ask me some question that had no relation to the subject we had been conversing upon.

After this I created opportunities for Yan Bol to question me. I lingered when he came on deck to relieve me. I sought to coax him into asking about the ship in the cavern, by loitering in his company instead of at once going below, and by speaking of the voyage, of the Galapagos Islands, of the uncharted island to which we were bound; but his mind appeared to have suddenly and completely turned round; what was before an eager, was now a blank countenance; indeed, he would look at me suspiciously when I talked of the voyage and the dollar-ship as though I had a stratagem in my head which must oblige him to mind his eye. Thereupon I ceased to trouble myself to attempt to convince Yan Bol that the captain's story was true, and that our errand was as real as a silver dollar itself is; and it was as well, perhaps, that this Dutchman found me no occasion to tax my wits by the invention of proofs for what I could by no means prove to myself. I did not like Greaves' looks when he talked of his dollar-ship; I did not understand his half-smiles at such times; I was puzzled by the dreamy expression of his eye, and by the light that had kindled in his gaze when he asked me, with an unspoken doubt behind his words, to convince Yan Bol that his story was true, in order that the crew might be satisfied.

It was a few days after my chat with him about the Dutch boatswain's questions that he asked me if I had succeeded in satisfying the fellow that there was a vessel, with a lazarette full of dollars, locked up in an island off the Western American coast? I told him that the man had bouted ship and was on the other tack now; that he shifted his helm when I approached him, exhibited no further curiosity, but, on the contrary, shrunk from the subject as though it vexed him. He made, or seemed to make, little of this. But that same evening, when I was sitting at supper with him, he said:

"Yan Bol will go to the devil for me now. I walked with him for an hour this afternoon, while you were below. He was frank. I like him none the less for being frank. He is a bit jealous of you. Mind ye, he said not one word against you. Fielding, not a syllable – though at the first syllable I should have brought him up, all standing. But the spirit of jealousy was strong in his remarks; it smelt in his words like a dram in a man's breath. 'Tis natural. You are an Englishman – he is a darned Dutchman. You came aboard through the cabin window, and his countryman, Van Laar, goes out as you walk in. But a plague upon forecastle passions! He was frank, as I have said, and told me that he had some doubts of the truth of my story, and that the rest of the men had not yet made up their minds about it. 'And what the deuce,' said I, 'is it to you or to the men whether my story be true or false? You were engaged for the voyage. It was a question of wages with you, and your wages will be paid.' 'Dot vhas right,' said this Dutchman. But I talked of the *Casada*, nevertheless, described her in the cave, gave him, in short, the story of my discovery that it might go the rounds forward; and then I told him that I had made up my mind to increase his share of the booty; his share of the sixty-one thousand dollars, I said, was to be according to his rating, which was the highest next yours; but I added that if he chose to work with a will and aid me and you to the utmost to carry this brig in safety to the Downs, I would give him a written undertaking to pay him a percentage on the whole value of the property, which sum would be over and above what he would receive in money as wages and as his share in the sixty-one thousand dollars."

"What did he say to that, sir?"

"He smiled, he thanked me, he let fall several Dutch words, swore that I was the finest captain that he had ever sailed under, and that his earnings out of this voyage would set him up for life in his native town. He was a fairly trustworthy fellow before. He is as honest now as is to be reasonably expected of human flesh. I am satisfied; and you need give yourself no further trouble, Fielding, to convince him that my story is true."

Well, thought I, this, no doubt, is as it should be, though it seemed to me that Greaves was making too much of Yan Bol, too much of his own anxieties, indeed, sinking the skipper in the adventurer, and a little heedless of Nelson's axiom that at sea much must be left to chance. If, thought I, he is cocksure that his ship and her dollars are where he says he beheld them, then how can it matter to him one jot whether his crew believe in his story or not? But conjecture and speculations of this sort were to no purpose. In a few weeks the problem would be solved; either the money would be aboard, or we should have found the ship broken up and everything gone out of her to the bottom – to such bottom as she rested upon, twenty or thirty feet, maybe, but as unsearchable to us, without diving equipment, as the floor of the mid-Atlantic; or we should have discovered that there was no ship and no island, and that ours had been the expedition of a dream. And still no matter, I would think. There are wages to be pocketed in the end, and I can only be worse off *then* by being so many months older than I was when I was fished up out of the Channel by the people of the brig.

The letter I had written to my uncle Captain Round, when I agreed to sail in the *Black Watch* in the room of van Laar, I had not yet been able to send. I forgot all about that letter when I went aboard Tarbrick's ship to arrange for the reception of the Dutch mate, and I had not witnessed in the little *Rebecca*, with her two of a crew, a very likely opportunity for communicating with Uncle Joe. But when we were somewhere about six degrees south we fell in with a large snow homeward bound. She was from round the Horn and proceeding direct to the Thames. I had several selfish as well as respectable and honourable motives for desiring to send the news of my being alive to my uncle, not to mention the pleasure it would give him and my aunt and cousin to learn that I was alive; I was down in his will for what you might call a trifle, but such a trifle as would prove very acceptable to me should it come to my having to continue the sea life for a living. There were other reasons why I desired that my uncle should know that I was alive, and let the one I have given suffice.

Our meeting with that snow was rendered memorable by a phenomenal caprice of wind. It was blowing a light breeze off our starboard bow; the hour was about two, the sky was like a sheet of pale blue silver, here and there shaded with curls and plumes and streamers of high-floating yellow-coloured cloud. There was wind enough to keep the ocean trembling, but at intervals, and at fairly regular intervals, there ran north and south a number of glassy swathes, oil-calm paths from the remotest of the northern airy reaches to the most distant of the recesses of the south. It was my watch below when we sighted the sail; I had dined. It was soul-consumingly hot in the cabin, and I came on deck to smoke a pipe and lounge amid the brine-sweet draughts of air, and in the pleasant shadows cast upon the white and glaring planks by the quietly breathing sails. Greaves was below. Presently Yan Bol, who was in charge of the brig, approached me. I had watched him staring at the approaching vessel through the ship's telescope, his vast chest rising and falling under his extended arms, which, clothed as he went – in pilot cloth, though the sun made him no shadow – looked as big as the thighs of an ordinary man. He approached me and said:

"Mr. Fielding, didt you belief in impossibilities?"

"No, Bol, I don't; do you?"

"By de tunder of Cott, den, I shall for effermore after dis, onless, indeedt, I hov lost der eyes I schipped mit at Amsterdam."

"What's the matter?" said I.

"Coom dis vay, Mr. Fielding, und you see for yourself." He crossed the deck. I followed him. He put the telescope into my hands and levelled a square fat forefinger at the sail that was now at no great distance. I viewed the vessel through the glass, but saw nothing remarkable. She was a motherly tub of a ship, with big topsails and short topgallant masts, and a cask-like roll in the sway of her whole fabric as the silver blue undulations took her.

"Well, what is there to see?"

"Tunder of God?" cried he in Dutch. "Lok, Mr. Fielding, how her yards vhas braced."

And now, indeed, I beheld what Jack might fairly call a miraculous sight. The wind, as I have said, was off our starboard bow, and we were, therefore, braced up on what is termed the starboard tack; but the stranger that was coming along was also braced up on the starboard tack, showing that she, like ourselves, had the wind on her starboard bow. For what did our two postures signify? This – that the wind with us was directly west-southwest, while the wind with the stranger was directly east-northeast. Here, then, were two vessels within a couple of miles of each other, so heading that one would pass the other within a biscuit-toss; here, I say, were two vessels steering in exactly opposite directions, but each braced up on the same tack, and each with the wind off the same bow!

"May der toyfell seize me if I like him!" exclaimed Bol, looking aloft at our canvas and then around the sea.

The sailors at work about the deck stared aloft and then at the approaching ship. They bit hard upon the tobacco in their cheeks. One of the Dutchmen called to an English seaman in the fore rigging:

"Dis vhas der ocean of Kingdom Coom. Der anchells vhas not far off vhen efery schip hov a vindt for himself."

The English sailor, with an uneasy motion of his body, swang off the rigging to spit clear into the sea.

"Arter this, mate," he called down to the Dutchman, "I shall give up drinking water when I gets ashore."

I looked into the cabin skylight, and, seeing Greaves at the table, begged him to step on deck and behold a strange sight. By this time both vessels had hoisted their ensigns, and each flag blew in an opposite direction.

"I have heard of this sort of thing," said Greaves, "but never before saw it. Lord, now, if every ship could have a wind of her own, as we and yonder craft have! There would be no weather gauge then – no complicated dodging for advantageous positions. Ha! Look at that now. She has taken our wind!"

The sails of the approaching vessel fell and trembled. A minute later the yards were slowly swung, and the canvas shone like white satin as it swelled to the same breeze that was breathing off our bow.

"I should be glad to send my letter home by that ship," said I.

"It may be managed," he exclaimed, "and without bothering to back yards or lower a boat. Get your letter."

I ran to my berth and returned with the letter, which Greaves posted for me on the passing ship in the following manner:

He sent me to procure a piece of canvas, a small number of musket balls, some twine, and an end of ratlin stuff. He put the balls and my letter into the canvas, and, with the twine, bound the cloth into a small, heavy parcel, to which he secured the end of the piece of ratlin stuff; then, giving directions to the man at the helm to starboard, so as to close the stranger, he sprung upon the rail and waited for the two vessels to draw together.

"Oh, the snow ahoy!" he shouted.

"Hallo!" responded a man who stood on the quarter of the vessel.

"Where are you bound to?"

"London."

"Will you take a letter for me?"

The man motioned assent and looked aloft, as though about to order his topsail to be backed. "I will chuck the letter aboard," said Greaves, swinging the parcel by its line, that the man might guess what he intended to do. "Stand by to receive it!"

Again the fellow, who was, probably the captain, motioned; and then, waiting until the two craft were abreast. Greaves, with a dexterous swing of his arm, sent the parcel flying through the air. It fell on the deck of the passing vessel just abaft her mainmast. The fellow who had answered Greaves, hail, running forward, picked it up, and held it high in his hand that we might see he had it. After this there was no opportunity for further communication; for scarce were the two vessels abreast when they were on each other's quarter, rapidly sliding a widening interval betwixt their sterns.

The snow was the *Lady Godiva*. I read her name under her counter. But her being bound to London, now that my letter was aboard, was information enough about her to answer my turn.

From this date down to the period of our arrival off the west coast of South America my clear recollection of every particular of this voyage yields me little that is good enough to record. Incidents so far had not been lacking, but south of the equator our sea life grew as dull as ever the vocation can be at its dullest. Heavens! how incommunicably tedious is the mechanic round of shipboard days! Wonderful to me is it that sailors in those times, when a single passage kept them afloat for months, remained human. And less than human some of them were, I am bound to say. Think of their lodging – a small, black hole in the bows of the ship, dimly lighted by a lamp fed with slush skimmed from the coppers in the galley, no fire in bitter weather, no air in hot; every straining timber sweating brine into the dark interior, till the floor in a head-sea was a-wash; till every blanket was like a newly wrung out swab; till there was not a dry rag in the hole of a living room to enable the poor devils to shift themselves withal. Think of their food – salted meat, out of which they could have sawn and chiselled blocks for reeving gear to hoist their sails with; biscuit that crawled on the innumerable legs of vermin, alive but unintelligent, for it came not to your whistle nor did it elude your grasp; tea from which the thirstiest of the fiery-eyed rats in the fore peak are known to have recoiled with lamentable squeaks and dying shrieks of disappointment. Think of their labour – the scrubbing, the tarring, the greasing, the furling and reefing and stitching, the kicks, the blows, the curses which accompanied the toil. Think of their pleasures – an inch of sooty pipe to suck, an ancient story to nod over, a song at long intervals.

Alas, poor Jack! What is it that carries thee to sea in the first instance? The love of freedom? Hie thee to the nearest jail; there is more freedom in it; better food, kinder words. The desire to see the world? What dost see unless thou runnest from thy ship? for in harbour all day long thou art sweating in the hold and stamping round and round to the music of the pawls; and when the night comes and thou goest ashore, if thou hast a shot in thy locker thou gettest drunk, and with whirling brains and blistered lips art thrust rather than conveyed to thy toil in the morning by the constable whom thy skipper hath sent in search of thee. And so much, therefore, Jack, dost thou see of foreign parts. But whatever may have been the cause that sent thee to sea, my lad, this will I affirm; that when once thou art afloat, there is nothing clothed in flesh, with an immortal spirit to be saved or damned, more deserving of pity.

But though we were a dull, we were a comfortable little ship. I never heard of any falling out among the crew. They worked well together. The common hope of the dollar that lay on t'other side the Horn was strong in them. It kept them well meaning. It was clear they all had full confidence in the captain's yarn, and their spirits danced with anticipation of the money they would jingle when they got home – the money in wages and share per man. This I used to think.

They made much of their dog watches when the weather was fine. One of the Dutchmen played on the flute; one of the Englishmen had a fiddle. The fellows would save their noon-tide grog for a dog watch, and make merry. Yan Bol sang as a bull roars, but his singing was vastly enjoyed. Never did any mariner better dance the sailor's hornpipe than the English sailor, Thomas Teach. He went through it grim and unsmiling, but his postures were full of that sort of elegance which is the gift of old ocean to such men as Teach. It is old ocean alone that can animate the limbs with the careless beauty of motion that Teach's arms and legs displayed when he danced the hornpipe.

And there was a sailor named Harry Call. He had served in American ships, and knew the negro character, and when he blacked his face he was good entertainment. Greaves liked his fooling so well that he would call him aft, send for the men, order Jimmy to mix a can of grog, and Call with his spare voice and negro pleasantries would agreeably kill an hour.

My own life was as pleasant as a seafaring life can very well be. Greaves had much to talk about. He had looked into books. He had travelled widely and observed closely. He was a person of much good nature. In truth, a more genial, informing man I could not have prayed for as a shipmate. Yet I would take notice of a certain haziness on one side of his mind. He loved metaphysical speculations, and would wriggle out of a homely topic to start a religious discussion. I humoured him for some time, but religion being one of those subjects that I did not much care to talk about, I soon ceased to argue, and then all the talking was his. He entertained some odd notions for a sailor, believed that every man had a good and bad angel, that when a man died his spirit slept with his dust. "Otherwise," he asked, "what is to bring the parts together again, inform them with mind, and render the whole sensible of what is happening?" I found that he had a leaning toward the Roman Catholic faith. I asked him if he was married. He answered "No." I then inquired why van Laar had threatened to take the bed from under him and his wife. "To vex me," said he.

He would be talking of religion and metaphysics, of dreams and a future life, of the state of his soul a million years ago, and of the inhabitants of certain of the stars, when I would be thinking of his ship in the cave and the dollars aboard of her. But as our voyage progressed, as we drove southward toward the Horn, he found little or nothing to say about his ship in the cave. You would have said he was done with the subject. He had so little to say, indeed, that I would wonder at times whether the purpose of this expedition was not slipping out of his memory as a dream, that is vital and brilliant on one's awaking from it, fades ere nightfall, and is effaced by the vision of another slumber, "It will be a confounded disappointment should it prove false after all," I would think; for, spite of my misgivings which sometimes I would nourish and sometimes spurn, I, during those tedious days and weeks running into months, I, in many a lonely watch on deck, in many a waking hour in my hammock, had built my little castles in the air, had furnished them handsomely for one of my degree, had gazed at them with fondness as they glittered in the light of my hope. Six thousand pounds! The money was a bigger pile in those days than it is now; to be so easily earned too! Why, in imagination I had bought me a little house, I had married a wife, I was gardening often in mine own little estate, and every quarter I was receiving dividend warrants; and there was good ale in my cellar, and no stint at meal times; and I was a happy young man, in imagination sitting, as I did, on the apex of that pyramid of promised dollars, whence I commanded a boundless prospect for a mariner's eye. And now if it was all to end in a hoaxing dream! Bless me! While I was on this side of the Horn how I pined for t'other side, how I thrashed the old brig through it in my watch on deck! With what ardour of expectancy did I every day sit down to work out the sights!

Chapter XV.
The White Water

THE *Black Watch* had sailed through the Downs in the middle of September, and on the morning of 12 December 1814, she was upon the meridian of Cape Horn, and in about fifty-seven degrees south latitude. This passage, for so swift a keel, was a long one. It was owing to diabolical weather between the degrees of forty and fifty south.

Greaves and I would sometimes say that the devil was afloat in a craft of his own within that belt of ten degrees. Head winds more maddening to the most angelic soul, calms more provocative of impious and affrighting language, it is not in the imagination of the most seasoned mariner to conceive.

But enough. We were off the Horn at last. Our bowsprit would be heading north presently, and, when our ship's forefoot cut this meridian again, the little fabric would (but would she?) be deeper in the water (by what division of a strake?) with a cargo of minted silver!

In 1814 much was made of the passage of the Horn. The doubling of that bleak, inhospitable, deep-seated rock was accepted, on the whole, as a considerable adventure. The old traditions of mountain-high seas and gales of cyclonic fury survived. The traffic down there was small; the colonies of New Holland were still raw in their making; and ships bound for Europe from that distant continent chose the mild but tedious passage of the South African headland.

The old dread has vanished. Experience has footed prejudice out of time. In furious weather the ocean off the Horn is as terrible as the North Atlantic, as the Southern Ocean, as any vast breast of water is in furious weather; and that is the long and short of it. Oh, yes; off the Horn you get some monstrous seas, it is true. I have known what it is to be running off the Horn before a westerly gale and to be afraid – seasoned as I then was – *to look astern*! But there is a safety in the mighty swing of those wide Andean heaps of brine which the sharper-edged surge of the smaller ocean does not yield.

The old freebooters and the early navigators are responsible for the evil reputation of the Horn. They returned from the wonders of foreign sight-seeing, from the joys of plunder and the delights of discovery, with their hearts full of astonishment and their mouths full of lies. There is Shelvocke's description of the Horn; it is heartrending reading in these days. The ice forms upon the page as you read; the atmosphere darkens with snow. And what, on the testimony of such a record, did Wapping think of that distant, ice-girt, howling navigation, with its enchanted islands and bergs, whose spires seemed to pink the moon? What did Wapping think when there was never a man in every company of a thousand jackets who had rounded the Horn and could tell of it?

We, passing the Horn on 12 December, found the southern hemisphere's midsummer there. We met, for the most part, with bright skies, a cheerful sun, not wanting in warmth, coming soon and going late, and a noble field of swelling blue seas. One iceberg we sighted. It was infinitely remote – a point of pearl on the sea-line.

"She vhas like a babe's milk tooth," said Yan Bol, pointing to it.

There was a fancy of milk in the whiteness of it; but, when I brought my eyes from the distant berg to Bol's face, I said unto myself – "What should *that* man know of a babe's milk tooth?"

Two disappointments await those who round the Horn with expectations bred of the reading of books. First, the weather. Often is it as placid as any quiet day that sleeps over the Straits of Dover, when the sky is streaked with the lingering smoke of vanished steamers and the white cliffs of France hang in the air. No; the weather off the Horn is not the everlasting saddle of the Storm Fiend. The seas are not always boiling, the hurricanes of wind are not always black with frost, heavy with snow, man-killing with ice-darts.

Next, the constellation called the Southern Cross. It hangs over you when you are off the Horn; often have I looked up at it, and never have I thought it beautiful. The smallest of the gems of the English skies is a richer jewel than the Southern Cross. A singular superstition is this widespread faith in the beauty of the Crux of the ancient mariner. The stars are unequally set; one is disproportionately small.

But now came a morning when we struck a meridian that enabled us to shift our helm for a northern passage, and then we had the whole length of the mighty seaboard of South America to climb. We were in the South Pacific at last. The island was hard upon three thousand miles distant; but it was over the bows – it was ahead! We had turned the stormy corner, and the verification of Greaves' yarn could be thought of as something that was about to happen soon.

Day by day we climbed the parallels, and all went well. Certain stars sank behind the edge of the sea astern of us, and as we sailed northward many particular stars which were familiar to our northern eyes rose over the bows and wheeled in little arcs, We made some westing that we might give the land a wide berth, for whether Great Britain was or was not at war with Spain, the Spaniards of that vast seaboard were scarcely less jealously and passionately tenacious in those days of their dominion in the South Sea, and under the Line to beyond Panama, than they were in the preceding century; and though we could not positively affirm that there was anything to be afraid of, anything curiously and sneakingly dangerous to be shunned (if it were not Commodore Porter, whose ship the *Essex* was believed to lie prowling hereabouts at this time), yet Greaves was determined to provide his bad angel with the slenderest possible opportunity for delaying or arresting the voyage to the island.

So we kept well out to the west, and fine sailing it was. For days we hardly touched a brace; the steady wind, growing daily warmer, sweetly blew the little brig along. It was the South Pacific Ocean. Many reports are there of the various tempers of that sea, but, for my part, northward of the parallel of forty degrees I have ever found it a gentle breast of ocean. Long and lazy was the blue swell brimming to our counter, drowsy the flap of the sunny canvas, soft the cradled motion of the ship. Once again the silver flying fish glanced from the slope of the violet knolls. The wet, black fin of a shark hung steadfast in our wake. What a world of waters it was! Never the gleam of a ship's canvas for days and days to break the boundless continuity of the distant sea-line. The men relaxed their labours, Yan Bol took no notice, and I, who was never a "hazer," was willing that they should lounge through their toil of the hours in a climate so enervating that one yearned to sling a hammock in some cool corner of the deck, to lie in it all day, to smoke and doze while the imagination slided away on the stream of the rippling music made by the broken waters and passed into the fairy harbours of dreams.

"By this time tomorrow," said Greaves to me one evening, "if this breeze holds, and our reckoning is true, and the island has not been exploded by a volcano or an earthquake, you will be having a good view of the ship in the cave – no, I am wrong, a good view of her you will not obtain from the sea, but you will be having a good view of the cave in which she lies, and I shall be very much surprised if you are not mightily impressed by the magnitude and beauty of that great hole or split in the rock, and by the indescribable complicated atmosphere or shadow within, caused, as I long ago explained to you, by the interlacery of the ship's gear and spars, visible and indeterminable."

"Visible and indeterminable! Captain, you put it as though it were some mystery of religion."

"Do you object, Fielding," said he, "to sailors, I mean quarter-deck sailors, expressing themselves as educated men would, nay, as average gentlemen would? Are you for keeping the quarter-deck sailor down to Smollett's platform of Hatchway and Trunnion? Must we swear, must we drink, must we behave when ashore like lascivious baboons and at sea like Newgate felons, who have burst through the iron bars and are sailing away for their lives, merely to justify the land-going notion that the best of all sailors are the most brutal of all beasts."

"I beg your pardon," said I; "I meant nothing."

"Visible and indeterminable. Are they not good words? Do they not exactly express what I want to convey to your mind? How 'der toyfell' would you have me talk?"

He looked at me and I looked at him. He then burst into a laugh, and we stepped the deck for a little while in silence. The time was something after half-past seven. The sun was gone, and night had descended upon the sea. It was a tropic night. The dark sky was full of splendid brilliants. A mild air blew from the westward and the brig, with her two spires of canvas lifting pale to the stars, dreamily floated over the black water that here and there shone with a little cloud of sea-fire, as though some luminous jelly fish was riding past, while here and there it caught and feathered back the flash of some large star, whose silver in a dead calm would have made an almost moon-like wake. Galloon marched by our side. Jimmy, forward, with a pipe in his mouth, lay leaning over the windlass and gazing aft, seemingly at the shadowy form of the dog, as though he hoped to coax the brute that way by persistent staring and wishing. The men, in twos and threes, trudged the forecastle. So still was the evening, so seldom the flap of canvas, so unvexing to the hearing the summer sound of the water lightly washing in the furrow of bubbles and foam-bells astern, that the voices of the men fell distinctly upon the ear; by hearkening one might have caught the syllables of their speech.

It had gone forward – taken there by Yan Bol, or whispered by the lad Jimmy, who by listening to the captain and me, as we discoursed at the cabin table at meals, would be able to pick up news enough to repeat; it had gone forward, I say, that, the weather holding as it was, and all continuing well, by some hour next day we should be having the island on the bow or beam, perhaps hove to off it, or with an anchor down. Expectation was strong in the men's voices. It was the very night for their flute or fiddle; for "Tom Tough," or "Britons, strike home!" or for some boisterous Dutch song in Yan Bol's thunder, for Call's lamp-blacked Jack Puddingisms, for Teach's hornpipe, for general caper-cutting, in a word, with a can of grog betwixt the knight-heads, and the fumes of mundungus strong in the back-draughts. But the humour of the sailors, this night, was to walk up and down the deck in twos and threes, and to talk of tomorrow and of dollars.

"If *La Perfecta Casada* – a fine-sounding name, by the way, captain," said I, "what is the English of it?"

"The Perfect Wife."

"The Spaniards," said I, "choose strange names for their ships. They have many *Holy Virgins* and *Purest Marias* at sea. I knew a Spanish ship that was called the *Holy Ghost*. Figure an English vessel so called. She meets another English vessel, which hails her: 'Ship ahoy!' 'Hallo!' 'What ship's that?' 'The *Holy Ghost*.' There is a looseness in this sort of naming that is not very pleasing to Protestant prejudice. I asked the mate of the *Holy Ghost*, 'Why is your ship thus named?' 'That she may not sink,' he answered. 'Hell lies downward. If the *Holy Ghost* goes anywhere, 'tis upward.'"

"You are in a talkative humour this evening."

"Well, it is like being homeward bound when the end of the outward passage is within hail."

"What were you going to say about the *Casada*?"

"I have never clearly gathered – supposing her to be still lying in that cave where you saw her – ."

"She is still lying in that cave where I saw her," he interrupted, repeating my words in a strong voice.

"I have never clearly gathered," I continued, "whether it is your intention to tranship her cargo – I mean the cocoa and wool?"

"I cannot make up my mind whether or not to meddle with those commodities," said he, "and so, because I have not been able to form an intention, you have not been able to gather one from our conversation. The weather will advise me. Then I shall want to know the condition of the cargo. The wool, cocoa, and hides in the hair may not be worth lifting out of a hold that has been aground in a cave since 1810. But there are a thousand quintals of tin, and there are some casks of tortoise shell – we shall see, we shall see."

"Mynheer Tulp," said I, "will, no doubt, be able to find room for all that you can carry home."

"Room and a market. But I am here for dollars. I believe I shall not meddle with the other stuff. We'll tranship as fast as the boats can ply, and then away."

I made no answer, being occupied at that instant with admiring the effect of a flash of lightning in the southwest – a clear and lovely blaze of violet which threw out the horizon in a black, firm, indigo line.

I went below with Greaves, at eight o'clock, to drink a glass of cold grog before turning in. Greaves had brought the chart of this part of the American coast out of his cabin, and we sat together conversing and looking at it. At intervals I was sensible of the burly figure of Yan Bol pausing near the open skylight, under which we sat, to peer down and to listen. But there was nothing Greaves desired to withhold from the crew, nothing he was not willing that any man of them should overhear if it were not, perhaps, the value of the money on board the *Casada*; though even their overhearing of this would be a matter of indifference, since they were bound to form an opinion of their own of the contents and value of the cases of dollars when they came to handle them.

Greaves had marked down upon the chart the position of the island in accordance with his observations when he hove to off it and sighted the ship in the cave on his way to Guayaquil. The position of the brig by dead reckoning since noon brought us, at this hour of eight, within twenty leagues of the spot, and, therefore, supposing Greaves' observations to have been correct, and supposing that the weak wind that was flapping us onward continued to blow throughout the night, we had good reason to hope that the bright morning light would give us a view of the tall heap of cinder cliffs before another twelve hours should have gone round.

Greaves was making certain calculations with a pencil on a sheet of paper, and I, with a pair of compasses, was measuring the distance of the island from the mainland, when we were startled by the roaring voice of Yan Bol, whose full face was thrust into the open skylight.

"For der love of Cott, captain, goom on deck und see vhat vhas wrong! Der sea vhas on fire. Quick! or ve vhas all burnt up."

"What does he say?" cried Greaves, who had been unable to promptly disengage his attention from his calculations.

"He says that the sea is on fire and that we shall all be burnt up," I exclaimed, picking up my cap; and, in a moment, we were both on deck.

"Der sea vhas on fire!" thundered Yan Bol as we stepped through the hatch.

I looked ahead over the bows of the brig, and the sea all that way was splendid and terrible with light. I call it light, but light it was *not*, unless that be light which is made by snow in darkness. It was a wonderful whiteness that seemed a sort of fire. It blended the junction of sea and sky into a wide and ghastly glare, and the light of the white water rolled upward into the sky as the clearly-defined edge of the milky surface advanced, as you see a blue edge of breeze sweeping over a silver surface of dead calm. The sea where the brig was sailing was black, as it had been before we went below, and in the deep, soft, indigo dusk over our mastheads the stars were shining; but the sparkling of the luminaries languished over our fore yardarms, and it was easy to guess that, if the coming whiteness spread, the sky and all that was shining in it would be hidden.

"Captain," cried Bol, "vhat in der good anchel's name vhas she?"

"A star has fallen," answered Greaves, "and is shining at the bottom of the sea."

"A star? Vhat, a star from der sky?"

"Where do stars grow?" said Greaves.

"Do you mean a shooting star, captain?" cried Bol.

"Yan Bol," said Greaves, nudging me as we stood side by side, "you have much to learn. Do not you know that the stars are often falling? They drop into other worlds than ours. Sometimes they plump into our earth, fizz into the sea, and lie on the ooze, shining for awhile and making queer lights upon the water like that yonder."

Bol breathed deeply. He could read, indeed; but he was as ignorant, prejudiced, and grossly superstitious as most forecastle hands in his day – fitter for the faiths of a Finn than a Hollander. He stared at the advancing whiteness, and seemed not to know what to make of the captain's discourse. "Yes," continued Greaves, "they are frequently falling. They are the stars which were loosed in the pavement of heaven when the angels fell. There should be many more stars than there are. Unhappily, when Lucifer was hurled over the battlements he swept away a number of stars with his tail and loosened many more, and it is those which drop."

"Der toyfell!" muttered Bol. "Von lifs und larns."

"It is a wonderful sight," said I, gazing with astonishment, not wholly unmixed, at the mighty whiteness that was coming along.

Already on high the verge of the startling milky reflection was over our fore royal masthead. You might look straight up now and see no stars. The line of the flaring whiteness upon the sea was a little more than a mile distant. The wind blew softly, and before it the brig floated onward, meeting the coming whiteness with an occasional flap of canvas that fell upon the ear like a note of alarm from aloft.

"Did you never before see the white water, Fielding?" exclaimed Greaves.

"Never, sir."

"I have sailed through it three times," said he. "Once off Natal, once in Indian, and once in China seas. I did not know it was to be met with on this side the world; but everything is probable and possible at sea. I tell you what, Bol," he exclaimed, calling across to the Dutchman, who had gone to the side to stare, and was holding on to a shroud, or backstay, with his big body painted black as ink against the whiteness that was coming along, "I believe I am mistaken, after all. It is not a star; it is an insect."

"I likes to handle dot insect. I likes her in der forecastle to read by und light my pipe by," said Bol, with a coarse, heavy, uneasy laugh, that sounded like the bray of an ass.

"It is a subglobular insect," said Greaves, nudging me again, "compressed vertically, convex above, concave beneath, wrapped in a transparent coriaceous envelope, containing a white, gelatinous substance. Repeat that to the men, Bol, will you, should the whiteness make them uneasy. Very few sailors," said he, addressing me, and talking without appearing in the least degree sensible of the wonderful and alarming milk-white light that was now almost upon us, "take the trouble to scientifically examine what passes under their noses. What, for example, is more often under a sailor's nose than bilge water? An Irish skipper once asked me what bilge water was. I told him that it was sulphuretted hydrogen, hydrosulphate of ammonia, oxide of iron, and compounds of lead and zinc. 'Jasus,' said he, 'and is that how you spell shtink in English?' "

As he spoke the brig, with a long-drawn flap up aloft, smote the sharply-defined white line, and in an instant was bathed in the unearthly light. We had not been able to see each other's faces before. Now the very expression of countenance was visible. The whole body of the brig was revealed as though by the light of the moon, and the ghastliness of the light lay in its making no shadow. The seamen stood staring and gaping; withered, they seemed, into a posture of utter lifelessness. But no shadows lay at their feet, no shadow stretched from the foot of the mast; I looked down, the planks lay plain, the seams clear, but I made no shadow. Nor did this magic light mirror itself. I glanced at the polished brass piece aft, but no star of reflection burnt in it, no gleam lay up on the cabin skylight. It was light and yet it was not light, and the wonder of it, and, perhaps, the fearfulness of it, to me, who had never beheld such a sight before, lay in *that*.

And now, by this time, the whole sea was as though covered with snow or milk, as far as we could extend the gaze. The sky reflected the light and the stars were eclipsed, but the reflection on high had not the glare of the ocean surface. I went to the side and peered over; the brig seemed to be thrusting through an ocean of quicksilver. The water broke thickly and sluggishly in small heaps from the bows, and the patches, as they came eddying aft, were like clots of cream.

The sensation induced by the progress of the vessel was as though she were forcing her way through a dense jelly. The slight heave of the sea was flattened; there was not the least visible motion in this surface of whiteness; the brig stood upright on it and the swing of the trucks would not have spanned the diameter of the moon. There was no fire in the water, no corruscation of sea glow, no green gleam of phosphor. To the very recesses of the horizon went sheeting this marvellous breast of milk-white softness that, though it was not luminous, yet flung an illumination as of the radiance of a faint aurora borealis upon the heavens.

"This is a beautiful sight," exclaimed Greaves.

"It will be a memorable one," I answered.

"I have never before," said he, "seen the white water so white, but the like of this phenomenon which I witnessed off the coast of Natal was heightened and beautified by a strange light in the heavens to the northward. It was a delicate, rosy light. I should have imagined it was the moon rising, had not the moon been up."

"Do I understand," said I, "that this sublime light is produced by a marine insect?"

"By nothing more nor less – so 'tis said. It is the marine insect that will sometimes give you an ocean of blood, and sometimes an ocean of exquisite violet, and sometimes, as I have heard, though it is something rare to witness, an ocean of ink."

"An insect!" I exclaimed. "And how many go to this show?"

"Oh, for a shipload of infidels now!" cried he. "D'ye see them looking up to God after gazing, white as the water itself, at the ocean?"

By this time the watch below had turned out, aroused, no doubt, by one of the sailors on duty. The men in a body had gradually worked their way from the forecastle to the gangway. They were all as plainly to be viewed as by the sickly light of a foggy day. No man spoke; not for minute after minute did the grunt or growl of any one of their hurricane throats reach my ears. The wild vast scene of whiteness terrified them. The impression produced was the deeper because this was the night before the day that was to heave Greaves' island out of the sea for our sight to feast on. For let it be remembered at least that the adventure we were on was highly romantic; the plain, illiterate Jacks would find something almost magical, something a little out of nature, according to their scuttle-butt and harness-cask views of life, in Greaves' discovery of an uncharted island, with a ship full of dollars in a hole in it. Also in these seas stood the Galapagos, islands of mystery and darkness, whose dusky rocks had not width enough of front to receive from the chisel or the knife the records of the bloody and diabolical tragedies of which they had been the theatre.

A man stepped out of the group; he coughed hoarsely and spat. His hand went to his forehead, and he scraped the sea bow of those times.

"Capt'n, I beg your honour's pardon," he said, "us men would like to know what sea this here is?"

"The South Pacific – always the South Pacific," answered Greaves.

"Will your honour tell us what's the meaning of this here chalkiness?"

"My lads, some clumsy son of a gun has capsized a milk can. Look for his ship, my hearts; she can't be far off." Some of the men stupidly gazed seaward.

"Vhas der island vashed by dis milkiness, captain?" exclaimed Wirtz.

"It stands in the bluest sea in the world," answered Greaves.

"This here's a sight," said Travers, "that may be all blooming fine to read about, but 'taint lucky, to my ways of thinking. Give me natur, says I."

He did not use the word *blooming*. This elegant expression was not to be heard in those days; but let it stand.

"Has none of you ever seen such a sight as this before?" called Greaves.

After a pause, "Ne'er a man," answered Teach.

"Then gaze your eyes full! drink your hearts full! Never again may you behold the like of this field of glory. Look thirstily! look till ye burst with the beauty that'll come into you by looking! Fear not, my sons – we shall be out of it all too soon. Gaze, my livelies, and silver your souls with this brightness as it silvers your cheeks. Bol, out whistle and pipe grog, that we may watch with enjoyment."

Bol blew. Jimmy, with Galloon at his heels, arrived with the can; the tot measure was dipped into the black liquor, lifted and emptied, and the dram seemed to give every man heart enough to look about him with common curiosity. One of the fellows fetched a bucket, dropped it over the side, and hauled it up full. I drew close. It was as though a pail of cream had been handed aboard.

I put my finger into the whiteness. It was as thin as salt water, nothing gluey or cheesy about it, though from the bows the whiteness rolled away from the rending slide of the cutwater as thickly and obstinately as melted ore, and astern there was no wake; it might have been oil.

For an hour we sailed through this sea of cream and under a dimmer sky of white. Bald and ghostly was that passage rendered by the shadowlessness of our decks. The sails swelled dark against the paleness; so clear was the tracing of the fabric of mast and canvas against the sky, that the course of so delicate a rope as the royal backstay could be traced to the head of the mast, and you saw the jewel block at each topsail and topgallant yardarm, clean cut as a pear on a bough against a sunset. Greaves came to a stand opposite me and looked me in the face.

"You make me think of my dreams of the dead," said he; "the dead are always pale when they come to me in dreams. Most people who dream of the dead dream of them as they remember them in life. There is light in the eye, and colour on the cheek. They always rise before me pale from their coffins." "Inspiriting talk, captain," said I, "at such a moment! But I hope I look no more like a dead man than the rest of us."

"If I were an artist," said he, "I would give many guineas out of my earnings for the chance of beholding such a light as this; this is the sort of light through which I would paint the Phantom Ship sailing. Figure that wondrous ghost out upon those white waters, the pallid faces of her men, to whom death is denied, looking over her side at the white sky, every timber in her glowing with the jewellery of rottenness – you know what I mean – the green phosphoric sparkling of decay. Cannot you see her out yonder, dully gleaming with dim green crawlings of fire as she steals noiselessly through this frothy softness, the hush of living death upon her, the silence of catalepsy? But what is the name of the painter, I should like to know, who is going to give us this light upon canvas? Oh, tell me his name. Fielding, that I may offer him all the ducats I hope to be in sight of tomorrow for his secret."

"Less my whack."

"Less yours. But mine, plus Tulp's. Damn Tulp; I'll drink his health." He called to Jimmy: "Two glasses of brandy-and-water, three finger-nips, James."

The liquor was brought, we chinked glasses, and down went the doses, to the benefit of *one* of us certainly; for I had not liked his talk of my looking like a dead man, and his fancies of the Phantom Ship with her crawlings of fire and cheeselike faces overhanging the side. Jack, if you are reading this, bear with me. I was a sailor, and, as a sailor, *you* will know that I would not relish such talk at such a time.

On a sudden the wind slightly freshened, with a melancholy cry, across the white water, and, as if by magic, the sea ahead opened black, with a few stars hovering over it. Some minutes later, the northern edge of the milky surface came streaming to our bows, and swept past us as though 'twas the edge of a mighty white sheet dragged by giant hands down in the south over the surface of the ocean. I watched the marvellous appearance receding astern, the sky unveiling its stars as the whiteness dimmed away, till it was pure nature once again, the heavens shining, the swell coming into the ocean with its long and lazy lift of the brig, the pleasant hiss of foam under her bow, and a little dance of jewels in the furrow astern.

It was my watch below, and I went to my cabin.

Chapter XVI.
Greaves' Island

I PULLED off my coat and lay down. Eleven o'clock was struck on deck before I closed my eyes. I was much excited. The prospect of the dawn disclosing the island kept me restless. Was there an island in this part of these seas for the dawn to disclose? and, if an island existed, would there be a cave in it, and would that cave contain a large Spanish ship, with five hundred and fifty thousand dollars stowed away in cases in her lazarette?

I reviewed Greaves' behaviour. He had been cool, I thought, seeing that this was the eve of the day that was to bring us off the island and put the dollars within reach of our oars. He had joked at the overwhelming apparition of the white water; he had talked of worms and fallen stars; he had treated a magnificent phenomenon without reverence; and, in one way or another, he had acted as though tomorrow were to be charged with no more than what today had held. These and the like reflections kept me awake. Shortly after six bells had been struck I fell asleep.

At midnight Bol aroused me to take his place, and I went on deck to keep watch until four o'clock. It was a quiet, rippling night; the moist breath of old ocean gushed pleasantly over the larboard quarter, and the brig slipped softly forward, clothed with studding sails. Several shadowy figures of the crew moved about the deck; their motions were restless; they'd go to the side, bend over, and peer ahead. At any other time it was just the night for a quiet snooze about the decks, with a coil of rope for a pillow, and the stars right overhead to watch until they winked one asleep. But the men were too restless to "plank it" this night. They guessed the island to be somewhere away out yonder in the dusk. They might hope at any moment for an order from the quarterdeck to back the main topsail yard. They were under the spell of the almighty dollar!

Bol hung near, waiting for me to arrive.

"Anything in sight, Bol?"

"Noting, Mr. Fielding," he answered out of the depth of his lungs; "but dere vhas time. She vhas not tomorrow yet."

"No more white water?"

"No, by tunder, Mr. Fielding. Enough vhas as goodt as a feast. I like der captain's notion of a star. She vhas a fine idea. Der verm vhas silly. How shall a verm shine in vater. Vill not der vater put her light out?"

I was in no humour to talk to him about phosphorus.

"You had better go forward and get some rest," said I. "Should daylight give us the island there will be plenty to do for all hands."

He grunted and moved forward, but not to turn in. His unwieldy shape joined other flitting forms, and I heard his deep voice rumbling first on one bow and then on t'other as he crossed the deck.

Greaves made his appearance three or four times during this middle watch. He did not stay. He would come up to me and say:

"Well, what do you see?"

"I see nothing."

"All the same, it's in sight, but you're not a cat, Fielding. Mind your helm. The difference of a quarter of a point might sink the island for us by daybreak."

He would then go to the binnacle and stand looking upon the card, address the helmsman, and after running his eyes over the canvas and stepping to the side, not to peer ahead like the men, but to judge of the rate of sailing by the passage of the sea fire through the deep shadow made by the hull, disappear through the companion way.

It was very dark at four o'clock in the morning, at which hour my watch ended. When eight bells were struck I went into the head and sunk my sight into the obscurity forward, running my gaze from beam to beam, for though it was very black there were stars sparely shining over the sea line, and by the obliteration of a handful of them might I guess the presence of land; but I saw nothing. I went aft and found Bol near the wheel and Greaves in the act of stepping through the hatchway. Eight bells had not long been chimed and the larboard watch had not yet gone below.

"While all hands are on deck reduce sail, Mr. Fielding," said Greaves. "Take in your studding sails and ease her down to the main topgallant sail."

"Ay, ay, sir."

Nothing more was said. Yan Bol went forward, I remained aft, whence I delivered the necessary orders. The heavier canvas was rolled up by all hands; the watch was then called – that is to say, the larboard watch were sent below. Daybreak was still an hour off. I said to myself, if the island is hereabouts there will be plenty to do when daylight comes. Let me sleep while I can; and for the second time that night I withdrew to my cabin and lay down, "all standing," ready for a call.

I slept well, and was awakened by a beating upon the door. The voice of the lad Jimmy called out:

"It's eight bells, sir."

"Any news of the island?" I cried.

I received no reply; in fact, the lad had run on deck the instant he had called the time to me. The berth was full of light and the glass of the scuttle was a trembling, brilliant, silver-blue disk, with the ocean splendour flowing to it. I stepped on deck, and the moment my head was clear of the companion way I beheld the island. It stood at a distance of about seven miles upon the lee or starboard bow. Greaves was pacing the deck, with his hands locked behind him and his head thoughtfully bent. Yan Bol stood in the gangway and all hands were forward breakfasting in the open; they grasped pannikins of steaming tea; they sawed with jack-knives at cubes of beef, blue with brine, locked by their hairy thumbs to biscuits, which served for trenchers; the muscles of their leather cheeks moved slowly as they chawed, chawed, chawed, cow-like; and cow-like still they moved their eyes slowly in their sockets to direct them at the island over the bow.

The morning was a wide field of day, a full heaven of tropic splendour, with a light breeze off the larboard beam blowing you knew not whence, for there was never a cloud for the wind to come out of. They had made all plain sail on the brig; she was floating forward, spars erect, under royals; the studding sails were stowed and the booms rigged in.

I stood staring for some moments, with my mind in a state of confusion. *There* was the island! The mass of it standing upon the light blue glory of water northeast was a hard rebuke to my scepticism. Yet – shall I say it – not the most mercenary of the munching Jacks in the bows could have felt a keener delight at the sight of that island than I. It signified dollars and independence to my ardent hopes. I had thought much upon my share of six thousand pounds, dreamt of the money often, had built many fancies tall and radiant upon Greaves' bond, and, sometimes had I believed that Greaves' story was true, and sometimes had I believed that Greaves' story was a dream, and therefore a lie. And now there was the island, down away over the starboard bow, a lump of shadow against the blue, to verify Greaves' assurance of an island being thereabout anyhow, and on the merits of that verification to warrant all the rest of the wonder of cave, of ship, and of a lazarette full of dollars!

For a few moments only I stood staring. Thought hath wondrous velocity, and in a few moments much will pass through the mind. I stepped up to Greaves as his walk brought him to me. I should have wished to give him my hand, but the etiquette of the quarter-deck forbade that.

"Captain," said I, in a low voice, full, nevertheless, of cordiality and enthusiasm, "I warmly congratulate you."

"And yourself," said he dryly.

"And myself," said I, "and all hands, including Mynheer Tulp."

"Seeing is believing," said he, still dryly. I looked at the island. "And yet," continued he, "though that land be there the ship and her cargo may be nothing more than a dream."

He had seen a little deeper into me than I had supposed. Finding him sarcastic I held my peace, and the better to cover my silence stooped to caress Galloon. He changed his voice and manner.

"My observations," said he, "of the latitude and longitude of that island were perfectly correct, you see."

"Perfectly correct, indeed," I echoed. "It is strange that so big a rock should remain uncharted."

"Nothing is strange at sea – in this sea particularly. The Spaniards are always for making their journeys by one road. Anything lying off that road they miss, unless they happen to be blown on to it, when one of two things happens; they perish, or they petition the Madonna and escape. If they escape, they have no more to tell about the rock or coast from which they narrowly came off with their lives than if they had perished. Why is that island uncharted by the Spaniards? Is it because no mariner among them has fallen in with it? Oh, they are lazy rogues all, they are lazy rogues all; timid, fearful navigators, execrable hydrographers."

"It is odd that no Englishman should have fallen in with it."

"That is as it happens to be."

I fetched the glass, and steadied it upon the rail, and looked. The island stood up large and livid, tawny in patches, a huge cinderous heap. The hue, and even the appearance of it, somewhat reminded me of Ascension viewed at a distance. One or two parts were robed with green. There was a tremble and flash of surf at the extremities, and I guessed that when the sea ran high, it would break very fiercely and dangerously against all weather-fronting corners of that lonely rock. Greaves came and stood beside me. I was conscious of his presence, and talked to him with my eye at the telescope.

"In what part of the island is the cave situated, sir?"

"Do you observe a lump of land swelling above the edge of the cliff to the left?"

"Yes."

"That lump or mound is the summit of the front of the rock in which lies the cave. We are opening it from the southward. I opened it, when I fell in with that land, from the westward."

"It is a volcanic pile," said I. "I observed points of rocks like chimneys. They may have smoked once upon a time."

He took the glass from me, leisurely inspected the island, and walked the deck in his earlier thoughtful posture, head bowed, hands locked behind him. I understood what was in his mind, and held off; he would have nothing to say until the wreck of the Spaniard stood before him in its dusky tomb. He mastered his anxiety, but would now and again pause and direct at the island a look that, with its accompanying play of face, expression of lip, suggestion of posture, told more of what was passing in him than had he talked for an hour.

He ordered the boy Jimmy to put breakfast on the skylight; and we ate, standing or walking, but exchanging very few words. Thus slipped the time away, and so slipped we through the water. The brig bowed as she went; a long breathing spell followed her astern, and the sails came in to the mast as she rose with the heave of the dark blue brine. The sailors lay over the forecastle head, waiting for the approach of the island and for orders. Now and again one would point and one would speak, but expectation lay as a weight upon their minds. It subdued them. For there was the island, to be sure, and the cave, no doubt, was round the corner, and in that cave might be the ship. But the dollars, the dollars, ah! Lay they there still massive, good tender as the guinea, plentiful as roe in the herring, noble coins to tassel a handkerchief with, to clink out the sweetest music in the world with to the accompaniment of deck-blistered feet marching across the gangway to the wharf, to the joys of the alley boarding house, to the delights of the runner's parlour – lay they there still in the mouldering hold within the cave?

So did I interpret the thoughts of the sailors, and I would have bet the last dollar of my share upon the accuracy of my construction of their several countenances and attitudes.

"Let her go off," said the captain.

The man at the helm put the wheel over by two or three spokes.

"Steady!" exclaimed Greaves. He viewed the island through the glass. "We are opening the reef," said he; and, taking the telescope from him, I instantly discerned the sallow line of a projection of rock, with a dazzle of sunshine coming and going along the base of the formation as the swell rose and sank there.

Deep silence fell upon the brig. All hands of us – nay, my beloved Galloon and the very brig herself – seemed to know that in a few minutes the cave would lie open before us.

And a few minutes disclosed it. I viewed the picture as though I had beheld it before, so clearly had Greaves painted it in his description, so familiar had it grown by frequent meditation. Almost abreast of us now, within a mile, lay a very perfect little natural harbour. The reefs swept out from either hand the island. They looked like piers. They needed but a lighthouse to have passed, at a glance, for roughly constructed artificial piers. Within their embrace lay a wide, smooth surface of dark blue water. A flat, livid front of rock overlooked, on the left, this placid expanse. Low down on the right of this rock ran a herbless and treeless beach, without scintillation as of sand or gleam as of coral – a dead ground of foreshore, mouse-coloured; a sort of pumice, with a small shelving to the wash of the water. But I had no eyes for that beach then, nor for any other portion of the island saving the vast, sullen, gloomy fissure which denoted the entrance of the cave right amidships of the tall face of flat rock.

Greaves let fall the glass from his eye. He swung it with an odd gesture of irritable triumph.

"Back the main topsail, Mr. Fielding."

I instantly delivered the necessary orders for heaving the ship to. The men sprang out of the bows, and rushed to the braces and clew garnets as though to a summons which signified life or death to them. The brig's way was arrested. She came with her head to the southwest, bringing the island upon her starboard quarter. All the time, while I sung out orders and while the men were hauling upon the braces, Greaves stood at the rail, his eye glued to the glass that was pointed at the cavern. He turned his head when the noise about our decks had ceased, and, observing me standing at a little distance regarding him, he beckoned.

"Look for yourself," said he.

I brought the tube to bear upon the cave, and for some moments saw nothing but the darkness of the interior. A singular appearance of darkness it was, burnished to the gleam of a raven's wing by the silver-blue atmosphere, by the azure glory floating off the surface of the natural harbour through which I viewed it. But after a little I seemed to make out a sort of intricacy of pale lines in that gloom. Well, *pale* I will not call them. They were of a lighter hue than the dusk out of which they stole to the eye. Then, knowing very well that that complication of shadow signified the spars, yards, and rigging of a large ship, I seemed to distinguish the form of the fabric; could almost swear to her bowsprit, to the tops, to the side she showed, to the crosses of the lower masts and fore and main yards.

"What do you see?" said Greaves.

"A ship," said I.

"Oh, you have no doubt?"

"I should have plenty of doubt," said I, "if you had not told me how to name, how to define that bewildering muddle of shadow."

"Give me the glass!" cried he suddenly, with a change and vehemence of voice that made the abrupt note of it wild as madness itself to my ears.

I started, gave him the glass, and watched him.

"My God!" he cried, "I fear we are too late."

"Captain," called Bol from the gangway, "dere vhas people valking on der beach."

The telescope fell with a crash from Greaves' hand. He gazed at me with an ashen face. "It was my *only* fear!" he cried. "Are we too late?"

"I see three people," said I, after looking awhile. "One of them is a woman."

"Are you sure of that?" he shouted.

"One of them is a woman," I repeated. "Two men and one woman. I see no more. One of the men is waving his hat, and now the woman is waving something white – a handkerchief. They are castaways."

Greaves snatched the glass from me.

"You are right, I believe," he exclaimed, after looking. "What should a woman be doing in a salvage or wrecking job? Yes; they are flourishing to us. I did not before observe that one was a woman. Get a boat manned, Mr. Fielding, and bring them aboard. I am mad till I learn what their business is there, who they are, what has brought them to *this* of all the hundred rocks of the Pacific."

"Which boat shall I take, sir?"

"The cutter. Let the crew go armed. Those two fellows and the woman may prove a piratical decoy, for all you know. Mind your eye as you enter the reefs, and hold on your oars to parley. There may be a big gang in ambush round the corner at the extremity of the flat there."

I have elsewhere told you that we carried three boats – a little one, which we termed a jolly-boat, stowed in a big one amidships, and abreast of these boats lay a third boat in chocks. This boat, whose capacity rose to a lading of from twenty to five-and-twenty people, we termed the cutter. Tackles were swiftly carried aloft. While this was being done the fellows who were to man her armed themselves with cutlasses and pistols. The boat was then swayed over the side, six men and myself entered her, and we headed for the island.

We gained the entrance of the natural harbour, and I bid the men pause on their oars while I looked and considered. I gave no attention to the singular aspect of the island, nor to the wondrous revelation of the ship in the vast cave. I could think of nothing but the three people on the beach. Were they decoys, as Greaves had suggested? Was there a crowd of formidable ruffians somewhere in hiding, close at hand but ready for a rush when the moment should arrive? I gazed carefully around, but saw- nothing resembling a boat. We might be quite sure that there was no vessel in the neighbourhood; the island was small, we had sailed half round it before heaving to. It was impossible to imagine that any craft with masts could be lying off the north side of the island without our having caught sight of her as we approached. But then it might matter nothing that no vessel should be in sight. Likely as not the ship in the cave had been discovered and explored, in which case the discoverer had acted as Greaves had – sailed away for a port to re-embark in a properly equipped expedition; a number of men had been thrown ashore to work at the caverned Spaniard, while the vessel to which they belonged to went away to put the horizon betwixt her and the rock, lest, by hovering and lingering close to, she should invite the attention of anything that passed.

These were my thoughts as I stood up in the stern sheets staring around. But the woman? Truly, methought, had Greaves conjectured that fellows engaged on such an errand as this of clearing the Spaniard's hold, would not burden themselves with a woman ashore, at all events. No noise came from the island. A low note of the thunder of the surf hummed from the north side, a great number of sea birds were wheeling about in the air over that northern part at too great distance for their cries to reach us.

"Give way," said I.

We pulled into the middle of the harbour, halted afresh, and now we had a good view of the three people, who, throughout this time of our tardy approach, continued to flourish to us, but without calling. The two men were apparently forecastle hands – foreigners. They wore grass hats, wide-brimmed, sombrero fashion; their clothes were loose blue shirts or blouses and blue trousers; they were barefooted; they were both of them hairy and dark, one of them of the colour of coffee. Their hair lay upon their backs in a snaky shower, and I caught a glance of earrings as they moved their heads.

The woman I could not very clearly make out. Her gown was of some pearl-coloured stuff – it had a look of shot silk, but I dare not attempt any descriptions in this way. She wore a large white hat with a white veil coiled round the crown of it, ready for dropping over the face. Some sort of mantilla she had on. She was a tall and graceful figure of a woman, and, as she stood a little apart from the men I observed the grace of a dancer in her attitudes of entreaty, in her gesticulations to us to approach.

We pulled closer in to the beach upon which those three were standing. One of the men cried out to us, the other clasped his hands, and the woman stood motionlessly, gazing.

"What language is that?" said I.

None of my men could tell me. The man continued to exclaim, gesticulating very eagerly and wildly. I listened, and thought he spoke in French.

"Are you French?" I sung out.

"Spaniards, *señor*, Spaniards," he answered, in Spanish.

"Do you speak English?"

He cried back that he understood a little English.

"Are there others, besides yourselves, on this island?"

He answered "No."

"What are you doing here?"

"We are shipwrecked," he answered, but in an accent I cannot imitate; the spelling would be meaningless to eye and brain.

"How long have you been here?"

He held up his right hand, the thumb pressed into the palm, that his four fingers might answer my question.

Here the woman exclaimed in Spanish. Her voice was clear, sweet, and rich. It came to the ear like music from the beach. There seemed no harshness of shipwreck, no weakness of privation or despair in it. She spoke with her face directed to the boat, but I could not understand one word she uttered.

"Do you wish to be taken off this island?" I cried.

"Yes, *señor*, yes," shouted the man who had answered throughout. "We starve here – we die here if you do not take us off."

I again looked very carefully about, fearful still lest some deadly trick was intended, but could see no sign of anything elsewhere on the island living or stirring. All was motionless; nothing came along with the wind but the sound of the creaming of waters, the throb and hum of surf at a distance.

"Back in, men," said I.

We got the boat stern-on to the beach. It was like a lake for the quiet lipping of the water there. The men held their places on the thwarts, ready at the instant of a cry to give way.

"Come, madam," said I to the lady.

She approached, comprehending my gesture. I took her by the hands and helped her to spring over the stern; then seated her. The two men jumped in, and we shoved off. I looked back and around as we pulled away for the opening betwixt the reefs. Nothing stirred.

The woman had very fine features. Her eyes were large, dark, and full of fire; her complexion a very delicate, pale olive; her mouth small and firm. Indeed, her mouth wanted but a corresponding and helping expression of sweetness and of tenderness in the other lineaments to be a lovely feature. She was clearly a lady. Her hands were small – models of hands to the finger-tips; her hair was extraordinarily thick, plentiful beyond anything I ever saw in a woman, and of a rich dead blackness. She wore a pair of long gold earrings, bulb-shaped, with a ball at each extremity in which sparkled a little star of diamonds. Some rings, too, she had – one on the forefinger of her right hand was a cross, formed of a sort of dark stone set upon gold, probably a signet ring. No other jewellery did she carry. Her clothes were of some rich stuff, but I could not give a name to the material; a magically contrived combination of dyes, swiftly blending and alternating with every move, and cheating the eye kaleidoscopically – the product of some Asiatic loom, an art that may have ceased as an art, and that has been extinguished by the neglect of taste. So much for my observations of this Spanish lady while we were making for the brig.

I found nothing remarkable in the two seamen. One had a pinched look; he was hollow in the eyes, and an expression of fear lay on his face. In appearance they answered to the beachcomber of the present day. They were hairy, dirty, and wild. A small silver crucifix gleamed in the moss upon the chest of the fellow who spoke English.

I had no time to ask questions. The men swung upon their oars with a will, and the brig lay scarcely a mile distant. I inquired of the lady if she spoke English. She bent her fine eyes very wistfully upon me, and shook her head on the Spanish sailor explaining what I had said. I again inquired of the fellow who understood my speech if there were others upon the island, and he answered, with energy and with passion, that there had been but three, as though he understood me to refer to his shipwreck. I asked if they had found water on the island. He answered "Yes," and pointed to some cliffs past the beach, where stood a small grove of trees and vegetation, resembling guinea grass, along with a thickness of green bushes coming down the slope.

But now we were alongside the brig. I helped the lady up the side; the two Spanish seamen followed. Greaves called down an order for the boat to keep alongside, and for two hands to remain in her. He then approached us, holding his hat while he bowed to the lady, who returned his salutation with a slow, very stately, elegant gesture, irreconcilable with the horrors from which she was newly rescued, and with the distress and apprehension in which she must continue until she reached her home, wherever *that* might be.

"She is Spanish, sir," said I, "and understands not a syllable of our tongue."

He called to Jimmy to bring a chair from the cabin, and placed it for her in some square of shadow cast by the canvas.

The crew of the brig, saving the two men over the side, were collected in the bows, and talked eagerly, and often looked our way and then at the island. Yan Bol, pipe in mouth, towered among the men.

Chapter XVII.
The Ship in the Cave

GREAVES read Spanish, but spoke it ill. He was a North-countryman, and was without musical accents for soft or swelling or vowelled tongues. On seating the lady, he looked at her and pronounced some words in her speech. My ear told me they were barbarous. They might have been Welsh or Erse.

"This man," said I, pointing to one of the Spanish seamen who stood near, "understands English."

Greaves was about to address the sailor; he broke off, and beckoned to Bol. The lumbering Dutchman came pitching aft like one of the bum-bowed boats of his own country over a swell.

"Station a man on the fore royal yard, Bol," said Greaves, "to instantly report anything that may heave into view."

"Ay, ay, sir."

The Dutchman went forward again, and a minute later the sailor named Meehan ran patting aloft.

"Fielding, should a sail be reported when I am ashore," said Greaves, speaking as though the lady and the Spanish seamen were not present, "fill on your topsail and stand away under easy canvas in a direction opposite to what the stranger may be taking. Keep your eye on her, and haul in again for the island as she settles away. Nothing must observe us hanging about here until we have got what we have come to take. I do not think it likely that anything will heave into view. I give you these directions while they are present to my mind."

I replied in the customary affirmative of the sea.

"Now for our friends," he exclaimed; "I will give them, ten minutes to make sure of them." He looked at his watch, and turned to the Spanish sailors. "Which of you speaks English?"

"Me – Antonio. I speak a little English," answered the sailor.

"Have you enough English to make me understand how it comes to pass that you are on this island? You may use a few Spanish words."

The Spaniard told this story. Their ship was *La Diana*. They had sailed from Acapulco – the date of their departure escapes me. Their ship was bound to Cadiz. She was a rich ship, and a vessel of six hundred tons. A few passengers went in the cabin, and her company of working hands, from captain to boy, numbered thirty-eight souls. They steered straight south down the meridian of 100 degrees west, and all went well till they were in about three degrees south of the equator, when a hurricane struck the ship. Neither I nor Greaves could clearly understand from the man's recital what then happened. The memory of suffering and horror worked him into passion. He talked in Spanish, forgot that he was talking to us, addressed the lady, who frequently sighed and moaned and lifted her eyes to heaven, while the other Spanish sailor, holding his clenched fists a little forward of his hips, shook them, nodding his head with a miserable, convulsed grin of temper, and horror, and tears.

We gathered that the ship's masts were swept out of her, that most of the seamen made off in the boats, that the captain ordered Antonio and his companion, whose name was Jorge, together with other seamen, to enter a boat to receive the passengers. This we understood. Then it seemed that though Jorge and Antonio got into the boat that lay lifting and beating alongside, threatening to scatter in staves at every moment, others of the crew did not follow. A lady was handed down – "the Señorita Aurora de la Cueva," said Antonio, with a nod of his head in the direction of the young lady – and scarcely had the two fellows grasped her when the boat's line parted and the fabric blew away.

What followed was just the old-world, well-worn story of a couple of days and a couple of nights of suffering in an open boat. Often has this form of misery been described; and a changeless condition of ocean life it must ever be, let the marine transformations of the coming ages be what they may. They fell in with Greaves' island. A heave of swell was running from the west; the two fellows were half dead with thirst and with the fear of dying. Spineless creatures they looked. If *they* were examples of the fellows who fought us at St. Vincent and Trafalgar, what was there in the victories of our beef-fed pigtails to brag about? They aimed for a head of reef to spring ashore, dragging the lady with them, heedless of their boat, the wretches, thinking only of a drink of water, and the boat went to pieces while they staggered inland.

Here Antonio swore horribly in Spanish. He smote his hands together, squinted fiercely at Jorge, and abused him with a torrent of words. The other hung his head and occasionally shrugged his shoulders. The lady kept her fine eyes fastened upon me. Her face worked slightly in sympathy with the speech of Antonio when he spoke in Spanish, and occasionally she sighed and moaned low; but her eyes rarely left my face. Never before had I been honoured by the intent regard of eyes so liquid, so beautiful, so full of fire, eyes whose lightest glance, when all was well with the owner, could hardly fail to be impassioned.

"Who is this lady?" said Greaves, breaking in upon Antonio.

The man again pronounced her name.

Greaves said: "She was a passenger?"

"With her mother, my captain. Both were proceeding to Cadiz for Madrid."

"With her mother! Then she is separated from her mother by the shipwreck?"

"The boat would have received the mother, but the line parted."

"Did the people you left behind perish, think you?"

Antonio replied with a shrug.

"You have been four days on the island, I understand, and there is water in abundance?"

"There is good water among those trees," said the Spaniard, pointing.

"And what food have you met with?"

He succeeded, with much difficulty, in making us understand that they had lived upon terrapin, crabs, and iguanas.

"Did you get fire for dressing your food?"

Antonio put his hand in his pocket and produced a little burning-glass.

"Fielding," said Greaves, "I am going ashore. Look to the brig and see to the lady. Take her below; let Jimmy put meat and wine upon the table. There's a spare berth for her, and by and by we will make her comfortable and keep her so till we can dispose of her. I wish she were not here, though." He made a face. "Go along forward, Antonio, with your companion. D'ye see that big man there? His name is Yan Bol. Ask him to feed you. Hold!"

Antonio and his mate faced about.

"Did you go on board the ship in the cave?"

"What ship, *señor*?"

"There is a ship in that cave," said Greaves, pointing.

"Did you go on board of her?"

The man placed the sharp of his hand against his brow and looked at the island.

"I know no ship – I know no cave, *señor*," said he.

"Go forward and ask that big Dutchman to feed you," exclaimed Greaves.

"When you think of it," he continued, addressing me as the men walked forward, "they would not be able to see the cave when on the island. It is clear that they did not notice the ship when they landed on the reef; they were too thirsty, poor devils."

"And how could they board the ship without a boat, sir?" said I.

"True," he answered. "I see too much. Fielding. I put on glasses and they magnify my meat, but they don't cheat my appetite. See to the lady."

He called to Bol to put a couple of lanterns into the boat and to send the crew of the cutter aft, and walked to the gangway. In a few minutes he was making for the island.

"Hail the masthead, Bol," cried I, "and ascertain if all is clear round the horizon."

The answer fell from the lofty height in thin syllables – there was nothing in sight. I beckoned to the lad Jimmy, who was standing by the caboose, and bade him furnish the cabin table with the best meal he could put upon it and to look alive. I then turned to the lady, and, with my hat in my hand, exclaimed:

"Will you let me take you below?"

She viewed me anxiously. Her fine eyes made a passion of even a trifling emotion in her. She did not understand, and so I had to fall to Robinson Crusoe's old trick of gesticulating. Heavens, how doth ignorance of another's tongue seal the lips! You are as one who walks dumb through many lands. Had this poor lady had power of speech in English, or could I have understood her Spanish, how would she have given vent to her full breast? I could see in her lips, in her eyes, in the movement of her features, how grievously was her heart in labour. Yes; in her face worked the anguish of enforced silence. I pointed to the cabin, made signs of eating, extended my hand to take hers, on which she rose, gave me a low bow, put her hand in mine, and I led her through the companion way.

Jimmy had not yet arrived with the meal. Still holding her hand, to deliver myself from the absurdity of gesticulating, I conducted her to a berth on the starboard side in the forepart of the living room, opened the door, and sought, with a flourish of my fist, to make her understand that it was at her disposal.

"*Lo hará muy bien*" – It will do very well – said she.

I afterward understood this to be her remark; *then* it was darker than Hebrew. In fact, I thought she referred to the emptiness of the berth. The bunk was without bedding; and that bare bunk and a little naked, unequipped semicircle of wooden washstand, screwed into the bulkhead, formed all the visible furniture of the interior.

I knew a few words in French, and tried her with a "*Parlez vous Français, señorita?*"

"*Nó, caballero,*" she answered.

I made a step into the berth, and motioned toward the bunk and the washstand, in the hope that she would be able to collect from my contortions that her comfort would be presently seen to. She inclined her head and slightly smiled, and the flash of her teeth was like sunshine betwixt her lips. Again I presented my hand, and she gave me hers; and I led her into the cabin where Jimmy was now busy. Galloon sat upon his chair, watching the lad lay the cloth. He pricked his ears and growled at the Spanish lady. I shook my fist at him, and his eyes languished, though his ears remained pricked. The lady exclaimed in Spanish, and fearlessly walked round to the dog and patted him. Galloon wagged his tail, but his ears, remained elevated, as though one end of him was in doubt while the other end was satisfied. I again noticed the beauty of the lady's hand, as she laid it on the dog, and the sparkling of the rings upon her fingers. Jimmy breathed fast and grinned much, and could scarcely proceed in his work for staring. I abused him for a lazy cub and bade him bear a hand.

The meal was spread. I motioned the lady into the chair occupied by Greaves, with further gesticulations desired her to help herself, and poured out a bumper of claret, of which wine Greaves had laid in a handsome stock, whether at Tulp's cost or not I could not say. I was greatly impressed by the self-control and dignity of this lady Aurora, as I understood one of her names to be. Hungry I could not question she was. Tempted, I might also feel sure she would be, by the food before her after four days of such living as the island beach and the grove of trees provided. Yet she helped herself to but a little at a time, first crossing herself with great devotion before lifting her fork, then eating with the well-bred leisureliness you would have looked to see in her at her mother's table. But the silence grew momentarily more oppressive.

"Jimmy," said I, "go forward and bring that Spanish sailor, Antonio, aft with you, unless he's still eating."

At the expiration of five minutes Antonio followed Jimmy into the cabin.

"Have you had plenty to eat?" said I.

His earrings danced while he nodded – he wore earrings like those you see on a French fishwife – his blood-stained, dark eyes searched the cabin.

"A very good ship – very kind men," said he. "When do you sail, *señor*?"

"I have not sent for you to question me," said I. "I desire you to interpret my speech to this lady. Tell her – " and, in few, I bade him inform her that instructions would be given for her cabin to be comfortably equipped, and that whatever the brig could supply was at her service.

She smiled and bowed to me on this being interpreted, and then addressed Antonio, who, however, found himself at a loss, and was obliged to act to make me understand. He feigned to wash his face, and unnecessarily passed his fingers through the length of his hair, and then, finding words, made me understand that the lady was weary, that she had slept but little, and then on the hard ground, and that she would be thankful to lie down and sleep. Thereupon I told Jimmy to convey my bedding to her bunk, also to place one or two toilet conveniences of my own in her cabin; and, after waiting to see my instructions carried out, I bowed low and sprang on deck, with my mind full of the dollars ashore, wondering likewise what Greaves' report would be, whether the dollars were still in the ship's hold, and when lie meant to go to work to discharge the vessel of her silver.

My first look was at the weather. It was boundless azure down to the lens-like brim of the sea – not a feather-sized wing of cloud – and a light air of wind with just enough of weight in it to hold the backed topsail steady to the mast. I looked at the island; the boat had entered the cave and was lost in the shadow. I picked up the glass, and levelled it; the dark lines of rigging and spar were faintly discernible, but the boat was deep in the dusk and not to be seen. It was the ugliest rock of island I had ever viewed, swart, sterile – save where the trees stood – gloomy, menacing with its suggestion of arrested fires. A few terrapin, or land tortoises, crawled upon the beach. Many birds, most of them white as shapes of marble, wheeled and hovered over the further extremity of the land with frequent stoopings and dartings, like our gulls over a herring shoal. I swept every foot of the visible surface of land with a telescope, but witnessed no signs of life of any sort. Nevertheless, the two long arms of the reef strangely civilized the beach and the face of cliff where the cave was, by their likeness to artificial piers. They formed a very perfect, spacious harbour in which, during a heedless moment or two, I caught myself looking for a cluster of rowboats, for some group of shipping, for cranes and capstans, for men walking, as though, forsooth, I gazed at the piers of a dock!

How it had come to pass that a big ship of seven or eight hundred tons should have backed and neatly threaded an eye of cave, and fixed herself within. Greaves had, doubtless, correctly explained. The commander of her had stumbled upon this island in thick weather; or he may have found the island aboard of him on a sudden in a black night. He had a reason for bringing up in the shelter of that harbour, and when his anchors were down it came on to blow dead in-shore. The ship dragged. Her stern made a straight course for the opening in the cave. Would they seek to give her a sheer to divert her from that entry? No. For there might be safely in that cave, but outside it was certain destruction. To touch was to go to pieces against such a steep-to front of cliff as that. But many are the conundrums submitted by the ocean, and victoriously insoluble are they for the most part. You may theorize as you will. Nothing is certain but this: there was a ship!

While I waited for the return of Greaves, I called to Bol to get a cast of the deep-sea lead. There was no bottom at eighty fathoms. I had expected from the appearance of the island to find a great depth of water to the very wash of the surf. No need, therefore, to bother with our ground tackle. And so much the better! Nothing like having your ship under control when the land is aboard. With an offing of a mile it would be easy to "ratch" clear any point of the island, even should it come on to blow with hurricane power; then it would be up-helm and a brief run for it, and a heave-to till the weather mended.

The two Spanish sailors sat, Lascar fashion, against the caboose. They sucked alternately at a short pipe which one of them had probably borrowed. When the lead-line was coiled away, Yan Bol rolled up to me and said in his voice of thunder, but very civilly:

"Dot vhas a scare."

"What was a scare?" said I.

He levelled a massive forefinger at the two Spaniards. I nodded. "Der captain vhas some time gone," said he. "I hope no man vhas before her."

"And that's my hope."

"How' many cases of dollars might der be, Mr. Fielding?"

"I don't know."

He looked as if he did not believe me, and said, "Veil, der more, der better for Mynheer Tulp und oders." He paused upon this word, *oders*. I gazed at the island. "Der more der better, certainly," continued he, "yet dey vhas not so plentiful but dot efery dollar might be shipped before dark. Tell me dey vhas plentiful some more dan dot, and, by Cott, Mr. Fielding, der crew's share vhas as a flea upon der dog dot scratch her."

"My name is Fielding, not Greaves, Yan Bol," said I.

"Oh, yaw, dot vhas right. But I likes to tink aloud sometimes, Mr. Fielding."

"Are not you satisfied?" cried I, suddenly rounding upon him and looking him full in the face.

"Perfectly satisfied, Mr. Fielding."

"Then why, by that devil who always seems to be busy in ship's forecastles, come you to me now with your growlings and your questions and your dots, and your Cotts and your dollars, Yan Bol."

"Growlings – questions! I likes to know when we get der dollars on board und make sail, dot vhas all."

"Strike a light with your eyes and keep a lookout for yourself, and hail the fore royal yard, will ye, and receive the man's report."

He went forward, and his roar swept straight aloft like a blast from the mouth of the cannon. There was nothing in sight at sea, the man called down. I looked toward the island and saw the boat at that moment stealing out of the cave. I mused on Bol while the boat swept across the satin calm surface of the natural harbour, the oars swinging like lines of flame in the men's hands. Was Bol going to give trouble? It was late in the day to ask that question. It would be impossible to rid the ship of him on this side the Horn, and by the time it came to t'other side – .

The boat arrived, and Greaves rose in the stern sheets; he rose, but he was supported too. A sailor grasped him by either arm, and he was helped with difficulty over the side of the brig. I was at the gangway to receive him, and assisted by seizing his hands as the men helped him to climb. He was pale as milk, and his mouth was drawn with pain.

"What is the matter?" I asked.

"I have had a fall," he said, speaking with a laboured breath. "I tripped and drove my whole weight against the sharp edge of a case in the lazarette of the ship yonder. I wish I may not have broken a rib. Help me, Fielding."

I took him by the arm, and Jimmy, who stood near, grasped him in obedience to my gesture by the other arm, and together we got him into the cabin and to his berth. He asked for brandy-and-water and drank a tumblerful, and then requested me to help him to strip, that he might see if he had broken any bones. He had hurt himself over the right hip, and the skin was somewhat darkened there, but the ribs were unbroken. He felt over himself anxiously, occasionally groaning, and said:

"No, my good angel be praised, the bones are sound. I am in torment from the pain of the blow. That must be it, and it will pass – it will pass."

"I would recommend you to lie perfectly still."

"No; I must be on deck. I can sit and keep watch and look about me while you go ashore."

I helped him to dress, and he seemed unable to speak for pain while he put his arms and body in motion. He then asked for another glass of brandy-and-water and sat, saying he would rest and talk to me for ten minutes.

"Are you in pain when you are still?" said I.

"No. I was too eager, and consequently careless, pressed forward, tripped, and should have set fire to the ship had I swooned, for I was alone and the fall flung the lighted lantern from me, and the candle lay naked and burning among the cases."

"Lord, how suddenly will a trifle become a frightful thing at sea!" said I.

"Where is the Spanish lady, Fielding?"

"In her berth, and perhaps asleep, sir."

"Well," said he, after a pause, "the dollars are there."

"I am glad to hear it, sir," said I, feeling the blood in my cheek, for I own that the news worked as a sort of transport in me.

"This cursed accident will hinder me from superintending the unlading of the vessel. You must undertake that job."

"You can trust me, captain."

"Up to the hilt I do. Open that drawer, and hand me the pocket-book you'll see." His extending his hand to receive the book made him wince. "There are a hundred and forty cases," said he. "You will take slings and tackles to hoist the cases out and lower them over the side into the boat. Be careful not to overload your boat. The money may be safely transhipped in three journeys; so divide one hundred and forty by three and your quotient is your lading for each trip."

"Ay, ay, sir."

"Be careful with your fire. I split open some of the boxes, as I told you, to make sure of their contents. Take tools and nails and battens with you for securing the riven cases. Be yourself in the lazarette while this is doing."

"Right, sir. Where will you have the cases stowed aboard us?"

"Oh, in the lazarette. I was prevented by my fall," he exclaimed, "from examining the rest of the cargo. Do you that when the money is transhipped. I will act on your report if the weather allows. But should there come a change when we have got the money, then damn your cocoa and tin – we'll be off."

"Shall I remain in the ship during the trips, or take charge of the boat?"

"Take charge of the boat, but see all your men in first."

I faintly smiled, for here was a direction that was a little particular, methought.

"Help me on deck, now. Fielding; and then go to work."

I thought to myself: "It is no time, this, to speak of Yan Bol. The matter must stand."

He leaned upon me, and, with pain and difficulty, gained the deck. All the men but one had come out of the boat, and the ship's company, saving that man and Jimmy and the fellows at the wheel and masthead, were assembled in the gangway. They hung together in a little crowd. Impatience burnt like fire in them – impatience and expectation and anxiety, now complicated by the injury their captain had met with. When we made our appearance they stared and shuffled, one and all, as though they were mutineers, scarce masking a madness of bloody intention, and about to make a rush aft to its execution. Is not the insanity that drink will run into the veins and brains a sweet little cherub compared with the demon that enters the soul of man out of the coin of gold or silver?

"Captain," cried Yan Bol, "I shpeaks for all handts. You vhas not hurt much, all handts hope?"

"Not much, my lads – not much, I thank you," answered Greaves, whom I had helped to seat in the chair Jimmy had placed for him, and who, while he remained motionless, seemed free from pain.

"Captain," again cried Yan Bol, in tones like to the noise of breakers heard in the hollow of cliffs, "again I shpeaks for all handts. Vhas der dollars safe?"

"Yes," answered Greaves.

The men roared out a cheer – a roaring cheer it was. It seemed to be repeated on the island a mile off, as though there was a crew ashore there.

I now began to sing out the instructions which Greaves had given me. Pieces of planking for nailing over the cases were flung into the boat;

lines for slings, tackles, tools, lanterns, and the like were handed down. The crew took their seats, and we shoved off, followed by a cheer from the fellows who remained behind. There went with me six men – two Dutch, the others my countrymen. The drift of the brig, though very inconsiderable, owing to the lightness of the breeze and the apparent absolute tidelessness of the sea, had veered the island a trifle southerly, and the brig lay on a line with the edge of the cliff where the cave was. The cave was, therefore, hidden from me. I stared with great curiosity at the island as we neared it, making for the head of the westerly reef to round into the lake-like expanse within. A more hideous heap of rock shows not its head above the water. The cliffs of it, where they run to any noticeable altitude, come down to the sea in twisted masses. You would have thought the process of this island's formation had been arrested at some instant when the red-hot mass of it was writhing and pouring into the ocean over the edges of its own heaped-up stuff. No iceberg ever submitted a more fanciful sky-line; but its toad-like hue, its several hideous complexions, made it a loathly sight. The spirit shrinks from this bit of creation as from some disgusting creature.

The cave was situated in the highest front of this island. The height of this front was above two hundred feet; how much above that elevation I know not. It was smooth and sheer, pumice-hued like the beach that swept from it into the northeast; so smooth and sheer was it that you would have said it had been split in twain from a like mass that had fallen and vanished. Assuredly some enormous convulsion had gone to the manufacture of that prodigious fissure or cave.

We pulled through the opening of the reefs, and I headed straight for the cave. So strong was my excitement that it felt like a sort of illness. I breathed with labour; the sweat lay like oil in the palms of my hands, though my hands were cold. It was not now the thoughts of the money. My excitement was no dollar madness then. I was oppressed, to a degree I find incommunicable, by the marvellous picture, as I was now beholding it for the first time, of the big ship clothed in the dusk of the mighty tomb into which she had backed and where she had brought up. I had had no leisure for the sight during my first excursion; had but glanced at it, my head being then full of the shipwrecked people we were bringing off, and of fancies of what might be lurking on shore. But now, our approach being leisurely, the expanse of water to be measured considerable, I could gaze, wonder, realize, until emotion grew overwhelming and became a sensation of sickness in me.

Were you to split a big stone open and find a live toad in it you would marvel. Hundreds would assemble to view the wonder, and a poor man might get money by exhibiting it; but how many much stranger things than a live toad imprisoned in a stone would I, as a sailor, exact the relation and sight of, ere admitting that half the sum of that marvel of a great ship at rest in a huge cave was approached?

At first sight the fabric looked like a piece of nature's handiwork as it lay in the gloom of the interior it had miraculously penetrated. It looked, I say, as though the volcanic spasm, which had shorn the lofty cliff into its bald front and wrought the prodigious fissure, had contrived the hundred fragments and ruins of rocks, the splinters, the serpentine lengths, the massive bulks, the pillar-shaped fragments into the aspect of a ship, building the wonder in a sudden roar of earthquake, and leaving it a faultless similitude.

"Oars!" cried I.

We floated forward with the arrested blades poised over the water. It was burning hot; the sun stood nearly overhead, and the surface of this strange natural harbour shone like new tin, tingling in fibres and needles of white fire back again into the light that it reflected. We were within a musket-shot of the entrance of the cave.

"On which side did you board, men?"

"To starboard, sir."

"Give way gently, and, bow there, stand by with your boathook."

Chapter XVIII.
We Tranship the Dollars

ALTHOUGH the hour was approaching high noon, and the day very glorious, no light was in the cave beyond the length of the ship's bowsprit. A wall of darkness came to the bows of the ship; it might have been something material, something you could lean against or stick with a knife; the daylight touched it and made a twilight of it at the mouth, then died out. The long and short of it is – it is my way, anyhow, of explaining the strange thing – the filthy coloured scoriae, the gloomy masses of cinder, pumice, lava – call it what you will – were unreflective; light smote the stuff and perished, or was not returned, so that a thin veil of dusk clothed with deepest obscurity any hollow it lay in.

The water brimmed blue to the mouth of the cave, and then, at a few boats' lengths, slept black and thick as ink, wholly motionless this day; though I might suppose that when a large swell ran outside the breakwaters, the smaller swell of the harbour put a pulse into the black tide of the cave, though without weight enough to stir the stern-stranded ship. Yet you saw much of her when you were still on the threshold of the cavern. Her huge bows sprawling with head-boards loomed out of the darkness, advancing the yellow bowsprit till the cap of it was almost flush with the sides of the opening. Had the jib booms stood, they would have forked far into daylight and, perhaps, long ago have challenged the attention of a passing ship, and brought her people to explore the Spaniard and enrich themselves. Her lower masts were yellow, and they showed ghastly in the gloom. She had immense round tops, black and heavy, and shrouds of an almost hawser-like thickness, with a wide spread of channels and massive chain plates. Most of the yards were across, and squared as though the machinery of the braces had worked to the music of the boatswain's pipe. Her sides were tall; she carried some swivels on her poop rail, and a few pieces calked with tompions crouched through a half dozen of ports, like motionless beasts of a strange shape about to spring.

To look up! To behold that lofty fabric and complication of mast and spar and rigging soaring to the dark roof, against which the topgallant masts had been ground away to the topmast heads!

Be seated in a small boat alongside a ship of six hundred or seven hundred tons, with such a height of side as this Spaniard had, lifting her platform of deck a full eighteen feet above the water for the eye to follow the ascent of the lower masts from; I say from the low level of a small boat, look up to the altitude of the starry trucks of such a ship as this *Perfecta Casada*; if you be no sailor, your eye will swim as you trace the mastheads to their airy points. To an immeasurable height will those spars seem to soar above you, yea, though they rise no higher than the cross-trees. But here was a vast cave in which a great ship – and a ship of seven hundred tons was a great ship in my time – could lie; and in this cave a lofty ship *was* lying, partly afloat, partly stranded; the darkness in which she slumbered magnified her proportions; she loomed upon the sight as tall again as she was, and half the wonder of this wonderful show lay in the height of the black ceiling against which her topmast heads were pressed, jamming her into the position she had taken up, as though a shipwright and his men had dealt with her.

The atmosphere struck cold as snow after the outer heat. A hush fell upon us as we floated in, with the bowman erect ready to hook on, and the silence was horrible, and the more horrible for the sound thrice heard in the hush that fell upon us, of a greasy gurgle of water, like a low, villainous, chuckling laugh.

But all this is description, and it takes me long to submit to you what I beheld in a few breathless moments of wonder, and awe, and admiration. We were here to load dollars, not to muse and marvel.

"Sort o' ole penguin smell knocking round, ain't there?" said one of the crew.

"Only a Dago could have managed this job," said another.

"Why don't Dagoes stay ashore? Blast me if even a Dutchman would have made such a muck of it."

"Hold your jaw!" I roared, in a rage; and my cry went in an echo through the cave, rebounding as a billiard ball from its cushion.

What is more diabolically and instantaneously fatal to sentiment than the vulgar talk of a vulgar Englishman? A Spaniard, an Italian, a Portuguese, a Greek – blasphemes in your presence, and his coarseness adds to the romantic colours of the idealism you are musing on; but let an Englishman come alongside of you, and drop an *h*, and emotion is shivered as by a thunderbolt.

The remarks of the sailor woke me up. We were alongside the ship, and the fellow in the bow had hooked on to one of the huge main-chain plates. I crawled into the channel, and over the rail, and dropped upon the deck. It was like entering a vault, and there was an odd, damp, earthy flavour in the air. I wonder, thought I, if there are two dead men in the forecastle, locked in each other's arms? But why locked in each other's arms? Ah, why? Fancy will give body to wild conceits at such a time and on such an occasion as this.

I stood a moment at the rail; the water flowed black as ink into the blackness over the stern. In the mysterious twilight that shrouded the ship, her decks and masts looked unearthly; it was hard to conceive that human hands had fashioned her, that the echoes of the mortal calker had resounded through her. I thought of the ship in Lycidas: "Built in th' eclipse and rigged with curses dark."

Sternward the craft died out in gloom. The roundhouse, or some such contrivance of deck structure, hung in a swollen shadow with the yellow shaft of the mizzen mast shooting straight up out of it. I seemed to catch a faint gleam of glass, a dim and ghostly outline of doorway, of skylight, of crane-like davits. The deck of a ship viewed at midnight, by the light of froth breaking round about, would shadowily and glimmeringly show as this Spaniard did from the gangway to the taffrail. But forward there was light; the radiance of the day hung, like a sheet of blue silver, in front of the opening of the cave, and against that brilliance – compact and undiffused, like the light upon the object glass of a telescope – the bows of the ship stood out in indigo, the tracery of the rigging exquisitely marked till it vanished in the gloom overhead.

I bade one man remain in the boat, and the rest to come on board and bring the lanterns, tackles, slings, and materials for securing the damaged chests of dollars. I then lighted one of the lanterns and walked aft, looking with the utmost curiosity around me, as though this ship, forsooth, instead of being a vessel of my own time, was coeval with this cave, and but a little younger than Noah.

The dollars were, I knew, stowed away down in the lazarette. This queer name is given to a part of a ship's after-hold. It is a compartment or division, and commonly used for the stowage of stores and provisions. The hatch that conducted to this place was in the cabin. I entered the cabin – a sort of deckhouse – and paused, holding my lantern high, and gazing about me. I observed a row of cushioned seats or lockers, three or four round scuttles on either hand, with dim oil paintings let into or framed to the panels between; lamps which, when lighted, might shine like the starry crescents of the poet, and two square tables, one at each end. The hatch was open. I descended and passed through a 'tweendecks, black as ink. The lantern light gleamed along a corridor, and revealed a short row of berths to starboard and larboard. And now, passing through the hatch in this deck, I stood in the lazarette. The floor was shallow; there were numerous stanchions, and the white cases, which contained the dollars, were stowed between those uprights. I approached a range of cases and found the top one split open. I squeezed my hand through and felt the dollars, packed in large rolls. They were as rough to the touch of the finger, with their milled edges, as any big surface of file, and cold as frost. There looked to be a great number of cases. I do not suppose that Greaves had attempted to count them. He abided by the declaration of the manifest, and since it was certain the cases had not been meddled with, no doubt the number and value were as the manifest set forth.

I halted inactively here for, perhaps, a minute, while, with lantern upheld, I ran my eye over the cases. The silence was horrible – no dimmest sob of water penetrated, no distant squeak of rat afforded relief to the ear. But here were the dollars! They were now to be secured, got into the boat, and conveyed to the brig. I called to the men, and they came below with the battens and hammer and nails. We had four lanterns burning, and there was plenty of light. In a few minutes this dead vault of hold was ringing to the blows of the hammers. I overhauled the cases and saw that every split lid was carefully repaired before ever I dreamt of suffering a box of the metal to be lifted. The men spoke not one word, unless it were an "ay, ay, sir," in response to a call from me. They chewed and spat with excitement, hammered and toiled with eagerness, and often did they roll their eyes over the cases, but they held their tongues. When the last of the boxes was repaired, slings were procured, a tackle rigged, and I, standing in the lazarette, tallied a quantity of the cases on deck, some of them large, and holding, as I should have reckoned by the weight, not less than three thousand to five thousand dollars apiece. I then followed the men, the gangway was cleared, and the chests lowered by tackles into the boat, where they were received and trimmed by three of the crew.

We pulled out of the harbour, deep, but not perilously deep, with silver, and when we rounded the reef I spied the brig at a distance of about a quarter of a mile away from the spot where we had left her. They had wore her and got her head round on the other tack, and clapped her aback afresh. There was a fellow stationed on the fore royal yard; I see him in my mind's eye, as mere a pigmy as ever Gulliver handled, as he sat jockeying the yard in the slings, one hand on the tie, his legs dangling, and the loose white trousers trembling, and a hand to his brow as he sent his gaze into the remote ocean distance. The sun made a blaze of the white canvas, and their reflection trembled in sheets of quicksilver, deep in the clear cerulean beneath the shadow of the vessel's side.

The *Black Watch* looked but a little ship after the lumping fabric in the cave. Yes, she looked but a little ship for the hundreds of leagues of ocean she had measured, since the hour when I was lifted over her rail nearly dead of Channel water. But small as she was, she sat in beauty upon the sea; the long passage had not roughened her, her sides showed like the hide of some freshly curried mare of Arabia. She rolled lightly, sparkles leapt from her, the colours about her deepened, paled and deepened again, and fingers of shadow swept through the blaze of her canvas.

As we approached I saw Greaves sitting in the chair in which I had left him; he sat under a short awning. There was a tray upon the skylight, and bottles and glasses, and I guessed he was eating his dinner. I looked for the lady, but saw nothing of her. Galloon watched our approach, seated like a monkey upon the rail with half a fathom of red tongue out. Bol and the others and the two Spaniards were congregated in the gangway. The big Dutchman waited until the boat drew close, he then roared in a voice that could have been heard on the other side of the island, "Hurrah, my ladts! Tree sheers for Capt'n Greaves." And when the men had cheered, he roared out again, "Und three sheers more for der dollars!"

By the time this unwarrantable uproar – but it was scarce worth correcting, seeing the occasion of it – had ceased we were alongside, and I sprang on deck. "How have you got on, Mr. Fielding?" called Greaves from his chair, without attempting to rise.

"Very well, sir."

"How many cases?"

I gave him the number.

"Get them aboard at once," he exclaimed, "and leave them on the quarter-deck till all are shipped. See those cases aboard, and then step aft."

The men speedily hoisted the cases out of the boat. Yan Bol was conspicuously forward and energetic in the hand he gave. I stood near, and heard him say, "I vhas pleased mit der Spaniards for leaving dis money. Dere vhas house, vife, beer, bipes, mit songs und dances in dese cases. Cott, vhat a veight! I likes to find more ships in a hole. Vhat drinks, vhat larks in von case only."

The sailors rumbled with laughter at the fellow, and some of the Englishmen eyed me askant to guess my mind. I was willing, however, that Bol should run on. Greaves was near, and able to hear and judge for himself. When the last case was out of the boat I walked aft.

Greaves said, "Send your boat's crew to dinner, and let others take their place for the next boat."

"With your leave, sir, I'll keep the men I have just returned with. They know the ropes and have nothing to learn."

"Be it so. Send the crew to dinner, but let them bear a hand; and you can make a meal off this tray here."

There was food in plenty, and wine. Having told the boat's crew to go to their dinner, I sat down with Greaves, and ate and drank. The weather continued extraordinarily beautiful, but the wind was failing, long glassy lines of calm were already snaking along the surface of the sea, and it was fiercely hot. The horizon swam in a film; you could have seen ten miles in the morning, and not five miles now from the deck. No sights had been taken; no sights were needed when there was an island, whose situation had been accurately observed, close alongside.

"We shall have the dollars aboard by four?" said Greaves.

"Easily, sir."

"Do you believe in the dollars now. Fielding?" said he, with a smile.

I answered, "Yes," colouring, and asked him how he felt.

"Easier," said he; "there is no pain when I sit. A severe bruise – no more."

"Yan Bol is a bit forward and outspoken for a foremast hand, don't you think, captain?"

"He is a Dutchman, and all Dutchmen are cheeky. The word *cheek* originates with the Dutch. Look at their sterns and look at their faces, if you want the etymology of the word *cheek*."

"I hope he'll remain cheeky only. For my part, I don't feel sure of the man."

"Too late – too late," said Greaves irritably and impatiently.

"I do not like that he should ask me the value of the treasure that is to come aboard, and I do not like that he should say that as the size of a flea is to the size of the dog that scratches it, is the proportion of the forecastle share to the whole of the money."

"If he gives me trouble," said Greaves, "I will shoot him. I will show you the rising moon through a slug-hole in the devil's skull. But do not accept Yan Bol too literally. Dutchmen will say without significance that which, in the mouth of an Englishman, might sound brutally malevolent and sinister."

"That may be, sir. I don't know the Dutch."

"I have made up my mind not to meddle with the cargo. Do not trouble to examine it. The money will be risk enough. Shrewd as old Tulp believes himself to be, and really is, the anxiety of running a quantity of tin won't be worth the purchase. If the cocoa is sweet, bring some of it off for the ship's use, and if you can meet with the four casks of tortoise shell, we'll find room for the stuff. Four casks are easy of transhipment, but the rest we'll let be."

This was good sense. It must have taken us some time to break out and tranship the tin and the wool and the hides in hair. The smuggling of such stuff, on our arrival home, would have taxed even the many-sided, hard-salted cunning of a Dealman; and, smuggling apart, without papers, how were these commodities to have been passed?

I allowed the boat's crew a quarter of an hour for their dinner, then summoned them; and, not to repeat the story of our first visit, by something after three o'clock that afternoon, the weather still holding marvellously radiant and all the wind gone, I had tallied the last of the cases of dollars over the side of the *Black Watch*, along with some crates of cocoa; but the four casks of tortoise shell I had been unable to meet with. Whether they had been omitted, or stowed in some secret place, I know not. Then, for an hour, I was busy in superintending the stowage of the cases of dollars in the brig's lazarette. While I was thus occupied,

Yan Bol, with a few seamen, was sent by the captain in the longboat to procure fresh water and fill up with terrapin and all else catchable that was good for the saucepan. The Dutch boatswain made two journeys before I was done, and was gone ashore again for more water and turtle when I arrived on deck after a wash and a clean-up. I reported the dollars stowed to the captain.

"Ninety-eight thousand pounds," said he. "It is worth the venture, I think."

"I can scacrely credit the reality now it has happened and all's well," said I.

"There are many men," said he, "who would be willing to be pressed, run-down, half-drowned, and picked up for six thousand pounds."

"Ay, indeed," said I; "and when I take up that money, Galloon, how much of it is to be your share, dear doggie?"

"The Spanish lady sleeps well."

"After four days of that island!" said I.

"What is to be done with her? I certainly cannot land her in a Spanish port. It will end, I believe, in our carrying her to England. I intend to court no unnecessary risks, and I should be courting a very unnecessary risk by looking close enough into a port to land her. No; she will sail with us to England. I hope she is amiable. I scarcely noticed that she was good-looking. I am no ladies' man – I do not care for women; and the deuce of it is, neither you nor I speak Spanish."

"She is a woman of degree," said I; "has fine manners, fine rings, and beautiful hands."

"You may have found a wife as well as a fortune in these seas, Fielding."

"Marry a Spanish woman for money!" said I. "Who'd lick honey off a thorn?"

"And why would not you marry a Spanish woman, money or no money?" said he. "Do not you know that the best and oldest blood in the world runs in Spanish veins? You seem to sneer at the mention of old blood."

"Not at all."

"Give me old blood in a woman. With old blood you associate all the elegances, all the graces and aromas in the bearing and conduct of human nature. Vulgarity makes a toad of beauty itself. Think of Venus saying ''Ave done,' and bragging of her jewellery."

"What is a lady?"

"I expected that question. Cannot you define what any chambermaid or boots can distinguish; what any shopman, waiter, poor sailor man like you or me, can instantly *recognize?* Marry, come up. What is more teasing than the question, 'What is a gentleman?' Cocky Mr. Macaroni, with his hat over his eye and his hair dressed in imitation of his betters, says, 'Vat's a gentleman?' and the beast knows the thing every time he sees it."

"How is the pain in your side?"

"Well, it makes me wince when I move as I did then. How strange," said he, sinking his voice and looking at the island, "that I, who have been dreaming of galleons all my life, should, of the scores whose keels have cut these waters, be the one chosen to light upon yonder ship of dollars."

"Shall you fire her before sailing?"

"No. We will leave her for the next man who may come along – for some poor devil to whom a few serons of cocoa and a thousand quintals of tin may be what the Cockney calls an 'object.'"

The sun was now low, and the west was on fire. The sea came like blood from the rim of the western line to midway the ocean plain, where the fierce light drained into thin blue that went darkening into melting violet eastward. The brig had drifted very nearly due south of the island, opening the reefs, and baring the harbour to our sight, and disclosing the verdure that clothed a portion of the northern rocks. The longboat lay alongside the beach, and the figures of her people came and went. I thought to myself, a pity if Yan Bol and his sweet and manly fellows don't take a fancy to the derelict, agree among themselves to attempt to warp her afloat, and consent to remain on the island if Greaves will give them the boat; food enough they will find in the ship and on the beach.

Though the island stood steeped in the red light of sunset, it reflected nothing of the western splendour. Grimy, melancholy, livid – an ocean cinder heap did it look in that fair evening radiance, a spadeful out of Neptune's dust bin. I picked up the telescope to view the ship in the cave before the shadows closed the wondrous object out, and with the tracery of the spars and rigging, dim in the lens, I conceived myself on board. I imagined the hour of midnight, I heard in fancy the distant groan of surf, I heard the sobs of the black water within the cave, a faint creak from the heart of the sepulchred vessel; and I figured fear growing in me even unto the beholding of apparitions, until a shiver ran through me as chill as though it had come out of the cold hold of the ship herself.

I put down the glass, meaning to laugh away my fancies to Greaves, and beheld the lady Aurora de la Cueva in the act of rising through the companion way.

Though Greaves and I had only just now been talking about her, I stared as though I had not known she was aboard. It was indeed strange, after all the months of Greaves and Yan Bol and the Dutch and English beauties forward, to find a woman in the brig; to see a fine, handsome, sparkling-eyed girl stepping out of the cabin as though she had been there from the hour of leaving the Downs, but secret. She bowed, I lifted my cap, Greaves struggled to his feet with his face full of pain. I begged him to sit, and ran below for a chair, which I placed near his for the lady Aurora. She had found out that he was in pain, that he had met with an accident, and was addressing him as I put her chair down, her large, Spanish, glowing eyes very wistfully fastened upon his face. He understood her, for, as I have told you, Greaves read Spanish indifferently well, and faintly understood it when spoken, but he wanted words and could not utter the few he possessed. He smiled and touched his hat, and then pointed to the island.

It was not for me to linger near them. I went to the rail and watched the boat and the movements of the fellows upon the beach, but I also found several opportunities in this while for observing the lady Aurora. She had slept and was refreshed. The fine, delicate, transparent olive of her complexion – I may say it was a very pale olive, well within the compass of the admiration of those whose love is for the white and yellow part of the sex – was touched slightly with bloom as from recent slumber. Her eyes were large and splendid with light, remarkable for their long lashes, and of a shade that made you think of the sea at night, black and luminous, their depths filled with wandering fires as she struggled with the oppression of silence or gazed at you as though she would speak. Her nose was slightly Jewish, rather small than big for her face, the nostrils the daintiest piece of graving I ever saw in that way. Her teeth were very good, strong and white, a little large. The quality of her clothes might have been very grand; one would judge of *that* perhaps by the rings, for this sort of thing goes on all fours as a rule; but the fit or fashion was monstrously vile to my taste. You guessed that underlying all that spread and sprawl of skirt and bodice there sat, or stood, or reposed the figure of a Hebe. Hints of secret perfections there were in plenty; but all grace of shape was overwhelmed by the cut of her gown; it stood upon her like a candle extinguisher, and in shape was not even fit for a nun.

"I am unable to understand the lady, Fielding," exclaimed Greaves. "Is Antonio forward?"

I spied the Spaniard leaning over the bows looking toward the island. He had gone away in the boat on the first journey to show the men where the water was. On her return with her freight of fresh water, he had crept over the side and sneaked forward to loaf and lounge and smoke in Jack Spaniard fashion. How did I know this? Because I knew that Antonio had been sent in the boat to point out the spring, and his lounging in the bows with a pipe betwixt his lips *now*, while the boat was ashore and the men busy, told me the little yarn of loafing from start to finish.

I called, and he put his pipe in his pocket and came aft.

"Interpret what this lady says," exclaimed Greaves.

She poured forth some sentences of Spanish. I could trace no fatigue, no reactionary debility, such as might attend the strain and passion of deliverance from peril tremendous above all words to her as a woman.

"The *señorita*," translated Antonio in effect – but, as I have before said, I will not attempt a written description of his articulation or phrases; I write that he may be intelligible – "wishes to know how long you intend to remain in this situation, and to what part of the world you are proceeding when you sail?"

"To England!" cried the lady, when Antonio had made answer out of the mouth of Greaves. "*Santa Maria purissima!* How shall I find my mother? If she has been rescued she will have been conveyed to some port on the South American coast, whence she will return to Acapulco, and there await news of me. To England! *Ave Maria!* The world will then divide me from my mother. Blessed Virgin! I did think this ship was proceeding to a South American port. To England! I shall never see my mother again."

She exclaimed awhile in this sort of language, but untheatrically. Nay, there was a dignity in her astonishment and concern; very little tossing of hands and uprolling of eyes. The main article in the outward expression of her grief and alarm lay in the piteous look she fastened on me, as though she would rather appeal to me than to the captain; as though, indeed, she considered that since I was the first to take her by the hand on the island, and to bring her off from a situation of horror, she was entitled to look to me for all further kindnesses.

"The *señorita*'s mother," said Greaves, "was, of course, rescued, and is, no doubt, safe and well?" Antonio turned his back upon the lady that she might not see him squint, and he shrugged his shoulders. "But we have no right to suppose," continued Greaves, looking sternly at the Spaniard, "that the ship which rescued the *señora* conveyed her to a port whence she could easily reach Acapulco. On the contrary, in all probability the ship was bound round the Horn, in which case the lady may be now on her way to Europe."

Antonio translated; the lady Aurora gazed at him somewhat passionately, and beat the air with a gesture of irritation, clearly unable to collect the captain's meaning from the fellow's interpretation of it. Antonio talked much and gesticulated with singular energy. The lady then appeared to comprehend.

"She says that her mother is rich," said Antonio, "and is well known as the widow of Don Alonzo de Cueva, the merchant of Lima. She will pay liberally to be conveyed to Acapulco, where she has a brother who is a priest. She will return to Acapulco because she is sure to believe that the *señora*, her mother, will seek her there."

"Tell the lady," said Greaves, "that I am truly sorry not to be able to put her ashore at any port where she would be within easy reach of Acapulco. When I have filled my water casks I am proceeding to England as straight as the rudder can steer the ship, touching nowhere, and giving everything that passes plenty of room. Yet this tell her, likewise, that on our way to England we may chance to fall in with a vessel bound to a port on this side the South American coast. Should we fall in with such a vessel, I will transfer the lady to her."

He spoke slowly, with the deliberateness of a man who is in pain while he discourses. Antonio made shift to render the captain's words intelligible to the lady. She asked, through the Spanish seaman, what Captain Greaves would charge to put her ashore at Lima or Valparaiso.

"It is not to be done," said Greaves; "beg her not to repeat that request."

She seemed to gather the matter of his speech by his manner. Her eyes came to mine, earnest, pleading, with a deeper shadow in their dark depths as though tears were not far off. It was a look that made me curse my ignorance of the Spanish tongue. Much could I have said to comfort and hearten her; but though I had been able to talk as fluently as she, it was not for me to intrude *then*. I was mate, and Greaves was captain; and I stood at the rail seeming to watch the island as it blackened to the fading crimson light, and to be keeping a lookout for the return of the longboat.

"Was not the lady's mother proceeding to Madrid?" said Greaves.

"Yes, capitan," answered Antonio.

"If the vessel which may have picked her up is going that way, why should she desire to return to Acapulco?"

"You have heard, my capitan, that the *señorita* believes her mother will return to Acapulco and wait for her there."

"How is the mother to know that the daughter is alive?"

Again Antonio squinted fiercely and shrugged.

"Is there reason to suppose that the widow imagines her daughter is saved? Is there reason to believe that the widow herself is saved? Supposing her to have been picked up by a ship bound south, why should not she proceed in the direction that, if pursued, must ultimately land her at Cadiz, or put her in the way of very easily reaching Madrid, for which city, as I understand, she and her daughter embarked at Acapulco? Interpret all this, will you?"

Antonio began to translate.

"Fielding!" exclaimed Greaves.

"Sir."

"Call Jimmy aft."

The boy arrived.

"I am going below, Fielding," said Greaves. "My ribs ache consumedly. I may get some ease by lying flat. Is the longboat coming off?"

The tall bulwarks prevented him from seeing the lower ranges of the island. I looked a moment; then, to make sure, levelled the glass, and said:

"They are at this instant shoving off, sir."

"Get in the water and then hoist your boat in," said he. "You can fill on the brig and stand north for an offing of about three miles; then heave-to afresh, and carefully observe the bearings of the island, lest it should roll down black or thick. If heavy weather happens in the night we will proceed, for we have fresh water enough aboard to carry us along. Otherwise, we will complete our watering in the morning, for I want to make a steady run of it to the Channel without need of a halt on any account whatever."

While Greaves was giving me his instructions, Antonio was interpreting to the lady Aurora, who frequently broke into short exclamations of "*Qué!*" "*Es esto!*" "*Será posible?*" and, while she thus exclaimed, she would look with an expression of dismay and reproach at the captain.

"If I rest my bones through the night," said Greaves, "I shall be easier or well again in the morning. Look in upon me with a report from time to time. Fielding, and tell Bol to visit me during his watch."

He rose from his chair with a face of pain, put his arm upon Jimmy's shoulder, and went below. I stepped to the gangway, calling to the fellows who were hanging about in the head to lay aft and stand by to discharge the boat and get her aboard. She came alongside deep, and it was dark before we had hooked the tackles into her. When she was stowed, the topsail was swung and the brig headed about north. There was a light wind out of the southwest. It set the water tinkling alongside with the noise as of the bells of a sleigh heard afar. The young moon lay in a red curl in the west, as though, up there, she was still coloured by the flush of the sunset that had blackened out to our sight. There was not a cloud. The stars were plentiful and bright, and the dusky ocean, flat and firm, showed as wide as the sky.

All this while the lady had remained on deck. It was about eight o'clock, and very dark. My watch had come round, and the brig would be in my charge till midnight; but, watch or no watch, I should have kept a lookout until I had secured the three-mile offing. The island was on the starboard quarter, scarcely distinguishable now – a dim smudge, like smoke.

Happening to look through the skylight, I saw the cloth laid for supper. Indeed, supper was ready. Salt beef and ham were on the table, together with biscuits, pickles, and a pot or two of preserves, a small decanter of rum for my use, and a bottle of Greaves' red wine for the lady. She had tasted nothing, as I presumed, since her arrival on board in the morning.

She stood at the rail, looking out to sea, a pathetic figure of loneliness, indeed, when you thought of what she had suffered, what she was freshly delivered from; when you thought again of her solitude of dumbness, as you might well term her tongue's incapacity aboard this brig of English and Dutch. Most heartily did I yearn to speak soothingly and hopefully, to bid her be of good cheer when she thought of her mother, to beg her persuade herself that her mother was rescued and sailing to Europe, even as she, the *señorita*, was thither bound.

"Weel, weel, there's Ane abune a'!" says the gypsy in the Scotch novel, and that was the substance of what I wanted to tell the lady Aurora.

And what did I say? Why, I just coughed to let her know that I was at her elbow. I had no other language than a cough.

She quietly looked round and began "*Yo no lo –* " then broke off, arrested by remembering that I knew not one syllable of her tongue.

I motioned to the skylight and pointed down, and made signs for her to go below and sup. She signed to me to accompany her. I shook my head, pointing to the sails and to the sea, and cursing my ignorance that obliged me to make a baboon of myself with my limbs and head.

She bowed and went to the companion hatch, and on looking down a few minutes later I saw her seated at the table. She had removed her hat; her brow showed white in the lamplight under the magnificent masses of her dead black hair. The jewels upon her fingers sparkled as, with a leisureliness that had something of stateliness in it, she helped herself to the food before her. Once again I admired the beauty of her hands, and then I turned my back upon the novel and beautiful picture of this fine Spanish woman to look to the brig.

Chapter XIX.
Off the Island

THE BRIG slipped cleverly through the sea. It was like gently tearing through silk with a razor to listen to the noise that floated aft from her cutwater. When I guessed the island to be about three miles distant I hove the vessel to. Yan Bol's pipe shrilled with an edge that seemed to fetch an echo from the furthest reaches of the dark sea. When the sails were to the mast the brig lay motionless under her topsails and standing jib.

I was about to go below to make a report to the captain, when the lumping shadow of Bol's bulky shape came along the deck,

"Beg pardon, Mr. Fielding," said he, with a loutish lift of his hand in the direction of his forehead, "how might der captain be, sir?"

"I am about to inquire."

"Dere vhas noting wrong, all handts hope?"

"No; a severe bruise. Nothing more serious, I trust."

"Vhas der brick to be hove-to all night?"

"Yaw."

"To gomblete der vatering in der morning, I zooppose?"

"Yaw."

"Vell, Mr. Fielding, der men hov oxed me to say dot if der captain vill give leave and she vhas not too sick to be troubled by der noise, dey vould like to celebrate der recovery of der dollars by two or dree leedle songs before der vatch vhas called."

This was another way of asking for a glass of grog for all hands. There could be no objection. The men had been much exposed throughout the heat of the day, and what could more righteously warrant a harmless festal outburst than the recovery and transhipment of a hundred and forty cases of Spanish dollars?

I entered the cabin. The lady Aurora was still at table, but had long since ceased to eat. She lay back in her chair, her head drooped, her hands folded in the posture of one waiting. When I entered she lifted her head and smiled, her eyes brightened, her lips moved in the first framing of a sentence; no word escaped her; she pointed to a seat, and half rose from her own chair as though in doubt where I was used to sit. I shook my head, nodded toward the door of the captain's berth, then at the clock under the skylight, holding up my fingers that she might guess I would join her in ten minutes; and so I passed on, hot in the face, and wondering whether it would be possible for me to communicate with her without making a fool of myself – for a fool I felt every time I gesticulated, which now I think must have been owing to my hatred of the French.

Greaves lay in his bunk motionless, on his back, but he was free from pain. Galloon sat on a chest near his head. I reported the affairs of the brig, the distance and bearings of the island, and the like. He asked how the weather looked.

"It is a heavenly night," said I.

"It is hot in this hole," said he. "Plague seize the awkwardness that tripped me and has floored me thus! One knows not what to do for a bruise of this sort. But patience – that's the physic for every sort of bruise, whether of the bones or of the soul. Jim tells me the lady has supped."

"She has, sir."

"I am sorry for the poor thing; but where is the woman that does not always want something more than she has? This time yesterday she would have given her hair – angels alive! what would she *not* have given? to be as she now is, safe aboard such a vessel as this; and now that she is safe aboard – rescued from raw terrapin and the risks of the society of two Spanish sailors (and I must like their looks better before I give them a handsomer name than *that*) – she craves to be with her mother – very natural, of course – who is, probably, at the bottom of the ocean, and she wants to be put ashore at Lima."

I delivered the request of the men, as expressed by Yan Bol.

"Oh, yes. Let grog be served out to all hands; and the men may sing, certainly. Disturb me? Not down here. And I like my people to be merry. Fortune has fiddled today; let the beggars dance."

Jimmy was in the cabin. I bade him carry a can of rum to the men, and went on deck, receiving, without knowing how to answer, a look of inquiry from the lady Aurora as I passed her.

"The men may make merry," said I to Bol. "There is grog gone forward. Tell them that the captain is free from pain; and will you keep a lookout in the waist – or in the head if you like, 'tis all one – while I get a bite in the cabin?"

"Yaw, dot vill I. By der vay, Mr. Fielding, vhas dere von hoondred und dirty, or vhas dere von hoondred und twenty, cases prought on boardt? Vertz swears to von hoondred und dirty; Friendt, von hoondred und twenty. I myself gounts von hoondred und dirty-two. Dere vhas a leedle vager in dis – shoost von day of a man's grog, dot vhas all."

"I made one hundred and forty cases," said I. "But are they all dollars?"

And bursting into a laugh, I left him to chew upon that thought, and returned to the cabin.

I bowed to the lady, and took the chair I usually occupied at the table. She rose, came to my side with a bottle of claret, poured some into a glass, and made as if she would wait upon me. I was not a little confounded.

Her handsome presence, her fine person embarrassed me. My career had but poorly qualified me for an easy address in conversing with ladies. Much of my life had been spent upon the ocean, in the society of some of the roughest of my own calling. For months at a stretch I had never set eyes on a woman, and when I was ashore, whether in foreign parts or in my own country, the girls I fell in with were not of a sort to teach me to know exactly what to do when I chanced upon the company of a Señorita Aurora.

I did the best I could with the imperfect and monkey like speech of the hands and shoulders to induce her to desist from waiting upon me and return to her chair; and in this I was helped by the arrival of Jimmy, to whom I gave several unnecessary orders, merely to emphasize to the lady the desire. I gesticulated that she should sit, and cease to do me more honour than I had impudence to support.

Presently she pointed to the bottle of claret – there stood but one bottle on the table – and looked at me in silence, but with an expression of such eloquence as Jimmy himself could not have missed the meaning of.

"Wine," said I.

"Vine," she repeated; and then to herself, "*Vino* – vine; *vino* – vine."

She next pointed to the piece of salt beef.

"Meat," said I.

"Meat – *carne*; meat – *carne*," she repeated.

She pointed to several objects. I gave her the English names, and she pronounced them deliberately, in a rich voice, invariably tacking the Spanish equivalent to the word, as though she wished me to observe it. I sat for about a quarter of an hour over my supper, and then, looking at the clock significantly, and then up through the skylight, that she might gather my intention, I arose, giving her a little bow. She rose also, and, pointing upward, tapped her bosom, most clearly saying in that way – "May I accompany you?"

"*Si, señorita,*" said I, expending, as I believe, in those words the whole of my stock of her tongue.

A fine smile lighted up her face, and she addressed me; and what I reckon she said was that it would not take me long to learn Spanish. She picked up her hat, and then, looking at the table, pointed, and showing her white teeth, said, "Bread – *pan*; meat – *carne*; vine – *vino*;" and so on through the words I had interpreted, making not one blunder either of pronunciation or indication of the object, saving that she called wine *vine*, and ham *yam*.

I conducted her on deck; I believe Yan Bol had been surveying us from the skylight; I perceived his big figure lurching forward when I emerged, and his way of going made me suppose that he had been looking through the skylight with his ear bent. "An old ape hath an old eye," thought I, as I watched him disappear in the darkness.

The crew were assembled on the forecastle and singing songs there. They had rigged up two or three lanterns and sat in the light of them, drinking rum-and-water out of mugs, and smoking pipes. A strange voice was singing at that moment; I listened, and guessed it to be one of the two Spaniards. The girl paused and listened too. She then ejaculated, "*Ay! Ayme!*" and went to the rail, and gazed out to sea.

There blew a soft wind, cool with dew, out of the southwest. I looked for the island, but the shadow of it was blent like smoke with the darkness. The ripples ran in faint, small ivory curls, and the water was full of roaming glows of phosphorus. The Spanish sailor ceased to sing. A fiddle struck up, screwing and squeaking into a tune which immediately set my toes tapping; a hoarse cough succeeded, and then rang out the roaring voice of Travers:

> "Eight bells had struck, and the starboard watch was called,
> And the larboard watch they went to their hammocks down below;
> Before seven bells the case it was quite altered.
> And broad upon our lee-beam we sight a lofty foe.
> Up hammocks and down chests,
> Oh, the boatswain he piped next,
> And the drummer he was called, at quarters for to beat.
> We stowed our hammock well
> Before we struck the bell,
> And we bore down upon her with a full and flowing sheet!
> (*Chorus*) And we bore down upon her with a full and flowing she-e-t!"

There were more verses. The chorus was always the same; it burst with hurricane power from the lips of the English seamen, who sang with passion, as though in defiance of the Dutch and Spanish listeners; and, indeed, the matter of the song was headlong and irresistible. The lady standing at the bulwark turned her head to listen, but when the noise had ended she sank her face afresh, put her elbow on the rail, leaned her chin upon her hand, and so gazed straight out into the darkness.

Much had she to think of, and her weight of memory would be the heavier, and the colour of it the sadder for her inability to communicate a syllable of what worked in her brain, when she thought of the wreck in which her mother may have perished, or of the livid cinder of an island on which she had been imprisoned for four days, of her present condition, and of her future. I wondered as I looked at her whether, if she had my language or I hers, she would be impassioned and dramatic in the recital of her adventures, or whether she would talk quietly, describe without vehemence of speech or motion, prove herself, in short, the dignified, apparently cold woman I found her in her compelled silence or speech? This I wondered while I watched her with an irritable yearning after words that I might speak. What had been the two sailors' behaviour to her on the island? Where and how had she slept of nights there? What had been her sufferings in the open boat? Who was she? Was she visiting Madrid to presently return to South America? She troubled my curiosity. She was as a book written in an unintelligible tongue, but curiously and beautifully embellished with plates which enable you to guess at the choiceness and profusion of the feast you are unable to sit at.

Now Yan Bol sang a song. His voice rent the night, and I observed the lady erect her figure as though she hearkened with astonishment. I walked aft to take a look at the compass, and to see that the binnacle lamp was burning well.

"Who is this at the wheel?"

"Jorge, *señor*."

"You don't speak English, do you?"

The man understood me, and shook his head. "Pretty cool fists," thought I, "to send this poor devil aft, while *you* enjoy yourselves with your songs and pipes and grog! Here is a shipwrecked man; what care you? He is a poor rag of a man, and very fit to be put upon; so it has been, Aft with ye and grip them spokes, while a better man than e'er a mumping Spaniard in all Americay comes for'ard and enjoys himself." But it was not a matter to be mended while the fellows were in the full of their jollification.

"*Como se llama esto?*" exclaimed a voice at my elbow, and a small hand, gleaming with rings, was projected into the sheen of the binnacle lamp.

I started, conceiving that the lady was still at the bulwark rail, deep in thought or listening to the singing.

"I do not understand," said I.

"Ow you call, *señor?*" exclaimed Jorge.

She pointed to the compass, wanting its name in English.

I pronounced the word and she echoed it very clearly; then lightly laying her hand upon my arm she took a few steps forward, and, pointing to the sea, asked again in Spanish what that was called. In this way I gave her some dozen words; and when I believed she was about to ask for more terms she, with her hand laid lightly on my arm, led me back to the wheel, and, pointing to the compass, pronounced its name in English, then indicated the sea, uttering the word, and so she went through the list she had got, blundering but once, at the word "star," which she pronounced *zar*.

By this time the singing had come to an end; the starbow-lines, as the starboard watch were then termed, were dropping below; the lady went to the skylight and looked at the time; then, coming up to me, she put her hand out and said:

"*Buenas noches, caballero.*"

I answered, "Good-night, *señorita.*"

She shook her head; by the cabin lamplight flowing up through the open frames I saw her smiling. She repeated, "Good-night, *caballero,*" in Spanish. Seeing her wish, I said good-night in the same language, imitating her accent.

"*Es admirable!*" she exclaimed, and then went toward the companion way, meaning to go below.

But I had resolved that this handsome, amiable, lovely Spanish lady should be made as comfortable on board us as the resources of the brig permitted, and I detained her by a polite gesture while I called to one of the men forward to send Antonio aft. The fellow was turned in and he kept us waiting ten minutes, during which the lady and I stood dumb as a pair of ghosts, she no doubt wondering why I held her on deck, though she did not exhibit the least uneasiness in her bearing so far as I was able to make out in the starlit darkness. When Antonio appeared I requested him to ask the lady if she wished for anything the brig could supply her with. Antonio translated sulkily and sleepily.

"No, *señor,*" said he, "the lady wants for nothing. She is wearied and entreats permission to retire to rest."

I was convinced that the villain had manufactured this answer to enable him to return speedily to his own bed. But I was helpless.

When the lady went below I told Antonio to send one of the men out of my watch to relieve Jorge at the wheel, and I then descended into the cabin to make a report to Greaves and to hear how he did. Jimmy was clearing up for the night. I inquired after the captain, and the youth told me he was asleep.

"Has he complained of pain?"

"No, master."

"Where's Galloon?"

"Along with the captain, master."

"Has the dog been fed today?"

"Oh, yes. He had a copper-fastened buster at noon – a heart o' oak blow-out."

"What did you give him?" said I, not doubting the lad's affection for the dog, but fearing that the poor brute might have been overlooked in the hurry and excitement of the day.

"As much beefsteak as he could swallow, master."

"There are no beefsteaks on board this ship," said I. "If the captain and Galloon were here we should have a concert. But I believe you when you tell me you have fed the dog."

"More'n he wanted, master."

I bade him put a spare mattress into my bunk – we carried a stock of spare bedding, a slop lot of Amsterdam stuff – and I then returned on deck. Two hours of watch lay before me, and my heart went in a gallop and my brain in a waltz through the earlier part of that time. I found leisure for thought now; the hush of the ocean night was upon the brig; no sound reached me from the forecastle. The stars shone brightly in the dark sky, and many meteors of crystal white fires ran and broke over our mastheads, bursting like rockets immeasurably distant, and leaving glowing trails, which palpitated for some minutes.

The hope of the voyage was realized. Underfoot lay half a million of dollars, and six thousand pounds of it were to be mine! Is it wonderful that my spirits should have sang, that heart and brain should have danced? But with this noble fulfilment of the half-hearted hope of many weeks was mixed the romance of the presence of a handsome Spanish woman in the ship. One thought of her as coming on board with the dollars – as the princess of the island pining for civilization and shipping herself and the treasure of her little dominion for the life and delights of a great and populous city of the Old World. She it was, I think, that set my brain a-waltzing, if it were the dollars which made my heart gallop and my spirit shout within me.

I tell you it was an odd, intoxicating mixture of the picturesque, the heroic, the romantic for a plain young sailor man like me to put his lips to and drain down. To be sure the influence of the Spanish lady upon me was no more than the influence of bright eyes, of white teeth, of a fine person, of a head of magnificent hair. And what sort of influence would that be, pray? Why, heart alive! Oh! what but a mingling of light with thought, an aroma to haunt all fancy of other things, giving a sparkle to the commonplace, putting foam and sweetness into cups of flatness. Do you who are reading this know how deep, know by the experience of months of weevils, corned horse, and the curses of constipated sailors, how deep is the deep monotony of life on shipboard? If the depth of this monotony be known to you, then will you understand why it should be that the presence, yea, the presence *merely* of a handsome woman, her glances, the flash of her white teeth, the eloquent hinting by movement and posture at a hidden shape of beauty, should mingle a few threads of gold with the coarse grey, brine-drenched worsted of the sailor's daily life – of such a daily life as mine; should touch with lustre his mechanic habits and trains of thought as the wake of his ship in the night of the tropic ocean is beautified with the fiery seeds and radiant foam-bells of the sea glow.

And now I have intelligently and poetically explained why it was that I walked out some time of the remainder of my watch on deck, with my blood in a dance and my spirits singing clearly. But as I paced I grew grave under the shadow of a fancy – not yet to call it fear. Suppose the crew should rise and seize the brig? This was a *notion* that was fixedly present to Greaves during the outward passage, because he had *known* when I doubted, that the half million of dollars were in the ship in the cave, and upon that conviction he could base acute realization of what *might* happen when the money was transhipped. I, on the other hand, had never seriously considered the possibility of piracy. The money must be in the brig before I could solemnly compass all the responsibility its possession implied. But the money was now on board, and six thousand pounds of it were mine, and my spirits fell as I paced the quarter-deck looking around the wide gloom and saying to myself: "Suppose this treasure of half a million of dollars should presently start the men into a determination to seize the brig! There were but two of us – Greaves and I – at our end of the ship. Could we count upon Jimmy? At the other end was now an addition of two Spaniards – cut-throats at heart for all one knew – with knives as thirsty for blood as an English sailor's throat for rum."

Why should I have thought thus? Nothing whatever had happened to put fancies of this sort into my head. Was it not the being able to understand that thirty thousand of the thousands in the lazarette were to be mine that set me reflecting with a sudden dark anxiety, when the question arose: Suppose the crew should rise and take the brig?

> The needy traveller, serene and gay,
> Walks the wild heath, and sings his toil away.
> Does envy seize thee? Crush the unbraiding joy,
> Increase his riches, and his peace destroy:
> New fears in dire vicissitude invade.
> The rustling brake alarms, and quivering shade;
> Nor light nor darkness brings his pain relief.
> One shows the plunder, and one hides the thief.

There was comfort, however, if not safety in this consideration: not a man forward, from Bol down to Jimmy, had any knowledge of navigation. What, then, would they be able to do with the brig if they seized her? They might spread a chart of the world and say: "Here we are *now*, and there is America, and there are the East Indies, and down there is New Holland, and up there is China, and if we steadily head in one direction, no matter at what point of the compass the bowsprit looks, we are bound to run something down, whether it be a continent or one of the poles."

Well, that is how sailors might talk in a book designed for the young. Before the seamen forward rose and seized this brig, that was now a very valuable bottom, as cargoes then went, they would ask of one another: "What are we going to do with the ship when we have her? Where are we going to carry her, and, having hit on a spot, how are we going to navigate her there?" This I chose to think, and, indeed, I had no doubt of it, and I drew comfort from the conclusion; but all the same, my spirits, having sunk, remained low throughout the rest of my watch.

I was uneasy. I caught myself arresting my steps when my walk carried me toward the gangway, whenever I heard the sound of a man's voice. O God, to think of what a hell of passions this tiny speck of brig was capable of holding! To think of the large and bloody tragedy this minim of the building yards could find a theatre for! Never had I so utterly felt human insignificance at sea as I did this night, when I looked over the rail and searched the smoky void of the horizon for the smudge of the island, till, for the relief of my sight, I watched a star.

"I'll tell you what it is, William Fielding," said I to myself, "your blood is over-heated, your spirits are over-excited. By this picking up today of a fortune – a noble fortune to you, my boy – of six thousand pounds, and by the sudden and novel companionship of a dark and splendid lady, the pulses of your body have been set a-hammering too fast. They must sleep, or excitement will make you sick."

Eight bells were struck. Bol came along, and I went below to see if the captain was awake. He addressed me on my entering his cabin. I reported the little there was to tell. He said that the pain in his side was easier; that he could move without the anguish of the afternoon.

"I shall lie by all night," said he, "and hope to be up and about again in the morning."

He then inquired about the situation of the island, the appearance of the weather, the sail under which the brig lay, whether any vessel had hove in sight, and added:

"If you should awaken in your watch, go on deck and take a look round; though I trust Bol."

I went on deck to give the Dutchman the bearings of the island and our distance from it. He was sullen with sleep. Likely as not, the can which Jimmy had filled contained more liquor than should have gone forward at once.

"Keep a bright lookout," said I. "There may come a shift of wind that will put the island under our lee, with nobody to guess that it's at hand until we're upon it."

"Ow, I'll keep a bright lookout," he answered; "but vould to Cott dere vhas no more lookouts for me! I vhas dam'd sick of looking out. I hov been looking out, by tunder, for ofer twenty year, and hov seen noting till dis day; and den she vhas to be carried round der Hoorn to Amsterdam before she vhas all right."

I went to my berth. Excitement had subsided since my few words with Greaves. I pitched into my bunk, and was sound asleep in a minute. I was awakened by the weight of a heavy hand and by the sound of a deep voice.

"Mr. Fielding, I do not like der look of der veather. I believe dere vhas a gale of vind on her vhay here."

"What is the hour, Bol?"

"She vhas a quarter-past dree."

I went on deck, and observed that the sky in the north was as black as pitch. Overhead the stars were dim and few, but they burnt freely and brightly in the south. I caught a moaning tone in the wind, that had considerably freshened since I left the deck; and the brig, hove-to under whole topsails, was lying over somewhat steeply, with the seas to windward slapping at her rounded side, hissing off in pale yeasty sheets, and flickering snappishly into the gloom to leeward.

"Call all hands and close-reef both topsails," said I.

I ran below to report to Greaves. A bracket-lamp burnt feebly in his cabin. He was wide awake, and his dark eyes, with the glance of the small yellow flame upon them, looked twice their usual size.

"It is coming on to blow, sir."

"Well, snug down and put yourself to leeward of the island, anyhow."

"Shall I heave her to, then, for watering?"

"Judge for yourself. The brig is in your hands. If it comes hard let her go. Keep a sharp lookout for the island. Have you its bearings?"

"Bol should have them," said I. "I have been turned in since midnight."

I regained the deck. The crew were yawling at the reef-tackles and singing out at the main braces to trim the yards for reefing. There was much noise. The wind was steadily freshening, and through the groans and pipings of it aloft ran the sharp, salt hiss of small seas, bursting suddenly and with temper under the level lash of the wind. I shouted to Bol, who came out of the blackness in the waist.

"Where do you make the island?"

"She'll bear sou'east," he answered.

I stepped to the compass.

"There's been a shift of wind since midnight. It was nor'-nor'west, and now it's come north. Since when?"

"Ow, she freshened out of der north in a leedle squall. Dot vhas vhen I called you."

I swept the wide, dark reach of the southern line of sea with the glass; but had the island been as big as England it would have been sunk in the peculiar smoky thickness of the dusk that yet, strangely enough, formed a clear atmosphere for the stars to shine through. I say I swept the ocean with the glass, but to no purpose. An old sailor once laughed at me for using an ordinary day telescope at night. I told him that what would magnify a coloured object would magnify a shadow; and he afterward owned that he talked out of prejudice; had looked through a telescope since in the darkness and discovered that I was right.

The men reefed the topsails smartly, and not being able to see the island, and not choosing to trust Bol's conjectures as to its situation, I headed the brig due east, setting the reefed foresail and trysail along with some fore-and-aft canvas to give her heels. It blackened rapidly overhead; every star perished. In a few minutes there was not a light visible up in God's heights; all the fire was below, and the sea was beginning to run in flames like oil burning. This shining in the sea was a blindness to the sight, for it brought the sky down black as a midnight fog to the very sip and spit of the surge. We held on, crushing through it, for the wind having swiftly swept up into a fresh breeze, had on a sudden roared into half a gale, and the brig was smoking forward as she plunged, with a heel to leeward when the sea look her, that brought the white and fiery smother within hand-reach of the gangway rails.

I stood at the binnacle; Bol was at my side; two hands were stationed on the lookout; the crew remained on deck. They had got to hear that Bol had lost the bearings of the island, and though the watch might be called, no man was going below on such a night of sudden tempest as this, with a hurricane away behind the windward blackness, for all we knew, and this side the horizon as deadly a heap of fangs as ever bit a ship in twain.

"I vhas glad if he lightened," said Bol. "It vhas strange if der island did not show on der starboard quarter there."

"It was strange," said I, mimicking him in my temper, "that you should fall asleep in your watch on deck with land close aboard ye."

"By Cott, den – ."

Rain at that instant struck the brig in a whole sheet of water. It came along with a roar and shriek of wind and wet. The cataractal drench was swept in steam off our decks by the black squall it blew along in; the fierce slap of it fired the sea, and we washed through an ocean of light, pale and green.

"By Cott, den – " bawled Bol.

"Breakers ahead!" roared a voice from the forecastle.

"Breakers on the lee-bow!" cried another voice.

It was like being blinded and shocked by lightning to hear *those* cries. They were paralysing. For an instant I looked and listened idly.

Then – "Hard a-starboard every spoke! Hard a-starboard every spoke!" I shouted, and flung myself upon the wheel to help the men there, roaring meanwhile to Bol to call hands to the main braces and to get the fore tack and sheet raised. He rushed forward, thundering. Never had Dutchman the like of such a voice as Bol.

The brig was in the wind; she was pitching furiously head to sea, the canvas thrashing in the blackness, the gale splitting in lunatic shrieks upon every rope and spar, the strange, hoarse shouts of the seamen rising and falling in shuddering notes upon the clamour that surged above as the water rolled below.

I had fled from the wheel to the side to look for the land, and was straining my vision against the wet obscurity in vain search of the white water of breakers, or of the overhanging midnight shadow that should denote the island close aboard, when – the brig struck! a violent shock ran through the length of her; every timber thrilled as though a mine had been sprung under her keel. "O God, that it should have *come* to it!" I thought.

"Round with that fore yard, men," I roared; "don't let her hang! *don't* let her hang!" Again the brig struck. A sort of raging chorus full of curses and the passion of terror broke from the seamen as they dragged. The rain cleared as suddenly as it had begun, the brig's head was paying off, and my heart swelled in thanks as she listed over to larboard, trembling to a blow of sea that rose in a mountain of milk upon her bow.

"Where are you, Fielding?" shouted the voice of Greaves.

"Here, sir."

He was standing in the hatch, gripping the companion for support, but his voice had the old ring. "What have you done with the brig?"

"White water was just now reported. I don't see it. I don't see the land – yet we struck."

"No," he answered coolly, "it was we who were struck. There is no land. Look there – and there – and there! Those are your shoals!"

At the moment of his speaking one of the sublimest, most beautiful sights which the ocean, prodigal as she is in marvels of terror and splendour, can offer to the sight of man was visible round about us. In at least a dozen different parts of the blackness that stooped to the luminous peaks of the seas I beheld flaming fountains, glittering lines rising and feathering to the gale, coming and going, blowing pale and yet splendid – every jet so luminous that the scoring of the darkness by it was as defined as the track of a rocket. They soared and fell in a breathing way, some near, some afar, ever varying their distances, and one snored like an escape of steam within a biscuit-toss of our weather beam, and the fiery shower flashed on the wind betwixt our masts with a hiss like a volley of shot tearing the surface of water.

"A school of whales," shouted Greaves. "One of them plumped into us. Now, get your topsail aback. Fielding, get your topsail aback, and stop her till the beasts go clear, or they'll be butting us into staves. Jump for the well and get a cast."

The men, hearing their captain's voice, were quieted. They came to the braces, and, without disorder or any note of cursing terror in their voices, brought the brig to a halt. I dropped the rod and found the vessel stanch; sounded the well four or five times, and always found her stanch. The wondrous luminous appearances vanished, and the blacker hours of the night before the dawn closed upon us in an impenetrable dye, but with less weight in the wind and with less fire in the sea.

"Furl the foresail and let the brig lie as she is till dawn," said Greaves, and walked slowly from one side of the deck to the other, looking forth, pausing long to look; then, with slow motions, he went below, and stretched himself at full length upon a locker, with a hand upon his side.

My watch came round at four; but, in any case, I should have watched the brig through the darkness. Some while before dawn the wind was spent, the stars glowing, the sea fast slackening its heave, with the muck that had troubled and drenched us settling away in a shadow south and west.

At last broke the day. Melancholy is daybreak at sea. There is nothing sadder in nature; nothing that so sinks the spirits of the watcher who suffers himself to be visited by the full spirit of the sight. On shore there is the chirrup and harmonies of birds, the rosy streaking of the sky over the hilltops; the vane of the church spire burns, the cock crows heartily, the farmyard is in motion, the smell of the country rises in an incense as the sun springs into the sky. But at sea the cold iron-grey of the breaking morn is reflected in the boundless waste. There is nothing to catch the light of the springing sun save the clouds. The vast solitude brims into the unbroken distance, and cold is the ashen sky and cold the picture of the ship, as it steals out of the darkness of the night. The melancholy, however, is but in the dawn's beginning. When the sun rises, there is a splendour of colours at sea which you will not find ashore. The ocean is a mirror that reverberates the light of day. Times are when the deep flings its own prismatic glories upon the sky. This have I marked at sunrise, when the flash of the luminary has sunk into the heart of the sea, when all is blueness and dazzle below, and, above, a sky of high-compacted cloud, delicate as flowers and figures of frost and snow upon a windowpane, charged with the colours of the great eye of ocean looking up at it.

"There's the island," said I to myself.

I snatched up the glass, and resolved the tiny piece of shading upon the horizon into the proportions of the ugly rock of cinders. It was twelve or fourteen miles distant down on the lee quarter.

"The deuce!" thought I. "What has been our drift? Where has the brig been running to? And yet Greaves told me he could trust Bol!"

I looked through the skylight, and immediately the captain, who lay upon the locker, opened his eyes and fastened them upon me.

"The island is in sight, sir."

"How far distant?"

I made answer. He asked a few questions, then bade me shift the brig's helm for the rock to complete our watering. Twenty minutes later we were standing once more for the island, with all plain sail heaped upon the brig, and a quiet air of wind blowing dead on end over the taffrail.

Chapter XX.
We Start For Home

WE WERE off the island again by nine o'clock. Greaves was wise to fill his casks; the water was sweet, the road home long, and our peculiar care was not to be forced to look in anywhere for supplies of any sort. Yet it was as depressing as a disappointment to return to the island. Is there an uglier heap of rock in the wide world? The black lava of the scowling Galapagos yields nothing more horrid. And the spirit of its dark and horrible solitude visited you the more sharply because of the crawling, stealthy life you beheld low down by the wash of the beach, remote from the inland loneliness; the creeping shape of the elephant tortoise, of the black lizard, of crabs as huge as targets, and no further motion save what's in the air, where the ocean fowl are glancing. That island was a fit tomb for the ship which it caverned. You thought of it as a grave, of the ship as a corpse; and the ugly heap of flat split cliff and black lava climbing into spires, and front of cinderous rock corrugated by the arrest of their glowing cataracts, fell cold upon the sight, and colder yet upon the heart.

We sent a hand aloft as before to keep a sharp lookout. The island lay square in the north, and while we hung hove-to off the reefs, at any hour something large and armed might come sailing up from the horizon at the back, and heave the breast of a royal over the western or eastern point ere we could guess that there was anything within leagues and leagues of us. Yan Bol took charge of the longboat and went ashore. It was a fine morning, but the sky looked dim, like a blue eye after tears; the sun had his sting of yesterday, but not his flash. A long swell swung through the sea, but the heave was out of the north, and we lay south, the land between; it was smooth here or we could have done little in the way of watering. The corners of the land illustrated the weight of the swell; the white water burst in clouds there, and the noise of it came along with the voice of a gathering storm.

Greaves was so much better of the pain in his side that he sat at breakfast and took a chair upon the deck afterward. He called me to his cabin, while we were heading for the island, and asked me to look at his ribs. There was a little discoloration, such as might attend a bruise – no more. I pressed the bones, but he did not wince. I dug somewhat deep in the soft part just under the liver, but he uttered no sound. The pain was very nearly gone, he told me; yet he looked pale, and his eyes wanted their former light and old activity of glance.

I was busy in bringing the brig to a stand while Greaves was at breakfast, and on passing the skylight and looking down, I saw the lady Aurora seated at table with him. When he came on deck after breakfast, she followed; Jimmy placed chairs and she was about to sit, but catching sight of me she approached, bowing low, with a fine arch smile, and her hand extended. I supposed she meant merely to shake me by the hand, but on grasping my fingers she retained them, and I felt a foolish blush upon my face, as she drew me to the binnacle stand, at which she pointed, saying, "compass." She then led me to the side, and projecting her glittering hand over the rail, said "sea." Then, looking aloft, she laughed and shook her head, and cried:

"No sar, *señor*."

"Star," said I.

"*Si* – star – *gracias*," she exclaimed.

"Had you not better mind your eye?" exclaimed Greaves, as we approached him. "Somebody's told her the value of your share in the chinks below, She's no clipper, but she's got a devilish fine bow and run, and you'd find her bends sweetly good, I'll warrant you, were you to careen her and clear her sides. By Isten! Fielding, she'll be forging ahead and taking you in tow if you don't mind your helm."

I made no reply. I did not greatly relish Greaves' humour. The girl's ignorance of our tongue was an appeal to our respect. But then I was twenty-four – an age of sensibility. Greaves was an older man, and though I love his memory, I must say the sea had a little blunted some of the finer points of feeling in him.

Madam Aurora took the chair which Jimmy had placed, and she and Greaves sat together, but in silence. Some business of the brig occupied my attention. Presently Greaves told me to go below and breakfast.

"I will look after the ship," said he.

I went below and made a good breakfast. There was a dish of terrapin; the Dutch sailor Wirtz, the burly, carroty man, with the deep roaring voice – but all our Dutchmen had deep voices – had somewhere learnt the art of cooking terrapin. He had stayed in the brig to dress this delicious meat, and Frank Hals, the cook, had gone ashore in his place in the longboat. I fared sumptuously, washing the delicate morsels down with some of the *Casada*'s cocoa, which had been prepared for the pot by Thomas Teach, who professed to have learnt what he knew under this head in two voyages he had made to the Dutch Spice Islands.

Galloon had followed me into the cabin, and bore me company. He sat upon his chair and gazed at me affectionately when I talked to him. Often had I talked out my mind to Galloon. Often in quiet, lonely watches, during the outward passage, had I held his ears, while his fore paws rested upon my knees, and given loose to the imaginations which the prospect of the promise of realizing thirty thousand dollars raised up in me. And then, again, I loved this dog as the saviour of my life. Never could I look in to his affectionate, liquid, intelligent eye, but that I would think to myself, and often say aloud to him, dog as he was, a poor four-footed beast, soulless, as it is commonly supposed, of affections to be best won by kicks and curses – that he had, by saving my life, become in a sense the creator of a man, the renewer of a being deemed by his own species immortal in spirit, so that what ever I did a dog would be answerable for; the existence of all passions in me, my pleasures and hopes and griefs; nay, my marriage, should ever I marry, and the children I begot, would be all chargeable upon a poor dog, God wot! a strange thing to reflect on by one who has been made to believe, all his life, that he is only a little lower than the angels, and yet true as the blessed sunlight itself; for if it had not been for Galloon, long ago I should have been – what? the roe of a herring, perhaps, the liver of a cod – instead of a man, capable of looking back, through a long avenue of years, and of moralizing thus.

When I came on deck I found Antonio standing in front of Greaves, cap in hand, translating for him and the lady. On my appearing, Miss Aurora exclaimed quickly and eagerly to the Spaniard, who turning to me, said, squinting as he spoke:

"The *señorita* has met you before."

"Where?" said I.

"At Lima, *señor*."

"Never was at Lima in my life."

He translated; she made a little dignified gesture of impatience.

"The lady says that she has met you at the house of – " and here Antonio named a Spanish merchant of Lima.

"No," said I, looking at her and shaking my head.

"Yes," she cried in English, and spoke rapidly to Antonio.

"She is not mistaken, *caballero*. Two thumbs are alike, but two faces never."

"You never were at Lima?" said Greaves.

"Never," I exclaimed, laughing.

"Let her have her way," said Greaves. "Contrive to have visited Lima, and to have been a bosom friend of Don –," and he named the Spanish merchant. "What does it signify? May it not mean that she is in love with you, and that her professing to have met you is a Spanish maiden's device to cover an advance, as a soldier would say."

Antonio continued to squint. I viewed him narrowly, and was satisfied that he had not understood the captain's words.

"Beg the lady to continue her narrative," said Greaves.

She addressed Antonio in a few sentences at a time. Occasionally her language was above his understanding; he would look at her stupidly, until she gave him another nod. How rich was her Spanish, how honey-sweet her utterance! It was like listening to singing. The memories which thronged her recital delicately coloured with blood her pale olive cheek; her eyes moistened or sparkled as she spoke, or watched while Antonio interpreted. Most of the time her gaze was fastened upon me. It seemed as though she put me before Greaves, as though the incident of my having had charge of the boat which brought her off the island, had established me in her gratitude as her deliverer.

Her story, however, was little more than a repetition of what has already been related. Her mother had been absent twenty years from Old Spain. On the death of her husband, she sold the estate and all her interest in the business, and went to Acapulco with her daughter, on a visit to her brother, who was a priest at that place; thence she and Aurora took shipping for Cadiz.

The lady broke off at this to implore us, through Antonio, to tell her, as sailors, whether we believed her mother's life had been preserved. Greaves answered that he considered it very probable that her mother was alive. Who was to tell that the ship had foundered? Who was to say that she had not outweathered the gale, been jury-rigged and worked by the survivors into port, the Señorita Aurora's mother being on board?

The girl's eyes glistened when this was translated. She smiled at Greaves and thanked him in Spanish. An expression of pleading then entered her face, and her look took a peculiar colour of beauty from the wistfulness and plaintiveness of it. Why would not the captain set her ashore at Lima, that she might rejoin her mother, who, on landing – it mattered not at what port on the coast – was sure to make her way to Acapulco?

But Greaves shook his head, smiling into her eyes, which were impassioned with entreaty.

"I must go straight home," said he. "Do not you know that there is a treasure in our hold, which obliges me to make haste to reach England? I will take care that you safely arrive at Madrid, even should it come to myself escorting you, *señorita*."

She bowed, looking sadly.

"Or here," said he, extending his hand toward me, "is a cavalier who will be honoured by conducting you to Madrid."

She slightly glanced at me, then fastened her eyes upon the deck and mused for a few moments; then addressed Antonio, who, turning to me, said – but in English, you will please understand, which I do not attempt to reproduce, that you may read without hindrance:

"The lady recollects that when she met you at Lima you spoke Spanish."

"I was never at Lima," I answered, colouring and then laughing.

"Depend upon it," said Greaves, "that the fellow she met was good-looking, or recollection wouldn't be so bright."

"What was the occupation of the gentleman?" said I to the lady, through Antonio.

"He was an English naval officer, had been imprisoned, but had been at liberty some weeks when the *señorita* met him."

"What was his name?"

"She does not remember; but you are the gentleman."

"Be it so," said I, laughing.

"On slenderer evidence have men been hanged," said Greaves.

Now came a short pause. Antonio shuffled his naked feet, sometimes looking straight, sometimes squinting, impatient to get forward and lounge. The longboat had made her second trip, and lay along side the beach. The figures of the men crawling from the grove of trees, trundling the casks among them, showed like beetles in the distance. It was about eleven o'clock. The sunlight was misty; the swell rolled with a dull flash in the brows of it; the wind hummed like clustering bees aloft, and swept the cheek as the breath and kiss of fever. The slewing of the brig, along with the sliding of the sun, pitched the glare upon the deck clear of the trysail, in whose shadow we had been conversing. I called to a man to spread the short awning. Antonio was going; the lady Aurora detained him.

"The *señorita* wants to know," said the Spanish seaman, "how long the voyage to England occupies."

"We mean to thrash our way home," answered Greaves. "We shall not take long. Let us call it three months."

"Blessed Virgin! Three months!" echoed the girl in Spanish.

A fine look of tragic horror enlarged her eyes. She distorted her mouth into a singular expression. The tension paled her lips and exposed her teeth.

Greaves seemed to admire her. For *my* part, I thought her now the most beautiful and wonderful creature I had ever heard of – a lady who might either be angel or devil, you could not tell which; or she might be both. Her face defied you, for it could put on twenty looks in the course of a short conversation, thanks to her heavy eyebrows, which were full of play and character, and thanks to the long lashes of her eyelids, whose drop or lift, whose languishing falls, and arch or scornful or playful erections, changed the meaning of her glances for her as she chose, rendering them, at her will, transparently eloquent or as inscrutable as a gypsy's gaze. She put her hand upon her dress, and Antonio interpreted.

"The lady's gown will not last three months, and then, *señor?*"

"Chaw!" cried Greaves, and, pointing with something of passion to the island, he exclaimed – "Ask the lady to put the clock back till the day before yesterday is reached, and *then!*"

On this being explained a flash of temper lighted up her eyes.

"I shall be in rags," said she, "before you reach your country."

"We have needles and thread on board," said Greaves coolly.

"You are men, and cannot conceive what it is to be a woman embarking on a long voyage, possessed of no more clothes than what she has on."

"How can we comfort her?" said I.

"Can the *señorita* sew?" said Greaves.

Certainly she could sew.

"Then," said Greaves, "if the *señorita* can sew, let her mind be at rest. I am the owner of a roll of fine duck, which is entirely at her service. There are yards enough to yield her as many dresses as she needs. Will she require stuff for trimming? Let her select a flag of two or three colours. Bunting makes excellent trimming. It is light and brine-proof."

Antonio bungled much, and squinted fiercely in the delivery of this; yet he contrived to make the lady faintly understand the meaning of Greaves' speech. She tapped on her knee with her fingers, and seemed to keep time with the beat of her foot to an air that she inaudibly hummed; her black eyes were downward bent, but at swift intervals the fringes lifted, and a glance of light sparkled at me or Greaves. I noticed a pouting play of mouth. In fact, her air was that of a girl who has been spoiled by indulgence since her childhood. One figured her as the goddess of the fandango, the burden of the midnight guitar, and the heroine of a score of sweethearts.

"Duck is very well for dresses, sir," said I. "She is thinking of under-linen."

"We are not to know anything about under-linen," said Greaves. "She must make what she wants. She doesn't seem grateful enough to please me. To bother me about dress now, after four days of that cinder, and the deliverance recent enough to keep most people hysterically sobbing and thanking God in fervent ejaculations!"

Antonio addressed her. I guessed he wanted to know if he could go. She spoke to him, and the man, awkwardly smiling, said:

"The *señorita* asks if you are Catholics?"

"Yes and no, for my part," answered Greaves, looking at her gravely, "I am heading that way. I believe I shall hoist the Papal flag yet, but it's not flying at present."

"Is the capitan a Catholic?" repeated the lady.

"Ay, but not a Papist," said Greaves.

"Are you a Catholic, *señor*?"

"I love God and hate the devil," said I. "That is my religion. It is broad, and there is room for many names upon its back."

"Is it customary for ladies, do you know. Fielding, for ladies who have just been rescued from the horrors of a volcanic island, from perils hideously increased by the association of such a yellow and by no means fangless worm as that" – dropping his head in a cool nod at Antonio – "to inquire into the religious faiths of their preservers?"

The lady Aurora spoke.

"The *señorita* wishes to know when you changed your religion?"

"Ah, when, indeed?" said I, laughing.

"You were a very good Catholic at Lima, *señor*?"

"Yes, when I was at Lima, I was a very good Catholic?" said I.

"Then you are the *caballero* the *señorita* supposes?"

"Damn ye, you squinting devil, you know better!" thundered Greaves. "Jump forward. We've had enough of this."

The man fled toward the forecastle, noiseless with naked feet. The lady looked frightened.

"Lima, *señorita* – *no!*" said I smiting my bosom with force.

She gazed at me earnestly with an expression of misgiving, then addressed me in Spanish. Greaves gathered her meaning.

"I believe she says you are not her man, if you are not a Catholic," said he; and then pointing at me, and looking at her, he cried out, "No Catholic – no Lima – not your man, in any sense of the word. Fielding, what's that Dutch devil Bol up to?"

I went to the side to look for the longboat. She was at that moment coming through the two points of reef. Her oars rose and fell in the distance in hairs of gold, and she seemed to tow a hair of gold in her wake as she came out of the calm breast of the harbour into the soundless heave of the ocean. I reported her approach and lay upon the rail watching her, and musing upon what had passed between the Spanish maid and us.

It was odd to think of a fine young woman, sitting on the deck of a vessel, that had but a few hours before taken her off the desolate island which was still in view, coolly inquiring into the religious beliefs of her preservers, and looking as though, if time had been given her, she would presently overhaul our consciences. To be sure, she hoped that if she found us Catholics, she would get more of her way with us, obtain pity, sympathy, enough to procure her direct conveyance to a near port. She left her chair, came close to my side, and stood looking at the boat; in a moment, pointing to it, she asked in Spanish for its name. I gave her the name, turning to look at Greaves, who was laughing softly, but with an averted face. She put more questions, pointing to the objects, and then lightly laying her fingers upon my arm, she signed that I should take her forward, glancing at Greaves as she did so, following the look on with a full stare at me, and a shake of the head eloquent as her speech. It was for all the world as though she had said in plain English, "I don't like that man; let us leave this part of the ship."

I made her understand as best I could, by pointing to the approaching boat, and then to the yardarm whip for slinging the casks aboard, that my duty obliged me to stop where I was. She bowed, but with a little flush, as though vexed by my refusal; indeed, in her whole instant manner, there was the irritation of your ladyship, of your exacting, well-served, much-admired, fine young madam, who is very little used to being disappointed.

I moved forward toward the gangway by two or three steps, that she might guess my work prohibited talk; and, in fact, conversation would have been impossible in a few minutes, for the longboat was fast nearing the brig, and the job of seeing the water aboard was mine; and that was not all, either. Greaves was captain; he was on deck, watching and listening. The influence of the presence of a captain is always strong upon the seaman, whether he be of the quarter-deck or of the forecastle. Habit worked like an instinct, and disquieted me. Had Greaves been below, I daresay I should have been very glad to keep the *señorita* at my side, if only for the enjoyment of meeting her full gaze; for the longer I looked at her eyes, the more did I wonder at their depth and life, at their transcendent powers of repulsion and solicitation, and eloquence of rapid expression; and the longer I listened to her voice, the more was I charmed by the sweetness and richness of it; and the longer I beheld her face, the more manifold grew its revelations. But its revelations of what? My pen has no art to answer that question. You gaze upon the face of the deep, and beauties steal out of it to your perception, and you know not how to define them, you know not how to indicate them. They come blending in an effect that enlarges as you look, and the sum of the steady revelation is a deepening delight and a constant growth of wonder. I hear you say, "Had a woman of Spain ever the beauty you claim or invent for this lady?" My answer is as simple as a look – I say "Yes." The Señorita Aurora de la Cueva was a woman of Spain, and she had the beauty, and more than the beauty, I feebly attempt to describe. I care not if all the females of Old Spain are as hideous as hobgoblins and witches; they may all be bearded like the pard, thatched at the brow with horse hair, their complexions of chocolate, their figures bolsters; the lady Aurora was beautiful, her charms I have scarce language enough to hint at, much less portray. This she was, and whether you believe me or not signifies nothing.

And I did not much admire the woman when I first saw her! thought I. In fact, had I rowed her aboard another ship and never seen her again, I should never have thought of her again. Is it to end in my making a fool of myself? Does a man make a fool of himself when he falls in love? A plague upon these cheap cynic phrases which creep into the national speech, and form the mirth of boys and the wisdom of the sucklings of literature. But I am not in love yet, anyhow, thought I.

"Oars I" roared Bol, in the stern sheets of the boat. "Standt by mit der boathook. Vy der doyfil doan somebody gif us der end of a rope?"

A rope was flung. My lady Aurora walked forward, calling and beckoning to Antonio. She arrived abreast of the galley and stood there, and talked to the Spaniard, pointing about her and clearly asking for the name of things in English.

"Fielding," cried Greaves.

"Sir," I answered, facing about.

"She will be making love to you in your own tongue before another week is out," he called.

"Such a voice as hers would keep anything not deaf listening as long as she liked."

"She has a very sweet voice," he exclaimed, "and she is a very fine woman. But should she pick up our tongue, you'll find the devil that's inside of her come drifting out horns first with the earliest of her speech. Talk of your fears of the crew! She's the sort of party to carry a ship single-handed, though the vessel mounted the guns and was manned by the complement of the *Royal Sovereign*. She is learning English for some piratic motive – it may be the dollars, it may be the brig – for she don't want to go, and I dare say she don't mean to go round the Horn without her mother. Bol, is this the last load?"

"Der last loadt, sir."

"Bear a hand then to whip the water aboard, and let us get away."

It was a quarter before one by the time we had chocked and secured the longboat and were ready to start on a passage that was to carry us over many thousands of miles of salt water. The breeze had freshened; soft small clouds, like shadings in pencil, were sailing up off the edge of the sea into the misty blue overhead; the lustre of the sun was still pale and brassy, and a look of wind was in the yellow of the disk-shaped spread of radiance, out of which he looked like an eye of fire in a target of gold.

"Make sail, Fielding," called Greaves, from his chair, on which he had been sitting ever since he came on deck, though in all those hours he had not once complained of pain. "Make sail and heap it on her. Bring her head due south, and let her go."

The braces of the yards of the main were manned, the wheel turned, the canvas filled as the fiery breath, that was now brushing the sea, and that seemed to come the hotter for the very dimness of the sunshine, gushed over the quarter. We squared away to it; and now the island slid by, opening features of its swart, melancholy, loathly rocks, which had been invisible before. The milk-white burst of surge made the base of the cliff in the wash of it black. I noticed a hovering of pale radiance upon the patch of verdure where the grove or wood stood. It was no more than a patch to our distant eye; it was like the dance of the South African silver tree. The verdure had the gleam of an emerald, and you thought of a gem on the sallow breast of death.

I was full of the business of making sail, yet could find an eye for the island as it veered away on the quarter. Greaves gazed at it intently, so did the lady Aurora as she stood at the rail, with her profile cut clear and keen as a marble bust against the sky over the horizon. The mouth of the cave yawned upon us, then narrowed, then thinned into a slice, then vanished round a shoulder of cliff.

"Pull, you toyfils! Shoomp und run!" bawled Bol, in his hurricane note, to the two Spaniards, who were loafing near the galley, lazily looking on at the work that was going forward. "Dis vhas not der islandt – dis vhas no shipwreck. Shoomp, or I make you fly mit a sharge of goonpowder in der slack of yer breeks."

The royals were sheeted home; trysail, flying jib, staysails set; for it was a quartering wind, and there was scarce a cloth that we could throw abroad but could do serviceable work. They called this sort of sailing in our time *going along all fluking*, the weather-clew of the mainsail up and the lee-clew dully lifting its weight of blocks and hawser-like sheets and thick frame of foot and bolt-rope.

"Set all stu'n'-sails," cried Greaves; and soon out to windward soared to their several yardarms and to their boom-ends those wide, overhanging spaces of sail, clothing the brig in surf-white cloths from the royal mast heads to the very heave of the brine, when she rolled her swinging-boom to windward.

"Pipe to dinner!" called Greaves.

The sweet, clear strains of Yan Bol's whistle found a hundred echoes in the hollows on high. Aurora gazed upward, as though looking for the birds. The men had worked hard, and were pale with heat and sweat. They had worked with a will in making sail. Even the Dutchmen had sprang along and aloft with a bluejacket's activity; for we were homeward bound! a cry in every marine heart magical in its inspiration of swift and eager labour. With dripping brows the men stood looking at the receding island, while Yan Bol whistled them to dinner; and when the burly Dutch boatswain let fall the pipe upon his breast to the length of its lanyard, all hands, moved by feelings which made every throat one for the moment, roared out a long, wild cheer of farewell to the island, flourishing caps and arms to it, as though its heights were crowded with friends who could see and hear them.

"Look at Galloon!" cried Greaves.

The dog was on the taffrail, and every bark he sent at the island was like a loud hurrah, with the significance the noise look from the wagging of the creature's tail and the set of the whole figure of him.

"He knows we are homeward bound," said Greaves.

"And that the dollars are aboard," said I.

Miss Aurora went to the dog, caressed, and talked to him. The lad Jimmy's head showed at the galley door. Greaves hailed him to know when dinner would be ready.

"Another twenty minutes, master."

"Heave the log, Fielding, and let's get the pace at the start."

All expression of pain was now passed out of his face; likewise had his natural, fresh colour returned to him. The triumph of this time had kindled his eyes anew, and there were pride and content in the looks which he cast around his brig and over the rail at the island. And I think if ever there was a man who had a right to feel satisfied with himself and his work, Greaves, at this time, was he; for, truly, something more than talent had gone to the discovery of the dollars in the caverned ship. Mere accident it was that had disclosed the vessel, but it needed the genius of a great adventurer to light upon the dollars, to note all the particulars of the Spanish manifest, to hold the secret behind his teeth till he got home, to inspire such an old hunks as Bartholomew Tulp with confidence enough to shed his blood, or, in other words, to disburse his money, in the furtherance of this enterprise of recovery.

I called a couple of men aft and hove the log. What is the log? It is a reel round which are wound many fathoms of line; at the end of the line is attached a piece of wood, sometimes a canvas bag, designed to grip the water when it is hove overboard. The line is spaced into knots, and the running of it is timed by a glass of sand. This log is one of the oldest contrivances we have at sea. With it the early navigators groped their way about the world. It found them New Holland and the Indies, and both Americas. It was their longitude and often their latitude. It was their chronometer and sextant. We use it still, and cannot better it. A simple and noble old contrivance is the log. May the mariner never lose faith in it! Crutched by the log on one side, and the lead on the other, he may hobble round the globe in safety, defiant of shoals, regardless of fogs.

I hove the log, and made the speed seven knots.

"A good start!" exclaimed Greaves, rising and coming slowly to the rail, and looking over. He walked without inconvenience or pain, and stood with a thoughtful face, gazing at the satin-white sheets of foam sliding past. Madam Aurora left Galloon and came to my side, but Galloon followed her – never went there to sea a friendlier, a more affectionate dog. The men were hauling in the dripping log line and reeling it up. The lady with a smile said with a very good accent, "How do you call it?" I laughed as I pronounced the word *log*. Oh, what should it convey to the imagination of a Spanish maiden?

She understood, however, for what purpose it had been used, and with eloquent gestures inquired the speed. I held up my fingers.

"*Quien lo hubiera creido?*" cried she.

"She is not grumbling, I hope," called Greaves from the rail, and he slowly approached us.

The lady looked for a little while very earnestly at the captain, with a world of meaning in her beautiful eyes – meaning so eloquent in *desire* of expression, that it was pathetic to witness the arrest of speech in her gaze and face. She then with grace and dignity motioned round the sea.

"It is very wide, and the voyage before us is a long one – I understand that," interpreted Greaves; and never did man peruse lineaments more speaking or translate glances more radiant and expressive.

She then placed the forefinger of her right hand upon her lips to signify silence or dumbness.

"Which means," said Greaves, "that you can't speak our tongue, and don't like the prospect, accordingly."

She then took her dress in her hand, putting on a most mournful countenance.

"Yaw, yaw," cried Greaves, with a little irritation, "we have discussed that matter, madam. But there is white duck below – duck for the duck, what d'ye say. Fielding? and there are hussifs in the fo'c'sle."

I believed that her dumb show was at an end. Not at all. Clasping her hands sparkling with the several rings she wore, and raising them in a posture of supplication to the level of her mouth, she upturned her face to the sky, and with an inimitable expression of entreaty, of piteous prayer rather, insomuch that her eyes seemed to swim and her lips to work, she stood while you could have counted ten.

"Sainted and purest of all the Marias, put pity into the heart of this British captain, and cause him to set me ashore, for the sea is wide and the voyage is long; and I am possessed by a dumb devil and cast among heretics; and I have but one gown; and, O Maria and ye saints! candles shall ye have in plenty, mortification will I undergo, prayers by the fathom will I recite, choice gifts will I make to Holy Mother Church, if ye will but soften the heart of the durned, slab-sided skipper who stands opposite me, interpreting my mind. There ye have it, Fielding. That's what her gestures said, that's what her eyes looked. But I tell you what – this sort of thing will grow tiresome presently. You must bear a hand and teach her to speak English."

"Dinner's on the table, master," said Jimmy, putting his head through the companion way.

"Call Yan Bol aft to stand a lookout while we dine, Fielding," said Greaves, "and give your arm to the lady and bring her below. She don't like me."

Chapter XXI.
A Fight

WE HAD swept the island out of sight before we left the dinner table. When I came on deck the horizon had closed somewhat upon us. The ocean was a weak blue, and ran with a frosty sparkle into a sort of film or thickness that went all round the sea. The breeze had freshened, and it whipped the waters into little billows, with yearning and snapping heads of foam, and it was pouring its increasing volume into the lofty height and wide expanse of canvas under which the brig was thrusting along in a staggering, rushing way, the glass-smooth curve of brine at the bow breaking abreast of the gangway with a twelve-knot flash of the foam into the throbbing race of the long wake.

We kept her so throughout the afternoon until six o'clock, when the evening began to darken eastward; we then took in the lower and topgallant studding sails, but left her to drag the fore topmast studding sails if she could not carry it, for this was wind to make the most of; we could not, to our impatience, come up with the Horn too soon; many parallels were there for our keel to cut before we should find ourselves abreast of that headland; degrees of latitude lying like hurdles for the brig to take along that mighty and majestic course of ocean.

That same night of the day of our departure from the island, Greaves came out of the cabin and walked the deck with me. He had been amusing himself for an hour below with the company of the Señorita Aurora. From time to time I had watched them through the skylight. He smoked a cigar; a glass of grog stood at his elbow, some wine and ship's biscuit before the lady. He held a pencil, and from time to time wrote, looking up at her; and she would bend over the paper, read, give him a dignified nod, take the pencil, and herself write.

But it seemed to me that she forced herself to endure this tuition. She held herself as much away from him as the obligation of writing and extending her hand and receiving the paper permitted. This went on till about nine o'clock. The lady then withdrew, and Greaves came on deck as I have said.

"This is fine sailing," said he.

"Ay, indeed. I would part with some of those dollars below for a month of it."

"I have been teaching the girl English, and have picked up some Spanish words from her. She is an apt scholar; her mind is as swift as the light in her eyes. It is clever of her to wish to learn English. We can't be always sending for that fellow Antonio. She seemed astonished when I talked of three months, but she knows – she *must* know – that the run might occupy a vessel more than three months. What change would the skipper of the craft she sailed out of Acapulco in be willing to give out of *four* months, ay, and perhaps five, in a passage to Cadiz?"

"She, perhaps, thought of herself as being without clothes when you talked of three months, and so cried out."

"Well, it is clever of her to wish to learn English. Here she is, and here she's likely to remain until we send her ashore in the Downs."

"But why?"

"Why?"

"Is there no chance of something coming along," said I, "in which we can send her to a port this side America?"

"She knows there is a big treasure on board."

"That's sure."

"She knows that it is Spanish money, and how got by us."

"True."

"Well, now, send her out of this brig with our secret in her head, and we stand to be chased by the chap we put her aboard of."

"Not if she be an English ship."

"I'd trust no Englishman in this part of the world. Figure a craft as heavily armed again as our little brig; figure *that*, and then count our crew forward there. I'll have no risks. I'll speak nothing. We have got what we came to fetch, and this is to be my last voyage. I am a rich man now. There are thirty-six thousand pounds belonging to me below. No, Fielding, the lady will have to go along with us. You shall teach her English, she shall teach me Spanish. She shall pour out tea, act the hostess, sing; the very spirit of melody swells her fine throat every time she opens her lips. She shall make dresses for herself and under-linen."

"And the two Spaniards?"

"They must go along with us too. They are a worthless, skulking pair of fellows, I fear; but we must keep 'em."

"They get no dollars?" said I.

"Not so much as shall buy them soap. We have saved their lives; that's good pay for such service as they'll render. What shall you do with your money?"

"Well, I have often considered, captain," I answered. "I believe I shall buy a little house, put what remains out at interest, and go a-fishing for the rest of my days. And you?"

"First of all," he answered, "I shall knock off the sea. I shall then strike deep inland and look for a little estate in the heart of a midland shire. I do not know that I shall marry. Should I marry, it will be with a lady of my own degree in life. I will play the gentleman only so far as I am entitled by my condition to represent one. I will be no sham. There is no yardarm high enough for the hanging of the men who, haying got or inherited money, set up as country gentlemen, still splashed with the mud of the gutter out of which their fathers crawled, shaking themselves – illiterate, vulgar, scorned by the footmen who stand behind their chairs, belly-crawlers, title-lickers, toadies. Faugh! I once made a rhyme on shams – four lines – the only rhymes I ever made in my life:

> "Pull up your blinds that all the world may see
> The house you live in and the man you be.
> The blinds are up, and now the sun hath shone:
> The house is empty and the man is gone."

"By which you mean to imply – " said I.

"By which I mean to imply," he interrupted, "that if the lines don't tell their own story they must be deuced bad."

He stopped to look at the compass. The night was dark, but the dusk had cleared. The clouds raced swiftly over the stars, and the wind blew strong, but with no increase of weight since we had taken in the studding sails. The brig rushed along, leaving a meteor's line of light astern of her. The dim squares of her royals swayed on high with the floating stroke of a pendulum. I admired the dark and pallid picture of the little fabric speeding lonely through this vast field of night.

Greaves came from the binnacle and stood beside me.

"Fielding," he exclaimed, with cordiality strong in his voice, "it rejoices my heart when I reflect that I, whose life you saved, should, by a very miracle of chance, be the one man chosen, as it were, to substantially, and I may say handsomely, serve you."

"I shall walk through my days blessing your name," said I, grasping the hand he extended. "And how have you repaid me? You have not only preserved me from drowning, you make me easy for the rest of my time."

"The accounts are squared to my taste," said he. "I am very well satisfied. Tomorrow I shall want you to take stock of the cases in the lazarette. You found them heavy?"

"All, sir."

"And all are full, no doubt. But you shall make sure for me."

"I shall want help," said I. "Whom shall I choose among the crew?"

"It matters not," he answered. "All hands know the money is there."

"Yes; but it is an *idea* to them now. When they come to see the sparkle of the white dollars!"

"There is no good in distrusting them," said he. "I am aware that your fears run that way. When we were outward bound your fears ran in another direction," he added dryly. "Let me tell you this, whether we choose to trust the men or not, they're aboard; they man the ship; they are the people who are to navigate her home. We *must* trust them," he repeated with emphasis. "In fact," he continued after a short pause, "I would set an example of good faith by letting them understand how entirely I trust them. Therefore, tomorrow, take Bol and two others of the men who were left aboard with me when you went to the *Casada*, and examine the cases in their presence, you testing, they moving the boxes for you."

I replied in the customary sea phrase; for this was a direct order, the wisdom of which it was no duty of mine to challenge. Shortly afterward lie went below.

It blew so fresh that night and next day, however, that the sea ran too high to enable me to get below among the cases. It was a spell of wild, hard weather for that part of the world, though it never blew so fierce as to oblige us to heave-to.

The gale held steady on the quarter and we stormed along, the white seas rising in clouds as high as the foretop and blowing ahead like vast bursts of steam from the hatchway.

Greaves pressed the brig, and she rushed through the surge in madness. I never before saw a vessel spring through the seas as did the *Black Watch* at this time under a single-reefed foresail and double-reefed topsails. She'd be in a smother forward, just a seething dazzle of yeast 'twixt the forecastle rails, everything hidden that way in a snowstorm, so that you'd think the whole length of her was thundering into the boiling whiteness about her bows; but in a breath she'd leap, black and streaming, to the height of the lifting sea, with a toss of the head that filled the wind with crystals and prisms of brine, while a long-drawn whistling and hooting came out of the fabric of her slanting masts, and the water blew forward in white smoke from the gushing scuppers.

Then came a change; the dawn of the third morning painted a delicate lilac along the eastern sky, and when the sun rose over the wide Pacific the morning was one of cloudless splendour.

At eight o'clock Yan Bol came aft to take charge of the deck. I told him that presently we would be going into the lazarette to take stock of the cases of silver, and that the captain would keep a lookout while he was below.

A dull light glittered in the eyes of the big Dutchman. He grinned and said, "Vill not she be a long shob, Mr. Fielding?"

"Yes," said I.

"How long shall she take a man to gount a tousand dollars? Und dere vhas hoondreds und tousands of dollars to gount below."

"Do you think I mean to count the dollars?"

"Yaw."

I arched my eyebrows at him, and then gave him my back.

"Veil, I vhas sorry. I like gounting money. Dere vhas a shoy in der feel of money if so be ash he vhas gold or silver – I do not love copper – dot makes me happier, Mr. Fielding, dan any odder pleasure. Ox me vhy und I tells you? Because vhen I gounts money she vhas mine own. No man gives me his money to gount. She vhas mine own; but leedle I have, and vhen I counts her it vhas after long years, so dot der pleasure vhas all der same as a pipe und a pot to a man vhen he comes out of der lockoop."

While I breakfasted I enjoyed some conversation in dumb show with the lady Aurora – dumb show for the most part, I should say – for a number of English words she now possessed, and I was astonished not more by her memory than by the excellence of her pronunciation. Her knowledge of a single word uttered by me seemed to light up the whole phrase to her perception. Her gaze would continue passionately wistful and expectant whenever she listened with a desire to understand, and whenever she seized or thought she had seized the sense of what was said, a flush visited her cheeks, her whole face brightened.

There was a degree of eagerness in this desire of hers to learn English that was a little perplexing. It was an earnestness, call it an enthusiasm if you will, that went beyond my idea of her need. It was intelligible that she should wish to make herself understood. She would now know that she was to be locked up in a ship with a number of Englishmen for three or four months; what more reasonable than that she should desire to make her wants intelligible without being forced upon so disagreeable and ignorant an interpreter as Antonio, and without seeking expression in grimaces and the lunatic language of the eyebrows, shoulders, and hands? What more reasonable, I ask? But her earnestness, her zeal, her satisfaction when she understood, caused me to wonder somewhat when I thought of her in this way. She was on a desert island a few days ago, with small prospect of deliverance from as frightful a fate as could well befall a woman. For all she knew her mother was drowned; she might be an orphan, and who was to tell what property belonging to her and her mother had sunk in the Spaniard from which she had escaped, supposing that vessel to have foundered? And yet spite of all this her spirits were good, her beauty growing as the lingering traces of her suffering died out. She took an interest in everything her eyes rested upon, questioning me like a child, questioning Greaves, nay, walking forward, as I have told you, to ask Antonio for the English names of things, and all the while her troubles, so far as she was able to express them, did not go beyond an anxiety as to clothes for herself and an eagerness to pick up our tongue.

These thoughts ran in my head as I ate my breakfast, while she talked to me by gesticulation, occasionally uttering a word or two in English, and listening with shining eyes to the sentences I let fall in my own speech. Greaves lay upon a locker. He listened, sometimes smiling, but rarely spoke. He complained this morning of an aching in his side where he had hurt himself, and said that he feared he had made a mistake in walking yesterday; he was afraid he had overworked the bruised ribs, but he looked well, and when he spoke there was a heartiness in his voice. It was as likely as not that he had angered the bruise by too much walking about the decks, and I advised him to lie up until the pain went.

However, the brig was to be watched while I went into the lazarette with Bol and the others, so I sent Jimmy on deck with a chair, and when I had breakfasted Greaves got up, put his hand upon my shoulder, and together we ascended the companion ladder.

Yan Bol was carpenter as well as bo'sun and sail-maker. I bade him fetch the necessary tools for opening the cases and securing them again. With us went Henry Call and another – I forget who that man was. We lighted a couple of lanterns, and going into the cabin lifted the lazarette hatch that was just abaft the companion steps. The lady Aurora came to the square hole to look at us, and inquired by signs what we were going to do. I shrugged Spanish fashion, and made a face at her, that she might gather that what we were going to do was entirely beyond the art of my shoulders and arms to communicate.

"Doan she shpeak no English, Mr. Fielding?" said Bol, as he handed down his tools to Call, who was already in the lazarette.

"No," said I.

"Veil, I, Yan Bol, teaches him herself in a month for von of her rings."

"Over with ye, Bol. Catch hold of this lantern."

He dropped through the hatch and I followed, and Miss Aurora stood at the edge of the square of the hole, holding by the companion steps and peering down.

There were one hundred and forty cases; we examined every one of them; it was a long job. I felt mighty reluctant at first to let Bol prize open the lids and gaze with the others at the dull, frosty glitter of the long rolls of dollars; but a little reflection made me sensible of the force of Greaves' argument. If the crew were not to be trusted, what was to be done? And was it not a mere piece of cheap quarter-deck subtlety on my part to hold that the *idea* of the dollars being aft was not the same as *seeing* them?

There was no need to watch very anxiously; the dollars were packed as tightly as though the metal had been poured red-hot into the cases and hardened in solid blocks. There was never a nail on Bol's stump-ended fingers that could have scratched a coin out.

"Vhas dere goldt here as veil ash silver?" he inquired.

"No."

"Oxcuse me, Mr. Fielding, but how vhas you to know?"

"How was anybody to know what these cases contained at all? Shove ahead, will ye, and ask fewer questions. Are we to be here all day?"

It was as hot as fire in this lazarette. Our blood was speedily in a blaze and our clothes soaked. The three Jews who were summoned from the province of Babylon to be hove into a burning furnace suffered not as we did. Bol's eyes took a gummy look and turned dull as bits of jelly fish; yet the three fellows were perfectly happy in staring at the silver and pulling the cases about. Every time a lid was lifted their heads came together in the sheen of the lantern, and rude sounds of rejoicing broke from them.

"How many sprees goes to each box?"

"There's an Atlantic Ocean of drink in this here case alone."

"Smite me, but if this gets blown the girls'll be coming down to meet the brig afore she's reported."

"She vhas a handsome coin. I likes to feel her in mine pocket. How much vhas she vurth, Mr. Fielding?"

"All that you shall be able to buy with her. Next case, and bear a hand."

"How many tousand dollars vhas tdere in all?"

"Enough to stiffen you with sausage and to keep ye oozy with schnapps."

We worked our way to the bottom case, and every case was chock-a-block, as we say at sea – filled flush – and the dollars by the lantern light resembled exquisitely wrought chain armour. I saw that every case was securely nailed; the boxes were restowed. We then climbed out of the lazarette, and Bol and the others went forward while I put on the hatch, padlocked it, and withdrew the key.

I plunged my fire-red face in water, quickly shifted, and quitted the cabin, tired, burning hot, but very well satisfied with the morning's work. Greaves was seated in a chair, and Miss Aurora walked the deck, in the shadow of the little awning, pacing the planks abreast of him. Her carriage, to use the old-fashioned word, had she been draped as the beauties of her person demanded, would have been lofty yet flowing, dignified yet easy and floating, graceful as the motions of a dancer who swims from the dance into walking; but the barbaric cut of her gown spoiled all. Never did I behold a woman's dress so ridiculously shaped. It was a grief to an English eye, for in my country the girls' costumes were just such as would have hit and sweetened by suggestion the form of Miss Aurora. Well do I remember the English girls' style of 1815; the neckerchief with its peep of white breast, the girdle under the swelling bosom, the fair up and down fall of drapery thence. Never do I recall that costume, with its hat of chip or leghorn, without a fancy of the smell of buttercups and daisies, the flavour of cream, the scent of a milkmaid fresh from the udder.

I handed the key to Greaves. He put it in his pocket and gazed at me inquiringly.

"It's all right, sir, to the bottom dollar," said I.

"Good!" he exclaimed.

"It is so much right," said I, "that I am disposed to think there is more money than the manifest represents."

"There are five hundred and fifty thousand dollars in one hundred and forty cases. I wish there may be more, but I suspect the entry was correct. What did the men say?"

"Yan Bol was all a-rumble with questions. There will be much talk forward."

"There has been much talk aft," he exclaimed, smiling. "Sailors are human, and those fellows yonder are to pocket twelve hundred dollars apiece besides their wages on this job. Let them talk. Let imagination run away with them. Let the fiddle be jigging in their ears; let their Polls be seated on their knees – in fancy. Keep their hearts willing, for this bucket has to be whipped home."

The lady Aurora looked and listened as she paced abreast of us. Her eyes, full of light, often rested on me. Greaves ran his gaze slightly over her figure, and, leaning back in his chair and looking away, that she might not suspect he talked of her, said:

"Our dark and lonely friend is mighty full of curiosity. I can believe that Eve was such another. When Eve walked round the apple tree and looked up at the fruit, with her head a little on one side, she wore just the sort of expression the dark and lonely party puts on when she motions a question."

"*Que hora es, señor?*" said the lady.

Greaves made her understand, by pronouncing the word "one" in Spanish and by gesticulating the remainder of his meaning, that it was drawing on to two o'clock.

"She may be hungry," said I.

"She shall be fed in a few minutes," said Greaves.

The girl seated herself on the skylight and watched the motion of Greaves' lips, listening, at the same time, with a little frown of attention to the pronunciation of the words he coolly delivered:

"I was observing," said he, with an askant glance at her, "that the dark and lonely party is mighty full of curiosity. She tried to pump me about the dollars below; wanted to know what you were doing in the hold; asked the value of the treasure."

"How did you understand her?"

"She beckoned to Antonio; but when I found she had no more to say than *that*, I sent him forward again with a sea blessing on his head. And when I was taking sights she put out her hand for my quadrant. I let her hold it. She clapped it to her eye – shutting the eye to which she put it, of course – fell to fingering the thing, and I took it from her. I wish she wasn't so handsome. A little moustache, a pretty shadowing of beard, the Valladolid complexion, and a few chocolate teeth would make the difference I want, to enable me to look my meaning when she teases me with questions. But who could be angry with the owner of those eyes?"

He gazed at her fully. She averted her face suddenly. I fancied I caught a fleeting expression of aversion, or, at all events, of distrust. She flashed her eyes upon me with a gaze as significant as though she understood what Greaves had been talking about, rose from the skylight, and motioned me to walk with her. Greaves left his chair and stepped slowly to the companion way. At this moment Jimmy came along with the cabin dinner. The lady, inclining her face to my ear, spoke low in Spanish, pointed to the cabin skylight, shook her head, then pressed her forefinger to her lip, all which, in plain English, meant: "I don't like him." I could have answered that she owed her life to him as master of the ship, and that his offhand manners were British, and meant nothing.

"Dinner," said I.

"Dinner," she repeated, smiling.

She repeated the word several times.

"Will you come?" said I.

These words she likewise repeated; then, giving me a little bow, she extended her hand, that I might conduct her below.

The evening of this same day was soft and beautiful, rich with the lights of heaven; the ocean so calm that some of the most brilliant of the luminaries found reflection in the water – tremulous, wire-like lines of silver; yet had the breeze body enough to give the brig way. It came fanning and breathing cool as dew off the dark surface of the sea, and the refreshment of it after the fiery heat of the day was as drink to the parched throat.

I walked in the gangway, smoking a pipe. It was shortly after eight o'clock. Yan Bol was aft with Greaves. The lady Aurora was in the cabin writing with a pencil. Some seamen were in the bows of the brig; their shadowy figures flitted to and fro, all very quietly. Voices proceeded from the other side of the caboose; the speakers did not probably know that I walked near. I could not choose but listen. One was Antonio, the other Wirtz, and the third Thomas Teach.

"What I don't understand's this," said the voice of Teach. "Th'ole man falls in with that there ship locked up in the island, and boards her. He finds the silver – why didn't he take it, instead of leaving it with a chance of the vessel going to pieces, or some covey a-nabbing the dollars afore he could come back for them?"

"Dot may seem all right to you," said Wirtz, "but see here, Tommy; shuppose der captain had took der dollars into der ship he commanded vhen he falls in mit der island; vhat do his crew say? Und vhen he arrives vhat vhas he to do mit der dollars? Gif dem oop to der owners of his ship? By Cott, he see dem dom'd first. If he keep der dollars for himself, how vhas he going to landt dem on der sly mitout der crew asking him for one-half, maybe, and making him like as he can hang himself for der rest? Dot's vhere she vhas. No, no," rumbled the man in his deep, Dutch voice, "der capt'n know his beesiness. Dis trip for der dollars vhas vhat you English call shipshape und Pristol fashion."

"Is the dollars to be run, I wonder, when we gets home?" said Teach.

"Do you mean shmuggled?"

"Yaw, smuggled's the word, Yonny," said Teach.

"Veil, if dey vhas not run dey vhas seized."

"Who's a-going to seize 'em?"

"Ox der captain,"

"I'd blow the blooming brains out of any man's head as laid a finger on my share," said Teach.

"Yaw, und you gif me der pleasure of seeing you hanging oop by der neck. Den I pulls off my hat, und I say how vhas she oop dere mit you? Vhas he pretty vindy oop dere?"

"When I gets my share," said Teach, after a pause, "I'm a-going in for a buster. There'll be no half-laughs and purser's grins about the gallivanting I've chalked out for myself. There's Galen always a-telling us what he's going to do with his money; sometimes he's a-going to buy a share in a vessel; then, no, dumm'd if he is, he'll buy a house and put his young woman into it; then no, dumm'd if he'll do that, he'll clap his money in a bank, and wait till the figures grow big enough to allow of his living like a gent for the remainder of his days."

"Vhen I gets my money dis vhas my shoke," said the Dutchman. "My girl shall teach me to eat. She shall puy me a silver fork. By Cott, I drink mine beer out of silver. Every day I hov veal broth, und sausages, peas und salad, stewed apple und ham, und pickled herrings mit smoked beef, und butter und sheese, und I shjjlits myself mit almonds und raisins."

"I like the taste of the Dutch!" cried Antonio, in a voice that sounded thin and almost shrill after Wirtz's. "When I get my money see what it shall bring me; white cod and onions from Galicia, Avalnuts from Biscay, oranges from Mercia, sausages from Estramadura" – here he loudly smacked his lips – "sweet citrons and iced barley-water and watermelons. *Vaya!* What have you to say now to your veal broth and salt herrings? And I will have Malaga raisins, and my olives shall come from Seville, and my grapes and figs from Valencia. *Vaya!* I am a Spaniard, and this is how a Spaniard chooses. All that is good may be had in Madrid, and all that is good will I have when my share is paid me."

There fell a short silence as of astonishment.

"Share!" cried Wirtz in a low, deep, trembling voice. "Share didt you say? Shpeak again. I like to hear dot verdt vonce more."

"Share! What share are ye talking about. Ye ain't thinking of the dollars below, I hope?" said Teach, in a tone of menace.

"I expect a share," said the Spaniard.

"Oxpect – say dot again. I likes to hear you shpeak," said Wirtz, with an accent that made me figure him doubling his fist.

"Aren't I a sailor on board this ship?" said Antonio.

"A *sailor*, d'ye call yourself?" cried Teach. "Well," he snapped, "suppose y'are, what then?"

"I have a right to a share."

"And do you tink you get a share?"

"I have a right to a share," repeated the Spaniard in a sullen note.

"Call her a shoke or I vill fight mit you," said Wirtz.

"I will not fight," said the Spaniard in a dogged voice. "I have a right to a share. The capitan will pay me and Jorge. We are sailors with you, and are helping to navigate this brig to your country. The dollars are Spanish; they are money of my own country. The capitan is a gentleman, and will not wrong me and Jorge, and we will receive our share as a part of the crew."

This was followed by a Dutch oath, by a crash and a low cry.

"Hallo, there – hallo!" I called. "What are you men about there on t'other side the caboose?"

I sprang across the deck, and, by such light as the stars made, beheld Antonio in the act of getting on to his legs.

"Mind! He may have a knife!" shouted Teach. The Spaniard, uttering a malediction, whipped a blade from a sheath that lay strapped to his hip, and flung it upon the deck. The point of the weapon pierced the plank, and the knife stood upright.

"I am no assassin! I do not draw knives upon men!" cried Antonio.

"Who knocked this man down?" I demanded.

"I – Vertz."

"You are a bully and a ruffian. This is a shipwrecked man, scarce recovered from great sufferings. He is half your size, too."

"He talked of his share, Heer Fielding, und my bloodt polled. We safe his life, he eats und drinks, und der toyfil has der impudence to talk of his share!"

"Forward there! What is wrong?" cried the voice of Greaves. "Where is Mr. Fielding?"

"Here, sir."

"What is wrong, I am asking."

"Come aft to the captain, the three of you," said I; and I led the way.

All hands were on deck at this hour. The forecastle was roasting, and the watch below lay about the forward part of the decks. The whole crew, therefore, heard the noise, were drawn by it, and followed me as I went aft, Teach loitering in my wake to tell those who brought up the rear that "the blooming Spaniard was swearing he'd a right to a share of the dollars, and that he was bragging as how he meant to spend his money in Madrid on onions and figs, when he was brought up with a round turn by Yonny Vertz's fist."

It is strange that unto the eye of memory the picture which the brig at this hour made should stand the most clearly cut, the most sharply defined of all my recollections of her. Why is this? Because, perhaps, of the accentuation that night scene took from the shadowy heap of the men assembled upon the quarter-deck, from the quarrel beside the caboose, from the significance that must come into any sort of difficulty aboard us from the treasure in the lazarette.

The sails soared dark and still in the weak night-wind; a brook-like bubbling noise of water rose from under the bows; the vessel was steeped in the dye of the night; but there was a faint shining in the air round about the illuminated binnacle, and a dim sheen hovered over the cabin skylight. The sea sloped vast and flat to the scintillant wall of the sky. The voices of the men deepened upon the ear the silence out upon the ocean. It was a night to set the mind running upon that saying and realizing it: "And darkness was upon the face of the deep; and the Spirit of God moved upon the face of the waters."

"What's wrong?" said Greaves.

The shapeless figure of Bol came trudging from the neighborhood of the wheel to listen.

"There's been some sort of discussion between Wirtz and Antonio," said I, "and Wirtz knocked the Spaniard down."

"Captain," exclaimed Wirtz, "all hands likes to know if der Spaniards you safe shares in der dollars?"

"Who began the row?" said Greaves.

"Señor," exclaimed Antonio, "I was speaking of the food that we eat in my country – ."

"Captain," bawled Teach, "he was a-bragging of the cod and onions, the nuts and barley-water he meant to treat hisself to out of his share, as he calls it, when he gets to his home."

"She made mine plood poil," cried Wirtz; "und he laughs at me when I speaks of vhat ve eats in mine own country."

"Señor," exclaimed Antonio, "have not Jorge and me a right to a share?"

"Of what?"

"Of the money in the cases – of my country's money – that you take out of the Spanish ship."

"Bol shall slit your nose if you talk like that. You rascal! Is it not enough that we have saved your life? And what d'ye mean by your country's money? Of what country are you?"

"I am of Spain, *señor*; born at Salamanca."

"There is no money in your country," shouted Greaves. "Ye are paupers all, cowards all, sneaks and rogues to a man." Yan Bol laughed deep. "Speak again of the money below being the money of your country, and we'll hang ye."

"*Señor*," said Antonio, "am I and Jorge to receive no money for working as sailors in this ship?"

"Not so much as will purchase you a rag to wind round your greasy ankles."

A half-smothered laugh broke from Wirtz and others.

"We ask, then, that you land us," said the Spaniard, whose audacity in continuing to address Greaves was scarcely less astonishing than the captain's extraordinary exhibition of temper and wilder display of words.

"Mind that you are not landed at the bottom of the sea, with a twenty-four pound shot to keep you there," cried Greaves. "Wirtz, did you knock that man down?"

"Yaw, captain," responded Wirtz, in a voice that made one guess at the grin upon his face.

"You are a big man, Wirtz, and Antonio is a little man. Wirtz, I wish you may not be a coward at heart. Know you not," cried Greaves, elevating his voice, "that it is written, 'Make not an hungry soul sorrowful; neither provoke a man in his distress.' The soul of Antonio is hungry for dollars and you have made him sorrowful; he is in distress, being shipwrecked and having lost all his clothes, and you have provoked him. Your grog is stopped for a week, Wirtz."

"By Cott, but dot vhas hardt upon a man," said the Dutchman.

"Now get forward, all hands," exclaimed Greaves, "but mark you this; any man who raises his hand against another on board this brig goes into irons and forfeits his share of dollars. This is to be a peaceful and a smiling ship. We are going to get home sweetly and soberly; then comes your enjoyment – the pleasures of beasts or men, as you choose. Let no man say no to this."

He walked aft; I thought he would stay to have a word with me. Instead he immediately descended into the cabin. The men moved forward, talking among themselves, some of them laughing.

Yan Bol came up to me and said:

"I tell you vhat, Mr. Fielding, der Captain Greaves vhas a very fine shentleman."

"Very."

"How he talks – mine Cott, how he talks! I would gif half mine dollars to talk like dot shentleman."

"He is an educated man, and speaks well."

"Yaw, veil indeedt. I like der sheck of Antonio in oxbecting a share. But he oxbects no longer, ha?"

I turned from the Dutchman and looked through the skylight, and saw Greaves sitting at table, leaning his head upon his hand. The lady Aurora continued to write, but once or twice while I watched, she lifted her eyes to look at the captain. I was weary and passed below to go to my cabin. Greaves had left the table and was entering his own berth, as I descended the companion steps. The materials for a glass of grog were on a swing tray. While I mixed myself a tumbler the girl rose and handed me the paper she had been writing upon. The sheets had been torn by Greaves from an old log book, and they were filled by her with Spanish names with their English meanings. I ran my eye over the writing, which was a very neat, clean Spanish hand, and nodded and smiled, and returned the pages to her, saying *Beuno*. Then emptying my glass I gave her a bow, bade her good-night in Spanish, received her answer of "Good-night, sir," well expressed in English, and passed into my berth.

Chapter XXII.
Greaves Sickens

THIS TIME gives a date to a change that came over Greaves. It was the change of sickness. He grew feverish, irritable, fanciful; his appetite fell away; the light in his eyes dimmed; sometimes he would put on a staring look, as though he beheld something beyond that at which he gazed.

I had been struck by his manner, and more by his manner than by his speech, when he lectured Wirtz and flung at Antonio, the Spaniard, as you have read in the last chapter. Yet of itself this would not have been a matter to rest very weightily upon my mind, seeing that all along I had considered Greaves as a little, just a little, mad at the root. But soon the incident took significance as being a first lifting of the curtain, so to speak, upon a new and somewhat crazy behaviour in my friend. I hoped at first it was the heat that unsettled his nerves and that the Horn would give me back my old, odd, hearty, generous shipmate and messmate. Then I feared that the blow he had dealt himself when he stumbled in the hold of the *Casada* had been silently and painlessly working bitter mischief in the organ of the liver, or in parts adjacent thereto. If the liver was hurt the strangeness of the man might be accounted for. I have suffered from the liver in my time, and know what it is to have felt mad; I say I have known moments – O God, avert the like of them from me and those I love – when I could scarce restrain myself from breaking windows, kicking at the shins of all who approached me, knocking my head against the wall, yelling with the yell of one who drops in a fit; and all the while my brain was as healthy as the healthiest that ever filled a human skull, and nothing was wanted but a musketry of calomel pills to dislodge the fiend that was jockeying my liver and galloping the whole fabric of my being down the easy descent.

It will not be supposed that the change in Greaves was sudden. It uttered itself at capricious intervals, and at the beginning was more visible in the mood than in the man.

For example, it was, I think, about four days after the little incident which brings the last chapter to a close. I had charge of the deck from eight to midnight. Miss Aurora had passed half an hour with me, sometimes asking questions by gestures distinguishable by the light of the moon, sometimes attempting strange sentences in English, all the words correctly pronounced, but so misplaced that with true British politeness I was forever breaking into a laugh at her. A moment there had been when she was in earnest. She came to a stand, her face fronting the moon so that I witnessed the working of it, her eyes with a little silver flame in each liquid depth dark as the sea over the side. She spoke in Spanish, with here and there a word of English. It seemed to me she referred to the voyage. I fancied that I worked out of her words the meaning that she desired to continue in the brig, and was content. How did I gather this, when I tell you in the next breath that I could not understand her? Well, it was my *fancy* of her meaning that I give you, but whether I understood her or not she motioned with an air of tragic distress, clasped her hands, looked up at the stars, and cried in English, "Sad – sad – not understand – sad." We then resumed our walk, and presently she left me.

Now it was that Greaves arrived. He smoked a long curled pipe of Turkish workmanship and moved noiseless in slippers. The moonlight whitened his face and silvered his hair and blackened his eyes till, elsewhere, I might have looked twice without knowing him. We were to the southward of the Lima parallel, our course south by west. The Bolivian coast trends inward. Our course gave us to larboard a wide sweep of open ocean and this we should hold down to the latitude of fifty degrees. After which the chance was small of our falling in with anything armed under Spanish colours.

We had made noble progress taking the days all round, and this night we were courtesying onward with a pretty breeze off the larboard beam – a wind that ran the waters gushing white to the bends, and overhead were all the stars and the moon in their midst dimming a circle of them, and under the moon the play of the sea was like a torrent of boiling silver.

"This is a desolate ocean," said Greaves.

"So much the better for us," said I.

"Oh, yes, so much the better for us. But the solitude of the sea is a burden that the heart don't always beat lightly under. Is solitude a material thing? It has the weight of substance when it settles upon the spirits."

I let him talk on. He was fond of big, fine words, and the stranger he became the more heroic grew his vein.

"Any more rows forward among the men?"

"I have heard of none."

"I had two men who fought through a voyage. They had sailed together before and fought throughout. 'They will fight while they meet on earth,' said the boatswain of the ship to me, 'and they will fight if they catch sight of each other at the Resurrection.'" He puffed a cloud of smoke upon the wind and looked round the sea. "I am unsettled in my faith," said he, "I am troubled by doubts. I believe I am almost Roman Catholic, but lack sufficient credulity to enable me to bring up in that faith. I will tell you what I mean to believe in," continued he, halting in his walk, compelling me to stand, and looking me full in the face; "I am going to believe in the transmigration of souls."

"Oh, you'll wish to choose your next body before deciding, won't you?" said I. "You wouldn't be a flea or a cockroach?"

"The flea and perhaps the cockroach have short lives," said he gravely, "and the next entry might be into something noble. But stop till I tell you why I am going to believe in the transmigration of souls. I had a dream a few nights since. I dreamt that I was a Jewess. I beheld my face in a glass and admired it vastly. My eyes flashed and were full of fire; my lips were scarlet. I wore something white about my head. I knew that I was a Jewess. Shadowy faces of many races of people approached, looked me close in the eye, felt my face with their hands, accosted me, and I could not speak. I was suffocated with the want of speech. But on a sudden I obtained relief. I opened my mouth and spoke, and the words I spoke were Hebrew."

"D'ye know Hebrew?" said I.

"A stupid question to ask a sailor."

"How do you know you spoke in Hebrew?"

"Because it wasn't Greek; because it wasn't Welsh; because – because – man, it was just Hebrew."

"And how does transmigration offer here?" said I.

"I was my own soul, informing the body of a Jewess. My soul, of course, couldn't utter itself, as it was fresh from the body of an Englishman, until it had filled up, as smoke might, every cranny and brain cell of the shape it possessed; until it had penetrated to the crypts and dark foundations of the woman's heart. Then, seeking vent, my soul broke through the lips of the Jewess. In what tongue, d'ye ask? In what but the tongue of her nation?"

"This," thought I, "is the lady Aurora's doing. She it is who's the Jewess of my poor friend's dream. The fiery eyes, if not the scarlet lips, are hers, and hers the arrest and suffocation of speech."

But I guessed it would anger him to put this; yet it grieved me to hear this nonsense in his mouth, and the more because his looks by the moon, that shone upon us while he discoursed, gave a gloomy accentuation of – what shall I call it? not yet madness; not yet craziness; let me rather speak of it as wildness – to his words.

He walked with me for above an hour, talking on this absurdity of transmigration, and reasoning illogically, and often with irreverence, on points relating to the salvation of man. It is a bad sign when religion gets into a man's head and acidly turns into windiness and nightmare imaginations, as a sweet milk hardens into curdy flatulence in the belly of the suckling.

I sought to shift the helm of his mind by talking about the dollars below; by speaking about the crew and my secret distrust of Yan Bol; by calling his attention to the look of his brig as she floated, with aslant spars, through the moonlight, flowing lengths of the sails curving in alabaster beyond the shadow in their hollows, the water, black as ink under her bowsprit, pouring aft in fire and snow. But all to no purpose. He looked and seemed not to see; he repeated, in a mouthing, absent way, my sentences about Bol and other matters, and immediately struck back again into his talk about heaven, his soul, the Jewess he had dreamt of, and the like.

But, even without seeing him, even without hearing him, I should have known that there was something wrong with the man by the behaviour of his dog. I do not say that all dogs have souls; but I am as sure that Galloon had a soul of his own, after its kind, as that my eyes are mates. As a change slowly came over Greaves, so slowly changed Galloon. I would notice the dog watching his master's face at table, and found a score of human emotions in the creature's expression. I'd see him lying at Greaves' door if the captain was within, when formerly he would be on deck cruising about among the men or skylarking aft with me. If I called him, he'd come slowly. There was no more capering up to me, no more buoyant greetings, no leapings and lickings and short, eager yelps of salutation in response to the many things I'd say to him. We make much of human love, I would think while caressing the dog or looking at him, and the love of man we call a passion; but the love of the dog we call an instinct. Yet is not the instinct nobler than the passion? Purity it has that is faultless. Is human passion pure to faultlessness? There is selfishness in human passion, but the love of yonder dog for its master is without selfishness. Many qualities enter into the passion of love; but the love of yonder dog is a primary quality in him. It is as gold among metals. Supposing analysis possible, then analyse the brute's affection, and you find not a hair's weight, not a dust-grain's bulk, of vitiating element.

The lady Aurora was quick to notice the change in Greaves. Her lids moved swiftly upon her eyes, and their lashes were a veil, and she had an art of glancing without seeming to glance. She did not like him, and would not appear to see him more often than courtesy obliged. Her rapid glances, therefore, on occasions when she would have found other occupation for her eyes, told me that she was struck by the man's looks, that she wondered at them and guessed their significance. I was no doctor. For all I could tell she might have some knowledge under that head. I fancied this from her manner of looking at Greaves.

So one day, when she and I were alone in the cabin, Bol on the lookout above, and the captain in his berth, I endeavoured to converse with her about my friend; but to no purpose. Intelligibility vanished in signs, shakes of the head, dumb pointings to the brow and ribs. She had, indeed, picked up a little English. She was able to pronounce the names of various articles of food, also had several English nautical terms at her tongue's end; but when it came to trying to talk about Greaves' state of health, there was nothing for it but to crook our brows, hunch our backs, and work meaning into nonsense with postures.

Yet I managed to discover that the lady and I were agreed in this; that Greaves had received some internal injury from his fall, that it was slowly sickening him, and affecting his mind.

Nevertheless, he went about as usual, punctually took sights, attended at meals, was up and down during the day and night. He was very rational in all the orders he gave to the men, in all direct instructions to me respecting shipboard discipline and routine. It was by fits and starts that his growing wildness showed, and always when he had me alone; and then the matter of his discourse was dreams and religion and death. Not that he talked as though he supposed his end was approaching; upon his words lay no shadow of the melancholy that is cast by the dread event when the heart knows, dimly and mysteriously, that it is coming. He chattered as if for argument's sake; postulated to disprove his own assertions, but he was seldom logical, often devout, filled to the very twang of his nose with fervour, and at other times, and on a sudden, as impious as young John Bunyan.

What think you of this character of a seaman, of a plain north-country merchant seaman; *you* whose ideas of the nautical man are gotten from Smollett's studies, from the delightful portraits of dear Captain Marryatt? But, Jack, bless ye! *you*, who have been to sea, *you* who have sailed ten times round the world, who have swung your hammock in a score of forecastles, and who have outweathered Satan himself in a dozen different aspects of ship's captains, *you*, mate, will approve this sketch, will recognize its truth, will tell the landlubbers that at sea are many varieties of men – men who swear not, who are gentle, faithful in their duty below; men who are a little crazy, who drink deeply and are devils in their thoughts and madmen in their behaviour, but trucklers and slaverers to those who hire them; men who are hearty, pimpled, broad of beam, verdant with the grog blossom and green in naught else, moist in the weather eye, and bow-legged by great seas.

One Sunday morning, when we had left the island a little more or less than three weeks behind us. Greaves said to me at the breakfast table:

"I shall hold divine service this morning on deck."

I stared, but said nothing.

"I'll read a portion of the Church of England liturgy to the men," said he, "and a chapter out of the Bible. What chapter do you recommend?"

I was at a loss.

"Give them something interesting," said I, "something that will carry them along with you."

"Right," he exclaimed, with a little light of vivacity in his somewhat sunken and somewhat leaden eye, "what d'ye say to a fight out of Joshua?"

"I do not think," I answered, "that a good fight out of Joshua could be bettered."

"I'll give 'em that chapter," said he, "in which the son of Nun corks the five kings up in a cave and then hangs them. Not that there's any moral that I can see in that sort of narrative. It is an Ebrew Gazette extraordinary – a pitiful, bloody business from beginning to end. But if the reading of a chapter of it causes even one of the sailors to take an interest in the Bible I shall have done some good."

"So you will."

"Do you know the men's persuasions?"

"Not I, captain."

"The Spaniards are Roman Catholics, of course. The Dutchmen and the others will be of us if they're of anything. When you go on deck tell Bol to see that the crew clean themselves, and let him muster and bring them aft for divine service at half-past ten."

"Ay, ay, sir."

Miss Aurora sat over against me at this meal as at most others; she stared at me as though something was wrong. I did not wonder; I had been unable to conceal my astonishment at Greaves' orders for divine service. Down to this moment he had never read a prayer to the men, never exhibited the least disposition to do so, never imported the faintest shadow of anything religious into the dull and swinish routine of the brig. It was somewhat late in the day to lay up on *that* tack, methought. But it was for me to obey, and I went on deck, leaving Greaves sitting. Miss Aurora followed, and touched my elbow as I passed through the companion hatch.

"What is it?" said she, in English.

"Nothing, nothing," I answered, smiling and shaking my head, for it would have given me a deal too much to act, with Yan Bol and the fellow at the wheel as spectators, to gesticulate Greaves' intention to collect all hands to prayers.

"No danger?" said she, speaking again in English.

"No, no," I responded heartily.

She touched her forehead, clasped her hands, and turned up her eyes to heaven with one of her incomparable expressions of tragic melancholy, sighed heavily, and returned to the cabin.

"Bol," said I, stepping up to the great Dutchman where he stood near the wheel, "you will see that the men clean themselves and muster aft by half-past ten for divine service."

"What's dot?" said he.

"Prayers."

He looked at Teach, who was at the helm, and a smile crawled over his face, as wind creeps over a surface of sea. His smile wrinkled his massive visage to the line of his hair.

"Brayers, Mr. Fielding! Dot vhas strange after all dese months. For vhat vhas ve to pray now dot der dollars vhas on boardt?"

"Reason the matter with the captain, if you choose. You have your instructions."

"Ay, ay, sir. Mr. Fielding, may I hov a verdt mit you?"

He spoke respectfully, and moved from the wheel. He was a man I had been careful to give a wide berth to throughout the voyage; but also was he a man whom, for my own peace sake, I had been at some pains not to give offence to. The familiarity of the fellow was Dutch. I never could make sure that it was more than a characteristic of his countrymen with him, and that he meant insolence when he spoke insolently, I bore in mind, moreover, that secretly he, and no doubt the rest of the crew, viewed me as an interloper – as one who would, probably, share far more handsomely than they in the treasure without having entered at Amsterdam or having formed a part of the original scheme of the expedition. This consideration, then, made me wary in my relations with Yan Bol.

He moved from the wheel out of earshot of the fellow there, and said, in a rumbling voice of subdued thunder:

"I oxbects dot der captain vhas not fery veil, Mr. Fielding?"

"He is not very well."

"She vhas a bad shob if he vhas to took und die."

"Yaw; but what is it you wish to say to me?"

"I hov nothing to say, Mr. Fielding, except vhat I hov said. Der men likes to know how her captain vhas. When I goes forwardt und tells dem dot dey most lay aft und bray, dey vhas for vanting to know if der captain vhas all right mil his headt Oxcuse me, Mr. Fielding, but vhas it all right mit der captain's headt?"

"We are talking of the captain," said I.

"Ay, ay, sir; and I shpeaks mit all respect. You vhas first mate; I oct second. It vhas right ve shpeaks together, when der capt'n's health vhas in trouble."

"You are able to judge of his state as well as I, Bol."

"No; you live close mit him. My end of der ship vhas yonder."

His voice seemed to deepen yet as he spoke these words, while he pointed with his vast square hand to the forecastle. I held my peace, sending a look to windward and at the wheel, as a hint to him to go. He stood a while viewing me and appearing to consider, all with a heavy Dutch leisureliness of manner and expression, as though his thoughts rose slow, like whales, to the surface of his intelligence, spouted, and sunk before he could harpoon them; then, saying, "Veil, brayers at half-past ten. Dot vhas a strange idea now der money vhas on boardt," he walked forward.

This being Sunday morning, the men had nothing to do, and lounged about the galley, smoking and conversing. I watched Bol approach them. He stood abreast of a knot and delivered his orders. *That* I gathered from the stares, the starts, the hoarse laugh, the rude forecastle joke sent in a growling shout across to a mate at a distance. A little later, however, the fellows came together in a body, somewhat forward of the caboose, some of them out of my sight until my steps carried me to the gangway. Yan Bol stood among them. It was clear to me that they were talking over this new scheme of a prayer meeting aft. I kept well away, and heard nothing but the rumbling of their voices; but it was easy to guess that the most of their talk ran on the captain's health and intellect, and I reckoned that, if they had already noticed any strangeness in him, this call to prayers would go further to prove him mad in their eyes than the insanest shipboard order he could have delivered.

Some while, however, before there was need for Bol to send the men to clean themselves, Jimmy came out of the cabin and said that the captain wished to speak to me. The morning was fine, the breeze steady, and the sea smooth. The deck was to be safely left for a short interval. I called an order to the helmsman and went below.

Greaves was pacing the cabin floor. The lady Aurora was in her berth, perhaps at her devotions. Galloon was upon a chair, wistfully watching his master as he measured the cabin. Greaves' face worked with excitement and agitation; his walk was equally suggestive of distress and disorder. Were there such a thing as news at sea, I might have supposed that something heart-shaking had come to him.

"Fielding," he cried, as I stood viewing him from the bottom of the companion ladder, "'I can't read prayers to the men. The devil's right. He's put it into my head that I'm too wicked, that I've been too great a sinner in the past, and am still altogether too vile to read prayers."

"Do not attempt to do so then," said I.

"I might be struck dead for profanity," said he. "There's a feeling here" – he laid his hand upon his heart – "that warns me I shall drop if I open my lips in the recital of a prayer to the men. Look how nervous I am!" he exclaimed, with a wild, hard smile; and approaching me close he extended his hands, which trembled violently, and then, turning up the palms, he disclosed the channels or lines in them wet with perspiration. "Tell the men," said he, "that I am too ill to read prayers. Next Sunday, perhaps – ."

He threw himself upon a locker, and hid his face upon the table. I watched him for a few minutes, then, going on deck, beckoned to Bol and told him there would be no prayers that morning. The Dutchman threw a suspicious look at the skylight and walked forward.

After this incident anxiety increased upon me until it became indescribably great. I had supposed that the hurt Greaves had done himself, through the connection which exists between the liver and the brain, affected his mind; but now, when he was growing worse, I reckoned he had struck his head as well as his side. Be this as it will, his intellect was giving way, his health every day decaying, and I say that when I grew sensible of this, when I understood that unless he took a turn and mended apace he must die, anxiety made my days bitter.

My old fear of the crew revived. That fear had been hushed somewhat by the behaviour of the men, but it grew clamorous when I thought of Greaves as dead and buried in the sea, of the treasure of half a million of dollars in the lazarette, of myself as standing alone in the brig, with no man in authority to support me, without even the moral backing of good-will I might have got from the men had I shipped at Amsterdam and formed one of the Tulp party.

The dead days became dreams and visions to my memory when I thought backward and recalled the *Royal Brunswicker*, Captain Spalding, my arrival in the Downs, the gibbet on the sand hills, the press-gang, the long outward passage to the island, and the hopes and fears which came and went when Greaves talked rationally of the dollars, then irrationally of dreams and the like, and so on, and so on. I did pray very eagerly in my heart that he would be spared. Indeed, I loved the man. He had saved my life, he had enriched me, he had proved a generous, cordial, and cheery shipmate and messmate. I say I loved him, and on several occasions, when I was on deck alone, walking out the weary hours of the night watch, did I look up at the stars and ask of God to deliver my friend from the death whose hand was closing upon him. These petitions would I murmur till my eyes were wet. It was hard that he should be called away in the prime of his time, after years of the stern and barren servitude of the sea, at the moment when a noble prize, gained, as I would think, with high adventurous skill, was his.

But I never could discover, at this time at all events, that he had the smallest idea he was in a bad way. What was visible to me and the sailors, to the Spanish lady, yes, and to his own dog, himself did not see – at least, by never a word that fell from his lips did he give me to guess he knew he was ill. Sometimes he'd complain of weakness and keep his bed; he'd wonder what had become of his appetite, that was all; he never went further. It was I, mainly, who took sights and kept the ship's reckoning, who, in fact, navigated the brig, and did the work of her master. Miss Aurora's sympathies with him were strong at the start – that is, when she saw how ill he was and how his illness was increasing upon him. She'd make efforts to anticipate his wants at table; with her own hands she'd boil chocolate for him in the caboose and bring it to the cabin; she let me understand she wished to nurse him. But whether it was because of simple dislike, or because his poor head, muddling the fine woman whom he had rescued with the speechless Jewess of his dream, excited in him some inscrutable fear or aversion I know not; he would have nothing to say to her, looked away when she spoke, repelled whatever she offered, often shrank when she approached – was so crazily discourteous, in a word, that I was obliged to take the girl aside and, by signs and such words as were now current between us, advise her to keep clear of him.

As to *her*, she spent much of her time in sewing and in attempting to master the English tongue out of some books which I borrowed from Greaves's cabin, and with such help as I had time to give her. We had plenty of needles and thread on board. Greaves, before his illness grew, had given Miss Aurora a handsome roll of pure white duck, or drill – I forget now which it was – to do what she pleased with. I had found some remnants of bunting, of different colours, that she might amuse herself, if she chose, with Greaves's notion of trimming her dresses; then I had borrowed a thimble from the forecastle. You will suppose that it was not a *tight* fit; but she managed with it. And so she went to work, sewing in the cabin or in her own berth; and I see her now, with my mind's eye, as she sits under the skylight, stitching away like any seamstress earning a living, the jewels upon her fingers flashing as her hand rises and falls.

One morning she came out of her berth dressed in a gown of her own manufacture. It was built on original lines, and it suited her. I believe she had shaped it to enable her to get about with ease, to allow her to step without inconvenience up the companion ladder and through the hatch, to pass through the cabin betwixt the table and the lockers without being dragged, and sometimes held, by the folds of her skirt, and to freely move in her little bedroom. The dress she had been cast away in had hardly permitted this liberty. It was voluminous enough to have yielded her three clinging skirts; it caught the wind when she was on deck, and blew out like a topsail in a squall when the yard is on the cap. I admired her vastly in this costume of her own making. The cut answered something to my own taste in female apparel; the waist rose high, the sleeves were tight, the dip and swell of her shape were defined. I had always suspected that a nobly proportioned woman lay awkwardly hid in the dress that had heretofore clothed her, and I guessed I had been right when I looked at her this morning and marked the curve of the breast, the width of the shoulders, the fine, swinging, lofty carriage.

The dress was snow white; it fell in with the colour of her face. Her cheeks seemed the whiter for the whiteness of her clothes. She had trimmed her dress with triple lines of red bunting, and, for my part, I should never want to see a prettier or more effective gown on a maiden for sea use.

She stood in the door of her berth, looking archly at me. Galloon growled, scarce knowing her for the moment. Greaves was in his berth, for by this time he was ailing badly. She looked down her dress, coloured slightly, then walked up to me and said:

"How you like it? How you like it?" turning herself about a little coquettishly.

Admiration will often make a man laugh; and I laughed to see her in that dress and laughed to hear her address me in English; and laughed yet again, but always admiringly, at her spirited, courting manner of turning her figure about, that I might get a view of her clothes.

"It is very good, indeed," said I.

"*Si*, it is very good," she repeated after me.

She then sought to express herself further, and, failing, signed to let me know that she had now two dresses, and that presently she would have three. I pronounced some word of applause in Spanish, which she obliged me to repeat, that I might catch the correct pronunciation, and we then sat down to breakfast.

I have told you that she wore some very handsome rings, and on this occasion it was that I took particular notice of a remarkable ring which she carried on her left hand. She followed my gaze, and stretched out her hand to my face. I imagined she intended that I should kiss her hand, for I was a fool in the customs of nations, and honestly knew not but that a man's kissing a woman's hand thus held out to him, almost to his lips, as it were, was some Spanish fashion of significant civility which she would expect me to attend to; so I bent my head and put my mouth to her hand.

She coloured, her eyes flashed, she looked confused; then smiled, shook her head, and pointed to the ring. I was young and ingenuous, and the blood rose to my face when I understood that I had blundered; but I held my peace, and looked at the ring. A moment later she pulled it off and put it into my hand. It was a very rich ring, formed of ten precious stones of different sorts and a medallion of the crucifix. I turned it about, admiring it. She watched me earnestly, and then, with a smile and a sigh, said:

"You are not Catolique."

"No," said I.

She motioned to let me know she could tell as much by my ignorance of the use of that ring; and then, taking the thing from me, she went through a pretty and dramatic pantomime, reciting "Aves" while she touched the ring, and winding up with a sentence out of the "Paternoster." She put on the ring after she had made an end of her pretty pantomime, and, looking again at me earnestly, repeated, with the same dramatic sigh:

"You are not Catolique."

"No," said I.

"You will be Catolique?" she exclaimed, in very fairly pronounced English, still wearing a wistful and impassioned expression.

I slowly shook my head. She sighed again and looked very downcast; but I was wanted on deck and could sit at table no longer, and so I left her.

Chapter XXIII.
The Whaler

ALL THIS while the crew went on quietly with the work of the ship, giving me no trouble nor occasioning me further anxiety than such as arose from my fear of how it might prove with us should the captain die. This will I say of Bol: a better boatswain never trod the decks of a vessel. I carried by nature a critical eye, and while Greaves lay ill my vigilance was redoubled; but not once had I cause to find fault with Yan Bol's part in the duties of the brig.

We wanted, indeed, the freshening of the paint pot, but in all other respects we were as smart a little ship, as we blew toward the Horn, as though we had quitted the Thames but a week before. Our brass guns sparkled, our decks were yacht-like with holy-stoning, our rigging might have been newly set up by riggers of the king. Every detail of the furniture aloft was carefully seen to, from the eyes of the royal rigging to the lanyards of the channel dead-eyes.

The men feared Bol; his vast bulk of beef and the granite lumps which swelled in muscle to the movement of his arms made him the match for any two of them. The delivery of his lungs was the cannon's roar. I have seen a stout fellow stagger as though to a blow – sway in the recoil of a man who is hit hard, on Yan Bol thrusting his huge mouth into the fellow's face and exploding in passion an order betwixt his eyes. But though the crew feared him they also liked him; he acted as second mate, indeed, but throughout with reluctance; was their shipmate and forecastle associate first of all, the man who ate out of their kids and drank out of their scuttle butt, who slung his hammock in their bedroom, showed them what to do and often how to do it, occasionally went aloft with them, yarned and smoked with them. So much for Yan Bol.

Greaves had a just and considerable admiration for him, the fullest confidence in him as a sailor, and counted him the best boatswain he had ever heard of; and I agreed with him. Going, however, rather farther, for I had distrusted the man from the beginning, and my distrust of him was now deeper than ever it had been, and I would have given half my share of the money in the lazarette had we been blown away from the island when he was ashore and forced to proceed without him.

The two Spaniards were bad sailors, lazy and reckless. Bol could do nothing with them. They skulked when there was business to be done aloft, were not to be trusted at the wheel, and it came at last to our putting them to help the cook and do the dirty work of the ship when they were not at sail-making – for, to be sure, they were smart hands with their palms and needles. There were no more fights, no more assertions by Antonio and his mate Jorge of their claims to a share. In talking to me one day about them Bol said it was the wish of the crew to turn them out of the brig at the first chance.

"The captain won't hear of it," said I.

The Dutchman asked why.

"Because," said I, "the Spaniards know that there is treasure on board. They also know it is Spanish treasure and how got by us. Suppose you tranship them; they arrive at a port and state what they know. The news that we have salved the treasure reaches the ears of the owner of it, who thereupon makes application for restitution. Our business is to keep clear of difficulties."

"Yaw, dot do I see. But hark you, Mr. Fielding, ve keep der Spaniards und ve arrive home, und der Spaniards go ashore, und den? I ox, und den? Vill dey not shpeak all der same as dey vould shpoke in von of der own ports down here?"

"I have considered that; so, too, has Captain Greaves. There is a remedy, but it does not lie in transferring them in these seas."

He shrugged his shoulders and the subject dropped.

But the long and short of Greaves's policy in this particular matter was; get the money home in safety first, bring off the treasure clear of the fifty sea risks and perils of the age – the gale, the shoal, the leak, the pirate, the enemy's ships of the State. It will be time enough to trouble yourself with what the Spaniards and others of the crew may whisper ashore when the money has been landed, divided, exchanged into gold of the realm, with plenty of leisure for a disappearance that might run into time should the news of the salving of the treasure of the *Casada* ever reach the ears of the owners of the silver.

We carried good strong winds to the southward. The days grew shorter, there was an edge in the weather let the breeze blow whence it would; the swell of the sea was long and dark. We bent strong canvas for rounding the Horn, and in other ways prepared for a conflict which in those days had a significance that has departed from that wrestle. The seamen put on warm clothes; there was never a need now for the small awning aft; the sun shone white, as though the dazzle of his disk was the reflection of his beam on snow. I say his light was white and often cold when we had yet to swim many hundreds of miles to fetch the parallel of the Horn.

In all the weeks we occupied in measuring our way from the island ere rounding the headland for the Atlantic we fell in with but one ship. It was our good luck, and there was nothing surprising in it either. In this present year of my writing my story it may be your chance to sail over a thousand leagues of Pacific water and meet with nothing. It was a lonelier ocean in my time than it is now. Northward, on the equatorial parallel, there was, indeed, some life, but southward the great liquid highway that now every year foams to the shearing stems of half a thousand stately ships, was, in the year of the *Black Watch*, scarce less barren as a breast of sea than when it was swept for the galleon by the perspective glasses of Dampier and Woodes Rogers.

We fell in with a little ship and spoke her, and the speaking her proved one of the most memorable of all the incidents in this strange expedition, as you shall presently learn if you choose to proceed.

Greaves was on this day very weak; he had risen to breakfast, sat like the spectre of death at table, his sunken, leaden, black eyes wandering from me to Miss Aurora with the seeking gaze of one who strives to collect his wits; then, rising with a little convulsion of his figure, he leaned with his hand upon the table and said, in a small voice, looking downward and slightly smiling:

"I must return to my bunk. It isn't the machinery that's wrong; the spring has slackened and wants setting up afresh."

I took him by the arm and helped him to his cabin and stood looking on, waiting to be of service, while Jimmy pulled off his coat and shoes. I believed he would speak seriously of his illness, for I guessed that if he felt as bad as he looked he would count himself a dying man. But he had not one word to say about his sensations or condition. When he was in bed I stood beside him, and he lay with his eyes wide open, viewing me steadfastly in silence. Presently he said:

"Why do you stand there? It's all right with me. Get back to your breakfast and finish it, Fielding. Whose lookout is it?"

"Mine, sir."

"Why do you stand there?"

"I wish to see if I can be of use to you," said I, making a step toward the door.

"I am truly obliged. Jimmy does all I need. I want you to think of nothing but the brig. I shall be quite well – I feel it, I am sure of it – before we have climbed far up the Atlantic. By Isten, Fielding, but it warms me to the very heart of my soul to reflect that you are in charge – you and not van Laar. Van Laar it might have been, with Michael Greaves helpless in his cabin, and the Horn coming aboard. Lord, Lord, wonderful are Thy ways!" said he, turning up his eyes. "Now get ye to your breakfast. The machinery is all right, I tell you; the spring's fallen slack, the old clock loses, but the tick's steady. Fielding, the tick's steady, my lad, and a few days will make the time right with me; so get on to your breakfast."

I re-entered the cabin and seated myself.

"The captain is bad," said the lady Aurora.

I answered with a sorrowful nod. She clasped her hands and looked at me across the table anxiously, and said:

"He die."

"*Que hacer?*" (What is to be done?) I answered, for by this time I had picked up a number of phrases from her.

She slightly shrugged her shoulders and shook her head, and, pointing upward, exclaimed in Spanish:

"It is as God wills."

Then, again fixing her fine eyes, full of fire and feeling, upon me, she, by nods and gestures, contrived to make me understand this question:

"Suppose the captain dies, how is the brig to get to England?"

I smiled and pointed to myself, and made her gather that, while I was on board, the brig was pretty sure, in some fashion or other, to head on a true course for England.

We continued to exchange our meaning in this fashion while I finished breakfast. Conversation between us was scarcely now the hard labour it formerly was. She had a number of words in my tongue and I some in hers; then, by being much together – or, as I would rather put it, having by this time held many conversations in our fashion of discoursing – we had got to distinguish shades of signification which had been wasted before in one another's gaze and gestures. Her looks were eloquence itself. Even now was I able to collect her mind when she talked to me with her face only; when she would talk to me, I say, for five minutes at a time merely with the expression of her face, never opening her lips. Her eyes were charged with the language of light and passions. She could look grief, dismay, concern, horror, pity, all other emotions, indeed, with an incomparable skill, force, and beauty of mute delivery.

I went on deck, and stepped to the side, as was my custom, to peer ahead. Bol, who stood near the skylight, called out:

"A sail!"

He pointed over the starboard bow, and looking that way, I spied the delicate white gleam of a ship's canvas. It was what we should call a fine, hard day, the atmosphere strong and tonical, cold, but without harshness or rawness. The breeze was fresh off the larboard beam, and swept with a rushing noise betwixt our masts – the breath of the young giant whose dam was the snow-darkened Antarctic hurricane. The surge was a long, steady sweep of sea, tall and wide, of the deepest blue I had ever beheld. The brig, with her yards braced well forward, the bowlines triced out, and every cloth that would draw pulling white as milk in the white sunshine from stay and yard and gaff and boom, was sweeping through the water with the speed of smoke down the wind. Magnificently buoyant was the vessel's motion. The yeast of her wake seethed to her counter as she courtesyed. Large birds were flying over the track of snow astern.

"What is that craft going to prove, Bol?" said I, taking up the glass.

"Dot vhas not long to findt out," he answered.

In those times our telescopes were not as yours are now. I levelled the long and heavy tube, but it resolved me no more of the ship ahead than this – that a ship she was.

"Shall ve shift our hellum und edge avay?" said Bol.

"I will let you know," said I, walking aft.

I waited a bit, looked at the sail again, and found we were picking her up as though she were at anchor. By this time, also, most of her fabric having lifted above the sea-line, I was able to tell that she was square-rigged, like ourselves, but that, unlike the *Black Watch*, she had short topgallant masts; whence, as you will suppose, I set her down at once as a trader. This and our overhauling her so rapidly – which means, suppose her an enemy, then she had no more chance of getting alongside of us than a land crab a scudding rabbit – determined me to hold on as we were.

You see I was in charge of the brig, and could do as I chose. Yet was it right that I should report the sail to Greaves, and I called to Yan Bol, who stood in the waist, and bade him keep a lookout for a few minutes while I went below. Jimmy came out of the captain's berth as I entered the cabin. The lad held open the door, and I passed in.

"I have come to report a sail right ahead, sir."

He turned his eyes upon me with such a look as you may behold in the gaze of an old man straining after memory.

"A sail?" he exclaimed.

"Yes, sir."

"Ay, ay."

He smiled strangely, fetched a long, trembling breath, and said:

"Suppose she should prove a galleon? We are rich enough, Fielding. Leave her alone – leave her alone."

"She is no galleon. She is a small trader, I reckon, and will be abreast of us and astern while we're talking about her."

"We have as much as we need," said he. "Don't imperil what you've got, man. D'ye know. Fielding, I fear my sight's beginning to fail me. Jimmy gave me the Bible just now. The type's big and it came and went in a dissolving way like a wriggle of worms in water. I would to God there was a priest aboard. I want to ask some questions."

He closed his eyes, and with them closed repeated, "I want to ask some questions."

I waited, supposing he would look at me. He kept his eyes shut; so, bidding Jimmy, who stood in the door, to have a care of his master, and to keep within reach of his hail, I returned to the deck very heavy in my spirits; for the departure of this man did then seem to me a question of hours instead of days, nay weeks, as I had lately thought, so ill did he look, so darkly and miserably did his manner and speech accentuate the menace of his face.

It was not very long before I made out the vessel ahead to be a whaler. I knew *that* by her heavy davits, crowd of boats and square, sawed-off look when she cocked her stern at us. I showed Dutch colours, scarce doubting as yet but that the stranger would prove a Yankee, for in those days, as now, many American vessels fished in those waters, pursuing their gigantic game into seas where the British flag was rarely flown – that is, over anything in search of grease. But the Dutch flag had not been blowing three minutes from our gaff end when up floated the red flag of England to the mizzen mast head of the stranger.

She was a little ship; to describe her exactly she was ship-rigged on the fore and main, while on her schooner mizzen mast she carried a cross jack and topsail yard. She lifted, ragged with weeds, to the heads of the seas, and washed along, heavily rolling and pitching, and blowing white water off her bows, whalelike. I shifted the helm to close her for the sake of the sight of a strange face, for the sound of a strange human voice. She was abreast of us some time before noon and there lay before us, foaming and plunging, as quaint a picture as the ocean at that time had to offer, liberally furnished as her breast was with picturesque structures. She was as broad as she was long, of a greasy rusty black, and when the sea knocked her over she threw up her round of bottom till you watched for the keel; and the long grass streamed away from her as she rolled like hair from the head of a plunging mermaid. Many faces surveyed us from over her rail. Her sails fitted her ill, and were dark with use. After every roll and plunge the water poured like a mountain torrent out of her headboards and channels; but I had read her name as we approached – her name and the name of the town she hailed from. She was the *Virginia Creeper* of Whitby.

Whitby! I had never visited that town, but I knew it in fancy through the famous Cook's association with the place almost as well as I knew in reality the little towns of Deal and Sandwich. It was just one of those magical English words to sweep the mind and the imaginations of the mind clean out of the countless leagues of the Pacific into the narrow miles of one's own home waters, there to behold again with a dreamer's gaze the milk-white coasts of the south, the chocolate coasts of the north, the red sail of the smack plunging to the North Sea, the brown sail of the barge creeping close inshore, the projection of black and tarry timber pier, with its cluster of bright-hued wherries, the length of sparkling white sand, the shingly incline, the careened boat, the figure of its owner worked upon it with a tar brush.

We foamed along together broadside to broadside, within musket shot, and I hailed the whaler and was answered.

The man who responded stood in the mizzen rigging. He wore a round glazed hat, a shawl about his throat, a monkey coat to his knees. He sang out to know what ship I was, and I answered that we were the *Black Watch*, of London, chartered by a merchant of Amsterdam, and that the captain and mate, and most of the crew were Englishmen. We were bound to London, I roared to him, omitting to answer his question where we were from. Then, in answer, he shouted that he was the *Virginia Creeper* of and from Whitby, ten months out, had met with shocking bad luck, and was bound out of these seas for the South Atlantic. All the whales had gone east. Sorry we were in such a hurry. He would have been glad to come aboard for a yarn, and for what news from home we had to give him. Were we still fighting the Yankees? A Yankee privateer had spoke him in the South Atlantic, and the captain of the vessel sent a mate aboard him with a box of cigars, and this message – that the whaler was a ship he never meddled with, no matter under what colour he found her; that he honoured a calling that had given his own nation her finest race of seamen; and when he sailed away he dipped to the *Virginia Creeper* as to a friend. All this I was able to hear. The man, who spoke as a Quaker, delivered his words with a strong, slightly nasal voice, and his words came clean as the sound of a bell through the washing hiss of the water and the roar aloft.

I found time to shout back that our captain was dangerously ill, and to ask the master of the whaler, as I supposed the man to be, if he knew aught of physic – of the treatment of injuries. He shook his head vehemently, crying "No!" thrice, as though he would instantly kill any hope the sight of him had excited in *that* way; and, indeed, what should a sailor know of physic and the treatment of such a sickness as was fast killing Greaves? I asked the question to ease my conscience and to satisfy the crew, who were listening. I figured him coming aboard and stifling a groan when he saw Greaves, vexing the poor, languishing man with useless questions put to mark his sympathy, and then coming out of the berth to tell me it was a bad case.

We sped onward. The voice would no longer carry, and the whaler veered astern almost into our wake, with a wild slap of her foresail, as she plunged a heavy courtesy of farewell at us.

My notes of what befell me in this memorable year of Waterloo gives much to my memory, but not everything; and I am unable to recollect the exact situation of the brig when we fell in with the *Virginia Creeper* westward of the Horn. I am sure, however, that we were something to the southward of the island of Juan Fernandez, somewhere about the latitude of Valdivia. This I supposed from remembrance of the climate. But be it as it may, it was now, on this date of our speaking the Whitby whaler, that I confidently supposed my poor friend Greaves would not live to see the end of the week. I have told you so; but guess my surprise when, on coming on deck at four o'clock that same afternoon, I found him seated on a chair, wrapped in a warm cloak. Yan Bol walked to and fro near him. They had been talking. I had heard the Dutchman's deep voice as I stepped through the hatch. But if Greaves had looked a dying man in his berth, he showed, to be sure, ghastly sick by the light of the day. I had seen much of him below, yet I started when my eyes went to his face now, as though, down to this moment, I had not observed the dreadful change that had happened in him. Galloon lay at his feet. The poor man smiled faintly on seeing me, and said in a weak voice:

"Did not I tell you I should be better presently? The machinery's sound, and, when that's so, nature is your one artist to make it the right time of day with ye."

I conversed a little with him. Yan Bol stood by. I told him about the whaler. He motioned with a trembling white hand, and said he had heard all about it from Yan Bol, Presently he wandered somewhat in his speech, and rose falteringly, sending a sort of blind, groping look round the decks; but he was too feeble to hold his body erect, and the swing of the brig, as she reeled to a sea, flung him roughly back upon his chair.

"Let me take you below," said I.

He looked at me as though he did not know me and talked to himself. I motioned to Bol with my head, and we each took an arm, and tenderly – and I say that there was a tenderness in Yan Bol's handling of the poor fellow that gave me such an opinion of his heart as helped me for a little while like a fresh spirit in that time of my distress, anxiety, and fear – very tenderly I say, we partly carried, partly supported, the captain into the cabin, whence he went, leaning on Jimmy, to his berth, looking behind him somewhat wildly at us who stood watching him, and talking without any sense that I could collect.

"Mr. Fielding," said Yan Bol as we regained the deck, "der captain vhas a deadt man."

"I wondered to find him out of his berth."

"He vhas von minute talking like ash you or me, und der next he vhas grazy mit fancies. I likes to know how dot vhas mit der brain. Von minute he oxes me questions about der vhaler, as you might; der next he looks at me und say, 'Vhas your name Yan Bol?' 'It vhas,' I answered. 'Vhat vhas der natural figure of der Toyfell?' he oxes. 'Dot vhas a question for der minister,' says I. 'Last night,' he says, 'dere vhas a full moon, und I saw a reflection like she might be a bat's upon der brightness of der moon. Dot reflection sailed slowly across. I ox you,' says he, 'vhas dot der reflection of der Toyfell – dot, you must know, is Brince of der vinds?' I keeps mine own counsel, und valks a leedle, und pretends dot der brig vants looking after; und vhen I conies back he oxes me anoder question dot vhas no longer grazy, but like ash you might ox. Now, how vhas dot, Mr. Fielding?"

"I am as ignorant as you," said I; "but his end is at hand. He will not long talk sensibly or crazily. God help him and bless us all! It is a heavy blow to befall this little brig – 'tis a heavier blow to befall the poor gentleman who has shown us how to fill our pockets with dollars; whose own share would make him a happy and prosperous man for life."

"Dot vhas so," said Bol; and our conversation ended.

Seeing that Greaves' mind was loosened, I no longer expected him to realize the near approach of death. I ceased, therefore, to be surprised that he did not speak to me about his condition. Sometimes I would ask myself whether it was not my duty, as his friend, to touch upon the subject of his state at some favourable moment when his faculties were strong enough for coherent discourse. He was dying. He must soon die. He could not live to round the Horn. How would he wish the money he had earned by this venture to be disposed of? Thirty thousand pounds was a large fortune. I knew that he was fatherless and motherless, but no more of him did I know than that. I had never heard him speak of his relations; indeed, throughout he had been silent on the subject of his parentage and beginnings, though he had never wanted in candour when he talked of his first going to sea, his struggles and failures and sufferings in the vocation.

But as often as I thought it proper to speak to him, so often did I shrink from what was, perhaps, an obligation. No; I could not find it in me to tell him that he was a dying man.

The weather grew colder, and we met with some hard gales out of the southeast, which knocked us away fifty leagues to the westward out of our course. It was Cape Horn weather, though we were not up with that headland yet. The dark green seas rolled fierce and high; the sky hung low and sallow and fled in scud. We stormed our way along under reefed canvas, showing all that we durst, and making good average way, seeing that the gale was off the bow and the seas like cliffs for the little brig to burst through.

Anxiety lay very heavy upon me all this time. I had confidence in Yan Bol's seamanship, but I had more faith in myself; and I was up and down in my watch below to look after the brig, till, when the twenty-four hours had come round, I would find I had not passed two of them in sleep.

The cold found the lady Aurora without warm apparel. The dress she had been shipwrecked in was of some gay, glossy stuff, plentiful in skirt, and as warm as a cobweb. What was to be done? It was not to be borne that she should sit shivering in the cabin for the want of apparel that would enable her to look abroad whenever she had a mind to pass through the hatch; so, after turning the matter over in my mind, one morning, soon after our meeting with the whaler, I ordered Jimmy and another to bring the slop chest into the cabin. It was a great box, and one of two. Both were of Tulp's providing. The old chap guessed he saw his way to making money out of the sailors by putting cheap clothes aboard for sale, and it was likely enough he would find his little venture in this way answerable to his expectations when we got home, for already one of the chests was emptied of two-thirds of its contents, the sailors (I being one of them) having purchased at an advance of about eighty per cent, upon what would be rated ashore as a very high selling price.

Well, one of the slop chests was brought up and put in the cabin. I had tried to make Miss Aurora understand what I meant – to no purpose. Now, lifting the lid of the chest, she standing by me and looking down upon the queer collection of sailors' clothing, I pulled out a monkey coat, big enough for the sheathing of even Yan Bol's bolster-like figure, and, holding it up, went to work to make myself intelligible. I put the coat on her. I then touched it here and there to signify that, by shaping a waist, and cutting in at the dip of the back, by shortening the sleeves and fixing the velvet collar to suit her throat, she might make a very good figure of a jacket for herself out of the coat. I then took a cap from the chest, and I placed it upon her head, advising, as best I could by signs and words, that she should stitch flaps to it to shelter her ears, with strings to keep the thing on her head in wind. I went further still, being resolved that the lady should go warmly clad round the Horn, and, calling to Jimmy, bade him bring me up a bale of spare blankets. I heartily longed for a Spanish dictionary, that I might give her the word *petticoat* out of it. However, she caught my drift after a little, on my selecting one of the finest of the blankets and putting it about her and holding it to her waist. She nodded and laughed.

I witnessed no embarrassment, and, in honest truth, there was no cause for embarrassment. Yet I do not suppose that an English girl – at least, that many English girls – would have made this little business of suggesting apparel, and hinting at clothing which a man is not supposed to know anything at all about until he is married, so pleasant and easy as did this Spanish maiden.

Well, her ladyship was now supplied with materials for warm clothing, and that same afternoon she went to work on the coat. Hard work it was. She wanted shears for such cloth as that, and managed with difficulty with a sailor's knife fresh from the grindstone; yet, by next afternoon, having worked all that day and all next morning, she had given something of the shape of her own figure to the coat. She put it on for me to look at. It wrapped her bravely; and when, with white teeth showing, she placed the cap on her head, her beauty – and beauty dark, speaking, impressive I must call it – took a quality of brightness, a piquancy that comes to beauty from male attire; in her case wanting when ordinarily dressed, of such gravity and dignity was her bearing, of such a natural, womanly loftiness were the whole figure and looks of her.

Chapter XXIV.
A Sailor's Will

AFTER a troublesome spell of stormy weather there happened a fine afternoon, and when the evening drew around the shadow was richer in stars than any tropic night I ever beheld. The wind was light; the ocean breathed in a long swell from the north; the atmosphere was frosty, but sweet and comfortably endurable.

We had sent down our royal yards, yet tonight was a night for royals and studding sails – a night to be made the most of. The ocean was off guard, asleep, and easily might we have stolen past the slumbering sentinel, clothed from truck to waterway in the tall, wide wings we had expanded in the north.

But the old villain was not to be trusted; 'twas but a snort and a stir with him down here, *then* a hideous black cloud flying at your ship, and hail and wind to which the stoutest must give his back.

So this evening we flapped slowly onward under topgallant sails and courses, and the long naked poles of the royal masts made a wreck of the fabric to the eye up aloft as they swung the dim buttons of their trucks under the stars.

It was seven o'clock. I had an hour to smoke my pipe in before my watch came round. I stood on the brig's quarter, leaning upon the bulwark rail. The sea ran in thick, noiseless folds like black grease, and I hung smoking and hearkening to a queer respiration out upon the water – the noise of the blowing of grampuses sunk in the blackness. Presently my name was pronounced. I turned, and by the light in the companion way beheld the figure of the boy Jimmy.

"What is it?"

"The captain wants to see you, master."

I knocked the fire out of my pipe.

"What is wrong?" said I, in a voice of awe, for even as the lad had called, my thoughts were busy with the dying man, and my heart heavy with sadness.

"The captain's very bad tonight, master."

This was the third day Greaves had kept his berth without attempting or expressing a wish to leave it. During these days he had been more than usually rambling and incoherent, insomuch that my visits had been brief because there was nothing to be said. I had looked in upon him merely to satisfy myself on his condition. I knew not how I should find him now, and sat me down on a chest beside his bunk. Galloon lay on the deck.

The lamp gave a strong light; Greaves saw me and I him very plain. There was an intelligence in his looks that had been wanting – his countenance was knitted into its old expression of mind, as though by an effort of the faculties.

"D'ye know, Fielding, I fear that I am very ill?" said he in a weak voice.

"You do not feel worse, I hope?" said I.

"I don't like my sensations. I don't understand them. It has crossed my mind that I am dying."

"Ill you are and have been, captain; yet less ill tonight, it seems to me, than you were yesterday. God preserve you! What can I do? Here we are, out upon the wild sea, nothing but Spanish ports to make for; but say the word and I'll head the brig for the port you shall name. We must forfeit our dollars, but your life stands first."

"It is too late," he said.

"For God's sake don't say that! Ought I to have sought help on the coast?"

"It is too late," he repeated, and sank into a silence that lasted a minute or two.

"Have you believed that I am dying?" said he.

"I have believed you ill – sometimes very ill."

"It will be hard to die here, all this way from home. The launch over the side makes a deep burial. I buried a man hereabouts last voyage, and – How deep is it? Has he touched the bottom yet? – with a twenty-four pound shot at his heels too."

"Don't think of such things."

"I am not afraid to die, but I wish there was a priest aboard – someone to help me to steady my thoughts. I believe in all that should make a man a good Christian. What's the time?"

"A little after eight, sir."

"What noise of hissing is that?"

"Grampuses have been blowing out to larboard; some may have come alongside."

"Ay, me!" he cried. "There is the hand of the devil in this snatching away of my life *now*, when the days show brightly, and my head is full of plans of goodness. How about the money, Fielding?"

"What money, sir?"

"Mine, mine," he exclaimed with irritation. "Yours you'll keep and welcome, and don't let the spending of it damn ye. Mine, I say. What't to become of it? If I die, what's to become of my money? Must it go to Tulp? By Isten, no, then!" he exclaimed, with a rather crazy laugh.

Have you no relations?"

"Tulp's no relation."

"Have you no relation whatever?"

"None, I tell ye."

"Few men can say that," said I doubtingly.

"Fielding, I am dying, and I will leave my money to God."

He spoke faintly, his appearance was very alarming; his eyes moved slowly and strangely.

"Tell me your wishes? If I live they shall be carried out."

He repeated in a low voice that he would leave his money to God.

"In what form can this be done?" said I, fearing that his mind was giving way again.

"I will leave my money to the Church," he answered.

"What Church?"

He made no answer.

"What Church, Captain?" I repeated, bending my face to his.

"Rome," he answered.

"In what religion did your mother die?" said I.

His eyes ceased to wander, he gazed at me steadfastly; but as he was silent, I again asked him in what faith his mother had died.

"She was a Protestant," he answered; "she belonged to the Church of England."

"Leave your money to the Church in whose faith your mother sleeps. Should not a mother's faith be the holiest of all to a child? Captain, there is no better faith than was your mother's."

"Who talks to me of my mother?" said he. "She married Bartholomew Tulp. Well, she was a very good woman. She has gone to God. She was poor – she married for a home, and to help me, as I have often since believed. I will leave my money to her memory. What time is it?"

I again told him the time.

"How is the weather?"

"A fine, quiet night."

"There is water in that can; give me a drink."

When he had drunk he asked me to lift the dog, that he might pat his head. He feebly, with a pale, thin hand, touched the ears of the poor beast; and as he did so, I thought of that time when I lay in a hammock, trembling and helpless, with a weakness as of death, and when he had lifted Galloon that I might kiss the dog that had saved my life.

"Who has the watch?"

"Bol, sir."

"Will you write for me, Fielding?"

"Anything will I do for you."

I seated myself at the little table that was near his bunk. It was furnished with ink and quills. I opened a drawer and found paper, and waited for him to speak.

"Tulp shall not have my money," said he; "the old rogue is rich, and he has a noble share in what is below. Too much – too much. And yet it was his venture. Let me be reasonable. He shall not have one dollar of my money, by God! If I die, and the money goes home, he will take it. I would see him damned before he touched a dollar of my money. Hasn't he enough?"

"More than enough."

"I will leave the money to the memory of my mother. The thought comforts me. I was her only child – I left her very young; I was not to her as I should have been. Write, Fielding."

He dictated, but ramblingly, with so much of incoherence, indeed, breaking off to talk to himself, to ask the time, to whisper some sea adventure, which he would go half through with and then drop, that, even if my memory carried what he said, it would be mere silliness in the reading. However, his wish was to dictate a will, which was to be embodied in a very few sentences. So when he had made an end and lay still, I wrote as follows:

> Brig *Black Watch*, at sea. February the 24th, 1815. This is the last will and testament of me, Michael Greaves, master of the above brig – at the time of signing this in full command of my senses. I hereby bequeath all the money I have in the world to the Church of England, in memory of my mother; and I desire that the money I thus bequeath may be devoted to a memorial that shall forever perpetuate the love I bear to the memory of my mother, whose soul is with God.

It was the best form of will I could devise, knowing little of such matters; but since it was his wish that the money should be dedicated to God, most reasonable was it that I, as an Englishman, should wish to see it bequeathed to the Church of my own and of his country. And I was the warmer in this desire in that the money was Spanish; by which I mean that nothing could be more proper than that the dollars of the most bigoted people in all creation, in religious matters, should go to the support of the purest, the most liberal, the very noblest of all churches. Bear ye in mind, it was the year 1815; when our esteem of the foreigner and his faith was not as it is.

"What have you written?" said he.

I read aloud.

"It will do," he exclaimed; "read it again." I did so. "Will not thirty thousand pounds build a church?" said he.

"It will build a ship," said I. "I know nothing of the cost of building a church."

"Write down that I want a church built," said he.

This I did.

"Write down," said he, "that I leave one thousand pounds to you, for having saved my life."

I hesitated and looked at him, and then said, "My dear friend, I thank you, but you have put enough in my way."

"Write it down, write it down," he cried. I wrote as he dictated. "Now," said he, "can I sign?" and he lifted his hand as though feeling for strength to control a pen.

I opened the door and called to Jimmy, who was putting wine and biscuit on the table. I asked the lad if he could write. He answered, "No." I put a pen into Greaves' hand, and he scratched his signature under the three clauses I had written down. His vision was dim, and he saw with difficulty when it came to his writing, but on my directing the point of the pen in his hand to the paper he wrote with some vigour. I bade Jimmy take notice of what I was about to read, and when I had read I signed my name, and the lad made his mark, which I witnessed.

All this was very innocent. I was a sailor, with no more knowledge of the law than a ship's figurehead, and little dreamed that I was rendering my interest in poor Greaves' will worthless by attesting it. But, as things turned out, it mattered nothing, as you shall read.

Jimmy went into the cabin to wait on the lady.

"Will you, or shall I keep this will?" said I.

"You," he answered. "I give you Galloon," said he after a pause, and now speaking with the faintness I had observed in him when I first arrived. "You'll love him, Fielding."

I put my cheek to the dog's face. "I am glad to have your wishes," said I. "Should you be taken before we get home I shall know what to do, if I outlive you." He feebly smiled. "Oh, but the risks of the sea are many – *we* know that. A man goes with his life in one hand. You are far from dead yet. It is I who may be the dying man."

"I wish there was a priest on board to settle my doubts," said he, scarcely above a whisper, and now his eyes began to look strangely again.

"What are your doubts?"

"Is there a hell, Fielding?"

"Not for sailors, captain."

He steadied his eyes, and smiled with an odd parting of his lips, that was like the first of a gape.

"Not for sailors, sir," said I. "Hell is here for them. There can't be two hells for the same man."

"I'd like to think that," said he. "I am afraid of going to hell. I've been afraid of dying ever since they put the notion of the devil into my head. I told ye just now I wasn't afraid of death. Nor am I, when I forget the devil. I forgot him then. Now he's back again. Give me some water and open the scuttle – it's grown blasted hot, hasn't it?"

He sat up on a sudden, and immediately afterward sank back. Again I gave him to drink, and opened the scuttle as he desired.

He now rambled. Some of his imaginations were wild and striking. They even struck an awe into me, though perhaps much of their impressiveness lay in their falling from dying lips. His poor head ran on religion – and sometimes he was to be saved, and sometimes he was to be damned; and then he would forget, and babble about what he meant to do when he got home; how so much of his money would go in giving clothes and food to the poor, and how he'd collect many kinds of animals and use them well, fearing them, for who was to tell what souls of men they contained; and there might be a human sorrow in the bleat of a goat, and a man's passion in the silence of a suffering horse.

I cannot tell you what he talked about. It matters not. Yet one strange thing that happened this evening let me note. It was this: he had sunk into silence, and I was about to quit his cabin for the deck. He had been talking very wildly, and sometimes, to my young, green, superstitious mind, almost terrifyingly; then had fallen still all in a moment, his eyes closed, his lips shut. I stooped to look at him, then turned to go, as I have said. My hand was on the door, when I heard his voice:

"Fielding, will ye sing?"

I went back wondering, and asked him what he said.

"Will ye sing?" he exclaimed.

I supposed this a part of his sad, dying nonsense, yet, to humour him, answered:

"I will sing for you, captain."

"Sing me 'Tom Bowling,'" said he.

I sat down, and Galloon laid his head on my knee. My voice was broken, but I strove to put a cheerfulness into it, and sang the opening verse of "Tom Bowling." He lay quiet while I sang. When I came to the end of the verse, he looked at me and, when I paused, believing he had had enough, he sang the closing lines in a feeble voice:

> "Faithful below he did his duty.
> And now he's gone aloft."

When he ceased, his eyes were full of tears. He put out his hand, and I took it, myself weeping, for the sight of his tears had unmanned me. I felt a gentle pressure. He then turned his face to the ship's side, and after I had watched by him for about five minutes, during which he breathed quietly but spoke not, I passed out and went on deck.

Whether Greaves feared death or not I don't know. I will not, however, believe he thought he was dying. Frequently will a man tell you that he is dying when his belief is the other way. His fears betray the secret of his hopes.

Happily, from this night Greaves lost his senses, sank into a lethargy, and lay motionless as death for hours; then awoke, but never to consciousness, though often he would call out from amid the darkness that lay upon him, with so much reason in his exclamations as made me imagine his mind was returned. Whatever he said that had sense was nautical. Once he put the brig about in his wanderings. He startled me, who had entered his cabin but a minute or two before, by a sharp, hard cry of:

"Ready about!"

He followed on with the proper orders, pausing with all the judgment you can imagine for the intervals, and, when he supposed he had got the brig on the other tack, the bowlines triced out, and the gear coiled away, he whispered awhile briskly:

"Now she stumps it," said he.

"Clap the jigger on that main-tack, my lads! Get a small pull of the weather main royal brace. Flatten in that jib sheet there. Damme, Mr. Walker, we don't want balloons on our jib booms."

So would he wander, and all that he said in *this* way was sensible.

When he lost his mind the lady Aurora offered to nurse him. He did not recognize her; and, down to the hour of his death, she was in and out of his cabin, dressing little delicate messes of fowl and tortoise and the like in the caboose, feeding him, damping the sweat from his face, ministering to him in many ways. He would have died quickly but for her. Jimmy had no knowledge of feeding or preparing food for him. Not a soul of the rough junks forward were fit for such work; and the business of the brig kept my hands full. The day before Greaves died, I entered his cabin, and found the lady on her knees beside his bunk. She looked slowly round on my entering, crossed herself, rose, and, putting her hand upon my arm, whispered in English:

"Shall he not die Catolique?"

I answered with one of those shrugs which I had got from her.

"He is Catolique," said she.

"No," said I.

"But, yes – but, yes."

"Very well," said I.

"He shall die Catolique," said she, "or – ."

And now, wanting words, she signed to let me know that, if he did not die Catolique, his soul went in danger. Happily, we had not language for argument. Her eyes sparkled; she looked at me hotly. There was the temper of the religious enthusiast in the whole manner of her.

"Her uncle is a priest," thought I. "There may be the blood of an Inquisitor in this fine woman," I thought. "Ay, and even though she was my mistress, and I her impassioned sweetheart, and even though she loved me with the jealous heat of a Spanish heart, all the same is she just the sort of party to order me," thought I, "to the stake, and watch me with an unmoved face while I was doing to a turn, if she supposed the burnt-offering of a shell-back would help her with the saints and give her Jack's soul a true course."

Here poor Greaves, who had lain motionless, suddenly let out. He seemed to be hailing a boat.

"Why the devil don't you pull your larboard oars? You infernal lubbers! what's the good of *all* hands pulling to starboard? Look at the boat. *This* is the ship, you fools – there! *Now* ye've done it. Plague take ye. Twenty stone of prime beef foundered! Lower a boat and pick 'em up. Lower a boat and pick – lower a boat – lower – ."

"He shall die Catolique," said Miss Aurora.

In what faith he departed this life is known to his Maker. Greaves went under hatches next day, in the afternoon, at one o'clock. A strong wind was blowing, a high sea running, it was bitterly cold; the windward horizon was sullen with the black shadows of clouds, out of which the dark green seas ridged in hills, with such a toss of spray from every foaming head that the wind sparkled with the flying brine. The brig laboured heavily. She was under small canvas, and the sea broke against her, in a sound of guns. I was watching her anxiously, intending, if it came harder, to heave her to. The blubbered face of Jimmy showed in the companion way.

"Master," said he, "the captain's dead."

I spied Bol to leeward of the caboose, and bawled to him to lay aft, and stepped below.

Yes, Greaves lay dead. The peace of eternity was upon his face, the peace that comes not until the noise of the clock falls upon the deaf ear. At every other moment the thick glass scuttle, through which the daylight came, rolled in thunder under water, and was hidden in whiteness; then a dark green shadow was in the cabin; then the light brightened, as the weeping glass was lifted. It was like being buried in the sea with the dead man, to stand in that cabin and listen to the roar of water round about, and mark the green dimness like daylight dying out.

I stood looking at Greaves. Beside me crouched Galloon. Every now and again the dog uttered a sort of low, sobbing howl. How did he know that his master was dead? *I* can't tell. He crouched beside me, I say, weeping in his way, and I dare swear that he better knew the captain was dead than I, who indeed guessed him dead by his looks, though I would not have buried him in that hour for a million.

I drew the head of the blanket over the poor man's face, and went to the door, with a call to Galloon to follow. The dog did not stir.

"Come," cried I, and approached him. He growled fiercely, and I saw danger in his eye. "Well, poor beast," said I in my heart, "you shall watch and mourn in your fashion;" and I came away, and sat down at the cabin table, and leaned my head upon my hand to let pass an oppression of tears that had visited my throat and was darkening my sight.

I had saved his life, and he mine; we had spent many weeks together, exchanged many thoughts, together paced out many a long hour of the day and night; he had been my friend, shipmate, messmate, and I knew not how warm was my love for him until now. The sea brings men close together, and there is the companionship of peril and a sense of isolation and remoteness that is binding. A man is missed at sea as he never can be missed ashore. Ashore is a vast field filled with distractions for the mind: the greatest ship is but a speck on the deep; you may walk the length of her, and descend to the depth of her in a few minutes, and over the side is the monotony of heaven and water, thrusting the spirit back upon its imprisonment of bulwarks, and compelling the mind to perpetual consideration of all the life that is contained within the narrow walls of timber.

I raised my head and found the lady Aurora sitting opposite me. She may have come from her cabin quietly or not; her movements were not to have been heard amid the straining sounds of that tossing interior.

"The poor captain is dead," said she.

"Yes," I answered.

"Blessed Virgin, he has suffered. He is now at peace," said she, partly in English, partly in Spanish.

"Were you with him when he died?" I called to the boy, who stood at the foot of the companion steps, white and grinning.

"Yes, master."

"Come here, my lad. Did he speak before he died?"

"Master, he lifted up his right hand and sung out 'from under!' then rattled."

"How did you know he was dead?"

"I saw father die, master, and last voyage the cook died, and I saw him go."

Miss Aurora looked as if she would have me interpret Greaves' dying exclamation. I drained a tumbler of rum-and-water to cheer me, and going on deck found Yan Bol standing beside the companion way waiting.

"Vhas der captain deadt?" said he.

"He is dead," I answered.

"Und vhat vas to become of his share, Mr. Fielding?"

"He'll not be cold for some hours, and he keeps his share till we bury him."

I walked away. When I turned the Dutchman still stood where I had left him, looking toward me. He then rolled forward and entered the caboose. There was no more weight of wind. In a few hours' time I should be keeping the brig more off for the Horn. I forget our latitude on the day of Greaves' death. It was something south of the parallel of the Horn, and our longitude was right for a shift of the helm. I walked the deck, thinking much of Greaves. What had killed him? He had been long a-dying, ever since his accident, indeed. No doubt that injury betwixt his ribs had brought about his death, and I reckoned his craziness to have been a consequence of that injury, though to be sure, his mind, as we would say at sea, had been launched with a list. But he was dead, and I was alone in the brig with a treasure of half a million of silver to carry home, and with a crew of men I did not trust.

No, it was not Bol's question that had startled me. The moment I came on deck, after leaving the dead captain, I realized my loneliness, and all my old misgivings stormed in upon me till, I give you my word, I stood with my back upon the helm, panting as after a run, with the sudden passion of anxiety that uprose.

Presently, after walking and reasoning myself into something of soberness, I thought I would have Yan Bol aft. I called; he put his head out of the caboose; I beckoned, and he approached, thrusting his pipe into his breeches pocket. It was his watch below, and he had a right to smoke on deck.

"The captain is dead," said I. "Let us talk of the affairs of the brig."

"I vhas villing to talk, but you valked off, Mr. Fielding."

"I walked off because I was fresh from the side of a friend who is dead."

"I vhas sorry, too. He vhas a goodt sailor. When did you bury him?"

"Tomorrow."

"He vhas steeched up by me himself. I makes a good shob of him out of respect to you, Mr. Fielding."

"What change is to come about? If I have charge of the brig, I can't keep watch."

"If you vhas not in sharge, Mr. Fielding, der brick vhas der *Flying Doytchman*."

"You'll be chief mate, then. Whom can you trust to act as second – to keep a lookout, I mean?"

"Plindfold me, und der man I touch is der man you vant. Vere der eggs vhas all ash one der voorst vhas der best."

"Let the men choose for themselves, then."

"Dot shall be – Und vhat vhas our port, Mr. Fielding?"

"Our port? Our port? – why – why – " I staggered in my speech, for, now that Greaves was dead, what name was I to give the place we were bound to?

"Vhas she to be Amsterdam?"

"No. You and I will talk of this later on."

He nodded emphatically, a large and heavy nod of approbation.

He left me after we had been talking for about half an hour. I then heard a melancholy noise of crying in the cabin. I went below, and found Galloon at Greaves' door, howling dismally. I told Jimmy to let the dog in, and resumed my walk and lonely lookout on deck. Lord, what a melancholy day was that in my life! The desolation of the sea was in it. I see that ocean now – its hills of liquid lead pour into foam, the grey shape of an albatross hovers off the quarter, there is a constant flash and leap of hissing whiteness at the bow, and the black running gear is curved to leeward by the gale.

I looked into Greaves' cabin before sitting down to supper. Galloon lay upon the breast of the dead man and whined dismally when I entered. I uncovered the face to make sure of the death in it, and the dog, when he saw his master's face, barked low and strangely, and licked the cheek of the dead. I hid the face once more and went out. The dog would not follow.

Little passed at table between the lady Aurora and me. The gloom of death was upon us, and I was too cold and sad at heart, too oppressed with anxiety, to attempt one of our broken and motioning talks.

At eight o'clock Bol came aft to stitch up the body in canvas. With him came William Galen, a freckled countryman of Bol's. I watched the brig while they went below; very dark was the night, with a sort of swarming of the seas to the vessel that gave her the most uncomfortable motion I ever remember. But the wind was sinking, and by this hour we had shaken a reef out of the topsails and had set the main topgallant sails, and the little ship rushed along wet and in blackness fore-and-aft, her head now something to the south of east, fair for the passage of the Horn.

Bol and his mate had not been above three minutes in the cabin when I heard a commotion below – the furious barking of a dog, deep roars, and thunderous shouts and Dutch oaths. I rushed into the cabin, crying to the sailors not to hurt the poor beast.

"She has tore mine breek," shouted Bol, "und bitten Galen to der bone of her thumb."

I bade them stand out of sight, and Jimmy and I went in; but the dog was not to be coaxed away from his master. There was nothing for it but to smother and carry him out in a blanket, and let him loose in an adjacent berth. The struggle with the beast capsized my stomach. He had crouched upon the dead body, and our catching at him and smothering him, and dragging him out of the bunk in a blanket, had given a horrid semblance of life to the poor remains. The half-closed eyes seemed to plead for repose, and, in the dance of the lamplight, the pale lips stirred, and, by stirring, entreated.

"Now for a neat shob," said Bol.

I went out sick, and was some time on deck ere I rallied. By and by Bol and his mate came up, and the boatswain said:

"She vhas all right now. How many men vhas dis dot I make up for der last heaf?"

"I don't know," said I.

"Veil, only dwenty-dwo. I steech opp half a leedle ship's company mit cholera. Dere vhas fifteen all toldt. Sefen diedt. I steech 'em opp. I tell you, Mr. Fielding, vhen dot shob vhas ofer I feels like drinkin'."

"Vhas he to be all night below?" said Galen.

"Yaw," said I.

"Aboot der vatches, Mr. Fielding?" exclaimed Bol.

"Let that matter stand till we bury the captain."

"Ay, ay, sir. Galen is der man, I belief."

"He vhas villing," said Galen.

I left the deck for a few minutes to view the body of my poor friend in his sea-shroud. Miss Aurora sat at the table. She drummed with her brilliant fingers, and her head rested on her left hand. Her face was unusually pale; her eyes large, alarmed, and fiery, and blacker, owing to her pallor, than they commonly showed.

"What is it?" said I, conceiving that something was wrong with her.

"*Ave Maria*, hark!" cried she.

I heard Galloon whining and complaining. Never did a more melancholy, depressing, heart-subduing noise thread the conflicting uproar of a ship in labour. I at once let Galloon into the captain's cabin, and paused a minute to view the shrouded figure upon which the dog had sprung; and I remember thinking to myself: "Great is the difference between the dead at sea and the dead ashore. At sea the dead man cannot be tyrannous; but ashore, how does he serve his relatives and the world which he leaves behind? A dismal funeral bell is rung for him, and the spirits of a whole district are dejected – the spirits of a wide district that may never have his name, or that, very well knowing his name, values not his loss at the paring of a finger nail, are sunk because of that dreadful knell. He obliges his survivors to draw down the blinds of the house in which he expires, and, for the inside of a week, they sit in gloom, a sort of pariahs, coming and going with fugitive swiftness, miserable all, until it is *convenient* to him to be buried. He defrauds his next of kin of good money by the obligation of a solemn and expensive funeral. He tyrannically robs his relatives by obliging them to put up a memorial to him. But at sea? A piece of canvas and a twenty-four pound shot; a little hole in the water, which is gone ere the eye can behold it! The dead cannot be tyrannous at sea."

"Señor Fielding," said my lady Aurora, rising and holding my arm as I was about to pass, "I cannot rest down here with the dead."

She did not thus speak, but this was my interpretation of her words and signs. I regarded her and considered. Where could she lie, if not in the cabin? This, for her, was a miserable, horrible time; in as wild a passage of shipwreck and adventure as ever woman lived through, and my heart pitied her. It mattered not when the captain should be buried; and, meeting her eyes again, and beholding the superstition and fear in them, I looked up at the clock, that showed the hour to be a little after ten, and, holding up my hands and afterward two fingers, I said, "*Doce de la noche* – twelve of the night;" and, pointing and signing, gave her to know that at midnight we would bury the captain.

She looked at me gratefully,

"I must go," said I.

"Stop – oh, stop a minute!" she exclaimed in English, and went to her berth, looking fearfully toward the door of the captain's cabin as she made her way, clinging and moving slowly, for very fierce and sharp at times was the jump of the deck.

Strange, thought I, that the flight of a soul should make a terror of the shell it quits! It would be the same with that fine-eyed woman, with her aves and crossings. She dies; and the caballero on his knees at her feet, the gallant cavalier who has courage enough for the holding of her sweetness and her perfections to his heart while her charms live, springs to his legs, fetches a wide compass to avoid the corpse, and sooner than sleep a night beside the body would go to a lunatic asylum for the rest of his days.

She came out of her berth clothed for the deck, wrapped up in her own comfortable slop-chest manufactures, but half an hour of the cold and blackness above sufficed; she went below again and sat under the clock waiting for midnight. I chose twelve because all hands would be astir at that hour. At twelve the starboard watch went below; Yan Bol would come aft, and then we'd bury the dead. Meanwhile I ordered a couple of the seamen in my watch to load the four nine-pounder carronades, that we might dispatch Greaves with a sailor's honours to his bed of ooze. Lanterns were lighted and hung in the gangway in readiness.

In those times the burial at sea, in such craft as the *Black Watch*, was a simple affair. Whether it was the captain at the top or the cabin boy at the bottom, it mattered not; it was just a plain, respectful launch over the rail, no prayers, a sail at the mast, and there was an end. We had no book containing the burial service aboard. Few merchantmen went to sea with such things. I thought over a prayer or two as I walked the deck, meaning that the petition of a brother-sailor's heart should attend the launch of the canvassed figure; in which, and in many other thoughts the time slipped by; the lady Aurora all the while sitting below under the clock, waiting for midnight, often lifting her black alarmed eyes to the skylight, and often looking around her with a slow motion of her head, and at long intervals crossing herself. This picture of her the frame of the skylight gave me. The glass was bright and the light of the lamp strong.

Eight bells were struck, and presently the shapeless bulk of Bol came through the lantern-light upon the main-deck. It was the blackest hour of a black night. Even the foam, lifting and sinking alongside in sheets, scarcely showed. We had made a fair wind with a shift of helm at eight in the evening, and were bruising and rolling through it at about nine knots, with a broad, dim, spectral glare under the stern.

"Is that you, Bol?"

"He vhas, Mr. Fielding."

"I propose to bury my poor friend at once. The lady cannot rest, with the body below. It will be a kindness to her, to all of us may be, and no wrong to him. Nay, God forbid – if I believed it hurried – but a few hours more or less can signify nothing."

"Noting. Der crew vhas pleased too."

"Well, get the body up – with all reverence, Bol; you know what to do."

I called to Jimmy to smother Galloon as before and stow him out of the road of the men till the body was on deck, and then I stationed Joseph Street and Isaac Travers at the carronades, to discharge them when the body left the plank. In ten minutes they brought him up; four carried him, and one was Bol. The *señorita* came on deck, and holding by my arm to steady herself, spoke to me. I said "yonder," and she went into the light cast by the lanterns on the lee side of the deck, and stood with her hand upon a rope.

They carried the body to the gangway where the lanterns were, and I went with them and they put one end of the plank on the top of the rail and two of them held the other end, ready to tilt it. I think all the seamen had drawn together to view this midnight burial. Antonio and Jorge were close to a lantern. They sometimes crossed themselves, and their eyes gleamed and restlessly rolled. They seemed heartily frightened. The others stood stolid and staring, some in shadow, some touched by the lantern beams. All hands bared their heads when the corpse came to the gangway.

Had this funeral happened in daylight I should have ordered the topsail to be backed. I agree with those who hold that the ship's way should be stopped when the body is launched. It would have been, however, but the idlest of ceremonies to back the topsail in this deep midnight hour. There was besides a large sea running, the fresh wind was off the quarter, and the brig would have needed a shift of the helm to have got an effectual stand out of her backed canvas.

Cold, oh how bitterly cold did that night grow on a sudden with the presence of that body, pale on its plank in the lantern light! A wilder cry sounded in the wind, a deeper dye entered the darkness, I prayed aloud briefly, but not for the hearing of the men: the hiss of the sweeping water alongside drowned my voice.

"Launch!" I cried.

As the canvas figure fled like a wreath of white smoke from the rail a sunbright flash of fire threw out the whole brig: the roar of a gun followed.

At that instant – at the instant of the explosion of the carronade – and while the two fellows who had tilted the body paused for a moment or two, grasping the end of the plank, a dark form seemed to spring from the deck at my feet; it gained the plank in a bound, and went overboard.

"Der dok!" roared one of the Dutchmen.

The second gun was exploded with a deafening roar.

"Was that Galloon?" I shouted.

"It was, sir," answered two or three voices.

"Hold your hand," I bawled to the fellow at the third carronade.

I sprang on to the rail to look over. No sanity in *that*, for what was there to see, what did I expect to see? We were going at nine knots an hour: the spread of yeast on either hand of us was a wild and roaring race that throbbed out of sight in the darkness abeam within a biscuit's toss, and that fled and vanished into the darkness abaft, within the span of the brig's main-deck.

"Are you sure it was the dog?" I cried from the rail.

"Yes, sir; yes, sir, it was the dog – it was Galloon," was the answer.

"It was the dog," cried Miss Aurora, coming close to me.

"Oh, poor Galloon!" I was struck to the heart. For some moments I stood motionless, staring into the blackness, while the brig stormed onward, rolling and foaming through the night. Was there nothing to be done? Nothing, I vow to God. Perilous it might have been to bring the brig to the wind in that hollow sea: but to save Galloon, who had saved my life, I would have risked the brig, the treasure in her, nay, the lives within her, so wild was I then. But the dog could not have been rescued without lowering a boat, and a boat stood to be swung and smashed into staves ere a soul entered her; and consider also the blackness of the Cape Horn night that lay upon the ocean!

"Are these guns to be fired, sir?"

"No. Oh, lads, I would not have lost that dog for twentyfold my share of the money below. He saved my life – he's still swimming out there – he's alive out there and may live. Where's Jimmy?"

"Blubbering here, sir," said a voice.

A couple of seamen ran him into the lantern light; I could have killed him.

"Did not I tell you to stow Galloon away?"

"So I did, master."

"Why is he perishing out yonder then, you villain?"

I turned my back and walked aft.

Chapter XXV.
Aurora Entertains Us

I'LL NOT swear I did not feel the loss of the dog more than I felt the death of Greaves. Should I be ashamed to own it? The captain's death I had long expected; it came without suddenness, it brought no astonishment. But the loss of Galloon happened in a breath. He was here, and then he was gone. He had gathered a human significance from my long association with him, my spoken reveries to which he seemed to listen, loving of eye and patient. For days and nights I was haunted by the thoughts of him, swimming round and round in that dark sea. He swam well, and I say that it was long an agony to think of him struggling out in that foaming water.

The lad Jimmy was broken hearted. So crushed was he that I had no heart to deal with him for indirectly causing the dog's death. For days he'd snatch minutes at a time to stand at the rail just where the plank had rested, just where Galloon had sprung overboard, and there he'd gaze astern with his face working and his eyes bubbling. The men let this maudlin behaviour pass without jeering. They reckoned him half an idiot. Yet the chap's grief went deep. He was alone in the world, and had nothing to love. Greaves had been kind to him, but he could not love the captain as he loved the captain's dog. Galloon had been his friend. Often used the lad to talk to him as a negro talks to a monkey or a pig. They'd lie together on deck, and had slept together, and now the dog was gone the boy's heart ached. He looked around him: there was no friend; he sent his fancies ashore and found himself alone there.

On the morning following Greaves' funeral I took possession of his cabin. I spent a couple of hours in overhauling his papers, for I could not bring myself to believe that he had been without a relative in the world, Tulp excepted. I could not realize such a thing as a man without a relation in the whole blessed wide world. Yet I found nothing to tell me that Greaves had not been alone. I carefully stowed his papers away with his clothes and other effects. To whom belonged his little property – his clothes, his books, his nautical instruments, and the like, together with a bag of thirty odd guineas and a quantity of English silver? To whom, I say? To Tulp?

I found nothing to connect Greaves with a home, with relatives, with friends – no miniature, no lock of hair, no memorial of ribbon or bauble. Never once had he hinted at any love passage. He'd speak of women with coldness, though with respect, as the child of a woman. Had you walked him through King Solomon's seraglio he'd have seen nothing worth choosing. Well, the yeast that had hissed to the plunge of his shape was his tombstone. He was bred a sailor, he had lived the life of a sailor, and was now gone the way of a sailor; yea, and true even in death was he unto the traditions of the sailor – for he had received the last toss, the sea had swallowed him up, and no man could swear that his name was as he had styled himself, nor affirm with conviction whose son he was.

When I had made an end with the captain's papers and effects I put on my cap, buttoned up my pea-coat, and went on deck. It was blowing a strong, fair wind. The brig still wore the canvas she had carried throughout the night. The sea ran high, it was much freckled with foam, and its frothing brows shone out like a hard light against the cold dark-green vapour to windward.

Bol paced the deck, thickly clothed. He wore great boots, had a heavy fur cap on, and a fathom of shawl was coiled round his immensely thick throat. He fitted the picture of that pitching and storming brig as the brig fitted the picture of that swollen and foaming sea. There was no sun. The dark clouds rushed rapidly across the sky; they were of the soft blackness of the snow cloud; the bands of topsails, the square of the topgallant sail, of a light sick as the gleam of misty moonshine, fled from side to side athwart the flying sky of shadow. The sea stood up in walls of ivory to every plunge of the bows – I never before saw foam look so solid. Where the bubble and foam-bell of it were too remote for the eye, *there* every ridge was like a cliff of marble.

Bol appeared surprised to see me. He supposed I was turned in.

"This is a wind to clap Staten Island in our wake."

"Potsblitz! as der Shermons say, dere vhas veight in dese seas too."

"Do you mean to live aft?"

"In der landt of spoon?" said he, with a smile wrinkling his face till he was scarcely the same man.

"Yaw. There is a cabin and bunk for your mattress. You are mate – first mate, entitled to live aft."

"I shtops where I vhas, Mr. Fielding. I vhas no mate."

"As much mate as I was."

"Veil, dot might be," said he; then added, "No, you vhas mate in your last ship. I am bos'en. I belongs forwardt."

"I want a second mate. Send the men aft, will you."

He went into the waist and put his pipe to his lips. His roar was like the voice of a giant singing the tune of the wind in the rigging. The men knocked off the several jobs they were on and came aft.

The fellows had a homely, comfortable appearance. The slop-chest had supplied the vacancies in their own bags, and they were clad as men who were starting on, not returning from, a long voyage. Their health was good. Some were fat, all hearty. I scanned them swiftly but with attention, and saw nothing to occasion uneasiness; and I believe I could not be mistaken, for of all living beings the sailor is the most transparent in his moods and meanings. A few I have known who were dark and subtle; they were not Englishmen, neither were they Dutchmen. The English sailor gets a face at sea that prohibits the concealment of feelings and passions, and, on board the merchant ship, he will look the thing that is in him.

"Am I captain? Is it understood?"

"Ay, captain, of course," exclaimed Teach after a pause, as though the men had waited for one of them to act as spokesman. "If not you, who? and if it's who, vhere do 'ee sling his hammock? Not forrads. All the larnin's been washed aft ont o'that."

"Mr. Yan Bol is your chief mate."

"Ay, Mr. Yan Bol is chief mate. Who but him?" said Teach.

"Now choose a second mate, lads."

"Is he to live aft?" said Friend.

"That's as he chooses."

"There'll be no man wants to live aft," exclaimed Street.

"I will live aft," said Antonio.

"Yaw, towed in der vake, you beastly man," thundered Bol. "Dot was aft for der likes of you."

"I will live aft, *señor*," said Antonio.

"Curse your impudence, I'll aft ye. Now, look. There are four Dutchmen and seven Englishmen, not reckoning two Spaniards."

"Don't count them Johnnies, sir," said Travers.

"It vhas oudt dey go mit dem soon, I allow," said Hals, the cook.

Paying no attention to these interruptions, I continued:

"A Dutchman is already mate. If I choose another Dutchman you Englishmen mayn't like it. Now then."

"Choose, sir," exclaimed Call.

"I choose Galen," said I.

There was a general grin, and Friend called out:

"We're satisfied."

"Then Galen it is," said I. "Galen, you now act second. Will you live aft, Galen?"

"May I pe dommed if I lifs aft!" exclaimed he, with a wide grin and a slow wag of his head.

"All right; that'll do. You can go forward;" and I went below, very well satisfied with the Dutchmen's refusal to live aft. Not for my own sake; indeed, there was a laugh here and there to be got out of the ignorance and talk and strange English of Bol and of Galen. I thought of my lady Aurora. How would *she* enjoy the company of those Dutchmen at table, the society of those heavy, lumpish forecastle hands, half-boors, half-savages? I suppose that never before in the history of marine disaster was a girl situated as was this *señorita*. Are you who read this a girl? Figure yourself, madam, on board a little ship; you are scarcely able to speak the tongue of the crew; your only associate is a rough seaman, your sitting room is a small, old-fashioned cabin, your bedroom a bit of a hole up in a corner, lighted by an eye called a scuttle, that winks at the leaping sea, your meals the pork and beef of the ocean, your diversions the fancies that come out of the running hills of water of the gale, out of the silent, swimming surface of the calm. Can you imagine the ceaseless heaving of the deck, the long days of the crying of the wind, the creaking and straining of a tumbling timber-built craft, the sullen roar of smitten and parted waters, the indescribable odours of the hold?

When I left the deck that day, after calling the men aft and choosing Galen to act as second mate, on stepping below, I found the lady Aurora leaning against the door of the cabin, with her arms folded upon her breast and her eyes fixed upon the deck. She did not immediately see me. I stood viewing her. She was attired in a white drill, or duck dress of her own making. It would have been cold wear but for certain hidden clothing she had contrived for herself. She looked a fine figure of a woman. She lifted up her eyes, released her breast from the embrace of her arms, and extended her hand. I brought her to a seat – it was what she wanted – and sat beside her.

We sat together for near an hour, because we both had something to say, and it took us long to communicate our minds, though, to be sure, these passages of laborious intercourse were never teasing or fatiguing to me, however *she* may have found them; for there was a pleasure not hard to understand in the mere watching her face when she talked or signed to me. Her expressions were rich and manifold; her eyes darkened, softened, brightened, shone with fire, dimmed as with tears, like the figure of a star in the sea over which the scattered mists of the calm night are floating.

But here will I put into plain English the words and signs we exchanged while we sat together at this time. It may well come to it, for I understood her and I know what myself said. Thus, then, ran this conversation:

"Señor Fielding, have the men rebelled?"

"No, why do you ask?"

"I stepped up yonder stairs just now and saw you talking to the men."

"It is true. I am captain, Bol is mate, someone must be chosen to take Bol's place."

But, oh, the time and difficulty to make her understand this!

"I am very sad today, Señor Fielding. The death of the captain makes me think of my mother. Most blessed and very purest Maria, does she live? Shall we meet again? Ay me, ay me," and here the tears stood in her eye.

"*Señorita*, this is what I wish to say to you. I have not the fears of the captain who is dead. If we meet a ship of your nation, if we meet a ship of any country sailing to Spain, or proceeding to a port in South America, east or west, I will put you on board her if she will take you."

"*Gracias*. I am content to stop."

"You are alone."

"It is true, *señor*." (Sigh.)

"There are few comforts for you in this ship."

"True, true, 'tis true. Yet could I be content if I knew my mother was alive."

"If you are content I am glad. I do not wish to speak a ship, yet I'll do so."

"No – I will go home in the *Black Watch*."

"I admire your spirit. You have borne up very bravely."

"To you belongs my gratitude, Señor Fielding. Throughout you have been amiable and tender. The poor captain liked me not. Why was that?" and here she bent her eyes upon me; their expression was a mixture of archness and temper.

"He was in pain, was a little crazy, and would not always be sure of the reasons of his moods."

"I am not used not to be liked." I bowed a very full acquiescence. "He was not as you are. But he is dead." Her hand flashed as she swept it before her face, dismissing the subject with a gesture. "Now that you are captain you will have plenty of leisure."

"I shall have time to spare."

"*Vaya!* Time to spare – and yet command! I shall want you to give me much of your time."

I looked at her eyes and laughed when I gathered her meaning, and answered: "All the spare time I have shall be yours, *señorita*. But how much of that spare time will it take to make you weary of my face and voice?"

"*Qué disparate!* (What nonsense!) You shall teach me English, and I will teach you Spanish."

"*Bueno!* Yet what is the reason of your desire to speak English?"

To this she made no answer. She cast her eyes down, and her face took a demure look.

"It is a rough language."

"It is a noble language, *señor*," said she, answering with her eyes cast down. Suddenly she looked up: the leap of her glance was like the light of a flash of fire upon her face, so swift and cunning was she in the management of her eyelids. "Do you love music?"

"Yes."

"I will sing to you when it is calm, and when you can hear my voice."

I thanked her for this promise.

"Are we not alone? We will be company one to the other. I have the actress's art, and can recite, and when you know some Spanish I will speak many beautiful and majestic lines to you. Have you playing-cards?"

"I fear not."

"*Eso me soprende mucho!* Many tiresome hours could we have killed with cards. Can you dance?"

"All sailors can dance."

"I will make you an accomplished cavalier. I will teach you to tell fortunes after the manner of the zingari, and you shall teach me English, and give me your company until I tire, or until the ship calls you from me."

We broke off here that I might fetch my quadrant, for it was drawing on to the hour of noon. Our conversation was not as I have set it down; it took us a long while to work our way through the above; but what you have read is the substance of what was meant and by our methods conveyed.

I went on deck puzzled and tickled, amused and astonished by the gay-spirited, fine woman below. Did she mean to make love to me? Did she intend that I should make love to her? What would my teaching her English and her teaching me Spanish, her singing to me, her recital of swelling Spanish rhymes, her gypsy tricks, and the rest of it end in – the rest of it, I say, backed by her impassioned eyes, the many arch and moving and tender and fiery expressions of countenance she was mistress of, her excellent person, and all that sort of sweet rhetoric which is found, the poet tells you, in the laughter and tears, the smiles and gesticulations, of a lady after the pattern of this Spanish maiden?

I took my quadrant on deck; the sun did not show himself, and I got at the situation of the brig by dead reckoning. The westerly gale blew fresh and strong, and I needed to keep the vessel under the tall canvas of the topgallant sail to run her free of the huge Horn surge, which chased us as though to the hurl of an earthquake. It was impossible to make too much of such a wind; at any moment might come a greasy Horn calm with a swell like a land of hills; to be swept with horrible suddenness by a black outfly right ahead. I saw no ice; the horizon lay open, distant seven or eight miles from the head of a sea. We were cutting the meridians spankingly, and three days of such sailing would enable me to head the brig northward for England.

And very nearly three days of such sailing did we get, during which nothing noteworthy happened, for the plain reason that so heavy and violent were the motions of the brig, the most seasoned among us found it difficult to come and go. Relieving tackles were hooked on; two hands steered day and night, and a third was always near in readiness. I have seen the gigantic feathering curl of the huge sea soar on either hand alongside to half the height of the foremast and fall aboard in froth, making it all sheer dazzle, like snow shone on, from the eyes to the main rigging, till the tilt of the brig aft, courtesying with her bows flat as a spoon upon the roaring smother of the on-rushing sea, sent the water in a cataractal sweep over the head, where it blew up in white smoke and drove away as though we were on fire.

This was a sort of weather to keep everything very quiet aboard. Hals cooked with difficulty; he scalded himself, broke dishes, and filled the caboose with Dutch oaths. The cold was bitter, and the chief work of the crew lay in keeping themselves warm. Yet no ice formed; no hail or snow ever drove in the sudden dark squalls which burst in guns of hurricane power out of the gale over the stern; we sighted not a berg, and yet the cold was frightful; the wind took the face like a saw, and you felt half flayed when you turned your back to it. The cold of the spray made its drops sting like lead, and it was as though you were shot through the head to be struck by a showering of the brine.

Her ladyship kept below. She saw very little of me; in those three days we made no progress in English and Spanish. The violent upheavals of the brig frightened her; then did her eyes grow large, her face look wild; if I was near her she'd grasp me and hold on to me and utter many exclamations in Spanish. I'd catch myself smiling afterward when I thought of those moments; how she used me as though we had grown up, boy and girl, together, never timid in her tricks of touching me, as free with me as a sister, and that's about it.

We were in longitude sixty-three or sixty-four degrees west when the westerly gale shifted into the north, and the wind blew in a moderate breeze out of that quarter. The cold lessened with the shift. The sailors moved with some trifle of alacrity, as though they were thawing. The decks dried, we shook out reefs, made sail, coiled down anew fore-and-aft; the smoke blew cheerily from the chimney of the caboose, and with taut running gear and white clothes robing her to the topgallant mastheads the brig renewed her comfortable, homely look.

This brought us to the afternoon of what I will call the third day of the gale. I had eaten some supper, talked awhile with my lady, visited my cabin, and returned on deck after an examination of the chart, resolved on a bit more of easting before changing the course.

When I passed through the companion way I heard Bol's voice. He and Galen stood at the bulwarks abreast of the hatch, their faces to the sea, and they conversed in Dutch, keeping their voices down and talking very earnestly. The large swell rolled quietly under the brig; the wind silenced the sails, and after the uproar of the preceding days the repose along the decks and up aloft was almost as the hush of a tropic calm upon the vessel.

I stepped to the binnacle. Teach, who was at the wheel, cleared his throat noisily and spat over the taffrail. The Dutchmen looked, and Galen, saying something sharp and quick in Dutch, walked forward. Bol glanced aloft with the air of a man in search of work for his watch; I walked a few paces his way, and he approached me.

"How vhas der vetter to be, sir?"

"The sky is high and hard, and the sun strikes clear fire into the west. Look at the edge of the sea; it sweeps clean as the rim of a new dollar. There is fine weather about."

"Veil, so much der better, Mr. Fielding. I have slept in more comfortable fo'c'sles dan vhas dis of der *Black Vatch* vhen she pitches heavy – more comfortable, but I doan say drier. No; der toyfell shall not pe more plack dan she vhas bainted. Dis vhas a dry brick, und dare vhas no schmarter sailor out of Amsterdam."

"I believe you."

He looked about him to let me see he did not heed the brig the less for talking. I was willing he should talk. I saw matter in his huge full face, and guessed, if he chattered, he might let me come presently at what had passed 'twixt him and Galen.

"Mr. Fielding, how far might she be from der Horn to der Channel?"

"A long stride. Would you have it as the crow flies? How many hundreds of miles will the zigzags of a ship tag on to a straight-line measurement?"

"Yaw, dot's how it vhas. No man at sea can say how far – she vhas from home. Der Cape of Goodt Hope, Mr. Fielding – dot, now, vhas a vast great roon from here?"

"Yaw; the whole width of the South Atlantic."

"She vhas vide."

"I'll teach you how to measure distances on a chart, if you like."

"Vell, I likes to know; but I doan believe dot I recollects tomorrow vhat you teaches him today. Mr. Fielding, vhere vhas Amsderdam Island?"

"Amsderdam Island?"

"Yaw. Der Doytch fell in mit her – veil, call it a hoondred year ago."

"There is an Amsterdam Island in the Indian Ocean."

"Dot vhas her."

"What of it?"

"Nothing, sir. Galen vhas saying how der Doytch vhas everywhere mit der names. New Holland, Amsderdam Island – look how dey roon."

"True," said I.

"Mind your luff, my ladt!" he called in thunder to Teach. "How vhas her headt?"

"East by north," answered Teach.

"East she vhas, und noting off."

He upturned his face to the canvas with an expression which let me see that certain whale-like thoughts were coming up to blow from the dark and oozy deep of his mind.

"Oxcuse me, Mr. Fielding – mit regard to der dollars. You promised a leedle vhile ago to talk mit me about der landing of dot silver vhen ve arrives,"

"What do you want to know?"

"Veil, Mr. Fielding, it vhas like dis. All handts vould like to know how dey vhas to be baid dere shares. If der money vhas schmuggled on shore, who bays me und der men? Dis vhas your peesiness like as ours, for you too shall ask who vhas to bay you herself?"

"On our arrival in the Downs," said I, willing to give him the information he desired, pleased, indeed, that he should seek it, since the manner of his question gave a new turn to my fancies of him, "I shall communicate with Mynheer Tulp and await his instructions."

"Suppose he vhas deadt?"

"I will suppose nothing. Tulp is alive until we know he is dead; and when we know that he is dead we will think of what's next to be done."

"Veil, dot's straight-hitting. I like her."

"You shall suppose Tulp alive. He will come on wings from the city of Amsterdam; and, when he is on board, every man will take his share of the dollars according to his paper of proportion. Tulp touches not one dollar until he pays us our share. We will then hold him to carry out whatever schemes he prearranged with Captain Greaves."

"Vell, dot vhas all right; but, Mr. Fielding, der ship's company likes to know if dere vhas any reesk vhen you gets her home?"

"Whom home?"

"Der money."

"Risk? I don't understand."

"Veil, dey puts it as she might pe dis vay. Ve vhas in der Downs. A boat cooms alongside, und somepody climbps on poardt und oxes, 'Vhat vhas your cargo?' 'Dot vhas my peesiness,' you say. 'Not at all,' he answers. 'I vhas a King's officer, I belongs to der Revenue.' How vhas it, den, mit her, der ship's company vould like to know, Mr, Fielding?"

"We should not be searched for cargo in the Downs – for men, perhaps; but who would meddle with the cargo?"

"Ay; but how vhas you to know dot for certain, sir?"

"Let us arrive in the Downs. The rest will be easy. Our difficulty lies in getting home. We are still fighting the Yankees, no doubt."

"Ay; but he vhas a Doytchman, Mr. Fielding."

"I hope whoever boards us will believe it," said I, with a shrug of the shoulders; and, catching sight at that instant of a dim, yellow spot against the sky across the round, large heads of the swell, I fetched the glass, and made out the object to be a ship bound westward. I watched her until she died out in the red air.

Bol drew off and we talked no more. His questions and remarks had struck me as honest, very natural, and to the point, seeing that the men expected him to speak what was in their minds, and that their united stake in the successful finish of this adventure, now that the money was aboard, was considerable. I did not perhaps much relish the persistent manner in which he had "Mr. Fielding'd" me. I could have wished him a little blunter. When Yan Bol gave me my name very often, distrust arose. On the other hand, there was nothing in his own suggestions nor in the fears of the crew to render me uneasy as to the safe disposal of the cargo of silver, should I be fortunate enough to reach the Downs. What excuse could be invented for overhauling a ship's cargo while she lay at anchor in those waters? You look for the wolves of the Revenue as you warp into dock; you look for them in the Pool; but I had never heard of them in the Downs – that is, I had never heard of them boarding a ship *there* to seek contraband matter.

A quiet evening came down upon the brig: the stars were many and glorious; there was a bright moon, and the temperature and the look of the heavens might have persuaded me we were ten degrees further north than where we were rolling. The brig was under all plain sail. The wind was about north, a moderate breeze, and the vessel pushed her way softly over the wide swell.

I brought the lady Aurora on deck for a walk, when the sun had been sunk about half an hour. All hands were enjoying the moonlight and the quiet weather. They paced in couples; they came together in groups and halted for a yarn; the hum of their conversation was a deep and eager note; but all the talk was subdued – I caught no sudden calls. Now and again a man laughed, and there was a frequent lighting of pipes by the flames of burning rope-yarns. The brig was made an ivory carving of by the moon. Every plank might have been chiselled out of the tusk of the elephant. Stars of silver glittered and swam in the glass of the skylight. The swell came along like folds of ink, but as every shoulder of black water swung into the glory of the moon's wake it flashed into a shining hill, and the splendour of those vast shapes was the more wonderful for the blackness out of which they rolled and the blackness in which they vanished.

Miss Aurora walked by my side; presently the play of the deck obliged her to take my arm. Galen had charge; he stepped to leeward out of the road of our weather walk and lay against the rail abreast of the wheel. The weariness of the sea was in that man's figure. As he stood there or leaned, the mere posture only of the clothes and the fat of him expressed with extraordinary force the sickening monotony, the profound dullness of the calling of the sea as that calling was in those years. The iteration of the ocean line; the ceaseless groan and heave of the timber fabric under one's foot; the eye-wearying flight of the sails to the masthead; the weeks and months of the same thing over and over again, ocean and sky, darkness and light, the weeping of mist, roar of wind, the cold of the dawn; the beef and the pork, the pork and the beef – it was *all* in that Dutchman's figure.

After we had walked the deck for half an hour the *señorita* informed me that she felt cold, and that the movements of the ship made her legs ache, and she proposed that we should go below and that I should give her a lesson in English. When we had entered the lighted cabin she saw in my face that I was in no particular humour to teach her English just then. She was quick in reading me: this had come about through much of our talk having been carried on with our faces. In truth, while I had walked with her on deck my thoughts had gone to Bol's questions about the disposal of the money, and my spirits had drooped a bit.

But her ladyship was not to be put off; she must coax me into an easy mind, and then no doubt I would give her a lesson in English. She removed the cap she had contrived out of the yield of the slop-chest, and turned herself about that I might help to take off the heavy pilot-cloth jacket which she had likewise cut and contrived for herself as you have heard. When this was done she seated herself abreast of the lamp, and laughing, and looking at me with sparkling eyes, she made me understand that if I would give her my hand she would tell my fortune.

I did not much like to give her my hand; it was coarse and horny with the toil of the sea. I extended the palms at a safe distance, and by motions informed her that the lines of the hand had been worn out – smoothed to the quality of the sole of an old boot by many years of pulling and hauling, by grasping the spokes of wheels, by the fingering of canvas, and the handling of capstan bars.

"No, no," she cried, "give me your hand, Señor Fielding."

So I went round the table and sat beside her. I winced when she took my hand; the contrast between my square-ended fist and her delicate fingers was a shock. She held my hand and pored upon it. The skylight was shut, and Galen probably thought that I did not observe him looking down at us. Holding my hand, her dark and shining eyes sometimes bent upon the palm of it, sometimes lifted full of archness and quiet mirth to my face, the lady Aurora told me my fortune. I comprehended but little of what she said; she spoke much in Spanish, motioned with one arm – always retaining my hand – viewed me with a face that was forever changing its expression, and occasionally she let fall certain English words. I guessed from what she said that I was to be rich, marry a handsome lady without money, have six children, and live to be a very old man.

Jimmy came into the cabin while she held my hand, and gaped at us from the bottom of the companion ladder. I bade him put wine, biscuits, and the material for grog upon the table and then clear out. When the lady was done with my hand she went to her berth and returned with a log book – a new volume of blank leaves headed for entries – which I had given to her out of several in Greaves' cabin.

"Now, Señor Fielding," said she in English, "you shall give me a lesson;" and, sitting down, she examined the point of her pencil and adjusted herself with the air of a lady who means business.

I glanced at the clock, poured out a glass of wine, and placed it on a swing tray in front of her, mixed myself a tumbler of grog, and took a seat over against her. The lesson consisted of dictation. I'd pronounce a sentence deliberately; she'd take it down: hand me the book; then our faces would meet across the table over the book, while I pointed out the blunders in spelling, and explained the meaning of such words as she did not know. She had filled several pages of the book on her own account, and some pages on mine.

The romance of it all! What more romantic as a detail of ocean life would you have? Realize that little moonlighted brig rolling over the black heaven of the sea, Cape Horn not far off, the Cross and the Magellanic dust overhead, nothing in sight, the moon's wake coiling in hills of silver under her, and in the heart of that lonely speck of brig two young people, again and again nearly rubbing cheeks together over a blank log book: one of them a fine, handsome Spanish woman, with dark eyes of fire and a smile that was like light with its swift disclosure of white teeth, and a beautiful little pale yellow hand that shone with jewels; and the other – and the other – .

She looked at the clock, and started, with a Spanish exclamation, and said, "I will sing. You have been good. I will sing to you." All this she said in English. Then, in dumb show, she played a phantom guitar, gazing at me with one of those asking looks which I could interpret as easily as I took sights. I shook my head to her signification of a guitar, and played on an imaginary fiddle; on which she nodded, crying with vivacity in Spanish, "It will do! It will do!"

I put my head into the hatch and called for Jimmy. Galen sent the name forward in a roar, and the boy arrived.

"Borrow me a fiddle," said I.

When he returned he held a fiddle and a fiddlestick; but this unusual appeal of the cabin to the forecastle had roused curiosity, and a number of the men followed Jimmy to the quarter-deck. I heard their softened footfalls, and caught a glimpse of their figures as they stood round about the skylight, scarce sensible that they were visible through the black glass. The lady took the fiddle and the bow from the lad, who withdrew. She put the fiddle to her neck, tuned it, and played a short, merry air. I had not known that she played the fiddle. I guessed she had asked for the instrument to twang an accompaniment upon. She played a second sweet and merry air; the melody was full of beauty and humour. Someone overhead tapped the deck in time to it. I took care not to look up, willing that the fellows should listen, though they had no business aft.

"How do you like that?" said the lady in Spanish.

"It is sweet and good. Give me more."

She put down the bow, and, laying the fiddle across her knees, twanged it. She kept her eyes fastened upon me, and, when she had tweaked the fiddlestrings, she shrugged her shoulders and laughed; then, before the laugh had fairly left her lips, she burst into song, singing with that clear, full-throated richness of voice which poor Greaves had predicted her the possessor of. She filled the cabin with her song. She would have filled the biggest theatre in Europe with it. Her voice was thrilling with volume and power, and her eyes were full of a gay triumph as she sang, as though she would say, "This is news to you, my friend."

I thought her spirit the most remarkable part of the performance. Here was a lady – a young and handsome woman, clearly a person of degree in her own country – amusing a young, rough sailor with her songs, fiddling to him, taking lessons in English from him, watching him with shining eyes, as though her heart was as charged with light as her gaze. Her voice, her face, the aroma of her manner, transformed the plain, grim little cabin of the brig into a brilliant drawing room, full of ladies and gentlemen, sweet with the scent of flowers, gay with the gleam of silk and jewel and epaulet. Who, while she sang, would have supposed that she had been shipwrecked not very long ago, living, with small hopes of deliverance, upon a desert island, in company with a couple of common, low seamen; ignorant whether her mother was alive or dead; still many thousands of miles away from her home – if Madrid was to be her home; with twenty hard fortunes before her, for all she knew?

She sang me three songs, and all hands, as I knew by the shuffling of feet, listened above, some shouldering warily into the companion hatch to hear well. I reckoned she knew she had a bigger audience than I, for once she lifted her eyes in the pause of a song and smiled in a conscious way.

"Now I am tired," said she in English, and put the fiddle upon the table with capricious quickness of movement. "Goodnight, Señor Fielding" and she gave me a low, but somewhat haughty bow, and went to her cabin, stepping the short length of the deck with the most translatable carriage in life: "*I have amused you, I have condescended; but I am always the Señorita Aurora de la Cueva. Vaya!*"

Chapter XXVI.
A Tragic Shift of Course

ALL WENT well with us through the month of February and through the early days of March in that year of God, 1815, until it came to pass that we arrived in the latitude forty-five degrees south, and in longitude forty-seven degrees west.

I was very hopeful in this time. The crew had been orderly, civil, and quick; strong, prosperous winds had swept us round the Horn and northward; we were homeward bound; we were putting the unfamiliar stars of the south over our stern; already some were gone, and some wheeled low. I walked the deck with gladness, and knew but two sorrows: that Greaves was not at my side to share in the rich issue of his own discovery and his own expedition, and that my poor, faithful, well-loved Galloon was drowned.

Little wonder that my heart at this time felt light, that my spirits sometimes danced. Let me but bring the brig to a safe anchorage off Deal, and I might hope – failing frigates and presses – that my business was done. I should have taken a long farewell of the sea. I should be a rich man; for to me in those days, *six thousand pounds* of English money was a great sum – aye, beyond my utmost hopes by one cipher at least. Yes; and even had I dreamt of *six hundred pounds*, how was I to earn it? Never could I have saved so much money out of the slender wage of the ocean. Why, let me even knock off another cipher, and put the figure at *sixty pounds*. Do many Jacks, after years of bitter toil, limp ashore – curved in the back, one-eyed, maybe, half-fingerless, rotted to their marrow with the beastly food, the stinking water of the jolly life of the deep, rotted to the soul by nameless sins and the slum-and-alley seductions of a hundred ports – are there many Jacks, I ask, whose savings, after years of labour, amount to *sixty pounds*?

There is an irony of circumstance at sea as there is ashore; but at sea this sort of irony is bitterer than ashore, because nothing can happen at sea that lacks a colouring, more or less defined, of the fearful significance of life or death.

In proof whereof list, ye landsmen, to what I am about to relate.

You will suppose that so shrewd, intelligent, and diligent a lady as the Señorita Aurora would not need to be thrown much in the company of an Englishman, would not need to be long instructed by him, would not need to spend many hours in studying for herself, before she acquired a very respectable knowledge of the English tongue. And let me tell you that, by this time, though she spoke slowly, with many pauses, though she wanted many words, she was already become a very good listener when I discoursed in my own speech. How long should it take an intelligent Spanish lady to learn English – to talk it freely and correctly? I don't know. My lady Aurora began (in questions) the study of the language, as you may remember, in the beginning of January; and now, in these early days of March, she understood me when I talked to her; when I talked to her slowly and pronounced my words carefully, and when I helped her with a sign or a Spanish word here and there.

I'll call the date the 12th of March: it was a Friday; I sat at dinner with Madam Aurora. Dinner! – yet I must give even that pleasant name to the midday repast, to the piece of beef in whose mahogany texture lurked scurvy enough to lay low a watch, to the boiled duff and the several messes of the caboose. But then our stock of poultry was growing small; we had need to be frugal; we were in the unhappy condition of not daring, or not choosing if you will, to look into a port for the replenishment of coops and casks.

I sat with her ladyship, and we ate of the yield of the *Black Watch*'s cabin pantry. The day was fine; the sun sparkled white as silver upon the skylight. The royal yards were aloft, and the brig was sailing with her larboard topmast studding sail out, making very little noise as she went, so that talking was easy.

Times had been when Miss Aurora questioned me about the dollars in the lazarette. She had asked me for the name of the ship they came from: I had answered her. *La Perfecta Casada*. She had asked me for the story of Greaves' discovery, and by our methods of communication I had spun her the yarn. When I had spun her the yarn, she informed me that she had heard of the loss of a Spanish ship called *La Perfecta Casada*, with all hands, as it was supposed, but this said, the subject dropped, and we rarely afterward mentioned the matter of the treasure in the hold.

Now, while we were at dinner this day, we talked of her shipwreck. She said there had been a quantity of antique valuable furniture belonging to her mother on board; otherwise, saving clothes and jewellery, the Señora de la Cueva had embarked no property in the ship. She spoke of the captain and officers of the vessel. The captain was a worthless seaman, a timid, ill-tempered, swearing fellow, a native of the Manillas. We drifted from this subject of the wreck to *La Perfecta Casada*. Our conversation was animated, despite the frequent interruption of gesticulations, the many hindrances of words unintelligible through their pronunciation, the frequent pausings for the needful term. She requested me to describe the cave in which the *Casada* lay. I fetched paper and pencil, and drew it for her as best I could. Then she asked me the value of the treasure, and I told her very honestly that it rose to above half a million of dollars of the currency of her nation.

"*Ave Maria!*" cried she, "what wealth to discover in a cave. It is like a tale told by the Arabs, *Santa Maria Purissima!* What a treasure for a mariner of the orthodox faith to dedicate to the Church! You will receive a handsome portion, I trust?"

"I will receive a share," said I.

"And the poor Captain Greaves – had he a share!"

"A big share."

"It will go to his mother?"

"He had no relations. It will go to his Church."

Her eyes sparkled. "My Church!" she cried, pressing her forefinger to her breast.

"Mine," said I, imitating her action with my forefinger.

She shrugged her shoulders, looked at me fixedly, smiled, and gave me several nods in the foreign fashion.

I felt no reluctance in talking to her about the treasure. Indeed, I had never sympathized with Greaves' nervous caution in this way. It was not as if he and I alone had possessed the secret of the dollars: all hands knew there were fifteen tons of minted silver in the lazarette. What on earth was the use of concealing the fact from this Spanish Indy, as if she only of all the souls on board the brig was to be feared by and by as the intelligencer?

I was in high spirits that day: the sunshine in the heavens was upon my heart; I enjoyed the company of the handsome lady; I found a growing and a deepening pleasure in viewing her when she talked; I delighted in the music that her voice gave to her English. All was well and we were homeward bound. I had a mind to talk of my dollars and my prospects, and whether she guessed my wish or not she helped me to the subject by asking me how much my share would amount to.

"Many figures in dollars," said I, "and in British gold just a little fat figure."

"Shall you buy a ship?" said she, smiling.

"No," said I, looking earnestly at her; "I will marry a wife and settle down."

She clapped her hands, threw her head back, and laughed aloud. "*Qué disperate.* Cannot you make a better use of your money than purchasing a wife with it? Señor Fielding, you shall buy a fine ship and trade to the Indies and grow immensely rich. Marry! *Qué disperate.*" She threw back her head again, and laughed out.

"I'll buy no ship," said I. "I will marry a handsome woman, and live happily with her on the seashore. She and I will go a-fishing for pleasure. You are not a sailor: were you a sailor, you would think of nothing but a wife and a home of your own and money enough for meat, tobacco, and the rest."

"Your wife," said she, "shall be another *Perfecta Casada*: she shall make you more money than any woman can bring you. You'll die a Catholic, and your fortune shall build a magnificent cathedral;" and now, without another word, she abruptly rose, made me a low, strange bow, as though forsooth we had met for the first time in our brig five minutes before, and went to her cabin.

She was frequently puzzling me in this way. She'd abandon herself, so to speak; be all charm, naïveté, smiles, and graciousness, then abruptly look poniards and corkscrews, and with a sweep of her fine figure make off. Was it her theory of coquetry?

I went on deck with a half smile in my thought of her odd, abrupt, capricious withdrawal, and amused, too, with thinking of how I now managed to make out a clear conversation with a girl who, a few weeks before, pointed at things with her finger and talked to me with her eyes. The time was about twenty minutes before two. John Wirtz was at the wheel. Bol, whose watch it was, talked with Travers and Teach in the gangway. Travers and Teach were in Galen's watch. I was surprised to find them aft; further aft, I mean, than that they had aright to be, talking with Bol, whose business it was to keep a lookout. Galen was on the forecastle pacing to and fro, under the yawn of the fore-course, with Henry Call and James Meehan; Friend and the two Spaniards were squatted upon a sail in the waist, stitching at it. Both watches then were on deck, and all hands saving Jim Vinten, the cabin boy, visible.

I found something strange in this: yet had I taken time to reflect I might have seen that the strangeness lay rather in the bearing of the men than in the circumstance of all the crew being in sight. I looked aloft: every cloth was doing its work; the whiteness of the sails overflowed the boundaries of the bolt-ropes with light, and the azure of the sky was a pale silver against the edges of the canvas. The foam spitting from the nimble thrust of the cut-water shot by fast alongside; the brig was sailing well. I stood with my hands upon one of the shrouds of the main, my eyes upon the sea line: turning a minute or two later I saw Yan Bol coming to me.

"Mr. Fielding," said he, "I likes to have a quiet talk mit you."

Travers and Teach in the gangway held their stations looking at us. Galen came to a halt on the forecastle with his face aft; Friend looked at us with his needle poised; the Spaniards went on stitching.

"What is it?"

"I shpeak for all handts. Do not be afraid, Mr. Fielding. She vhas all right and every man vhas good friendts."

"Afraid!" said I, looking at him steadily, though I was conscious that the blood was gone out of my cheeks. "I think you said *afraid?*"

"I ox pardon, I vhas – ."

"There is no Dutchman in this ship – there is no Dutchman in all Holland that can make me afraid. Use another word and bear a hand. I mean to get an hour's sleep this afternoon."

"Dere vhas nothing I hope to stop you sleeping soundtly as long as you please."

"What do you want?"

"Mr. Fielding, ve vants the brig's course altered."

"Ay, indeed. For what part of the world?"

"I hope you shall not sneer. By ter tunder of Cott, all handts vhas in earnest."

"Dot vhas so," exclaimed Wirtz at the wheel, in his deep voice.

I observed that Galen had come aft and was standing with Travers and Teach at the gangway, within easy earshot of our voices: in fact, they were almost abreast of us t'other side of the deck, and our ship, as you know, was a little one.

"You want the brig's course altered? For where?"

"For Amsterdam Island."

"Yes, that island in the Indian Ocean which the Dutch discovered and gave a name to, and which you were talking about to me lately."

"Mr. Fielding, ve vhas all good friendts. I like to talk mit you as a mate mit his captain. Ve vhas respectful, but, by Cott, ve vhas in bloydy earnest also." He smote the palm of his left hand with his huge right fist and looked round, on which Galen, Teach, Travers, and others came aft. Friend flung down his palm and needle and joined the group; the Spaniards rose to their feet, but remained where they were.

I knew myself pale. I was startled – I was thunderstruck; down to this instant the crew had given me no hint to suspect their willingness to work the brig to the Channel. I fetched some laboured breaths, recollected myself with a prodigious effort of resolution, and after looking first at one face and then at another, during which time I was eyed with great eagerness, with here and there the hint of a threat, but generally with countenances not wanting in respect, I exclaimed, "Who will tell me what it is you want?"

"Shall I speak, Mr. Bol?" said Teach.

"Shpeak," cried Bol in his voice of thunder.

"The matter's simple as countin' your toes," said Teach, addressing me. "There's a cargo of silver down in the lazarette, ain't there? The captain's dead – him it rightly belonged to as the discoverer of it. He's dead, and us men are agreed that his share – a lump we allow – should be divided among all hands, you being one of us."

"Dot's so," said Bol.

"We don't want no blooming fuss," continued Teach; "the job's to be handled so that it shall be agreeable to all concerned. Here's the brig, and the money's below."

"Dot vhas so," said Galen. "Dis vhas a shob over vhich ve all shakes hands."

"If we carried the money home," continued Teach, "what's going to happen? Mr. Tulp'll claim the captain's share as well as his own. And what's to be his own? And what's to be your'n, Mr. Fielding? And what's to be our'n? Tulp 'ud suck egg and smash the shell agin our faces. Our rights goes hell's own length beyond the measly hundreds that's to be our fo'c'sle allowance of dollars."

"No need to curse and swear, Thomas," exclaimed Friend. "Mr. Fielding's a-taking of it all in. Give him time. Before a man lets go he sings out. We haven't sung out. I'm for kindly feelings in this here traverse."

"The shares you are promised along with your wages," said I, "should satisfy you. I will see that every man is paid."

"Vhat vhas your share, sir?" said Wirtz at the wheel.

"Ain't it worth naming?" said Meelian after a short silence.

Call laughed.

"'Taint as if you was here through Mr. Tulp's ordering," said Teach.

"You have chosen me captain," said I.

"The brig saved your life," exclaimed Street; "you owes us a good turn."

"Captain you are and captain we wishes you to remain," said Teach.

"Dere vhas one ting dot vhas proper you should recollect, Mr. Fielding," said Bol. "How about der wars dot vhas on? If we carries der treasure oop der Atlantic ve stands to lose her. Down here dere vhas peace und comfort."

"Are not our heels a match for anything that's afloat?" said I.

"Yaw," answered Bol, "and vhilst ve roon a shoe comes off; den vhere vhas ve? Look at our gompany. Look at our goons."

"What's your scheme?" I exclaimed.

"Is it for me to speak?" said Teach.

"Shpeak, Thomas," cried Bol.

"Our scheme's this, sir. We want you to carry the brig to Amsterdam Island, where we mean to heave the brig to, weather allowing, land the silver, bury it, and sail away for New Holland."

"Out with it all, Tom," said Travers.

"There's a party as is settled at Port Jackson," continued Teach. "He's a relation of mine. He'll do for us men what Mr. Tulp did for Captain Greaves; if this brig's to be given up, he'll find us a schooner or some such craft. We'll fetch the silver in her, and he'll receive it, and divide it among us, making a share for himself. His share'll be what our'n is, no more nor less. That'll be right. We find him the money and he finds us the vessel, and it's share and share alike. I am for fair dealing. Straight was straight with me afore I went to sea; I wor straight as a little 'un; straight's the word still; and I han't kinked yet. What are we doing? Robbing any man of his rights?" cried he, looking around into the faces of the others. "I say no. The captain's dead. If he were alive his rights 'ud carry the brig home, barring events. But he's dead; his money falls into shares for us men to take up – for us men and you, sir. As for Mr. Tulp – look here. Suppose he never hears again of the brig? Is this a-going to break any man's heart? How is he to know that we've got the silver? How is he to know Captain Greaves' yarn warn't a lie? What's his venture? Just the cost of the hiring of this brig. Well, by our not turning up we save him in wages. That's wrote off, and that means pounds in good money. The brig don't turn up, and what then; she's gone to the bottom; she's been taken. It'll hentertain Mr. Tulp when he ain't hard at work making money, to guess what's become of us; and how'll our mysterious disappearance leave him? Vy, one of the richest gents in the city o' Amsterdam."

Every eye was fastened upon my face while Teach addressed me. The fellows' looks were eloquent with expectation ihat I should be instantly convinced, satisfied, impressed, eager to execute their wishes. Jimmy was staring at us out of the door of the caboose and I called to him:

"Fetch me the bag of charts and a pair of compasses."

He brought the things. I found a chart of the world – a track chart.

"Spread this on the skylight," said I, giving it to Teach. He and Travers held it open on the skylight. "Do you know the situation of the brig at this moment?" said I.

The men drew shouldering round me to look; Yan Bol stooped his huge form and ran his wide and heavy face over the chart, his nose within an inch of it as though he hunted for a flea. Not a man could point to, nay, not a man had the least idea of, the place of the brig on the chart.

"Here's where we are now," said I, "and here's Amsterdam Island."

They huddled yet closer in a hairy, warm, hard-breathing group to look at the island.

"There it is, and here are we. Can you collect sea distances by looking on a chart?"

"No."

"Damn your ignorance. It's out of that this trouble's come. Look, you Bol, you Dutchmen who are the cooks of this devil's mess – look how I take this pair of metal legs and make them walk – look – every step signifying the flight of a ship in a week of prosperous gales. Look – peer close – value every one of these lines at twenty leagues; count them, Bol, count them."

"She vhas some vhays off; dot's allowed," answered Bol. "But dere vhas der island, und dere vhas ve, all in goodt time."

"Why *that* island?" said I, stepping back from the chart to command the men's faces.

"Because I knows her," answered Galen. "I vhas off her. Shi vhas an uninhabited island. She vhas lofty, mit goodt hiding ground. She vhas never visited."

"Dot's vy," said Bol.

"I'll not carry you there."

"Ye'll turn it over, sir," said Friend.

"I'll not help you to rob Mr. Tulp of his share."

"Dere vhas no robbery. Ve vhas lost at sea, mit all hands," said Galen.

"I'll sail you home and, if you choose, will give you my bond to pay you so many of the dollars as we'll agree to. But I'll not take you to Amsterdam Island. So what will you do?"

"What'll *you* do, sir?" exclaimed Teach.

"My duty."

"Dot vhas not even half-way," said Bol.

I called to Jimmy to restow the charts and bring them below, and descended the companion ladder. I was alone, and glad to be alone. The looks and questions, nay, the presence of her ladyship would have been intolerable to me just then. I sat down at the table and thought, then jumped up and paced the cabin like a madman. It had come about as I had many a time feared, but more darkly than ever my imagination had foreboded. The road to Amsterdam Island ran through a hundred and fifty degrees of longitude. Suppose – an incredible suppose! – an average of a hundred and fifty miles a day; two months then in making the island! and afterward? The silver was to be landed and buried, and we should head on for Port Jackson in New Holland, where my throat would be cut if the spirit of murder left the crew a hand to cut my throat withal.

And the money being buried, good-night to my six – my seven thousand pounds – to my fine prospects, my giving up the sea forever, and settling down ashore with a wife. Tulp? God bless you, no. It was not of Tulp I thought. What was he to me? I was no servant of his, under no obligation of fidelity to *him*. It was the six thousand pounds which ran in my head and set my brains boiling – the six thousand and the one bequeathed to me by Greaves.

I paced the cabin like mad. What am I to do? How was I to preserve my share of the dollars? There were eleven, and with me twelve, of us now to the brig's company; the men were not likely to count Jimmy and the two Spaniards as partners. Teach – was it Teach? – talked of an equal division; *that* would work out fifty thousand dollars a man; twenty thousand ahead of my present share. They'd promise me more, I daresay – offer me what I chose to take – Yes, and knife me, or drop me overboard in the hour of the coast of New Holland heaving into sight.

Nor was that all of it either: I conceived the fifteen tons of silver buried in the island of New Amsterdam: we arrive at Port Jackson: Teach's friend – think now of the respectability of a friend of Teach! – finds a little schooner. Would the fellows return to the island with me? or would they pick up some cheap ruffian of a navigator, leaving me to wait for them?

If the money was buried my share was gone for good, my life not worth a hair of my beard. What was to be done?

While I paced the cabin I had observed that the men continued to hang about the skylight. I supposed that they were looking at the chart. By this time the skylight lay clear: Jimmy came below with the bag of charts and the pair of compasses; I heard the voices of men singing out in pull-and-hauling choruses, and the brig heeled over a little.

There hung under the seat that Greaves used to occupy a tell-tale compass: I looked at it and found the brig's course east by south. I immediately went on deck and found the yards braced forward and both watches hauling down the larboard studding sail. Bol walked the quarterdeck and Galen was shouting orders from the forecastle.

"Who's captain here?" said I, stepping up to the great Dutchman.

"You, Mr. Fielding."

"What are you doing with the brig?"

"Heading her off for Amsterdam Island."

"So. Then you know your way there?"

"No, sir. Der shart explains dot der island vhas in der east: so east it vhas mit der brig till ve vhas goodt friendts, Mr. Fielding, und shake hands und agree. And maybe he vhas all right mit you now, sir," he added, looking at me out of the corner of his little eyes.

"I want time to consider," said I, realizing my extreme helplessness, and by that realization urged more than half-way to the acceptance of my fate, whatever it might prove, without further struggle.

"Mr. Fielding," cried Bol, throwing out his arms and addressing me in that posture, "vhat vhas it how he vhas mit der brig und mit Mynheer Tulp while she vhas all right mit *you*? Mindt, I doan say dot if der captain had lif dot dere vhas no trouble. Vhat?" he shouted, in a voice of thunder: "a leedle footy sum of sixty tousand dollar for all us men vhen Tulp vhas to get der half of der half million and you yourself, Mr. Fielding, maybe vhas to take but a leedle less dan Captain Greaves herself. Vhas it right?" He thumped his bosom. "Vhas she a beesiness dot vhas good ash between man and man?" He thumped his bosom again. "Vhas not you a sailor? Vhas not der sailor gruelly used? Vhas she not right to stand up for herself when der shance comes? Mr. Fielding, in der sight of der crew, gif me your hand und shake mit me und ve vhas der happiest of families from dis hour."

"I'll not give you my hand. I want time to think." His face darkened. I continued: "If I refuse to navigate the brig to Amsterdam Island and on to Port Jackson, what then?"

Wirtz, who was at the wheel, hearing this, called out in Dutch. Yan Bol gazed at him slowly, then leisurely brought his face to bear upon mine and eyed me fixedly.

"Mr. Fielding," he said, slowly, "I likes to shake you by der hand und it vhas a good ting to be a happy barty. But if you doan navigate us you vhas of no use, und we puts you into dot boat mit der two Spaniards und sends you away, hoping dot it shall be well mit us all."

* * *

I remained in my berth during the greater part of that afternoon. I was nearly mad and afraid to trust myself on deck. The insult, let alone the significance, of Bol's threat to send me adrift with the two Spaniards, was crushing, because it found me entirely helpless. Bligh, of the *Bounty*, had been so served; others who deserved far better usage at the hands of their crew than Bligh, of the *Bounty*, had been put into boats in mid-ocean and dispatched to their doom. In the next hour I might find myself adrift with the two Spaniards, the brig a white gleam on the horizon, the lady Aurora alone with the crew, the money as utterly lost to me as if it had gone to the bottom.

So I remained in my berth and thought, and all the afternoon I sat thinking till the evening darkened upon the porthole, till the fire had gone out of my blood, and the machinery of the brain worked calmly.

Thrice, or perhaps four times, did Miss Aurora beat upon my cabin door and call my name. I heard her ask the lad Jimmy if I was ill, if I was mad, what had happened, why did the Señor Fielding hide himself? The half-witted boy knew not how to answer her. She knocked upon my door again. I told her that I was hard at work, and promised to join her presently.

When the dusk fell, I opened the door of my berth and entered the cabin. I stepped at once to the tell-tale compass, and saw that the brig's course was still east by south. The lamp was alight and the meal of the evening was upon the table. The breeze was light, the heel of the brig trifling. I guessed she was under the same canvas I had left her clothed in at noon. I saw the stars shining through the skylight glass, and heard a steady trudge of feet overhead, as of two men, perhaps three, walking the quarter-deck. I looked round for the lady Aurora, and, while I did so, her white dress, with its fanciful decoration of bunting, filled the companion way, and she came down. Her eyes were bright, her looks without excitement or alarm, her cheeks faintly coloured by the breath of the evening air she was fresh from. It was clear – I saw it in her – she knew nothing of what had passed.

"At last, *señor*," said she, approaching as though to give me her hand.

She stopped, looked at me earnestly, and slightly wagged her head in a strange foreign way.

"You are ill?" she said.

"No; I am hungry. Let us sup."

She removed her hat. I helped her to take off her jacket. While this was doing she was silent. She took her seat in silence, and viewed me without speech, reflecting in her own face the expression in mine, as I might suppose, for now was her look of ease gone. I waited until we had eaten and drunk, occasionally breaking the silence by commonplace remarks; then, closing my knife and fork, and draining my mug. Hooked up at the skylight, round at the companion way, leaned my head on my elbow across the table, and told my companion, as best I could, what had happened, and what was still happening, aboard us.

Her intelligence was so keen, she was so apt in the interpretation of my looks and gestures, so quick in collecting the meaning of my words, that I found no difficulty in making her understand. She exclaimed often in Spanish; the shadows of many emotions swept her face; she stared with horror when she understood that the men meant I should carry the brig to the Indian Ocean, and that the vessel's head was already pointed, according to their notions of navigation, for the Island of Amsterdam. But she received the news with a degree of calmness that was an astonishment and a reproach to me when I thought of my own distraction. I scarcely imagined she grasped the full meaning of the crew's intention, till, pointing downward, by which she signified the brig's hold, she said:

"The *Casada* had a demon on board. It is now the spirit of this ship."

This she conveyed in Spanish and English. I understood her.

"Yet I mean to keep a hold of that demon," said I, thinking aloud rather than talking to her. "I'd put the vessel ashore sooner than let the scoundrels plunder me of my share and divide – Jesus Maria! only think! – fifteen tons of dollars among them!" and I smote the table with my fist, and the blood, hot as flame, flushed my face.

Then the following conversation passed between us, managed as before. I give you the clear sense picked out of the interruptions, gestures, sentences, and looks:

"What shall you do, Señor Fielding?"

"Advise me."

"I – a poor, helpless woman, ignorant of the sea? Yet does it not seem to you that, unless you comply, they will send you away with Antonio and Jorge."

"Yes."

"Then you will comply."

"And after?"

"After?" she cried. "Who knows? Many things may happen to deliver us from this dreadful situation; but, if you defy the crew, and they put you and my countrymen into a boat, we are surely lost."

I assented with, a gesture.

"They are ignorant of navigation?" said she.

"Utterly."

"Could not you steal the brig to a part of some coast where we are likely to fall in with ships of war?"

"If they suspected treachery they'd hang me at the yardarm."

"*Ave Maria!* Where is this New Holland?"

"It is very far from here."

"How far?"

"It may be four months and perhaps five months from this place."

"Mother of God! Is Spain to be reached from New Holland?"

"Yes, but the world grows old before such voyages are ended."

She cast down her gaze in thought. The noise of the tramp of footsteps had ceased; I reckoned we were being watched, but I would not lift up my eyes to know. I rose and paced the cabin, having formed my resolution; and now I considered with whom of the crew I should speak. I abhorred Yan Bol for the horrible threat he had uttered, for the enormous insult that threat implied, and I dared not put myself alone with him – yet. I went to the companion ladder and called up the hatch for Jimmy; my cry was re-echoed, and in a minute or two the boy made his appearance.

"Tell Friend to come to me – here."

"Señor Fielding," said the lady Aurora, "you will comply with the men's requests?" I motioned an assent. "If not we are lost. I have been thinking. You are in their power. *Paciencia!* If they send you away, I – I – Aurora de la Cueva – " and in pronouncing her name she touched her breast two or three times, "am alone with men who will be the murderers of you and my countrymen. I count upon your protection. Think of me alone in this ship with your men."

She clasped her hands and turned her dark and shining eyes upon the little stand of muskets. A peculiar expression slightly curled her lip as she looked at those weapons.

"I'll not leave you."

She put her forefinger to her mouth, and at that moment I saw a man's legs in the hatch.

"Is it down here I'm wanted, sir?" said the voice of Friend.

"Come along."

He descended, pulled his cap off, and stared with looks of misgiving and surprise. Peradventure he thought I had a design on his life, and meant to slaughter the crew one by one, courteously inviting them below for that purpose. He was a sailor of a mild cast of face, rather quiet in manner, and had the most civil and least swearing tongue in the brig.

"Sit down. I've a message for the crew. I am sick of that huge, bloody-minded Bol's yaw-yaw-yawling jaw. Your English is mine. You'll answer some questions, perhaps?"

"I will, sir."

"The scheme's this: we said to Amsterdam Island, there unload the silver and bury it. Why Amsterdam Island?"

"Because it's straighten the road to Australia, uninhabited, and never visited."

"Why do you not proceed direct to Botany Bay, keeping the money aboard?"

"I'll tell you," he answered, putting down his cap, leaning forward, and addressing me with his forefinger on the palm of his left hand. "It's a matter we've argued out for'ads, and we're all agreed; for this reason. There'll be nothing easier than to wreck the vessel within a day's walk of Port Jackson. If we keeps the money aboard we shall be casting it away with the brig. Is the risk of our losing the money along with the brig to be entertained? Why, certainly an' of course *not*. The money's to be hid first. D'ye ask, why we don't hide it on that part of the coast where we cast the brig away? Because the privacy there ain't the privacy of an uninhabited island; there's savages and settlers a-knocking about; runaway convicks and chaps in search of 'em; and no man would reckon the money safe until it was dug up. Next step, then, after losing the brig, will be to tramp it to Port Jackson, shipwrecked men. There Teach has a friend. That friend's an old pal of Teach's, and when last heard of was a-doing well. He'll find us in a schooner or some small vessel, and when we've got the money he'll show us the ropes."

"What's Teach's friend?"

"Dunno, sir."

"Was he a convict?"

"Dunno, sir."

"You think this a devilish clever scheme, don't you?"

"It'll come off – it'll come off," he answered.

"I'll work you up twenty safer, surer, and easier schemes than that," said I.

"Maybe; we likes our'n," he answered, with a quiet grin and a slow look at the lady Aurora, who was listening with the strained, vexed, impatient look of one who hears but understands little of what passes.

"Amsterdam Island is in the Indian Ocean," said I.

"So they say."

"No vessel under three hundred tons may navigate the Indian seas. Do you know that?"

"When I was in a Company's ship I think I heerd something of the sort, but there's no law where Amsterdam Island is, and if there was – we aren't pirates, anyhow;" and he made as if he would rise.

"It's a damnably wicked scheme, a hanging scheme, and as stupid as it's wicked. D'ye know what Yan Bol told me today? … Friend, I'm an Englishman talking to an Englishman; and this threat is an accursed Dutchman's. Yan Bol told me today that if I refused to navigate the brig to Amsterdam Island, you men would send me adrift in one of the boats, along with the two Spaniards."

"Mr. Fielding," he exclaimed earnestly, "it was talked of – it is talked of. You'll be making it mere talk, sir, I'm for working this traverse on the smooth. Let good will grease the ways, says I. Why, ain't it for you as well as for us? You're no servant of Tulp's, and the captain is gone dead, and if we says, 'Here stow more'n the allowance of dollars ye was to have, only steer us true and take a sheepshank in your tongue,' who wouldn't be you? It's easy terms for a swilling measure. And that's my sentiments straight."

"You can go forward, Friend," said I, "and tell Mr. Yan Bol and the men that I have thought the matter over, that I consent to remain captain of the brig, and to navigate her to Amsterdam Island."

Chapter XXVII.
Bol's Ruse

"WHAT DEMONS!" exclaimed the lady Aurora when Friend had left the cabin. "You do well to consent. May the Holy Virgin watch over us and deliver us!" She cast up her eyes and crossed herself with great devotion.

When Friend was gone with my message I leaned upon the cabin table thinking. The Spanish lady chattered. I did not heed her. I had no hope, saw no prospect, could imagine no issue. True, much might happen; but then, what would be good for my safety – for my own and the safety of Madam Aurora – *might* prove fatal to my fortune, and my dollars were with me the first of all considerations.

I wanted my six thousand pounds: I wanted the thirty thousand pounds which formed Greaves' share, that I might deal with it in accordance with his instructions. I wished to realize the happy dreams I had been dreaming throughout the voyage. It was maddening to think of the whole fifteen tons of silver falling into the hands of the blackguard fellows forward; and yet the devil's luck of the business, as it now stood, was this, that what was bad for *them* was bad for *me* – by which I mean that if the brig was captured by an enemy, or boarded by an Englishman and the money discovered; if she foundered or was stranded with the dollars aboard, I might indeed escape with my life, I might be delivered along with the lady Aurora from the situation I was now in – but my dollars would be lost to me, and with them my sweet and jolly prospects.

I went into my cabin, brought out a chart, and putting it under the lamp laid off a course for the Cape of Good Hope. I likened my feelings to those of a man who is wakened by a jailer and told that all is ready, that he can order what he likes for breakfast, and that the chaplain will wait upon him presently. I struck the chart a blow with my fist, and hissed a curse at it like any stage ruffian. We were to be bound the other way now. We were sailing to the inhospitable ends of the earth; the stars of the south were to arise again; the star of the pole must remain a dream of home.

The tragic suddenness of it all, when only at dinner that day I was rejoicing in spirit over our progress north, and telling my Spanish companion what I meant to do with my share of the dollars!

I replaced the chart, drank a tumbler of grog, and stepping on deck, marched to the wheel and looked at the card. Call grasped the spokes.

"Let her go off. The course is – " and I gave the fellow the course.

The swollen, dusky shapes of Bol, Galen, and others of the crew trudged in the gangway. It was a fine, clear night, I sang out:

"Trim sail and then heap it on her. Set stun's'ls and let her go."

My voice was instantly echoed by Bol.

"Hurrah, my ladts! Man der braces. Clear avay der foretopmast stun's'l. Hurrah for beesiness! All vhas right now. Dis vhas a happy ship."

I stood beside the wheel while the men trimmed and made sail, Bol roaring at them, deeply thunderous, with excitement and satisfaction. Presently the great Dutchman came up to me.

"Mr. Fielding, vhas he a disgrace to shake handts now?"

I gave him my hand, and the brute squeezed it. He then looked at the card, observed the course, and said, "Dot vhas for der Cape!"

"Yaw."

"He vill not bring der land aboardt? All hands would gif der Point of Agulhas a vide berth."

"I'll run you as far south as you choose."

"Veil, I dessay a hondred mile vhas sout enough."

"Is the fresh water going to carry us to Amsterdam Island?"

"Dot vhas to findt out. If not, dere vhas plenty of rain in der sky before dere casks gif out. But she vhas not longer to Amsterdam Island dan to England, and dere vhas water to last to England, so dot vhas all right, I hope. Dere is fresh water on der island."

"And your provisions?"

"She vhas to be seen to likewise."

"You'll find nothing to eat at Amsterdam Island; nothing to carry you on to Port Jackson."

"Vhen der money vhas hid dere vhas St. Paul hard by, mit goats, und cabbage, und fish for drying."

I cursed him behind my teeth. The villain looked far ahead; all hands knew what they were about, while I saw nothing an inch beyond my nose.

"Mr. Fielding, ve vhas all gladt dot you remain in sharge. Mitout you ve vhas at sea indeedt. You vhas now von of us. Dere vhas no robbery. Tink a leedle, Mr. Fielding. How vhas Tulp to know dot ve hov der dollars? Tink a leedle, sir. Ve gifs him our vages – our verk costs her not von stiver. Der captain vhas deadt – der money by der law of expeditions like ash dis vhas, I mean expedition dot vhas all der same as privateering, belongs to der surfifers. Suppose I die? Veil, my share goes by rights to you und der oders. Dot vhas onderstood. Now, Mr. Fielding, vhat vhas your share to be?"

On his asking me this question I walked off.

It was fine weather till past midnight; the wind then came out of the northeast in a heavy squall of wet, and after this for several days it blew very fresh. The rain drove in clouds over the sea; the dark sky hung low, and our reeling trucks were swept by the shadows of the flying scud. Yet in these heavy, boisterous days Yan Bol and two or three others contrived to take stock of the quantity of fresh water and provisions on board. Bol sent Jimmy to me with the particulars, and asked leave to attend me in my cabin while I worked out the figures. I sent word back that an Englishman might come – Teach or Friend – bidding Jimmy add that I understood Bol's English with difficulty. The truth was I hated the villain; wished to have no more to do with him than the work of the brig forced upon me. He had threatened me with an open boat, he was at the bottom of this seizure of the brig and her cargo of silver; the project of casting the vessel away was his I did not question. Could I have served any purpose by taking his life I'd have shot him with less compunction than I'd wring a fowl's neck.

The man who arrived was Teach. He had washed his face and buttoned himself up in a clean pilot coat to pay the cabin this visit. He was a smart seaman: a sharp-looking rogue, with curling hair and a long, lean nose, and little, darting eyes. He knocked on my cabin door, and I bade him come in.

"Oh," said I, "is it you? Sit down."

Without further words, I took pencil and paper and fell to my calculations. Bol's figures lay before me, I guessed they were correct. He'd naturally go to work anxiously, that we might not be starved or driven by thirst from the Amsterdam Island scheme. There was so much beef, so much pork, so much ship-bread, and such and such a quantity of peas, sugar, flour, and the like; there was so much water. We were fifteen souls in all, counting the girl and the two Spaniards; and my figures worked out thus – that, at the usual allowance, we had provisions for seven months and water for three.

I gave Teach these figures, and then put them down in black and white for the crew, and handed him the paper.

"There's plenty of provisions," said he, looking at the paper upside down, "to last all hands to Australia. Fresh water we'll take in at Amsterdam Island."

"Ever at Sydney?"

"No, sir."

"Who's your friend?"

"A man named Max Lampton."

"D'ye know that he's now at Sydney?"

"He was there two years ago. If he's dead his son'll be living. But he ain't dead. Max is one who takes care of himself. No drink – no baccy – regular as a clock – a steady man."

"What do you expect of him?"

"He'll show us what to do with the money; 'vart it into paper and gold for us."

"Fifteen tons!"

"It'll take time. We sailors aren't going to make a job of it without help, anyhow."

"Is it a clever idea to bury this silver in Amsterdam Island, first of all?"

"Ay, blooming clever! Where's there such another island to answer our turn? We can't cast the brig away with the money aboard, that's sartin."

"You mean to cast her away?"

"Why, what are we to do with her?" said he, talking all this while with his little eyes rooted on my face. "Carry her to Port Jackson? What's the yarn we're to spin? Where are we to ha' come from? Where was we to be bound to? We've thought it o'er. We don't like the notion. She's a pretty boat, but she must go. There's a blooming lot of us. Are we all to be trusted? Are we all going to stick to the same yarn if it comes to close questioning? Any durned fool can be a shipwrecked sailor. There's a-many durned fools piking it now as castaways on the British roads, a-yarning spunkily, and saving money."

I thought to myself, "And you'd trust me, would you? You'd allow me to be one of your shipwrecked party, eh? And if I am *not* to be one of your shipwrecked party – and most surely you don't intend that I *shall* be – what's to happen betwixt this and New Holland? How have you hearts of oak arranged to get rid of me?"

I looked down and sat silent in thought. He stirred, as if to leave, and said:

"We're too many, sir."

"For the dollars?"

He grinned, and answered:

"No. There are dollars enough for all hands. We're too many mouths for the stock of provisions and water."

"Yan Bol has threatened to send me adrift, curse him! Do you mean that I should go first to shrink your company!"

"No, no!" he answered, in a voice heavy and almost savage with emphasis; and he thumped his knee with his fist. "We can't do without you – you know that, Mr. Fielding. And that brings me to something I'll tell you in a minute or two. It's them Spaniards. What's the good of them?"

"No cruelty! So help me God! if there's cruelty I drop my command! Mark me, and report what I tell you."

"There'll be no cruelty," said the man sullenly; "but them Johnnies'll have to walk."

"And the lady?"

"Ain't she in your share?" said he, and his face relaxed. He drove his quid out of one cheek into the other, and when he had chawed a little while, he said, "But what's to *be* your share?"

I crooked my eyebrows and surveyed him steadily.

"Won't you give it a name, sir?"

"Shall I get it by naming it?"

"Mr. Fielding, we can't trust you if you can't trust us."

"What share will you give?"

"A big share."

"Bol and the rest of you know the worth of what's below. Make me an offer in writing. It'll content me."

"Give me a figure to go upon," said he standing up. "Tell us what you was to get if Captain Greaves had carried the brig home."

"Six thousand pounds, and a thousand from Captain Greaves – seven thousand pounds."

An oath broke from him – he checked himself; struck his thigh hard, picked up his cap, and looked at me sideways. Then, stepping to the door, he exclaimed:

"Good pay compared to the forecastle allowance."

I began to whistle, and drew on paper with the pencil I had calculated with. He again eyed me sideways and went out.

I believe it was on the fifth day of the heavy weather that Teach had paid me this visit. Next morning, while I was breakfasting with the Spanish lady, Jimmy – the boy as I call him, though he was a great, hulking, strong, sprawling lad as you know; half an idiot in many directions, but quick and even intelligent in some – this lad came into the cabin and said that Bol asked to speak to me. I would not have the Dutchman below, neither would I leave my breakfast; so I bid the lad say I'd be on deck by and by. Down he comes a minute later with a bit of dirty folded paper in his hand.

"Master," says he, "Mister Bol didn't know you was at breakfast. Will you read this, and tell him, when you go on deck, if it's to your satisfaction?"

The dirty piece of paper was like to the sheets that had been used for the Round Robin. It was the fly-leaf of some old book, yellow with age and pockmarked with brine. A Dutch scrawl in faint ink half covered it. The precious document ran thus:

> Meester Fielding, dis vhas a bondt. All handts agree. Suppose dere vhas fifteen ton silver – veil, two tons vhas yours if you sail der brick true und does her duty by oos ash we does by him. Dot being right ve all makes our marks and sines her names ash oonder. ~~If you goes wrong dis bondt vhas tore oop~~, und vot vhas las' wrote stans for noting. Dere vhas no more paper.

Then followed the crosses and names of the men, as in the Round Robin. I burst into a laugh. Heartsick as I was, this stroke of farce, happening in the great tragic occasion of that time, proved too much for me. I put the paper in my pocket.

"At what do you laugh?" said the lady Aurora.

"At a piece of Dutch humour," said I, laughing again.

She looked eagerly, and wished to know if the crew had done anything to please me – anything to lighten my anxiety.

"They have given me two tons of silver," said I with a sneer, pointing down that she might understand me.

She shrugged her shoulders, and asked no more questions about the crew's bond. I reckoned she saw in my face as much as she was interested to hear. I observed her fine eyes fixed upon the stand of muskets and cutlasses and watched her; not speculating on her thoughts, merely observing her face. I beheld no marks of anxiety in her handsome features, of such passions of uneasiness and continued distress as you would look for in a woman situated as she was. The glass in poor Greaves' cabin had assured me that what had befallen us had not sweetened or coloured my own visage. I was growing long of face; yellowing daily, and my eyes had sunk. This Spanish girl, on the other hand, was still bright and spirited with all the health she had regained aboard us. I watched her while she looked at the weapons; she turned her face slowly upon mine, and our eyes met.

"Why," she exclaimed – and now began one of those brief conversations which I am forced to put into plain English for reasons I have given you – "why, Señor Fielding, do not you lock away those swords and firearms?"

"Why should I lock them away?"

"The crew may take them."

"What then?" said I, "we should be no worse off. I am alone: forward are ten stout, determined men; armed or unarmed, 'tis all one."

"There are two," said she.

"Yes, Jimmy is a strong lad, and might be useful, and I dare say he is on our side at heart, but he is wanting," said I, touching my head. "I dare not trust him."

She smiled and said, "I did not mean the youth. I am the other."

I asked her to explain. She rose and seated herself beside me. The skylight was partially covered with tarpaulin, and what was visible of the glass was blank as mist with wet. The brig was full of noises. She was rolling and pitching very heavily, and the thunder of seas bursting back in heavy hills of foam from her weather side trembled like discharges of cannon through the length of her. Nevertheless the *señorita* came and sat by my side, and put her lips close to my ear, though had she shrieked her ideas from the extreme end of the cabin, or even up through the hatch, nobody on deck would have heard her.

Her manner was tragic and mysterious. It was not put on. The thoughts in her bred the air, and she had the face and figure for a very curious high dramatic expression of emotion of any sort.

"Why," said she, speaking so close that I felt the heat of her face, "do not we kill the men who are robbing you and carrying me away?"

"All of them?" said I.

"Not Jimmy, and not my two countrymen. Look! suppose I bring Antonio here and tell him that he and Jorge are in danger of their lives, and that they must fight with us and kill the crew. There are you, me, my two countrymen: there is Jimmy," she held up her fingers. "Five to ten, and everything is ready," said she, pointing to the muskets.

"I would not trust your two countrymen. They are cowards. I would not risk such a business for your sake. Failure would mean my being killed: that *must* be; and how would the men whom *we* did not kill deal with you?"

"All could be killed," said she. "I myself will kill in this cabin that great Jean Bol, as you talk to him. I will creep behind and stab him. Send for Galen; I will kill him too; then Teach. Three then are *gastados!* (expended!) For the rest – ". She shrugged her shoulders and leaned back to observe the impression produced upon me by her talk.

"Madam," said I, looking at her eyes, which were all on fire, and her cheeks, which were coloured, hot with the devilish fancies which worked in her, "your spirit is fine, but somewhat too deadly for one of my cautious character."

"I wish for release," she cried, with a great sigh, and her eyes suddenly clouded; "I wish for my mother and for home. I thought the English were brave, *vaya!* Your men will kill you if you do not kill them. Are you afraid to kill them? *Ave Maria!* Good men die in thousands every day."

She began to tremble, and rose as if to pace the cabin; the motion of the brig was too heavy to permit that. I took her hand to steady her – it had turned from the heat of fever to the coldness of marble. "Just so!" thought I; "aren't you one of those delicate assassins who prog and faint? Who'd stick friend Yan, then swoon, and leave me to deal with what would follow his roars?"

"We'll burn no powder just yet," said I, "and we'll keep our poniards in our breasts. Amsterdam Island is a long way off; many things may happen."

"*Pu! Quita allá!*" she exclaimed, with pale lips and dull eyes, and trembling, and then rising with a murmur of anger and a manner of haughty contempt she went to her berth.

When she was gone there ran in my head a strange fancy of Defoe concerning a beautiful demon lady. You may read of it in that author's *History of the Devil*, which is, I think, the best biography of the landlord of the Black Divan that ever was written. I could not but vastly admire the spirit of the woman in offering to shoot down the ten men; but I thought there was something damnable and fiendish in her proposing to make a shambles of the cabin by sticking Bol and the others she had named, while I talked to them. A demon spoke through her Spanish blood *there!* And yet her fine eyes and fine figure were in my memory of her counsel, and found a sort of fascination for what should have affected me as quite abominable.

I sat a bit, coldly considering her ideas. True it was that I could have killed Bol cheerfully; but to slaughter the whole ten of them, even if their assassination was to be contrived! Bol, to be sure, had threatened to send me adrift: he may have meant no more than a threat; my life was not immediately in danger; my knowledge as a navigator warranted me the good usage of the scoundrels till the coast of New Holland arose, and 'twixt this and *that* there lay some months: the men had dealt respectfully with the girl – left her indeed to me, as though they counted her a part of my share. No! I could not consent to shoot them down; I could not consent to them – one at a time.

I went to the stand and took out a musket to judge the quality and age of the lot: it was a Dutch musket, long, clumsy, and murderous. I took down a cutlass and tried the blade – all this mechanically: my mind was rambling. I scarce knew what I was about; I bent the blade and the steel snapped and the point of it sprang with the twang of a Jew's harp through the air. Some of Tulp's purchases! thought I, then replaced the broken half of the blade in its scabbard, and hung up the cutlass in its place.

This trifle begot a new scorn of Tulp in me. The rogue would even cheat himself, thought I. He would ship cannons that burst and blades that shiver to save a guilder or two, and risk the lives of us men and his dollars by the ton for some lean-paring of saving that would scarce put an onion to a man's bread and cheese. What do I care for Tulp, thought I? What is his brig to me now that poor Greaves is gone? Had Greaves owned relations among whom he wished his money distributed the thing would wear a different face; but as it stands, Tulp and the brig being nothing to me, why should I not throw in my chance with the crew, elbow Bol out of his leadership by sheer enthusiasm, sincerity, knowledge of the ocean roads? The fellows groped in their black ignorance after some scheme, and brought up this muddy project of Amsterdam Island with Sydney beyond. Could not I devise something much better than *that* for them, something safe and quick – compared at least with *their* programme: something they should hearken to and eagerly adopt when they saw me and knew me and felt me to be in earnest?

Yan Bol came up when I put my head out of the hatch.

"Vhas dot bondt all right?" he roared that his voice might carry above the shouting in the rigging and the fierce hissing of the sea.

I nodded.

"Two ton. Only tink. Dere vhas much skylarking in two ton of silver. How many dollars shall go to her?" said he.

"Dollars enough for me," I shouted, and passed on to the compass and took a look at the brig and around me. I hated the villain; I hated his roaring voice, and his English; besides, speech soon grew difficult, even to physical pain, on that clamorous deck.

It was not much later on, however, that the crew gave me cause to think twice before throwing in my lot with them. By this time we had stretched far across the Atlantic; the month of April was drawing to an end. Much heavy weather had we encountered, but it had been of a prosperous sort, rushing us onward with hooting rigging, and reeling bands of canvas, with such a spin of the log-reel that many a time and oft three and sometimes four men were required at the great scope of line to walk it in.

On the day of the little business I am going to tell you about I went on deck and found a very fine morning. The blue sky sank crisp with mother-of-pearl-like cloud to the pale edge of the sea. The sun, that was risen about half-an-hour, shone white as silver in the east, whence blew a pleasant breeze of wind, dead on end for us, however, so that our yards lay fore and aft and the little brig under every stitch of plain sail looked away from her course.

I saw Bol to leeward gazing at the sea off the lee bow. I never addressed that man now unless there was something particular to say, and after having satisfied myself with a quarterdeck stare around and aloft, I began to walk. Bol turned his head and perceived me. He approached, and pointing his finger at the sea on the lee bow, said:

"Do you see dot ship?"

I looked and spied a sail hidden to me until this by the brig's canvas.

"How is she standing?"

"Our vays."

She was about five miles distant. Bol had been using the glass. It lay upon the skylight. I examined the sail, and found her a small topsail schooner. With the naked eyes, by the look of her, as she floated out there in the frosty whiteness of sunshine, I had guessed her twice as big as we. She was coming along leisurely. The wind was off her quarter, and a light wind for fore-and-aft canvas.

"Vhat vhas she, tink you, Mr. Fielding?"

"Don't you know a ship by her rig?"

"I mean, vhat vhas her peesiness? Vhas she some leedle man-of-war?"

"Perhaps a trader, bound across the Atlantic."

He went forward as far as the gangway and beckoned. Wirtz, who stood on the forecastle, called out the name of Galen, and then walked aft to Bol, along with Friend and Street. Galen came out of the caboose eating. His jaws worked with some mouthful he had crammed betwixt his teeth. There was but little discipline in all this, you will say. There was none whatever. There had been very little discipline on board the *Black Watch* since illness had forced poor Greaves to give up and hand the command over to me. Was the fault mine? The long and short of it was, the men had never recognized me as mate in the room of Jacob van Laar. They had worked for the safety of the ship and because of Yan Bol. I was an interloper. They had made me feel it, times beyond counting, in their sailors' way; and now, though nominally captain, I was no more nor less than pilot, with authority only in the direction of the general safety.

All this I very much understood as I walked the deck, appearing not to heed the group of men in the gangway, and wondering what matter they were settling among them. Presently Bol came aft, took the telescope to the men, and one after another of them levelled it at the little sail off the bow. I never caught what they said, though my steps sometimes brought me pretty close.

They turned their faces my way sometimes. Street went over to the boat that lay stowed in the longboat amidships, looked into her, and returned to the others. I then thought to myself, "Are they going to signal that craft and put me aboard her?" I went into a violent passion over the suspicion, and came to a stand at the bulwarks, nearly opposite the spot where they were grouped, and stared, I have no doubt, with a very black face. Indeed, my conjecture had put me into such a rage that I heeded not, by a snap of the finger, what they might think, I tried to cool myself by reflecting that they could not do without me; but the mere notion that they meant to turn me out of the brig, and make off with Madam Aurora and the fifteen tons of silver, taking their chance of what might follow, worked like a madness in me.

They stood together, I dare say, about ten minutes talking. In this time the sail had grown, and was visibly a topsail schooner, low in the water, of a clean, black, slaver-like run. The sun flashed in flame from her wet sides, and I thought at first she was firing at us. Meehan, I think it was, sung out:

"Better see all ready, mates!" and went to the boat, he and others.

Bol alone stayed, looking at the schooner. He then came to me.

"Mr. Fielding, I shall vant to command for a leedle vhile. Me himself vhas skipper till our peesiness vhas done."

"What do you mean to do?" said I.

"To shtop dot leedle hooker. I shall vant to hail her. Of course, Mr. Fielding, you vhas der captain all der same; but you hov a soft heart, and so I vhas der skipper in dis shob."

"I don't understand you."

"It vhas like opening your eyes in a minute. You vhas not to interfere, dot vhas all."

He went to the flag-locker, took out the English ensign, and ran it aloft, union down, at the trysail gaff-end.

"Back der main topsail, some hands!" he bawled. All hands were on deck. Hals came out of the caboose to look on or to help. Some of the men laid the canvas on the main a-back, and others unshipped the little gangway preparatory to launching the boat, smack-fashion, through it; and among those who hove the little boat out of the bigger one, and ran her to the side, were the two Spaniards. Meanwhile, the schooner had hoisted English colours. They blew out from her main topmast head. The telescope gave me the character of the bunting. To the naked eye it waved and trembled like a red light against the pearly crust which covered the sky that way.

I guessed by her showing her colour that she was going to halt when she came abreast. What did my crew mean to do? What scheme had the beggars suddenly hit on and were going about with a unanimity that held them all as quiet as the backed topsail aloft?

It was about now that Miss Aurora came on deck. She looked up at the sails of the brig, at the flag flying at our trysail gaff-end, at the approaching schooner, the open gangway, the boat lying in it, the men hanging about the little fabric.

"Holy Mother!" cried she, and in a step or two she was at my side. "What is it? What is wrong? What is happening?"

Bol, who stood with others near the boat, hearing her turned. The huge man approached and was calling out before I could answer the girl.

"Mr. Fielding, der lady must go below."

"Must!"

"Yaw, by Cott! I vhas skipper for dis leedle while. You vhas not to be seen, marm. Dot vhas so I play no bart mit you on deck."

He came to the companion way, and with a face full of blood and temper, pointed down the ladder, exclaiming in his deepest thunder, "Quick, if you please. Doan' be afraid. It vhas all right. No von vhas hurt over dis shob."

"Go," said I, "do as he bids you. See how those fellows are watching us."

She obeyed me with an extraordinary look; the expression of a naturally fierce spirit contending with womanly terror; I'd think of it afterward always as if the girl had had two souls – one of flame, a gift of fighting blood older than the Moors perhaps; the other just a woman's.

"My ladts," bawled Bol to the men, "keep yourselves out of sight. Aft some of you, und standt by to swing der topsail yard. Manage dot your heads vhas not seen."

Those who came aft and those who stayed forward crouched under the bulwark: the two Spaniards hid with the others. Observing this, Bol called to Antonio:

"Oop you stand, you and Jorge. You vhas der crew."

They stood up, looking at the Dutchman wonderingly, with a half grin that was pathetic. I began to smell a rat, as they say. The schooner came sliding along, and when she was within ear-shot her topsail was swung and she halted to leeward of us. Her crew gazed at us from their forecastle, and three men stood on her quarter-deck. She was pierced for a few guns, but her ports were closed, and I saw no pieces of any sort upon her decks, though the easy, longdrawn roll of her gave us a good sight of the white planks, with the great main hatch and a tiny smoking caboose, and a fellow in a red shirt at the end of the long tiller. She was a sweet little picture, a far prettier model than the brig, handsomely gilt at the bow and quarter. "Lord!" thought I, "if I could but make those men yonder know what sort of stuff we carried down aft and the piratic trick those crouching scoundrels and that vast heap of flesh called Bol are playing me!" Yet, suppose the crew should permit me to shout out the yarn, would yonder chaps board us? We were nearly as numerous – our livelies would be fighting for treasure dear to them as their own ruddy drops; and look at our little grin of carronades and those long, shining engines on the forecastle and aft!

Bol got on to a gun. One of the men on the schooner's quarter-deck hailed.

"Ho, der brick ahoy! Vhat sheep vhas dot?"

It was the hail of a Dutch voice! I burst into a laugh – I must have laughed out at that Dutch hail had I been standing with a noose round my neck under a yardarm. Yan Bol stood idly straining and gaping a moment or two when he heard those Dutch tones. He then sent his deep voice across the water in a roar:

"She vhas der *Black Watch* of London to New Holland."

"Vat vhas wrong mit you?" shouted the Dutchman in the schooner.

"Ve vhas a seek ship und in great distress. I vill sendt a boat to you, ash I vhas veak und cannot cry out."

He floundered off the carronade on to the deck, and rolling over to the gangway, called to the two Spaniards, who stood there:

"Ofer mit dis boat. Quick now, and row aboardt dot schooner, und ask him to take you home. Der rest," he shouted with a look fore and aft, "keeps hid till I give der signal."

The bustle of the burly fellow was so heavy and eager, so much of elbow, knee, and thrust went to the launching of that boat, that the two miserable Spaniards were swept into the job as a man is hurried along by a crowd. They scarce knew what they were to do even while they were doing it; and then in a minute it was done, the boat alongside, and Bol bundling both the Spaniards into her through the open gangway.

"In you shoomps! Dot vhas der vhay! Quick! If dot schooner vhas missed your life vhas not vorth der shirt on your pack. Oop mit dem oars, Antonio, und shove off. Avays you goes, mit our respects und vill der captain restore you to your friendts!"

I went to the side. On seeing me Antonio who, with an oar in his hand, stood up in the boat looking along the line of the brig's rail with a wild, pale face, cried out in his incommunicable English:

"Señor Fielding, do not let Mr. Bol go away until he sees that the schooner will receive us. We have but these oars," he cried passionately, "no water, no provisions."

"Pull for her – she'll take you," I cried.

"Roundt mit der topsail," thundered Bol.

The seamen sprang to the braces, and in a very few moments had filled on the brig's canvas. The vessel sat light on the water and quickly felt the impulse of her sails. The boat containing Antonio and Jorge slipped astern; the two wretches were not even *then* rowing; but the moment the brig got way one of them – it was Jorge, I think – yelled out like a woman; they threw their oars out and hysterically splashed the little tub of a boat toward the schooner.

There was no sea to hurt them. The swell ran firm and wide, rippling only to the brushing of the wind. I dreaded lest the – schooner, on beholding our sudden show of men, should suspect what with our visible brass pieces and the suggestive sheer of our hull – a piratic device, and make off. If that happened the Spaniards were lost; Bol certainly would not return to pick them up. The mere fancy of our leaving them out in this vast sea to horribly perish worked in me like ice in the blood, and as I watched I was all the while thinking, "What shall I do to save them if yonder schooner fills in a fright?"

But the schooner did not fill; that her people were amazed by our behaviour I could not question, but they did not offer to run away. Possibly they thought we were executing some manoeuvre, and would shift our helm presently for the boat we had dispatched to them.

The Spaniards splashed along in their passion and fury of distress. Their boat was already a toy; they themselves dolls. They got alongside the schooner, and, seizing the glass, I watched them scramble over the rail, and continued to watch. They went up to the three men on the quarter-deck, and both fell to violently gesticulating and pointing at us. I could no longer tell which was which; one of them shook his fist at us, the other motioned with violent dramatic gestures toward the hold of the schooner. I might swear he was telling the men about the dollars, and furiously motioned that we might guess, *if* we watched him through the glass, what he was talking about.

Bol hauled the ensign down, and called to a man to roll it up.

"Vhas dot a neat little shob, Mr. Fielding?" said he, coming and standing beside me.

"Would not the schooner have taken the men without all this neatness?" I answered.

"Maybe and maybe not. Ve vhas not going to reesk it."

"You have lost the boat. Why did you require the lady to leave the deck?"

"She vhas soft-hearted, und dis shob vhas to be neat und quiet. Look!" he roared suddenly; "dere swings der topsails. Down coomes der flag. Gif me der glass, Mr. Fielding." He put his eye to the tube, and in a moment bawled, "Der boat drops astern; she vhas empty."

He pitched the glass on to the skylight and uttered an extraordinary roar of laughter.

Half an hour later the schooner was no more than a shaft of white light down in the west, with Yan Bol singing out orders to trim the sails of the brig and head for the boat, whose bearings had been taken, that we might recover her.

Chapter XXVIII.
I Scheme

NEVER once in all this while, and my story is covering many days, was I visited by the palest shadow of a scheme of release. And why? Because the *schatz* – the treasure – the dollars and I were one. All plans of escape provided that I left my dollars behind me. But I wanted my money. I had lived in a golden dream. The abandonment of the treasure was an unendurable consideration. I believe I could have faced death on board that brig with something of coolness. The contemplation of it would not have been frightful; the calling of the sea hardens the sensibilities and accustoms the soul to more things than the wonders of the Lord; but I could not consider with coolness the idea of the men possessing themselves of the fifteen tons of silver, burying the half-million dollars in the Island of Amsterdam, then perhaps being unable to find out where they had hidden the money, or hindered by who knows what of the unforeseen from ever getting to the island again.

I say I fell half mad whenever my head ran on that forecastle device. The thought of it regularly threw me into a fever. I have walked my cabin for a whole glass or watch at a time, as bad a murderer as any man can well be in heart only, killing the crew in imagination over and over.

Yet not the leanest vision of a scheme offered itself. Suppose I had attempted to recapture the brig by slaughtering the men after the manner proposed by Miss Aurora; by her stabbing them in the cabin while I engaged their attention, and then by her and me shooting the others; suppose this wild, ridiculous, horrid proposal practicable – all the crew being hove over the side – what was I to do with the brig, I, whose assistants would be a woman and a tall, clumsy, idiotic lad? Navigate her to the nearest port? Ay, but that was just what I durst not do if I wished to keep my dollars. Greaves had been strong on this point; he'd touch nowhere – rather reduce all hands to quarter allowance than touch, lest by entering or hovering off a port he'd court a visit that should carry him every dollar ashore.

Well, then, since I dared not convey the brig to a port, was I to wash about the sea with Miss Aurora and Jimmy for my crew, until I fell in with a ship willing to put me two or three men aboard? Yes, that sounds nicely; but what would be the risks before we fell in with a ship willing to assist? Many days, many weeks might pass before we sighted a sail, for I am writing of the year 1815, when the ocean we were afloat on ran for countless leagues bare to the sky, nearly all the traffic steering northward, Mozambique way.

But what was the good of this sort of speculation? The crew were alive; I was one to ten; I was without an idea; and every day was diminishing something of the meridians betwixt us and the Island of New Amsterdam.

I did not in this time give Miss Aurora a lesson in English. I do not remember that she asked me to give her a lesson. We had many long earnest conversations about our situation, by which she profited, for I spoke mainly in my own tongue. She did not favour me with another song, she nevermore asked for the fiddle, nor did it once occur to me to request her to oblige me with a recital in the rich and beautiful tongue of her nation. Yet she was now speaking English very fairly well. She was seldom at a loss, and conversation was easy without signs, nods, or gesticulations, saving an occasional shrug of her shoulders, the naturally impassioned action of her hands when she talked eagerly and hotly, and the many expressions of face which accompanied her speech.

She did not again offer to assassinate Bol and the others; she had read in my face what I thought of that proposal, and her fiery and scornful flinging from me because I would not consent was a flare of temper that was out before we next met. On one occasion, however, we quarrelled rather warmly, and I was sulky with her afterward for some days. She told me that I thought more of my dollars than of her life. I coloured up and answered that that was not true; I valued her life, and would restore her to her friends if I could; but I also valued my dollars. I had worked hard for them, and was not to be robbed by the blackguards forward of a considerable fortune.

"You think only of your dollars," said she; "you do not scheme, because your dollars are in the way of every idea. Is this how an English cavalier should treat a poor, unhappy, shipwrecked lady? Señor Fielding, I should be first with you; nothing should occupy your attention but the resolution to release me from this horrid situation and the dangers which lie before us;" and then she towered with her figure, and swelled her breast and flashed her eyes at me.

There was more of truth in her words than I relished to hear from her lips, and it was this perhaps that angered me. I begged her to advise; she shrugged her shoulders, and with an arch sneer which rather improved than deformed her beauty, said that if I were a Spanish sailor I would be ashamed to ask counsel of a woman.

"If I were a Spanish sailor I would be ashamed of myself," I said.

"Why do you not scheme to release us?"

"Scheme to release us? Shall I blow up the brig? That will make an end."

"It would not be the Señorita Aurora, but the Cavalier Fielding and his Spanish dollars which would hinder that," said she.

"If, by jumping overboard and swimming, I could put you in the way of reaching Madrid, I'd do so," said I; "but it's a long swim hereabouts to anywhere."

"You would not jump overboard and leave your dollars," said she, "If you were the gallant and respectable gentleman I have long supposed you, you would think of nothing but my deliverance. Why am I to be carried away to the extreme ends of the world? What is to become of me when your odious Hollanders and Englishmen have wrecked this brig?" and here she sank upon the table and sobbed.

"What am I to do?" I cried, not greatly moved by her tears; indeed, I was too angry with her to be affected by her sobs. I had used her very kindly; I had never failed in such rough sea courtesy as my profession permitted me the poor art of; I did not like her sneers at my love for my dollars; and I less liked the pinch or two of tart truth that acidulated her language. "What am I to do?" I cried. "Bol will not tranship you. He'll speak to no more vessels now the two Spaniards are gone. I can't sneak you away in a boat. Let any land but that of Amsterdam Island heave into view and the sailors will slit my throat. Why do you lie sobbing upon that table, madam? Pray, hold up your head and listen to me. What was your scheme, pray? A hideous one, indeed; and one that would not profit us either. It would fail, were we devils enough to attempt it: and then God help you and me! Many are the saints, but none would then be powerful enough to serve you."

She raised her head. The fire in her eyes was by no means dimmed by her tears. Her sobbing and posture had reddened her cheeks.

"The navigation of this brig is in your hands. Wreck her!" she exclaimed.

"And be drowned?"

"Wreck her in such a way that we shall not be drowned."

"Come, you shall not teach me my business. If I am not a Spanish sailor, I'll not take counsel of a woman either."

She snapped her fingers at me, and showed her teeth in an angry smile; turned, and I thought was going to her berth. Instead, she stopped and looked at me over her shoulder, made a step, and her whole manner changed. Her demeanour was, all of a sudden, a sort of wild tenderness. Why do I call it *that*? Because it suggested – the memory of it still suggests the moment's sportiveness of a tigress with its young. Her eyes softened: her face grew sweet with a look of pleading; she put herself into a posture of entreaty, her hands outstretched and figure a little stooped. Acting, or no acting, it was as good as good can be. You would have said she loved me had you watched her eyes. The contrast between the rascally snap of the finger and this pose of appeal was sharp and strong; – but how mean that stage for so rich a performance the lifting, uncarpeted deck of a little, plain, ship's cabin, with its austere furniture of table and lockers, and a skylight bleared with the greyness of the day without?

"Señor Fielding, let *me* be first with you."

Another reference to the dollars! It vexed me greatly, and saying, "It always has been so," I gave her a cool bow and went on deck.

We had quarrelled before, but lightly, for the most part, and were friends again in an hour. This quarrel, however, ran into two or three days. She would not leave me alone. Did I mean to scheme for our salvation? Was she to be first with me? Was I ashamed of myself to be devoured by avarice? What was the good of dollars to a dying man? and was I not a dying man if I did not rescue her and myself from the crew of the brig? I don't say she used all the words I put into her mouth. No; she was not so fluent *then* as all that; but I understood her very easily – rather too easily – when she sneered at me for thinking more of my dollars than of her.

Finding, however, that I continued resolutely sulky, answering her shortly, passing through the cabin instead of sitting with her as before and talking, she grew alarmed, felt that she had said too much, and made her peace. She made her peace by coming to my cabin. I was looking at a chart of the Southern Ocean when somebody knocked. My lady entered.

"*Ave Maria!* What will you think of me for coming to you thus and here? But my heart is too full of remorse for patience. Blessed Virgin! How long is half an hour when one is impatient: And I have been waiting for half an hour outside in the cabin. I have angered you, and I am sorry. You have been good to me, and you are my friend. And how do I show my gratitude? Forgive me, *señor*;" and with that she put out her hand.

It was very true than Yan Bol had declared the men would speak to no ship until the silver was out of the brig. And in my opinion they were right. As we made for the Island of New Amsterdam we increased the chance of falling in with war-ships and privateers. For Amsterdam Island is in the Indian Ocean, at the southern limit of those waters, it is true, and in those times many vagabond vessels were to be found in the Indian Ocean on the lookout for the big rich ships, the tea wagons and spice and silk carriers bound to and from China and the Indies.

But it so happened that after we had lost sight of the little schooner which had taken the two Spaniards aboard, we met with no other sail – none, I mean, within reach of the bunting or speaking trumpet. At long intervals a tip of white showed in some blue recess of that sea, infinitely remote, pale as a little light that lives and dies and lives again while you look. Never before had the measurelessness of the ocean affected me as now. The spirits of vastness and loneliness which came shaping themselves to the imagination out of those month-wide breasts and secret solitudes of brine grew overwhelming to the mind – to my mind I should say; and often of a night when the deck was quiet and the sea black and the stars were shining, I'd feel the oppression of a mighty presence – of something huge and near.

And then consider the doses of salt water I had swallowed and was yet swallowing! I was fresh from very many months of the sea when I was picked up off an oar in the Channel and swept outward again into the world where the salt spits like a wildcat, and where the sound of the wind is not as its noise ashore; and I was still at sea with months of water before me in any case if I was not put an end to.

So, even had the crew been willing to speak a ship that the lady Aurora might be transferred, no opportunity to do so came along; nothing hove in sight but a star of sail in the liquid distance, and *this* only at long, long intervals.

I'll not tell you of the weather we fell in with between Cape Horn and the distant island we were steering for; what do you care about the weather and the weather of so long ago as Waterloo year? Otherwise I could fill you several pages with pictures of hard gales, in one of which the brig lay for a wild, terrifying time with her lee rail under, her hull scarce to be seen for the smother that filled her decks, and I could please you with pictures of soft calms in which our stem tranquilly broke the cold grey water that reflected on either hand of the vessel the silver sheen of her overhanging wings; and I could give you pictures of merry breezes that swept us onward fast as the melting head of the blue surge itself ran. Enough!

One afternoon I sat upon the edge of the skylight frame with my arms folded and my eyes fixed upon the sea. The sun was warm, the breeze brisk. A pleasanter day had not shone upon us for a fortnight past. My lady Aurora seated on a cabin chair at a little distance from me was intent on an English book, one of the new volumes which had belonged to Greaves, Her posture was very easy and reposeful; her dark eyes wandered slowly down the printed page; often she was puzzled by the meaning of a word and frowned at it; you would have supposed her a person without a single cause for anxiety, a lady who was sailing to her home, which might now not be very far off.

Yan Bol was in charge. He had been standing for some considerable time beside the wheel, occasionally exchanging a sentence in guttural Dutch with Wirtz, who held the spokes. At last he came along the deck and stood in front of me.

"Vhat might hov been der situation of der brick at noon, Mr. Fielding?" he inquired.

I gave him the ship's place.

"Dot vhas close!" he said.

"It was," I answered.

"Donnerwetter!" he thundered, "der island vhas aboardt!" and he looked ahead at the sea as though he expected to behold the Island of New Amsterdam.

The lady Aurora, leaving the book opened upon her lap, raised her eyes and listened.

"How close vhas der island, Mr. Fielding?"

"Roughly, sixty leagues."

"Den, she vhas here tomorrow?"

"That is as the wind wills," said I.

He went forward by twenty or thirty paces, and putting his hand to the side of his mouth – not that his voice should carry the better, but to qualify the liberty he was taking by making an "aside" of it, so to speak, to the eye – he called to Galen, Meehan, and two others who were on forecastle:

"Poys, she vhas here tomorrow. Der distance vhas sixty leagues at dinner-time."

Galen accepted the news with a heavy Dutch flourish of his hand. Yan Bol returned to me. In the minute or two of his going forward I had been thinking, and with the swiftness of thought had concluded to ask him certain questions.

"Do you mean to bury the silver?"

"Dot vhas der scheme."

"You will need to dig wide and deep if your pit is to contain all those cases."

"Yaw, dot vhas so."

"What are you going to dig your pit with?"

"Dere vhas two shovels in der fore-peak. Whateffer else vhas useful ve takes mit us."

"Do you object to my asking you these questions?"

"Nine, nine, Mr. Fielding," he answered, "you vhas von of us, ve hope. Two tons of der silver vhas yours. Vhas it not right you should know what vhas to become of her?"

"Then, since in all probability we shall be off the island some time tomorrow, I'd be glad to hear now how you mean to go to work. I have asked no questions before. I had expected that you would come to me with your arrangements, and for advice,"

"Vhat advice vhas vanted? A man vhas green dot requires to be learnt how to make a hole in der earth, und put his money into it, "und cover it oop."

"You will need to make a very big pit."

"Yaw, she vhas a wide und deep pit dot ve dig."

"How long d'ye reckon that it will take you to dig that pit with such tools as you have?"

"Dere vhas no reckoning. Ve gets ashore und falls ter verk."

The lady Aurora closed her book, arose, brought her chair close to the skylight, and reseated herself. Bol looked at her, then fastened his eyes upon me.

"Am I to be left in charge of the brig?"

"You vhas, Mr. Fielding."

"What of a crew do you mean to allow me? It may come on to blow hard while you are on shore."

"Dere vhas crew enough," said he, with a queer expression in his eyes.

"How many?" I demanded sternly.

"Dere vhas four, und dere vhas der ladt, Jim. Dot vhas men enough for der braces," said he, looking up at the sails.

"Four men and the boy," said I aloud and musingly; "well, I daresay I shall be able to manage with four men and the boy."

"Dere vhas yourself to gount."

"Oh, I do not forget myself. Do you take charge of the landing and burial of the money?"

"Yaw, me himself. I likes to know vhere she lies."

"You will pull around the island and reconnoitre first, I suppose, before you land?"

"Vhat vhas dot?"

"Before landing the silver you will take care to make sure there is nobody upon the island? *That's* what I mean. Risk your own share, if you like, but my two tons must lie till I fetch them."

"She vhas an uninhabited island mitout house or foodt. Dot vhas certain sure. But we foorst takes a look, Mr. Fielding. Oh, yaw, by Cott, we foorst takes a look."

"You have come a thundering long way to hide this money." He nodded. "And there's the devil's own trouble to be taken afterward. First the voyage from here to Sydney; then the trusting of Teach's friend. Max Lampton, with this big, rich secret; then supposing *that* to prove all right, the return to Amsterdam Island – this fine brig, meanwhile, having been cast away – in some crazy little schooner, with the risks of a trip to New Holland in a bottom that may drop out under the weight of fifteen tons of silver."

"Ve vhas not all dom'd fools," said he, with a slow smile; "dere vhas no grazy bottoms mit us. Dis brig vhas fine, yaw," said he, with a leisurely look round the deck, "but she must go."

"It's the maddest scheme that even sailors ever lighted upon," said I, "but let's have the rest of it. Having dug your pit you come back for the cargo?"

"Yaw."

"It may take you a day to dig your pit."

"And b'raps two," said he.

"You will load about four tons a journey."

"Call her five," said he.

Here I observed that Galen, Teach, and one or two others having observed the big Dutchman and me close and earnest, yet very audible in this talk, had approached with sneaking steps to within earshot, where they feigned to occupy themselves, one in coiling down a rope, another in dipping for a drink out of the scuttle-butt, and so on. This decided me to drop the subject.

I walked to a corner of the deck called the starboard quarter, and folding my arms leaned against the bulwarks. A dim and faint idea had come to me in those few instants of time when Yan Bol went forward and called out to his mates on the forecastle with his immense, hairy, square hand beside his mouth, and this idea had slightly brightened while I questioned him. It was an idea that would be quite glorious if successful; otherwise it would be a forlorn and beggarly idea, a treacherous, cut-throat idea, exactly fit to play my heavy stake of silver and the Spanish maid into the hands of the men, and to secure me the quickest exit that could be contrived by the knife or the yardarm.

Madam Aurora watched me. I wish you were a man, thought I. Are you a person to fail one in a supremely critical hour? You offered to stick three men in the back; have you the courage to stick one man face to face?

I regarded her steadfastly, reflecting. I better remember her on that particular afternoon than at any former time. Would you like to know how she was dressed? I will tell you exactly. She wore a seaman's plain cloth jacket, fitted by her own hands to her figure; it sat well and was tight and comfortable for those latitudes. She wore the dress she had been clad in when we took her off the island; she had turned it, or in some fashion rearranged it, and it was no longer the hideous garment I had thought it. She wore a cloth cap; it sat like a turban upon her thick, black hair, and laugh now, if you will! she wore a pair of sailor's shoes, whence you will guess that what grace of *littleness* she had, lay in those hands of hers I have admired so often. Not at all. Her foot was perfectly proportioned to her hand. She had small, delicately-shaped, highly-arched, and altogether lovely feet. The shoes she wore I had found in the second of the slop-chests; they were embellished with buckles; the Dutch shopman probably stowed them away by mistake; they might have been designed for some dandy lad of a Batavian quarterdeck; they were *small*, and small they *must* have been, for they fitted Aurora.

This is the picture of her as she sat, intently regarded by me, who lay against the rail with folded arms, deeply considering. Teach and the others had sneaked forward again. Bol stumped the weather gangway. He was usually respectful enough, whenever I came on deck, to carry his vast carcass to a humbler part of the brig than I occupied. Miss Aurora rose and walked up to me.

"What are you thinking about?" said she, speaking in her own way, a way I have not yet attempted to write, and shall not here give. "Do I look ill, that you stare at me?"

"I am thinking."

"I am not blind. I might suppose I saw mischief in your face, if I thought you capable of mischief."

A pair of slow but shrewd Dutch eyes, and a pair of big but attentive Dutch ears overtopped the spokes of the wheel. I made her glance at Wirtz by myself looking at him. She understood the meaning in my face, and returned to her chair. I crossed the deck, and passing my arm round a lee backstay, gazed at the horizon ahead, thinking with all my might.

I remained on deck about half an hour, and then went below. I took a book out of the shelf in my berth, and seated myself at the cabin table, as far removed as possible from the skylight, but not out of sight of one who should peer through the glass; the size of the cabin did not admit of such concealment. After the lapse of a few minutes I was joined by Miss Aurora, who pulled off her cap and placed herself beside me.

There could be nothing suspicious in our sitting close together. Many a time had we sat very close together indeed, at that cabin table, under the skylight, when I was teaching her to speak the English language, and wondering whether, under *other* circumstances, I should discover myself to be rather in love with this fine young Spanish woman; and many a time had the men looked down and observed us, and grinned, I have no doubt, and uttered such remarks, one to another, as the very low level of their forecastle intelligence would suggest.

"What has caused you to stare at me, Señor Fielding?"

"I have wished to satisfy myself that you are to be trusted."

"*Ave Maria!* Trusted! Do not wrap up your meaning. I dislike people who wrap up their meaning."

"Could you kill a man?"

"For my honour and for my liberty, yes," she replied after a short silence, rearing herself in her swelling way, and flashing one of her wicked looks at me.

"Would you faint when you had killed him?"

Her manner instantly changed. She slightly shrugged her shoulders and answered, "A little thing has made me faint. At Acapulco I slept at a friend's house. I awoke, and by the moonlight saw a mouse upon my bed, after which I remember no more. But nothing heroic, nothing exalted in horror, would make me faint, I think. I could look upon a man slain by me for my liberty or for my honour without swooning." This was, in effect, her answer to my question.

"Have you ever killed a man?" said I.

"No," she answered hotly; "but when he is ready for me I shall be ready for him;" and, unbuttoning the breast of her coat, she thrust her hand into the pocket of her gown and pulled out a poniard or stiletto. It was a blue, gleaming blade, about seven or eight inches long, sheathed in bright metal, with a little ivory hilt that sparkled with some sort of embellishment of gem or ore. In all the time we had been associated she had never once given me to know that she went armed; but I afterward discovered she was a young woman who knew how to keep a secret.

"Hide that thing!" I cried with a glance at the skylight.

She pocketed it, giving me a fiery nod. "Never," said she, "have you asked me whether I was afraid to be alone with Jorge and Antonio on the island. *Vaya!* Do your English ladies secrete knives about them? It is a wise custom. But you wish to find out if I am to be trusted, if I can kill a man for my liberty or for my honour. Try me," she cried, snapping her finger as she waved her hand close to my face.

"I have a scheme," said I, "for getting away with the treasure and the brig and you."

"The treasure first," she exclaimed, smiling till her face looked to be lighted up with her white teeth. "You will have to be quick. Is not tomorrow the day of your Amsterdam Island?"

"Ask the wind that question," I answered.

"What is your scheme?"

"It is a magnificent scheme providing it succeeds. If it does not succeed better had we never been born. Shall we desperately attempt it?"

"*Qué es eso* – what is it? what is it?" she cried; and then a passion of excitement seized her, and her hands trembled.

"I will tell you the scheme in a minute. It depends not upon me and you only. I shall require the help of the lad, Jimmy. Is he to be trusted?"

"Your scheme – your scheme!"

"Is he to be trusted?" I continued, feigning to read aloud from the book that was before me, for I had thought I heard a man stop in his walk overhead. "My scheme is not to be thought of unless this youth will help us. You are a very observant lady. I have often seen you look attentively at Jimmy."

"*Vaya!* If I have looked at him it was without thought, and because I had nothing else to do. What a face to gaze at attentively!"

"Do you think he is to be trusted?"

"You continue to ask me that question," she exclaimed, petulantly twisting her prayer-ring as though hotly engaged in the aves. "First tell me your scheme, and then I will give you my opinion on Jimmy's trustworthiness."

On this, feigning to read aloud to her while I talked, that anyone above might suppose we were at our old game of playing at school, I communicated my scheme to her. A scheme it was: a distinct idea and project of deliverance; but several conditions, partly of chance, partly of contrivance, must attend its success. She listened eagerly, never removing her eyes from me, and once she was so well pleased that she clapped her hands and fell back with a loud laugh. This was not a behaviour to object to. No man, warily observing us, would guess our talk, the significance of this long and intimate cabin consultation, from the hard laughter of the *señorita*, and the merry noise of the clapping of her hands. In truth I never could have imagined such spirit in a woman. She had clapped her hands at the one feature whose disclosure would have turned another woman faint, she being to act in it. It was this stroke of our projected business that had made the cabin ring with her laughter.

"How long will the work occupy?" said I.

"It matters not," she answered. "I will take no rest until I have finished it."

"You will not, however, begin until I have talked with Jimmy? If I see reason to distrust him, we must think of another plan."

"Promise him plenty of dollars if he is faithful," said she, "and threaten him with death if he fails you."

We continued for some time longer to talk over my scheme. I then walked to the stand of arms, and looked, with much irresolution in my mind, at the muskets and the cutlasses, and at several pistols hanging near. My instincts cautioned me to disturb nothing.

"No," said I, wheeling round to the lady; "those weapons must remain as they are. The magazine is down there," said I, pointing to a part of the deck that formed the ceiling of a small compartment just forward of the lazarette. "It is entered by that hatch, and, therefore, if the men require ammunition – and it is likely as not they'll go ashore armed – they must pass through this cabin to get at the magazine. Nothing must be disturbed."

At this point the lad arrived to prepare our supper. Miss Aurora walked to her berth. I sat upon a locker and watched the youth, as he went round the table furnishing it for the meal. I have elsewhere described him. Since the date to which that description belongs he appeared to have grown somewhat; he had broadened; his face had gathered from the dye of the weather something of the manly look of the sailor; but that was all. It was still a stupid, insipid, grinning face. He breathed hard, and put down the knives and forks and plates with the characteristic energy of a weak-minded youth who is always very much in earnest. He was more than usually in earnest now, because I watched him. I took the altitude of his head, and guessed him taller than I, who was a pretty big chap, too. I took a view of his hands. Methought they fell not far short of Yan Bol's in magnitude. They were not fat, like the hands of Yan Bol; on the contrary, they were bony and rugged with muscle and veins. They were hands to hold on with – to hit hard with.

Presently, reflection in me became a torment; nay, without straining words, I may say that it rose into anguish. Should I put my life and the life of the girl into the hands of that youth, who was little more than an idiot? I waited until he had prepared the table for supper. I could then endure the agony of irresolution no longer, and I rose and walked to my berth, bidding him follow me. When he was entered I shut the door. He stared at me, slightly grinning, but his look had a little of wonder and fear in it.

"Jimmy," said I, "you're often in the forecastle, aren't you? You follow the talk of the men, I guess. Where do you sling your hammock?"

"In the eyes, master."

"You hear the men talk. Do you understand 'em?"

"Why, ay," he answered, staring at me without a wink from the full, knock-kneed, muscular stature of him; for he stood before me as a soldier – as he used to stand before Greaves when he received a lesson on the difference of dishes.

"What's going to happen to this brig?"

"Why, master, they're going to unload the silver and hide it in Amsterdam Island; and then we're a-going to sail away for the coast of New Holland, where you're to wreck us; and then we comes back for the money."

"After?"

"Dunno what's going to happen arter."

"What's to be your share of the dollars?"

"There's been nary word said about my share, master."

"D'ye know why?"

"'Cos they don't mean to give me none."

"That's so. There's ne'er a dollar meant for you, Jimmy. Don't you think that's hard?"

"I'm a poor lad, master. What comes, comes to the likes of me. When the captain died I lost my friend;" and grasping his fingers he cracked his joints one after another, yielding first on one leg and then on the other, as though he was about to break into a main-deck double shuffle.

"Did Captain Greaves ever promise you a share?"

"No, master."

"But you have a claim, and he was not the man to have overlooked it D'ye remember Galloon?"

"Remember him, master? Remember Galloon?" said he, lowering his voice.

"Galloon was an honest dog. Had he been able to speak, his advice to you would always have been 'Jimmy, be honest.'"

He looked somewhat wild and scared, as though he imagined I was going to charge him with a wrong.

"It'll be a wicked act to cast this fine brig away, don't you think? Galloon wouldn't have loved ye for helping in such a job."

"It'll be no job of mine, master."

"Both Galloon and Captain Greaves," said I, "would have wished you to be on the right side, no matter whose side it might happen to be. Are you on the right side or the wrong side? Are you on the side where home lies, where a share of the dollars lies, where safety lies; or are you on the side where New Holland lies, where there are no dollars for you, where there's no home for you, and where you may be finding a gibbet as one who helped to cast a ship away? – if the men don't first chuck you overboard as being in the road."

He continued to listen with increasing eagerness and agitation, cracking his joints again and again, while he advanced his head, setting his mouth in the form of a half-arrested yawn. When I had ceased he nodded repeatedly, maintaining silence, with a face that seemed to mark him too full for utterance. He, then, in stammering and choking voice, exclaimed, while a grotesque smile touched his countenance into a dim intelligence, even as the eastern obscurity is tinctured by the lunar dawn:

"Master, I sees yer meaning. I ain't on the side where the gibbet is. I would sail round the world with you, master,"

Twenty minutes later he followed me out of my berth, and went on deck to fetch the cabin supper from the galley.

"Are you satisfied?" said the lady Aurora, who was seated at the table.

"Perfectly," I answered.

Chapter XXIX.
Amsterdam Island

I HAD hoped to make the Island of Amsterdam next day; had the wind prospered we should have sighted it according to my reckoning; but in the morning watch, a little after daybreak, the breeze fell, shifted, and came on to blow ahead in hard rain squalls.

Yan Bol aroused me. I was sleeping soundly. I had been busy throughout the long night – busy after a manner of secrecy that had rendered my toil not less exhausting to my mind than to my body. Throughout the night I had been occupied with the boy Jimmy in paying furtive visits to the magazine, and with the help of the lad I had stowed away in a cabin locker a few round shot, cartridges for the long gun aft, some canister, pistols which I had loaded, and to whose primings I had care fully looked, a few brace of handcuffs, and some bilboes or leg-irons, such as Greaves had obliged Mr. van Laar to sit in.

This work had run into hours, because I had to await opportunities to carry it on – the changes of the watch, men's movements above – and throughout it was the same as though a musket had been levelled at my head, so frightful was the peril, so deadly the consequences of detection. For besides the risk of my movements aft exciting attention, there was the chance of Jimmy being missed forward. Luckily he was what is termed at sea "an idler," and an idler at sea has "all night in." No man can tell by merely looking at a hammock whether it is occupied or not, and I counted upon such of the men as might give the lad a thought believing that he lay buried in his canvas bag in the eyes of the brig.

Yan Bol aroused me. I went on deck and found a sallow, roaring, wet morning. The brig was heading points off her course, bursting in smoke through the headlong leap of the surge, with the topsail yards on the caps, reef tackles hauled out, a number of men rolling up the mainsail, and two on the main and two on the fore struggling with the wet, bladder-like topgallant sails.

I was bitterly vexed. Postponement might mean frustration. My scheme was ready for instant execution; my heart was hot as a madman's to *have* at the project and accomplish it; and now I might be obliged to wait a month and perhaps as long again as a month! For here was just the sort of wind to blow us half-way back the distance we had already measured; and I could do nothing until the brig was off Amsterdam Island, the weather quiet, the maintopsail to the mast, and Bol and the longboat ashore.

There was nothing, however, to be done beyond heaving the brig to under a rag of main staysail, and letting her lie with no more way than she would get from the hurl of the seas and the gale up aloft.

And yet, in one sense, this foul weather was as fortunate a thing as could have happened; I'll tell you why. I had taken care to persuade Yan Bol that I had turned over the crew's scheme of burying the money, had thought better of it, was, indeed, now thinking well of it as, on the whole, the easiest way to secure the treasure for a method of distribution to be afterward considered; but I had never flattered myself that he believed me fully sincere. In fact, I had shown too much amazement at the start, reasoned against the imbecile project too vehemently afterward. But now, when this change of weather came, my disappointment was so great, my mortification so keen, that even Yan Bol, with his slow eyes, and heavy, dull, ruminant intellect could not look me in the face and mistake.

We stood together while the men rolled the canvas up, their hoarse cries, as they triced up the bunts, going down the gale like the yells of gulls. The rain swept us in horizontal lines; the water smoked the length of the brig as though her metal sheathing were red hot; the Dutchman's cap of fur clung to his big head like a huge, over-ripe fig. The mist of the sudden gale boiled round the sea line, and we laboured in the commotion of our horizon, whose semi-diameter could have been measured by a twenty-four pounder.

"Holy Sacrament!" roared Yan Bol in Dutch. "Dis vhas der vindt to make anchells of men!" and he shook his immense fist at the windward ocean, and thundered out, "Nimin dich der Teufel, as der Schermans say!"

"Han't I had enough of this?" I shouted, sweeping my hand round the dirty, freckled green of the seas, which were beginning to heap themselves with true oceanic weight out of the granite shadow of the wet. "I'd had months of it when I was picked up off the oar, and I've had months of it since, and months of it remain." And I bawled to him that we wanted no more hindrances from the weather, that it was time the dollars were buried, that it was time, indeed, we were thrashing the brig to that part of the Australian coast where we should agree to wreck her. "I want my money," I cried. "I want to settle down ashore."

"Vhere vhas ve bound to now?"

"Dead west and all the way back again."

"Vy zyn al verdom'd! Vere vhas der island?"

"Somewhere close. The brig must be kept thus while it blows on end. I may have overshot the mark, and the island may be leeward of us now – so keep your weather eye lifting."

Together we stormed at the disappointment awhile in this fashion, I more hotly than he, and with more sincerity, perhaps, for I was maddened by the weather. The brig was reduced, as I have said, to a fragment of staysail, but she was light, and blew to leeward like a cask. I threw the log-ship over the weather quarter, and the line stood out to windward like the warp of a fisherman's trawl. For three days and three nights it continued to blow, and we to drift. The flying sky blackened low down over the sea, and the surges came out like cliffs from the windward shadow. I obtained no sights, and knew not our situation. I never could at any time have been cocksure of the position of the brig; the mariner, in those times, went to sea but poorly equipped with nautical instruments. His Hadley's quadrant was indeed an improvement upon the cross-staff of his forefathers, and he had a chronometer or watch which those who went before him were not so fortunate as to possess; not because watches of exquisite workmanship were not to be procured, but because nobody had thought of Greenwich time. But the sailor of 1815 was nevertheless not equipped as the sailor of today is. Charts were misleading; the ocean current worked its own sweet will with a man; consequently, I am not ashamed to own that I never could have been cocksure of the brig in reference to land, and more particularly to such a speck of land as Amsterdam Island makes, as you shall observe by casting your eye on the chart. The fear that the vast lump of rock might be to leeward in the thickness kept me terribly anxious. I was hour after hour on deck. My anxiety went infinitely deeper than the possible adjacency of the island; but the crew believed that I was only worried for the safety of the brig; and this, as I had reason to know, raised me high in their opinion.

So that, as I say, the foul weather blew for a useful purpose; but, by delaying me, it involved risks. Jimmy had my secret; he was exactly acquainted with my scheme. Suppose the half-witted fellow should babble; nay, suppose he should talk in his sleep! When I had explained my project to him I believed that the brig would be off the island next day. It was wonderful that my hair should have retained its colour; that the machinery of my brain should have worked with its established nimbleness. *That*, I say, was wonderful, considering the bitter anxieties of the navigation, the fear of Jimmy involuntarily or unconsciously betraying me, the conviction that I was a dead man if that happened, and that the lady Aurora would be barbarously used through rage and the spirit of revenge and brutal wantonness.

Fine weather came at last. It was the fifth day of our westerly drift. The sea flattened and opened, the sky cleared, the wind fell dead, and then, over the green rounds of the swell, there blew a draught of air from the northwest. The sun shone brightly before noon. I got a good observation, and calculated our distance at about two hundred miles from the island. All sail was heaped upon the brig, every studding sail boom run out, everything that would draw mast-headed; and, at four o'clock of that afternoon, the little ship was sweeping through it at twelve knots, roaring to the drag of a huge lower studding sail, every tack and sheet, every backstay and halliard taut as a harp-string and shrill with the song of the wind; with all hands standing by watching for something to blow away, and ready to shorten sail, should the yawning hurl of the fabric grow too fierce for spars and spokes.

You know the month; the date I forget. The day, I recollect, was a Friday. It had been a very dark night, blowing fresh down to about the hour of eleven, during which time we had given the brig all her legs, forcing her to her best with large reefless breasts of canvas. Not a star showed all through the night. An eager lookout was kept for the Island of New Amsterdam, which, I guessed, should be visible, were there daylight to disclose it.

It is a lofty mass of land, rising amidships to an altitude of near three thousand feet; and a frequent heave of the log had assured me that already, in these hours of darkness, we were within its horizon. I swept the sea line. It was all black, smoky gloom. No deeper dye than that of the universal shadow of the night was visible. Toward midnight the wind slackened. We rolled on a deep-breasted heave of swell, which, I reckoned, would be raising a mighty smother of yeast at those points and bases of iron terraces which confronted this long lift of ocean. The swollen sails dropped; the brig flapped along like a homeward-bound crow at sunset. Amid intervals of silence I strained my ears, but not the most distant noise of breakers did I catch.

This went on till a little while before the hour of daybreak. The weather was now very quiet, and the brig floated stealthily through the darkness, under small canvas. I had no mind to pass the island and find it astern of me, and perhaps out of sight, at sunrise.

I went into the cabin, when dawn was close at hand, to drink a glass of grog and puff at a pipe of tobacco. The lady Aurora was in her berth. She had been about during the night; had once or twice joined me on deck, and we had conversed cautiously as we walked. I sat upon the locker in which, some nights before, I had stowed away the materials for my scheme. How long was the execution of that scheme going to take? Would the lady Aurora's courage be equal to the part I had allotted to her? Was Jimmy's half-addled head to be depended upon ill the instant of a supremely tragic crisis, when action, saving or delaying time by a minute or two, might make all the difference between life and death?

Thus thinking, I sat upon the desperately-charged locker, puffing at my pipe and drinking from my glass. Suddenly the thunder of Yan Bol's voice resounded through the little interior:

"Landt on der starboardt bow!"

I sprang to my feet, and gained the deck in a heart-beat. Dawn was breaking right ahead. A melancholy, faint green light lay spread low down along the sky; against that light ran the horizon – a deep black line; and on the right, or about three points on the starboard or lee bow, there stood against that green light of dawn the pitch-black mass of the Island of New Amsterdam, defined as clearly upon the growing light as the fanciful edges of an ink-stain on white blotting-paper.

It was not the Island of St. Paul's. *That* I knew. It was, therefore, Amsterdam Island; and, filled as I was with anxiety and distracted by many contending passions, a momentary emotion of pride swelled my heart when I beheld that island, scarcely five miles distant, within three points under the bows of the little brig.

Yan Bol stood beside me with folded arms. The ear-flaps of his hair cap helmeted his face; his skin was green with the faint light ahead; he looked like a mariner of Tromp's day in casque-like cap.

"So dot vhas der island? Dot vhas New Amsterdam, hey? *Potsblitz!* Vhas not der Doytch everywhere in her day? But dot day vhas gone. Und dot vhas der island, hey? Veil, she vhas in good time, und I likes der look of der vetter. Vhere vhas der landing-place, I fonders?"

I told him I couldn't say; I was without a chart of the island. Its configuration, to our approach, was that of a lofty mass of coal-black rock southeast, with a down-like shelving of the stuff into the interior, and a facing seaward of rugged, horribly precipitous cliff. I should say it scarcely measured five miles north and south. The ocean looked lonely with it, as a babe makes lonelier the figure of the lonely woman who carries it; the melancholy picture of the deep at that moment – of that picture of faint green dawn blackening out the forlorn pile of island and the indigo sweep of the sea-line on either hand of it, and all astern of us the thickness of the smoky shadows of the departing night – is indescribable.

The sun rose right behind the island. It shot out a hundred beams of splendour before lifting its flaming upper limb; it was then a fine morning; the water of this Indian Ocean brimmed in a dark and beautifully pure blue to the base of the iron-like steeps; the flash and dazzle of rollers were visible at points, the sky was hard and high with a delicate shading and interlacery of grey cloud, and the wind was small and about northwest.

I looked south for the Island of St. Paul; it was invisible from the altitude of our deck, though I dare say on a fine, clear day it may be seen from the top of Amsterdam Island.

"Vere vhas the landing-places, I fonders," said Bol.

I fetched the glass and carefully covered as much of the island as our bearings commanded. While I kneeled I felt a hand upon my shoulder.

"*Que tiempo hace?*" inquired the lady Aurora in a cool, collected voice, looking down into my face.

I answered in Spanish that the weather was fine and promised to keep so.

"Good-morning, Mr. Bol," said she.

"Goodt-morning, marm. I hope you vhas veil dis morning? Dot vhas der island at last. She vhas a Doytchman's discovery. I likes to tink of der Doytchers all der vay down here."

The lady Aurora made no reply, probably not having understood a syllable of Bol's speech. I put the telescope into the Dutchman's hand, and bade him look for himself. The lady arched her brows at the island, and glanced interrogatively, round the sea, fixing her eyes upon me full with a look of meaning. I faintly inclined my head. Often had I read her meaning in her face when I had failed to grasp her words, so facile and fluent was the eloquence of her looks.

All the crew save Hals and Jimmy were collected on the forecastle-head, staring at the island. The caboose chimney was smoking, and Hals' head frequently showed in the caboose doorway while he took a view of the land. Galen constantly pointed and talked much, and was the centre of a little crowd. Bol stood up, and said he could see no signs of a landing-place.

"There'll be one on the eastern side, I dare say," said I. "You're bound to have a landing-place somewhere. I wish I had a chart of the island. The last survey I remember was d'Entrecasteaux's. It is enough, of such an island as this, to know that it exists. Look at it!"

The sun was hanging over it now; its light revealed many slopes of the land falling to the precipitous edge of the cliffs. A most horribly barren rock did it seem – desolate beyond the dreams of the wildest fancy of an uninhabited island. There may have been some sort of growth on top; I know not; I saw no verdure. All was cold, naked, iron-hard cliff, swelling centrally into a prodigious summit, around which even as I watched dense white masses of mists were beginning to form and crawl, reminding me of the magnificent growth and fall of lace-like vapour on Table Mountain – the fairest and most marvellous of all the airy sights of the world when viewed by moonlight.

I hauled the brig in to within a mile of the land, then, observing discoloured water, I ordered a cast of the hand-lead to be taken; no bottom was reached. We shifted the helm, trimmed sail, and stood about southeast, rounding the point which I have since ascertained is called Vlaming Head, so named after the Dutch navigator who was off this island in 1696. Here we found fifty fathoms of water, and black sand for a bottom. The rollers broke very furiously against the base of Vlaming Head. Foam was heaped in a vast cloud there, as though the sea was kept boiling by a great volcanic flame just beneath.

We trimmed sail afresh and steered northeast. The land rose black and horribly desolate; but the swell being from the west the sea was smooth, and the tremble of surf small along the whole range this side. All this while we eagerly gazed at the coast in search of a landing-place – of any platform of sand and split of cliff by which the inland heights might be gained. Bol's round face grew long, and he swore often in Dutch. Many of the men came aft to be within talking distance of the quarter-deck, and hoarsely-uttered remarks and oaths fell from them, as they gazed at the precipitous front of the island and beheld no spot to land on.

The wind was scarcely more than a light draught of air, owing to the interposition of the land; it was off the bow, too, by this time, and we were braced up sharp to it. I told Bol to send the crew to breakfast while the brig made a board into the northeast to enable her to fetch the northern parts of the island, where now lay our only chance of finding a landing-place. Impatience worked like madness in me, and no man of all our ship's company could have been wilder to behold a landing-place than I.

The breeze slightly freshened as we stood off from the island. I put the brig into the hands of Galen, and went below to get some breakfast. Miss Aurora and I conversed in subdued voices; she ate little, and was pale, but I saw courage in her mouth and eyes. While Jimmy waited I told him that, if we found a landing-place, our business might be settled before sundown. "Before sundown," said I to him, "we may, but I don't say we shall, be sailing along, the island astern, old England before us, and a handsome promise of dollars for you, my lad, when we arrive. Are ye all there?"

"All there, master," said he, feeling his wrist.

"You've gone through your lessons o'er and o'er again?"

"O'er and o'er, master."

"This job'll make a fine man of you, You shall knock off the sea and choose a calling ashore. What would you be? Oh, but don't think of that yet. Have nothing in your mind but this," said I, holding up my hand and twisting it as though I screwed a man by tile throat. "Afterward turn to and whistle and dance till you give in."

His grin was deep and prolonged. The feeling that he was now being enormously trusted by me bred a sort of manliness in him. Methought he was a little less of a fool than he used to be; his gaze had gathered something of steadfastness, his grin something of intelligence.

When our stretch had brought the northern point of the island abeam, we put the brig about and headed for the island on the starboard tack; and now, after we had been sailing for some time, the telescope gave me a sight of what we were all on the lookout for. The northern point of the island sloped to the edge of the sea, in perhaps half a mile's length of surf-washed margin. The surf was but a delicate tremble. The climb to the height was steep; but fair in the lenses lay the half-mile of landing-place, whether sand or beach or rock I knew not.

"Yonder's where you'll be able to get ashore," I cried, thrusting the telescope into Yan Bol's hands.

"What dy'e see?" bawled Teach, who overhung the bulwark rail.

"A landing-place, my ladts, und she vhas all right," thundered Bol, with his eye at the telescope.

"Anything alive ashore?" cried Teach.

"All vhas uninhabited," answered Bol.

"Ne'er a hut?" shouted Teach.

"Vhas dot uninhabited, you tonkey? Dere vhas no shtir. Dot vhas der country for my dollars until by um by. Hurrah!"

He rose slowly and heavily from his posture of leaning, and put the glass down. I took another long look at the island we were approaching. There was majesty in its loneliness; there was majesty in the altitude its dark terraces and inland heights rose to. A crown of cloud was upon the brow of its central height, and the sunshine whitened into silver that similitude of regal right – as real and lasting, for all its being vapour, as any earthly crown of gold!

"There's your island, and there's your landing-place," said I, thrusting my hands into my pockets. "What's the next stroke, Yan Bol?"

"Vhat vhas der soundings here?" he answered, going to the side and looking down.

"What do you want with the soundings?"

"Shall you not pring oop?"

"No, by thunder!" I cried. "What? Bring up off that island with four men and a boy to man the capstan should it come on to blow a hurricane on a sudden out of the eastward there, putting that black coast dead under our lee? No, by thunder! If we are to bring up I'll go ashore with you; I'll not stay with the brig; I'll not risk my life. Oh, yes! It will kill the time to hunt for the dollars at low water after the brig's stranded and gone to pieces, eh? Bring up?" I continued, shouting out that all the men might hear me; "send plenty of victuals ashore if that's your intention. I'm no man-eater; and what but Dutch and English flesh will there be to eat if it comes to anchoring?"

"Mr. Fielding knows what he's talking about," sung out Teach; "I'm to stay aboard for one, and I guess he's right. No good to talk of slipping if it comes on to blow; we aren't flush of anchors, and the end of this here traverse is a blooming long way off yet."

"How vhas she to be?" cried Bol, looking round the sea.

"How was she to be?" I exclaimed. "Why, heave to under topsails and a topgallant sail."

"Suppose she cooms on to blow und ve vhas still ashore?"

"Well?"

"Veil, der vetter obliges you to roon, und you lost sight of der island und us. How vhas dot, mit noting to eat ashore, und der vetter tick und beastly for dree veeks, say?"

"Look here, Bol," said I, speaking loudly, "you are wasting valuable time in talking damned nonsense. You're all for supposing. *I* choose to suppose because I am to be left in charge of this brig, frightfully short-handed, and don't mean to depend upon her ground tackle. D'ye understand me?" He gave one of his immensely heavy nods. "But *you* – there are always chances and risks in a job of this sort, and recollect 'tis your own bringing about – 'twas you and Teach yonder who contrived it."

"Vell?" he thundered impatiently.

"Get your boat over as smartly as may be when the time arrives. Load her with as much silver as you may think proper to take for the first jaunt. Stow a piece or two of beef and some barrels of bread – you say there is fresh water ashore?"

"Blenty," said the Dutchman.

"You can bring off the victuals when your job's ended," said I.

"Mr. Fielding, you're right," said Teach. "Yan, 'tis only agin the chance of our being blowed off. If that's to happen, ye must have enough to eat till we tarns up agin. But what's that chance?" cried he, with a stare up aloft and around. "If the fear o't's to stop us, good-night to the burying job."

Bol trudged a little way forward; the men gathered about him and held a debate. I marched aft with my hands in my pockets as though indifferent to the issue of their council, having made up my mind. But for all that it was a time of mortal anxiety with me.

After ten minutes Bol came aft and told me that the crew were agreed the brig should be hove to. There was no anchor at the bow, and precious time would be wasted in making ready the ground tackle. Next, we should have to haul in close to land to find anchorage, and the crew were of my opinion that the brig was a perished thing with such a coast as *that* close aboard under her lee, should it come on to blow a hard inshore wind.

"Und besides," he continued, "ve doan take no silver mit us today. Our beesiness vhas to oxplore. Ve take provisions und shovels, und der like, vhen ve goes ashore now, und ve begins to dig if ve findts a place dot all vhas agreed vhas a goodt place for hiding der money."

"Then turn to and get all ready with the boat," said I; "we shall be in with the land close enough in a few minutes. I want a mile and a half of offing – nothing less – otherwise I go ashore in the boat and you stop here."

"Hov your way, sir; hov your way," he rumbled in his deepest voice. "Vhat should I do here? Soopose ve vhas blowned away out of sight of der island; how vhas I to findt her?"

Saying this he left me, and in a few minutes all hands were in motion. I stopped them, in the middle of their labours over the boat, to bring the brig to a stand. We laid the main topsail aback, and since it was now certain that I should not be able to put my scheme into execution that day, I ordered them to reduce the ship to very easy canvas; the mainsail was furled, the forecourse hauled up, the trysail brailed up, and other sails were taken in, one or two furled, and one or two left to hang. The fellows then got the longboat over. They swayed her out by tackles, and when she was afloat and alongside they lowered some casks of beef and pork and some barrels of bread and flour into her. We were handsomely stocked with provisions, and I foresaw the loss of those tierces and barrels without concern.

The *señorita* came to my side, and we stood together at the rail, looking down into the boat and watching the proceedings of the men. It was a very fine day; the hour about one. The island lay in lofty masses of dark rock within two miles of us, bearing a little to the southward of east. The great heap of land filled the sea that way. The searching light of the sun revealed nothing that stirred. I saw not even a bird; but that might have been because the sea-fowl of the island were too distant for my sight. An awful bit of ocean solitude is Amsterdam Island. The sight of it, the reality of it, makes shallow the bottom of the deepest of your imaginations of loneliness. The roar of the surf, at points where the flash of it was fierce, came along in a note of cannonading. You'd have thought there were troops firing heavy guns t'other side the island.

The men threw the fore-peak shovels into the boat, along with crowbars, carpenter's tools, and whatever else they could find that was good to dig with. They handed down oars, mast, and sail. I particularly noticed the sail. It was a big, square lug with a tall hoist. The biggest galley-punts in the Downs carry such sails. The fellows lighted their pipes to a man. They grinned and joked and put on holiday looks. It was a jaunt – a fine change – a jolly run ashore for the rogues after our prodigious term of imprisonment. Besides, every man possessed a great fortune; every man might reckon himself up in thousands of dollars! I could not wonder that they grinned and wore a jolly air.

The following men entered the boat: John Wirtz, William Galen, Frank Hals, John Friend, William Street, and lastly, Yan Bol. Hals, as you know, was the cook. They took him, nevertheless – perhaps because he was suspicious, and wished to see for himself where the pit was dug; perhaps because he was an immensely strong man – short, vast of breech, of weight to sink, with his foot, a shovel through granite. And the following men were left behind to help me to control the brig: James Meehan, Isaac Travers, Henry Call, Jim Vinten, and Thomas Teach.

The men in the boat shoved off, hoisting the big lug as they did so. The devils sent up a cheer, and Bol flourished his hair cap at me and the lady. I returned the salute with a cordial wave of the hand, and the lady bowed. They hauled the sheet of the lug flat aft, that the boat might look a little to windward of the landing-place, where, so far as I could distinguish, there was a sort of split, or ravine, which would provide easy access to the inland heights and flats. I watched the boat's progress through the water with keen interest and anxiety. Flattened in as the sheet was, the little fabric swam briskly. The wind was small, yet the boat drove a pretty ripple from either bow and towed some fathoms of wake astern of her.

"We'll *chance* it, all the same!" thought I, setting my teeth.

Chapter XXX.
My Scheme

I WATCHED the boat until she entered the tremble of surf. 'Twas a mere silver fringe of surf, so quiet was the water on this, the lee side of the island. The sail of the boat shone in that slender edge of whiteness like a snowflake; then vanished on a sudden. I looked through the glass, and saw the men on either gunwale of the boat running her up the beach clear of the wash.

I was so provoked by that sight, that I was mad then and there to start on my scheme of release. The resolution seized me like a fit of fever, and the blood surged through me in a flood of fire. I went to the lee side of the deck to conceal my face. In a few minutes I had reconsidered my resolution and was determined to wait. For, first, the afternoon was advancing; the boat was not likely to stay long ashore; her sail might be showing out on the blue water, under the dark height of cliffs, ere I was half through with what lay before me. Next, the wind was very scant; it was scarce a four-knot air of wind, though the brig should be able to spread the canvas of a *Royal George* to the off-shore draught. There was nothing, then, to be done but wait; to pray for a continuance of fine weather and a little more wind.

The brig lay very quiet. The swell of the sea ran softly, and the hush that was upon the island – such a hush as was on the face of the earth when it was first created – was spread, like something sensible, throughout the atmosphere; and this silence of desolation was upon the breast of the sea. I kept the deck throughout the afternoon, often looking at the landing-place. The boat lay high and dry, watched by a single figure; the others were gone inland. They had sailed away without firearms – an oversight, I reckon; or they might have asked of one another, "What was the good of going armed to a desolate island?" Yet I had a sort of sympathy for that lonely figure down by the boat when I thought of him as unarmed. Frightfully lonesome he looked, with the great face of the cliff hanging high up behind him and spreading away, huge and sullen, on either hand. I guess, had I been that man, I should have yearned for a loaded musket. Crusoe carried two, and went the easier for the burden.

The sun would set behind the island. It was sinking that way when I spied the sail of the boat. The men had their oars over, and she came along pretty fast, I calculated her speed, and cursed it. She drew alongside, some of the men halloaing answers to questions bawled by Teach and the others, who were on the forecastle. Bol scrambled up, and shouting for all hands to get the boat inboard and stowed for the night, he stepped up to me, who was standing aft with Miss Aurora, Call being at the wheel.

"She vhas all right," said he, thick of voice with fatigue.

"What was all right?"

"Veil, first of all, she vhas der prettiest leedle islandt in der whole vorldt for hiding money in. Ve looked about us – all vhas still. Dere vhas birdts in der air, und dot vhas all, und dey vhas still too. Dere vhas no sign of man ever having landted upon dot island. Mr. Fielding, she vhas still undiscovered."

"Did you find any fresh water?"

"Blenty. Sweet und coldt."

"Have you dug your pit?"

"Donnerwetter, no! Dot vhas to take a morning. Der ground vhas hard like dis." He stamped his foot. "Dere vhas no caves; ve look for a hole, und dere vhas nothing so big ash a monkey might hide in."

"Have you stowed the provisions securely away?"

"Dot vhas all right, Mr. Fielding. Everyting vhas ready for der morning." He cast his gaze round upon the sky.

"Have you found a place for the burial of the money?"

"Yaw, a first-rate place," he answered, with a glance at the island. "Shtop till der shob is over, den you und Teach und der odders dot stays mit you goes ashore und you take der bearings of der place for yourself."

"I'll do that. It's fair, Bol."

"She vhas fair," he answered. "If you vhas villing, marm," he continued, addressing Miss Aurora, "you shall go mit us likewise. Dere vhas noting so goodt for man, fimmin, und beast as a leedle run ashore after months of board ship."

She did not understand him. I explained, giving her a look; she addressed me in Spanish and English.

"The lady will be glad to go ashore, and looks forward to it," said I.

Nothing more was said. The huge bulk of the man seemed wearied out to the heels of his feet; and, indeed, the straining and climbing involved in the ascent of those inland steeps must have sorely tested the muscle and bones whose load was Bol's fat. He went forward and sat down. The men had swayed the longboat inboard, had chocked her, and were now shipping the gangway and clearing up.

I considered a little and then resolved to let the brig lie as she was. We had a full two-mile offing, which was enough with a short lee-shore to deal with in case of a heavy, sudden inshore gale.

The sun went down behind the island, as it had risen behind the island, to our gaze when coming from the east. The western sky was a sheet of red splendor, and the island stood in a deep purple against it until the light went out of the heavens, when the land floated in shadow upon the dusk like a vast thick smoke hovering. Never a light kindled by mortal *there*! The whole mighty spirit of the great ocean solitude was in that shadow. A few clouds hung high, and the stars were bright, with a merry fair weather twinkling among them that made me hopeful of clear skies and brisk winds.

The night passed quickly. I lay upon the cabin locker, fully dressed, and was up and down every hour. The air was soft and mild, for Amsterdam Island lies upon the pleasantest parallel in the world,, where the atmosphere is sweet and dry, where it is never too hot, though at night-time it may be sometimes cold, and the wonder is that you should find such hideous barrenness and nakedness as you observe in this island in the most temperate, cheerful, and fruitful of climates.

Miss Aurora retired early, at my request. I was afraid of her on the eve of such a day as tomorrow might prove. She was a little heedless in her questions, talked somewhat loud, as the foreigner will when he discourses in our tongue, and to provide against all risks of our betraying ourselves by sitting in company below, or walking the deck together, I told her to go to bed.

At midnight Bol relieved Galen. I walked with Bol awhile, and all our talk was about the island, the depth at which the money should be buried, the mark that was to denote the treasure, and so forth. He wanted to know if money was to be injured by lying in the earth; I answered that the metal out of which money was made came from the earth. What would be a good mark to set up? I told him he was a carpenter and ought to know; but I advised him not to bury the money so carefully that we should never afterward be able to find out where it lay hid. He said it would not do to erect a cross, or any sign that indicated human handiwork, lest men should land after we had left the island, and, guessing at the meaning of the mark, fall a-digging. The place they had settled on he informed me was at the foot of a peculiar rise of land of a very strange shape. He described this rise of land and its appearance seemed to be that of the head of a cat. Once beheld it could never be forgotten. It was the wish of the men, however, when the money was buried, and I went on shore to view the spot and take its correct bearings from different points of the island, that I should make a sketch in black and white of the peculiarly-shaped rise of land or little hill; this would be copied, and each man hold a drawing of the hill for himself with all particulars written underneath.

"I'll do whatever is reasonable and right," said I.

"Dere vhas two ton belonging to you, Mr. Fielding."

"I don't forget."

In this walk we settled the next day's proceedings. I advised Yan Bol to take three tons of silver with him ashore when he started early in the morning with his digging party.

"Shall ve not dig der pit first?"

"Yaw, but also take a portion of your cargo with you. The boat's capacity of five tons was right enough for Captain Greaves' island; but here a roller may catch and capsize you, even as you're going ashore, unless you show the best height of side you can manage. Three tons a trip won't hurt – I'll not advise more."

"Yaw, dot vhas right. I himself vhas for tree. But vhy take der silver ashore before der pit vhas dig?"

"To save time. Then, with three tons, you'll have boxes and chests to enable you to gauge the depth and space you require. You don't want to dig forty feet when ten may do."

"No, by Cott, Mr. Fielding, nor would you if you only shoost knew how hardt vhas dot land. Veil, you vhas right. A leedle at a time, und ve starts tomorrow mit a leedle; und vhen der pit vhas dig ve comes back for more."

"How long will it take you to dig the pit?"

"Veil, dot vill be ash she shall turn out. She may mean a morning's shob, but all vhas right und safe, I hope, before der sun vhas sunk."

I went below and slept for an hour. The men got their breakfast early. Hals lighted the caboose fire before the sun was up, and the hands breakfasted when the east was still rosy with the dawn into which the sun had sprung in glory. I say in glory, for it was a very perfect morning, the sky of a deep blue, and the sea of a silver azure with the sunlight upon it. The breeze was light out of the north; but, if it held, it fanned with weight enough to serve my turn.

The men got the boats over as on the previous day. Yan Bol rolled up to me, who had come on deck long before sunrise, and said, "Mr. Fielding, how many cases vhas dere in tree tons?"

"About twenty," said I, "they won't all run alike in size. If they were all alike of course there'd be thirty."

"Veil, ve takes twenty."

"Yes, a little at a time, if you please. Two tons are mine. If you capsize, who bears the loss?"

"Dere vhas no capsize," said he. "Look what a beautiful day she vhas! Und how many dollars, Mr. Fielding, vhas dere in tree ton?"

"One hundred and ten thousand dollars."

He rounded his little eyes and smacked his huge lips, and could find no more to say than, "Veil, veil!"

He and Galen and three or four others shortly afterward went below and got into the lazarette, whence they handed out twenty cases of the silver. I feigned a prodigious interest, roaring out to the fellows in the boat, as I hung over the rail, to trim more by the head, to trim more by the stern, to keep the stuff amidships for the sake of stability; and then I bid Teach observe that three tons were to the full as much as should go per trip. "For," says I, "look well, and you'll find her a ton deeper than, in my opinion, her safety allows. But what are we sending ashore? Is it Thames ballast? Or is it something more precious than all your eyeballs put together? I'll have my two tons go alone. No other man's ton shall go along with mine," and so I went on shouting.

All being ready the crew of the boat entered her. They were the same as on the preceding day. I regretted this, for I had hoped that Teach or Travers or Meehan – Call I did not fear – would have taken the place of Friend, who, as you know, was the mildest man of the whole bunch of rogues; but I kept my mouth shut; I durst make no suggestion that way. We are all good men, the fellows would have said; what reason has he in wishing Friend to remain?

Call was at the wheel. I sung out to Meehan to lay aft and loose the trysail, adding, that the others might hear me, that the brig wanted more after-sail to keep her head to. The three men lay aft, and in a few minutes the sail was set.

In this time the longboat was slipping through the water toward the land. When the trysail was set I asked Meehan, who claimed to be a bit of a cook in his way, to boil me a pot of cocoa; I had been up all night, I said, and had breakfasted ill (the girl and I had not breakfasted at all). Travers and Teach went on to the forecastle; I watched them light their pipes, coming to the galley for a light, and returning to the forecastle; they leaned upon the rail in the head, and watched the boat.

"I shall be wanting a word with Teach below shortly," said I to Call; "does he know the Sydney coast? I'd like him to hit upon a spot for casting this brig away – something to keep in mind. There's no chart aboard that's going to help me in that job. Keep a lookout. Don't leave the wheel, and mind you hallo if I'm wanted."

I entered the cabin, and found the lady Aurora standing at the table, and the lad Jimmy near the door of my berth.

"The hour has come," said I, feeling myself grown pale on a sudden, "and the man's at hand. How is it with you?"

I gently grasped her wrist and looked at her.

"Only be quick, Señor Fielding. It is this waiting and waiting that tries the nerves," she answered in effect.

"How is it with you, Jimmy?"

"I'm ready, master."

"Where's the bag?" said I to the *señorita*.

"It's there" said she, pointing to a locker.

"Sit upon it, for I am about to send."

I entered my berth and brought out a chart of the continent of New Holland. I carried it to the table on the same side on which the lady had seated herself, and spread it, putting, as I well remember, a metal mug at each corner to keep the curled sheet flat. I then stepped to a scuttle and peered through it, and descried the sail of the boat close in with the island. I turned to the table again and called to Jimmy.

"Go now and send Teach here," and when he was gone I overhung the chart in a posture of anxious scrutiny; though in this while I several times glanced at the lady Aurora, who was sitting just behind me, and observed that she sat very still, her face as composed as at any time since I had known her, her eyes bent upon a book which she had taken from the table before sitting. The motion of the brig was gentle; the cabin became warm, almost hot; a little while before I descended I had looked through the skylight at Jimmy, who stood beneath, and he had quietly closed and secured the frames.

Teach came down, and behind him was Jimmy. He descended the steps without the least manner of suspicion. He wore a round hat, and his feet were naked, the bottoms of his trousers being turned up midway the height of the calves of his legs. I bade him uncover in the presence of a lady; he asked pardon, and threw his hat down upon the deck.

"Here's a chart of New Holland," said I, pointing to it. "D'ye know anything of the coast down Port Jackson way?"

"No, sir," said he.

"Where's this brig to be wrecked? Come you here." He came to my side, and I put my finger upon the line that denoted the coast near Port Jackson, holding my left hand behind me. "All hereabouts is wild ground, I reckon – and if the brig's to be stranded, the spot should be within a comfortable tramp of the town of Sydney," and as I pronounced these words I motioned with my left hand, on which, as swiftly as you fetch a breath, the lady Aurora whipped a big bag, thickened for the face with wadding, over the head of Teach, dragging it down to his shoulders and holding it there, and all as nimbly as the hangman pulls down the cap over the malefactor's face. In the same instant of her doing this I grasped Teach by his right arm and Jimmy seized him by his left, and pulling out a pair of handcuffs from my pocket I brought the fellow's wrists together and manacled him.

His first struggles were furious; but how should he be able to help himself in the grasp of two men, each of whom was out and away stronger than he? He kicked and plunged with frantic violence, but he could utter no sound. He was fairly suffocated by the thickly-lined bag which Miss Aurora had whipped down over his head.

Not an instant was to be lost; moreover, I had no intention to kill the man, though I reckoned by the gathering faintness in the capers he cut that his senses were going. Grasping him by the arms Jimmy and I dragged him aft and thrust him into a spare berth that lay between mine and the cabin I had occupied in Greaves's time. Miss Aurora followed and handed me a gag of her own manufacture. I pulled the cap off the man and found him nearly gone; we sat him on a locker with his back against the ship's side and I gagged him, taking care to see that the nostrils were clear. So there he was, gagged, handcuffed, and very nearly dead, and there was nothing to fear from him at present.

I shut the door of the berth and went again to the chart, while Miss Aurora sat behind me upon the bag as before. I slipped a second pair of handcuffs from my left into my right pocket, and then told Jimmy to send Travers below.

"If he asks you what I want," said I, "answer that Mr. Fielding and Teach are talking about casting away the brig and looking at the chart of Australia."

In a few moments Travers arrived. He was closely followed by Jimmy. He descended the steps without the least appearance of misgiving. I perceived, however, that in a moment he began to cast his eyes about for Teach.

"D'ye know anything of the coast of New Holland, Travers?"

"Nothen, sir."

"Teach and I have been talking about casting this brig away. Teach'll be here in a moment," said I, with a significant sideways motion of my head toward my berth, which I was willing the fellow should construe as he pleased. "This is the spot which Teach recommends," said I, putting my finger upon the chart. "Draw near, will you. You'll understand my meaning when your eyes are on the drawing of the coast."

He came at once to my side, cap in hand. I bade him observe the conformation of the coast, and while I spoke I made a motion with my left hand, whereupon, with lightning speed, the cap was on him! The man halloed faintly inside: 'twas like a voice from the height of a tall chimney; then, Jimmy and I bringing his brawny arms together, I slipped the handcuffs on.

He was a more powerfully built man than Teach, but without that devil's desperate spirit. He appeared to understand what we meant to do, felt his helplessness, and after a brief, fierce struggle stood quiet. We ran him, silent and suffocating in his bag, to the forward cabin on the larboard side, by which time he was nearly spent for want of air, so that, when we drew the bag off his head, he was black in the face. I waited a few minutes till he rallied somewhat, then gagged him with a second gag of Miss Aurora's manufacture. We next pulled off his boots, to provide against his kicking at the door, and threw them into the cabin, and shutting him up I went to the locker in which I had stored my borrowings from the magazine, as you have heard, and thrust a couple of loaded pistols into my pocket.

My lady Aurora had fallen into a chair: she was deadly white and trembled violently, and seemed to be fainting. I told Jimmy to give her a glass of brandy and follow me on deck. I dared not pause now, no, not even though her life should be risked by my going. I went on deck and stood a minute at the companion. Call was at the wheel, carelessly grasping the spokes. I looked toward the island; the boat was clearly ashore, her sail lowered, and nothing therefore to be seen of her, at that distance, with the naked eye.

Taking no notice of Call I walked to the caboose and looked in, expecting to see Meehan at work there boiling my cocoa. The caboose was empty, but the fire burned briskly as though freshly trimmed, and a saucepan was boiling upon it. I stepped swiftly to the fore-scuttle, that is to say, to the hatch by which the sailors entered or left the forecastle, and, when I was within a few feet of it, I spied Meehan's head in the act of rising to come on deck. I sprang and struck him hard, crying out, "Keep below till you're wanted." He fell backward, and I instantly drove the cover of the scuttle over the hatch and secured it by its bar.

Call remained to be dealt with. As I walked aft Jimmy came up out of the cabin. Call was very white. He let go the wheel, and cried out, "Mr. Fielding, where's my mates?"

"Where you'll be in a minute, my man," said I, pulling out one of the two pistols I had pocketed; for I had not foreseen in the case of Meehan so easy a capture.

"There's no need to show me that," said the fellow in his small voice, nodding his head at the pistol, "I follows your meaning, and I'll work as a good man if ye'll take me on."

"No, I won't trust you. Not yet, anyhow; though I should be mighty glad to believe you trustworthy."

"Try me, sir," he exclaimed.

"No, by – ! Jimmy, lay hold of that wheel and keep it steady. Call, get you forward," and I pointed with my pistol to the forecastle.

He went like a lamb, and I followed at his heels. Indeed, I needed no weapon with this man; in strength I was twice his master; in nimbleness and the art of fisticuffs he was not within a league of my longest shadow. I could have tossed him by scruff and breech over the rail, and have drunk a pint with the same breath I did it in.

When we came to the scuttle, I told him to open it and descend. Meehan roared out, when he saw daylight; I answered that I would send a bullet through his brains if he made any noise, that his and Call's wants should be seen to presently, and that I was going to sail the brig home to save the men who had been left with me from the gallows.

"Where's Teach and Travers?" bawled Meehan.

"Dead – dead – dead!" I cried, then closed and secured the scuttle as before, and ran to the cabin.

I found my lady very much better. She had drunk a little brandy, and was eating a biscuit; the trembling had left her, and her face was steady.

"All the men are secured." said I.

She clapped her hands and cried, "You have been very quick," and then laughed with hysteric vehemence; and, no doubt, to satisfy me that she was composed, she at the same moment got up from her chair, and said, "What is next to be done?"

"Follow me," said I.

I went on deck, and pointing the glass at the landing-place, took a long look. The fellows had hauled the boat high and dry; I could not see what sort of a beach it was; the boat lay beyond the thin line of feathering surf. There were figures about her in motion. I counted all the men who had gone in her. The telescope was poor – poor even for that age of marine spy-glasses – and I was unable to distinguish clearly. But the boat was high and dry, and the men were out of her and busy with their cargo; *that* was certain; so I put down the glass, and, going to the wheel, called to the *señorita* to come to me.

"Hold it thus," said I.

She at once stationed herself in Jimmy's place and grasped the spokes. Then, followed by the lad, I ran to the cabin, and, together, out of the locker we brought up three rounds for the long brass pivoted twenty-four pounder. We likewise loaded with all possible speed six muskets, which, with the remaining pistols that lay in the locker, we conveyed on deck. When this was done, I charged the long gun, taking care to see that all was ready for quickly reloading.

"Now, Jimmy," said I, "it is time to swing the main topsail yard and be off." The wind hung in the north; it was a little pleasant breeze, with just enough of weight to tremble the water into a darker dye of blue with the summer rippling and wrinkling of it, and to put a dance into the blinding sparkles under the sun. I went forward with the lad, and first we hoisted the standing-jib; then went to the main braces and, the wind being very light, we swung the yards easily. The topgallant sails had been clewed up on the previous day, and had hung by their gear unstowed all night. Both yards were heavy, for the *Black Watch* was very square in her rig; so to masthead the canvas we led the halliards to the little capstan on the quarterdeck, and set the sails with fairly taut leeches. A couple of staysails we also ran aloft, by which time the brig had wore. We then trimmed for the northerly draught, and in less than twenty minutes from the start of the operations the brig was standing eastward, and slowly gathering way, with Jimmy at the wheel, holding the little ship steady to my directions, myself near him, glass in hand, watching the men ashore, and the girl at my side.

I had reckoned on this – that, when the men saw me fill on the brig they'd suppose something to make me uneasy had hove into sight, or that I was manoeuvring to take up a new position. I guessed they'd never imagine for a long while that I was running away with the brig. I had taken particular care for weeks past that they should observe nothing in me to excite distrust. And then there were Teach and the others; and I counted upon Bol's and upon Bol's mates' confidence in the loyalty of those shipmates. So they'd watch us for some time without suspicion; and every minute was precious, because every minute the distance widened and the pace briskened.

Thus had my calculations forerun, and now I stood with the telescope at my eye, watching and waiting.

Five minutes passed – no more. I had turned to look at the compass and to glance aloft; and now I levelled the glass afresh.

"They're after us!" I cried.

In those five minutes they had launched the boat and, as I looked, were hoisting the sail and throwing their oars over. I was mightily startled at first. I had never imagined they'd prove so keen in their guessing; but reflection speedily cooled me, and brought my nerves to their proper bearing.

The boat gained on us slowly. The pace of the brig was about four miles an hour; the boat's a mile faster than that. Presently I could count the steady pulse of her five oars. I had no fear, but I was very eager to come off with the brig without killing any of those men. The lady Aurora said:

"They're catching us up."

"Yes," said I; "and if they can come within hail they'll make me a hundred fine promises and entreat me to take them on board; and, a few minutes after they are on board, my corpse will be floating astern – another shocking example of forecastle gratitude. I'm done with 'em," said I, scarcely supposing while I talked that she wholly understood me; and, putting my hand upon the long brass gun, I moved it until the muzzle was over the boat.

I knew the little fabric was out of range, but I wished the men to see the feather-leap of white water, the flash of the missile, that they might understand I shot with ball; and, having everything to my hand, I bid Miss Aurora step a little aside, and fired. The gun roared in thunder, and belched out a big cloud of smoke. I dodged the smoke to mark the flight of the ball, which hit the water several cables' lengths this side the boat. If the spurt of it was plain to me, it was plain to them. I put Jimmy to the gun to clean it while I watched the boat. She continued in pursuit;

but now, by aid of the glass, I made out something white flying at her masthead – a signal of truce, as though the fellows and I had been at war. Some man must have torn up his shirt to produce that flag; for there were no white handkerchiefs in the longboat, and nothing to answer to what was flying save what one or another carried on his back.

"I want no truce! I want no peace! I want to have nothing whatever to do with you!" I cried, while I went about to load the long gun again.

This time I resolved to load with case as well as round, that the splash might emphasize my hint. I asked Aurora to hold the wheel, and bid Jimmy rush into the cabin and bring up some canister out of the locker. I clapped in some case on top of the ball, took aim, and fired. The brig thrilled to the explosion. I wondered to myself what the imprisoned fellows forward and the two men below would be thinking of this bellowing of artillery.

The ball and musket-shot struck the sea before I saw the splash; the smoke of the gunpowder hung a bit, clouding aft before blowing clear, and I could not spring to the side in time to see. I ordered Jimmy to make ready the gun for loading afresh, being now hot in heart with the noise of the firing and angry, too, with the stubborn pursuit of the devils astern; and I told Miss Aurora that, if they did not shift their helm, I'd blow them out of water.

"I want no man's life," I exclaimed – "not even Yan Bol's; but if they creep much closer, and I can manage to plump a ball among those – ."

But here my speech was arrested; for, having talked with my eye at the glass, I saw them lower the lugsail on board the longboat; they then pulled her around and hoisted her sail afresh.

"There she goes!" cried I.

"*De veras!* Oh, glorious! Oh, glorious!" exclaimed the *señorita*, dropping the wheel to clap her hands.

"Yes, there she goes," said I, "the second hint sufficed. I wish the shot may not have hurt any man of them. Was she out of reach? Yes, there she goes. Wise ye are, Yan Bol. I should have sunk you. Never should you have gained footing aboard this brig. And has not the breeze slightly freshened too since you started in pursuit? Ay, there is a little foam in our wake, and the glance under the sun is keen. We should have run you out of sight, Yan Bol, and you in pursuing would have run the island out of sight, and then without compass, without provisions, without water, how would ye have managed, you scoundrel Dutchman?"

I put down the glass and clapped the boy on the shoulder.

"Jimmy, you have done well. Yours'll be a good share of dollars for this job. Now jump, my lively, and get some breakfast for the lady and me – and some breakfast for yourself."

The poor fellow, grinning with delight, fled forward with the speed of a hare. I took the wheel from the *señorita*, and she stood beside me.

"What'll dose men do?"

"They will return to the island."

"Will not dey starf?"

"They have plenty of provisions, and they have a good boat."

"What will dey do with de money dey have taken?"

"May it founder them! The dogs! To force us down here when we should be in the Channel, or at home! Here am I now with this big brig on my single pair of hands, and you and the boy as helps and four horrible scoundrels to sentinel and feed."

I felt sick with heart-weariness at that moment. An eternity of waters stretched between me and England in the measureless miles of Southern Ocean, in the measureless miles of south and north Atlantic. How was I to manage with one half-crazy boy and a girl to help me, and four prisoners to guard?

"De dollars are saved," said the *señorita*, bringing her eyes with a flash in them from the boat to my face.

"You are the greatest heroine the world has ever produced," said I.

"It is a day of glory for you, and your money is safe," said she.

I looked at her a little sullenly; I was in no temper for irony.

"If de money is safe, I am safe," said she, "for one goes before de other, and to be safe I am content to be second."

I heeded her not; her tongue was a rattle, and very heedless at times. After a little, finding I did not speak, she looked at the boat through the glass. Long practice had now enabled her to keep open the eye she applied to the telescope. I, too, gripping the spokes, gazed astern; the sail of the boat was like the wing of a white butterfly out on the dark blue, that thrilled with the breeze. The island hung massive and rugged in the sky, but already was it growing blue in the blue air.

At this time Jimmy came along with some breakfast. He put the tray upon the deck. The pot of cocoa Meehan was to have cooked had overboiled and was burnt. Jimmy brought us some fresh coffee, salt beef, and biscuit. The girl and I ate and drank, Jimmy meanwhile holding the wheel. My lady asked me how the prisoners were to breakfast? Could they feed themselves with handcuffs?

"No," said I.

"They'll need to be regularly supplied with food," said she. "Who'll feed them?"

"*Parece que quiere hacer buen tiempo,*" said I to change the subject.

When I had breakfasted I held the wheel that Jimmy might eat. I was forever racking my brains to conceive how I was to manage, alone as I was with the youth. The girl was of no earthly use. Indeed, for the matter of that, the boy himself did not know how to steer, and was a poor sailor aloft, though as "an idler" he was expected, and was used to help the men in reefing and in putting the brig about. I was grateful for the beautiful morning with its gentle breeze. "Perhaps," I said to myself, "I shall have worked out some theory of navigating the brig with the aid of Jimmy, before a change of weather happens."

The lad took the wheel, and I went below to remove the gags from the men. I had a brace of loaded pistols in my pocket, and I pulled out one of them, and looking to its priming, I walked to the berth in which we had thrown Teach, and opened the door. The man's posture was that in which we had left him, saving that his head had fallen forward. I did not like his looks, and felt afraid; I went up to him and took his arm; he did not stir. I lifted his head by the chin, and saw death in his eyes. On this, full of horror and pity, I removed the gag. It was a piece of drill with a lump of stuffing stitched amidships to fill the mouth. Aurora had made it, as she had made the bag with which we had stifled the two men. The stuffed part of the gag that had filled the man's mouth was soaked with blood, and when I pulled the gag off, and the head fell forward, a quantity of dark blood followed.

No doubt he had ruptured a blood vessel; in any case, his death was not to be laid to the account of the gag, in other words, to our having suffocated him. Nevertheless, I was as greatly shocked, and viewed him with as much horror as though he had died by my hands.

I then bethought me of Travers and rushed, with my heart beating hard, to his berth, dreading to find him dead likewise. The man was standing upright, looking at the sea through the scuttle. He turned when I entered, and presented his gagged face to me. I thanked God to find him alive. So far we had managed all this business bloodlessly. I am one, and ever was one, of those who count human life the most sacred thing under God's eye.

I had thrust the pistol into my pocket at the sight of Teach, and now kept it there in the presence of this man Travers, gagged and handcuffed as he was. He motioned piteously with his head, lifting his fists a little way toward his face. I at once took the gag off, and threw it aside. He tried to speak; he fetched many breaths, during which some froth gathered upon his lips; he then, in a dim, husky voice that seemed to rise from the bottom of his chest, exclaimed:

"Water!"

I ran into the cabin and filled a mug with fresh water; he remained standing where I had left him. I put the mug to his mouth, and he drank long and deep. The water refreshed him, and he found his voice.

"What are ye going to do with me?" he asked.

"Keep you under hatches," said I.

"Where's Bol and the others?"

"Ashore on the island."

"Left to their fate, sir?"

"You know better. Have they not the longboat, plenty of provisions and water? If Captain Greaves were alive he'd yardarm the four of you – no, not the four; Teach is dead."

"Did you kill him?"

"He's dead," I shouted in a rage; "I have killed no man. You would have killed me – there is no stain on my conscience."

"Are ye carrying the brig home?"

"Where else?"

"Teach dead!" he muttered. "Mr. Fielding, for God's sake, take me on. You'll find me a true man."

"Which d'ye choose – the bilboes or those bracelets?"

He answered me with a savage stare. I turned to go.

"Leave me some water," he called.

I filled the mug afresh, placed it where he could put his lips to it, and locked the door upon him.

Chapter XXXI.
A Quaker Skipper

I LOOKED in upon Teach again. The sight was piteous. The handcuffs gave a wild pathos to that picture of death. The sight was not to be borne. I removed the handcuffs, and then took a steady view of his face, and felt the man's wrist to make sure that he was dead. He was stone dead; and I went on deck.

Miss Aurora leaned upon her elbows on the rail, looking at the Island of Amsterdam, that was fading into a dark blue cloud. I said:

"Teach is dead."

She started, and shrunk back and stared at me, and instantly reflected the expression she saw in my face. Her features then relaxed, and, slightly shrugging her shoulders, she exclaimed:

"He was not a good man. Yet good men are dying every day. Teach's time had come. Did we kill him?"

"I don't think so."

"That pleases me. I would have killed him for my honour or for my liberty. It is God's doing, and it must be good."

I found that Jimmy kept the brig to her course fairly well, and roamed about the deck for awhile by myself, considering how I should act if we did not presently, and, indeed, speedily, fall in with a ship to help us with the loan of two or three men. I then asked Miss Aurora to hold the wheel, and took Jimmy below with me to help clap the bilboes on to Travers, that I might relieve the poor devil of his handcuffs. While I put the bilboes on, Travers asked me why I refused to give him a chance to turn to.

"You've had a chance of proving yourself an honest man for weeks past. I'll not trust you now."

"Mr. Fielding, we meant to act square by you."

"Yes, by knocking me over the head when I'd served your turn."

I sent Jimmy in a hurry for provisions and water to place in this prisoner's berth. The beast couldn't read, or I should have tossed him a book or two. I was eager to regain the deck, for her ladyship was on no account to be left alone at the wheel. Travers asked for his pipe and tobacco. I told him he should have them; and then, threatening to shoot him through the head if he made any noise, attempted to break out, or acted in any way to imperil the safety of the ship, I locked him up.

I put a loaded pistol into Jimmy's hand, keeping a brace in my pocket; and, finding that the brig made a straight wake to the set of the helm, as surrendered by me to Miss Aurora, with the request that she would hold the spokes steady, I went forward with the lad, lifted the hatch, and sung out.

Both men came under the hatch and looked up. I let them see that the boy and I were armed, and said:

"Call, I am here to give you a chance. If you'll come on deck and help me to carry on the work of the brig, good and well."

"I asked to turn to afore," said he, putting his hand on the coaming as though to come up.

"I'm willing to turn to," said Meehan.

"I'll abide by Call's behaviour," said I.

"It's cussed hot and black down here," exclaimed Meehan. "Ain't ye going to let us have a light?"

"You shall have a light," said I; "but mind your fire. We have the boats, and I shan't lift the hatch."

"What made ye clip me o'er the head?" he growled. "I'd ha' stepped back had ye arsted me."

"Come up, Call."

The man rose instantly, and stood blinking to the splendour of the morning.

"Go aft and take the wheel," said I. "The course is as you find it."

I was about to put on the hatch cover.

"Ain't I to be let up?" said Meehan.

"No."

"Ain't I to have anything to eat and drink?"

"Yes."

"Hell seize the blooming lot of ye!" said he, and disappeared in a single stride.

I closed the hatch cover, but opened it shortly after to hand down a beaker of water, a quantity of provisions, and oil for the forecastle lamp. I say to "hand down"; but the ruffian was so sulky that he refused to answer to my call, and I had to tell him what I had brought, and to threaten him with thirst and starvation, before he would come under the hatch to receive the things. The belch of heat and of foul atmosphere was so disgusting when I first lifted the cover, that I guessed the fellow would suffocate if I did not give him some fresh air. The cover opened on strong hinges. I procured a bit of chain; then inserted a wedge to keep the cover open to about half the length of your thumb. I now passed the chain through the staple and the eye of the bar, securing the links at a place out of reach of our friend's knife. This done, I went aft with Jimmy, and could scarcely forbear laughing to observe the lady Aurora in the posture of haranguing Call. She stood up before him, and menaced him with her forefinger; and she was saying as I approached:

"If you do not behave well it is death; I am a Spanish lady and know not fear. I will kill any man for my liberty or for my honour, and my liberty I must have, but I have it not while I am in this little ship. I desire to be at Madrid. Be honest and help Mr. Fielding, and your reward will be great. I tell this, I – I – the Señorita de la Cueva – she tells you this on her honour as a Spanish lady." She touched her bosom with her forefinger, then looked round and saw me close by.

"I am willing to prove a true man," said Call, "this here mucking job was never my relish. *I* was never for casting this here brig away. But how's one voice to sound when a whole blooming squadron of throats is a-hollering?"

"Jump aloft and stow that topgallant sail along with Jimmy," said I.

With the help of this man Call I snugged the brig down to topsails and forecourse as a provision against change of weather. I kept him on deck all day, and he ate on deck under my eye; he behaved well, yet I dared not trust him; while I slept he might liberate the other two, and then truly should I be a dead man; for of course Meehan and Travers secretly raged against me, and would take all the risks of washing about without a navigator and of being hanged if they were boarded and the truth discovered; all risks would they accept, I say, to be revenged upon me. I took Call below into the cabin and made him help me drag Teach's body out of the berth it lay in; I then put his legs in irons to keep him quiet through the night. He protested violently, and his remonstrance often rose into coarse, injurious language.

"I'll trust you presently, but not now," said I, and so I locked the door and came away. I heard him swearing, and then he began to sing as I went on deck.

It was some time between eight and nine o'clock. All the stars were out, the sky was cloudless, and the evening as beautiful as the morning had been splendid. The wind had shifted into the east, and was a small soft wind; it held our little show of canvas steady, and the brig rippled quietly onward over the wide dark sea. I stationed my lady Aurora at the wheel and entered the cabin with Jimmy; there we made fast a cannon ball to the feet of the dead man Teach, and picking him up we carried him to the gangway, which we opened that his plunge might be from a little height only. I was a sailor; for many months Teach had been a shipmate of mine; I had hated him – but he was dead and his last toss at a sailor's hand must be decorous and reverent. So we dropped him gently feet foremost and he went down instantly, leaving behind him a little cloud of fire that was sparkling even when it had slided into the vessel's wake.

Four days passed. I will not stop to explain how we managed; shall I tell you why? Because, when I look into the mirror of my memory for the vision of what happened in those four days I find the presentment dim, vague, foggy. These things I recollect; that I did not trust Call, that I freed him from time to time that he might take a trick at the wheel, threatening to stop his food and water if he refused, and that every night at eight bells or thereabouts I put him away with the bilboes on. That I kept the other two men imprisoned, supplying them every morning with provisions for twenty-four hours. That I held the brig's head for the Cape of Good Hope, praying daily for the sight of a ship and beholding nothing. That for two days after our losing sight of Amsterdam Island, the weather continued very glorious, then darkened with a wind that breezed up out of the southward and blew fresh, but happily never too hard for our whole topsails.

These things I remember.

I was awakened on the night of the fourth or, let me say, in the dark hours of the morning of the fifth day by the boy Jimmy calling my name. I had wrapped myself up in Greaves' cloak, sat me down near the wheel, at which I had been standing for two hours, and had fallen into a deep sleep without intending to sleep. The lad had taken the helm from me; when he called I sprang to my feet.

"What is it?"

"See that light, master?"

I looked and saw what I supposed was a ship on fire. A ruddy glare was colouring the sky at the extremity of the sea about three points on the lee bow. I thought to myself, if she is a ship on fire and beyond control, her people will help me to navigate the brig home. The fancy, the hope, elated me; I was wide awake on a sudden, though I had sat down dog tired.

A long swell was rolling out of the south, and a five-knot breeze was blowing off our larboard quarter. I put the helm up for the light, and when I had it fair ahead I gave the spokes to Jimmy, and fetched the telescope out of the cabin where, on a locker, lay the lady Aurora sleeping. The telescope resolved the red light into several tongues of flame which waxed and waned; I had then no doubt whatever that the fire was a burning ship, and forthwith fell to walking first to one then to the other side of the brig, for long spells at a time overhanging the bulwark rail, straining my sight into the darkness, and hearkening with all my ears.

By and by, recollecting that an empty tar barrel stood upon the forecastle, I resolved to make a flare. I rolled the barrel aft, kindled it, and Jimmy and I flung the barrel overboard.

It burnt finely, and lighted up a great space of the sea. If the people of the burning ship were in the neighbourhood they'd know by the fire upon the water that help was at hand, and rest on their oars till daybreak, which was hard by.

When the dawn broke the ship was about a mile distant. Smoke was rising from her decks. I sought in vain in all directions for a boat. I saw no fire now on board the ship, and when I pointed the telescope I perceived that she was hove to, and that the smoke was local as though it rose from chimneys. Between us and the ship was a vast lump of red stuff that lifted and fell; it was scored and flaked with white, and its redness was that of blood. The sun came up and touched it, and now I perceived – by this time we had neared it – that the loathsome bulk was a part of a great whale, freshly "cut in," as it is termed. A number of birds were on it, and they tore the horrid mass with their beaks, and many birds hovered over it.

I looked very hard at the ship. I seemed to know her. Her numerous davits and crowd of boats bespoke her a whaler, and I knew by the sight of that vast heap of whale which had gone adrift that she was "trying out" – that is, boiling down the blubber that came from the whale. In fact, my nose told me of what was going on when I was half a mile away.

The flash of the sun on the skylight awakened Miss Aurora; she came on deck, and cried out on beholding the whaler.

"This is a very wonderful thing," said I. "Do you know that ship?"

She stared hard and shook her head.

"She is the *Virginia Creeper*, whaler, of Whitby," said I, "we spoke her t'other side the Horn."

"She is on fire," cried the girl, "and – *Ave Maria!* What is that?" she exclaimed, pointing to the bloody mass of whale that was on our beam.

We floated slowly down to the ship; the wind had blackened at sunrise, and our canvas was small. The sky was dark in the south whence the swell was running, and a bright blue all about the north and east. We approached the ship, and I saw many men on board of her watching us. Some of the faces showed in the telescope of a copper colour, and I guessed they were natives of the South Sea Islands.

Miss Aurora teased me with questions, with sounding exclamations in Spanish and English. I begged her to hold her tongue. I wanted to think. Should I give the whole plain story of our voyage to the captain of that ship? Should I tell him that I had twelve tons of silver on board, and three prisoners of a crew who had possessed themselves of three tons, but who had meant to plunder the whole and bury it, and then wreck the brig? I hastily paced the deck, staring at the whaler and thinking with all my might. But a moment arrived when I could think no longer. I put the helm over, gave the wheel to Miss Aurora to hold, and with the help of Jimmy got the main topsail aback.

The two vessels then lay abreast within a cable's length. A man stood in the mizzen rigging of the whaler; he was the same person that had hailed us in the Pacific. I jumped upon a gun and sung out, "Ho, the *Virginia Creeper*, ahoy!"

"Hallo!" answered the man near the mizzen rigging.

"We are but three, as you see," I shouted, "Will you send a boat and come aboard? Our distress is great."

The man responded with a quiet motion of his hand, lingered a moment or two as though to take a further survey of us, then called out an order, and a few moments later he had entered a boat and was being pulled across to us.

I received him in the gangway, and giving him my hand said, "We have met before."

"Indeed, friend," said he, "where might that have been?"

On my recalling the circumstance, he said in a sober voice, and without any air of surprise, "I remember." Then looking leisurely at Miss Aurora he said, "Is that thy wife, friend?"

"No," I answered; "she is a shipwrecked lady."

"And what art thou and what's thy name?"

I made answer, observing him narrowly. He was a Quaker, as you will suppose; a fellow of a very serious, composed appearance, close shaved, with coal black eyes, wary and stealing in their manner of gazing, a large expressionless mouth, and a pale skin that had suffered nothing from the weather. He wore a soft cone-shaped hat, the brim very wide, and was skewered to his throat in a coat with a double row of large metal buttons. His legs were encased in jack boots. The garb was somewhat of a change from the glazed hat and pea jacket of his South Pacific costume.

"This is the *Black Watch*," said he, looking slowly along the decks and then slowly up aloft.

"Yes," said I.

"When we spoke thee thy captain was sick."

"He is dead."

"Is that thy distress?"

"No, sir. If you will step into the cabin I'll tell you a very strange story, but as this brig must be watched – yonder lad at the wheel being merely our cabin boy – will you hail one of your mates and request him to take charge while we converse?"

He walked gravely and quietly to the side, and looking over, bade his men in the whale boat fetch Mr. Pack. Presently Mr. Pack arrived. He was the mate of the whaler. The captain told him to watch the brig, and followed me into the cabin, the lady Aurora going before us.

I put a bottle of spirits upon the table. The captain shook his head at the bottle and looked around him, presently fixing his eyes on Madam Aurora, at whom he continued to stare after I had begun to talk to him. He had lifted a hat and disclosed a flat, almost bald head. Without further delay I entered upon my narrative, and coaxed his gaze from the lady to me. He heard me through without a syllable of comment, without a grunt of surprise. His composure was perfectly wooden. I observed no further sign, indeed, of his heeding me than an occasional grave nod of the head, such as he might bestow on a minister whose discourse from the pulpit pleased him.

I ceased. The dark Spanish eyes of the lady Aurora burned, with impassioned anxiety, upon the composed countenance of the Quaker skipper.

"Wilt thou be pleased to repeat the sum?" said the captain slowly and deliberately, without the faintest colour of wonder in his tone.

"Five hundred and fifty thousand."

"Of which thy men took three tons?"

"Yes," said I.

His lips slightly stirred to a sudden pressure of rapid calculation. "And what dost thou think the men will do with those three tons of dollars?"

"Bury 'em," said I. "They will leave the island in the boat – not for awhile, I dare say – but they will not carry their dollars with them. They'll not risk putting to sea with three tons of dead weight in addition to the provisions they'll want. Or put it that they would not take the chance of falling in with a ship, of transferring the money to her, and of standing to the lies they'd have to tell to account for their possession of the silver."

"Thou art right," said the captain, with a sober nod.

"They will bury the money," said I, "swear one another to secrecy, and then return for the silver when they can."

"Thou art right," repeated the captain, with another sober nod.

"Now," said I – "but let me ask your name?"

"Jonas Horsley," he answered.

"Captain Horsley, this is my proposal: I want help; I want three or four men to enable me to carry this brig home. I also want to hand my prisoners over to you – the three of them, able-bodied fellows, as good as the best of your own hands, I daresay. Further, I want as much fresh water as you can spare. In return I'll give you the clew to the burial-place in Amsterdam Island. If you sail promptly you'll arrive before the fellows depart. They're bound to wait awhile for a ship before taking their chance, six of them, in an open boat, every man ignorant which way to head for land, even if they had a compass. Furthermore, that you may make sure of my gratitude, you shall take a case of the dollars in the lazarette."

The *señorita*'s eyes sparkled. She vehemently nodded approval. Captain Horsley viewed me steadily, with an expressionless countenance.

"Friend," said he, after a short pause, "might the chests in thy lazarette be all of a size?"

"They slightly vary."

"And the biggest might contain – ?"

"About four thousand dollars," said I.

He continued to regard me expressionlessly; his composure raised my anxiety into torment. My lady's face worked with half a dozen emotions at every heart-beat.

"Hast thou breakfasted?" said Captain Horsley.

"No," I answered.

"Thou hast the means, I trust, of providing a meal?"

"We have plenty of provisions."

"Thou may'st consider all things settled," said he, slowly turning his head to gaze at the lady Aurora. "I will break my fast with thee and the lady. It is a pleasure to converse with you both. When we have eaten and drunken I will ask thee to show me thy lazarette, and I will choose a chest, and we will then exchange the men."

"Give me your hand on it," I cried, and my heart was swollen with delight; but the taking and lifting of that man's hand and arm was like pumping out a ship.

We went on deck, and brought up a sailor out of the whaleboat to stand at the helm while Jimmy prepared breakfast. Before breakfast was served I took Captain Horsley into the lazarette and showed him the cases of silver.

"Do all those chests contain dollars?" he asked.

"All."

He made no further remark until, after considering awhile, during which time his eyes roamed shrewdly over the chests, he pointed to one of the biggest, and said:

"That will do for me."

"It is yours," I answered.

"Friend," said he, after a short pause, due to reflection, by no means to embarrassment, "I should be glad to know that I am receiving dollars. Suppose we lift the lid."

I fetched a hammer and other tools, and nails, and when the chest was opened he brought the lantern close to the money, and after staring and running his hand over the milled edges, he said:

"These be good dollars."

I then hammered down the lid and we went up into the cabin, where we found breakfast ready.

I much enjoyed this strange man's conversation. He was cold and grave, very slow, and a trifle nasal of speech, and his trick of "theeing" and "thouing," and the meeting-house turn of his phrases in general seemed to ill fit the character of a hearty English sailor. Yet he had plenty to talk about, had followed the sea for many years, had been long in the whaling business, was a considerable man at Whitby, and even had news to give me, for I was at sea in the *Royal Brunswicker* when he sailed on this cruise. A British sea Quaker was something of a rarity in my time; I presume he is extinct in these days. Many American whalers were commanded by Quakers, but the board-brims of our island loved less the pursuit of the game than the safer business of tallying the blubber cargo over the side into their warehouses.

While we breakfasted I gave him a description of the proposed burial-place as it had been sketched to me by Yan Bol. He composedly entered the particulars in a pocket-book. I asked him to write down my uncle's address at Sandwich, that he might let me know whether he fell in with or took off Yan Bol and the others and recovered the silver. He gravely promised to write to me.

We then went to business; and Captain Jonas Horsley's first step was to accompany some men into the lazarette and superintend the transhipment of his chest of dollars. This done, he asked me how many men I wanted. I answered that I had spoken of three, but that I would be glad of as many as he could spare. He answered that he would let me have five in exchange for my prisoners. One of them was a Kanaka, or South Sea Islander, who had long sailed in whalers, and was a very good cook. The others, he said, would volunteer; but I might make my mind easy. All his men were livelies of the first water. What pay would I give?

"I will give," said I, "whatever will bring them to me."

"They sail by the lay. Thou must take that into consideration," said Captain Horsley.

"Shall we say two hundred and fifty dollars a man for the run home?" said I.

"I will let thee know," said he. He got into his boat, and was rowed across to his ship, whose tryworks were still smoking and filling the air with a disgusting scent. There was no increase of darkness in the south, and north and east the blue sky was splendid with the sparkling of the morning; but a movement worked in the southerly swell that hinted at a fresh wind presently. Captain Horsley, however, did not keep me long waiting. First, he sent me one of his largest boats with a stock of fresh water and hands to stow the casks. His men took back my empty casks in return for their full ones; then two boats came off full of men, in one of which the captain was seated. Parties were distributed to bring up the prisoners. Meehan scowled when he saw the whaler, hung back, and fought like a devil, saying that he was a sailor, and no whaleman, and cursing me and the brig and the whaler – whatever his eye rested on, in short – until they tumbled him into the boat alongside, where I heard him roaring out to me to pay him his wages and to hand him over his share of the dollars. Call and Travers walked quietly to the gangway. Travers stopped before putting his foot over, and asked me if he was not to be paid for the work he had done.

"Mynheer Tulp is your owner," said I. "Call upon him when you return to Amsterdam. He'll pay you, I daresay."

He then began to swear, upon which Captain Horsley motioned to his men, and he and Call were forthwith bundled into the boat.

"These are thy men, friend," said the captain, pointing to four seamen and a Kanaka, who stood apart. "Four are Englishmen, and of my own town, anxious to return home. They each ask three hundred and fifty dollars."

I looked them over, as the phrase goes, put a few questions, and, being satisfied that their quality was right, I said:

"You shall have three hundred and fifty dollars a man. Captain Horsley knows I can pay you, and the agreement shall be signed when we have filled upon the brig."

The clothes and chests belonging to Meehan and the other two were then got up and put into the boat. Captain Horsley gave me his pump-handle of an arm to shake – or, rather, to work. I thanked him cordially for the assistance he had rendered me. He listened till I had done, and said:

"Friend, thou hast made my kindness very much worth my while."

He entered his boat, after bowing with the most grotesque contortion I had ever beheld to the lady Aurora. The brig's topsail was then swung; we raised a loud cheer, which was lustily re-echoed aboard the whaler; and, in a few minutes, the *Black Watch* was heeling over from the breeze, with her head for a course that was to carry us home, and one of my new men trotting aloft to loose the main topgallant sail.

***

On this same day, in the afternoon, I, with two of my new men, very carefully took stock of the fresh water aboard, and I discovered that we had enough to carry us to the English Channel. This discovery was a stroke of happiness. I had allowed for a long passage, knew that we were already weedy at bottom, that every day would add to the growths, and that before we were up with the equator we might be sliding very thickly and sluggishly through the sea. Spite, however, of my computation of long days, there was fresh water enough to yield us such an allowance as no man could grumble at.

The men shipped from the whaler proved very good seamen; all four Englishmen were Whitby men; they were held together by that quality of local patriotism which I think is peculiar to our country; they were all anxious to get home, and owned that they had intended to run from the *Virginia Creeper* at the first opportunity. The prospect of taking up three hundred and fifty dollars a man kept them very willing, alert, and in good spirits. One of them, a man of about forty, with iron-grey hair, who boasted that Captain Cook had once asked him the time – when and where I forget – this man came to me on the Sunday after he and the others had joined my brig, and asked me to lend him a Bible. I lent him a Bible that had belonged to Captain Greaves, and Jimmy afterward told me that of a dog-watch this man would sit and read out of the Bible to his mates, the Kanaka listening very attentively and occasionally interrupting by a question.

All this was as it should be; I had been living and moving for weeks in intellectual irons, so to speak; as much in irons as the figure that had fallen from the gibbet; I had gone in fear of my life – could never imagine what was in store for me should I be forced to New Holland with the brig; had for weeks and weeks despaired of my little fortune on which I had counted in Greaves' time, upon which I had built such fancies of happiness as would visit the heart of a young sailor. *Now* I breathed freely, slept without anxiety, paced the deck and realized that every fathom of white wake was diminishing the vast interval between home and the situation of the little vessel. I had no other fears than such as properly fell under the heads of sea risks. *These* I must take my chance of – fire, the lee-shore, the sudden hurricane, privateersmen, the Yankee cruiser; but the direst of the items of the catalogue of oceanic perils were as naught to my apprehension after what I had suffered at the hands of Yan Bol and his men.

We rounded the Cape; we crept north; we hoisted the Dutch flag to passing ships; the stars of the south sank; our shadows every day grew shorter and yet shorter at noon, and all went well. Having but six men of a crew I worked, on occasion, as hard as any of them; often sprang aloft to a weather earring, helped to stow a course and stood a trick if the fellows had been much fagged by the weather. Nevertheless, though I was very often full of business and hurry, I found plenty of leisure for the enjoyment of the society of the lady Aurora. This was peculiarly so in the fine weather of the southeast trades, in the calms of the equatorial zone, in the steady blowing of the northeast wind. She persevered in her English, and many a lesson did I give her; she recited to me, for I now understood the Spanish tongue fairly well. But though she recited with great power she could not declaim as she sang. I always thought her singing beautiful and enchanting. The fiddle to which the original crew had been used to dance and sing, Jimmy found in a hammock; he brought it aft, and to the twang of it the *señorita* would again and again lift up her voice, her large, rich, thrilling voice, to please me.

One day we sat together in the cabin. We were a little northward of the Island of Madeira. The weather was very mild and fine, the time of year the beginning of August. I had been reading aloud to the girl out of

The Castle of Otranto, and she had followed me very closely, interrupting seldom to inquire the meaning of a word. When I had done she exclaimed:

"I will now give you a brave recital. You shall enjoy it. I have seen you wear a red silk kerchief; lend it to me."

I fetched the kerchief and she bound it round her head, then lifting a locker she drew out a tablecloth, in which she wrapped her figure as in a sheet, holding the folds with her left hand and leaving her right hand free to gesticulate with. She then declaimed a set of verses, written in the jargon of the Spanish gypsies by that famous poet of Spain, Quevedo. It was a very fine performance. I understood but little of the queer dialect, but I enjoyed the rich music of her voice, the swelling and melting melodies her mere utterance gave to the verses; I gazed with delight at her impassioned eyes, and at the wild, romantic figure she made, draped as she was in a sailor's kerchief and a cabin tablecloth. Was it not Nelson's Emma who, with a scarf only, contrived a dozen different representations of characters, was fascinating in all, and so pathetic in some that her audience wept?

"How do you like me as a Spanish gypsy?" said she, pulling off the kerchief, dropping the tablecloth, and shaking her head till her long earrings flashed again.

"So well that I want more," I answered.

"No," said she; "come on deck."

She put on her hat, I carried a chair, and we seated ourselves in the shade of the little awning under which we had often sat and gesticulated, and endeavoured to look our meanings in Greaves' time. But now she spoke English very well indeed, while I had enough Spanish to enable me to converse with her in that tongue, though I never could catch the sonorous note of it, nor give the true twist to some of the words.

We sat together. The brig was sailing placidly over a wide surface of blue sea; the horizon was a bright line of opal against the dim violet of the distant sky, and abreast of us to larboard was a full-rigged ship, her hull below the sea line, and her canvas showing like little puffs of steam. The Kanaka was at the wheel; he was cook indeed, but when he was done with the caboose I put him to the ship's work. One of the sailors who had charge walked in the waist; the other three were variously engaged.

I found myself gazing very earnestly at the lady Aurora, and thinking of her and of nothing but her, I was still under the influence of the witchery of her recitation, and then again I thought I had never seen her look so handsome. Am I in love with you? I wondered. Thought is as swift as dreams, and you may dream in your sleep through a thousand years in the time of the fall of an ash from the grate to the hearth. "Am I in love with you?" I said to myself, earnestly regarding her, her eyes being then fixed upon the distant sail. "I have a very great mind to offer you marriage.

What will you say if I propose to you? Will your eyes flash, and will you show your teeth, or will you put on one of your tender, brooding looks? I have often thought that you would make as fine, useful, accomplished a wife as any young fellow need wish to live gayly and comfortably with. You sing deliciously. I don't doubt you dance perfectly well. You can be saucy and quarrelsome in such a manner as to lend a new flavour to sentiment. You have a stately, handsome person; you are extremely well-bred, I am sure. I must take my chance of your relatives. Some of them may be grandees – let that be hoped for the sake of my children, who, if they take after me, will wish to be respectably connected. I'll offer you marriage," I thought to myself.

"Our troubles are nearly at an end," said I.

"It is time," she answered, keeping her eyes fastened upon the distant ship.

"We have been very closely associated, *señorita*."

She now regarded me, and for an instant there was a peculiar softness in her gaze; she then seemed to find an expression in my face that alarmed her; I saw the change; she grew nervous, and her effort to control herself confused her.

"Yes, we have been much together, Mr. Fielding. I shall always regard you as the saviour of my life, and never shall I forget your gentle and courteous treatment of me."

"I trust you never will. My desire is to live forever in your memory."

She looked troubled and frightened, and then sorry, as though she had pained me.

"You have said you will give up the sea when you arrive in England?"

"Oh, yes; I shall have been three years continuously at sea when I reach home. I'll take a home and settle down ashore."

"Is your fortune in the Spanish dollars all that you possess?"

"All. It is seven thousand pounds." I pronounced these figures with emphasis.

"It is not much," she exclaimed.

"Indeed! I think it a very good fortune."

"For a single man – *si;* but put it out at interest, and what you receive shall not be handsome. Oh, it is a fortune for a bachelor – yes, but in no country, not even in Germany would it be regarded as a handsome fortune for one who would live in style. *Vaya!* Have I not advised you to buy a ship and trade with distant nations, and end your days as rich as a prince of the blood royal of England?"

"I do not intend to take your advice," said I. "I will not risk my money in adventures. What I have I will keep. It is a considerable sum – it is enough for two."

She slightly shrugged her shoulders again, and turned her eyes away with an expression of concern. Suddenly she looked fully at me; her face was dark with a blush that glowed from the roots of her hair to the rim of the collar of her dress; I could not express the meaning in her face at that moment; I felt it without understanding it.

"When I am settled in Madrid, Mr. Fielding, you will come and see me, I hope? Often, I trust, will you visit me? Who more welcome, of all the friends of Aurora de la Cueva, than Señor William Fielding?"

I thanked her, with slight surprise. I had expected, from the looks of her, something very different from this.

"Would it not please you to live in England?" said I.

"No," she answered vehemently; softening, she added, "my establishment will be in Madrid."

I was conscious that I changed colour. I looked at her hand – at that pretty hand of beringed fingers, on which very often had I admiringly fastened my gaze. When I lifted my eyes, she faintly smiled.

"Your establishment?" said I.

"Yes; my establishment."

"Do you mean your mother's establishment?"

"*Ave Maria!* No. My poor mother! Where is she? *Ay, ay me!*" she cried, looking up at the sky with a sorrowful, admirably managed roll of her dark eyes. "My mother's establishment was at Lima, as you have often heard. She broke it up on the death of my father; and, if she be alive – oh, may the Blessed Virgin grant it – she will live with me at Madrid. It was her intention to dwell with us. She is growing in years and has many infirmities, and is unequal to the fatigues and anxieties of an establishment of her own. But of whom am I speaking? She may be dead – she may be dead!"

"Pray," said I, "have I been all this while enjoying the society of a charming woman without guessing that she was married?" and here my eyes sought the rings upon her left hand again.

"I am not married," she answered.

"Maybe, then, you are engaged to be married?" said I.

She made me a low bow, and held her head down till a second deep blush should have passed.

"I make you my compliments, *señorita*," said I, turning in my chair to look at the ship that, by heading on a more westerly course than ourselves, was sinking her canvas.

"It will interest you to know," said she, "that I am engaged to be married to a countryman of yours. Do you wonder why I did not long ago tell you this? I did not imagine that it would interest you. When I embarked at Acapulco I was proceeding to Madrid to get married. I had known Mr. Gerald Maxwell only three months – think! when we were affianced. Do you ask if he is a Catolique?"

"I ask nothing," I answered.

"Oh!" she cried, giving me a look made up of pity and reproach – a deuced insufferable look, I thought it – "he is a true Catolique. All his family for ages have ever been of de ortodox faith. His father established a rich business at Lima, and his son came from his education in England to be a partner. He went to Madrid last year to represent his house in Spain. We should have been married, but my mother's grief would not allow us to rejoice; so he sailed for Europe, and it was agreed that, when my mother had settled her affairs, she should follow with me. *Santa Maria purissima!* He will think I have perished."

All this is, in effect, what she said; but her speech, of course, did not flow so easily as you read it.

"Did your friend, Mr. Gerald Maxwell, during his three months' courtship, teach you English?"

"No; he was too busy."

"In those months he was too busy to teach you a word of English?"

"*Ave Maria!* Do not speak angrily, nor lose your temper. Mr. Maxwell was often absent for days. He had no opportunity to teach me English."

"*That*, happily," said I, bursting into a laugh, "was to be reserved for me."

"Oh, Señor Fielding, you have been so good," she cried in Spanish; and then she laughed loudly also.

"'Tis what a famous poet of my country," said I, "has termed a most lame and impotent conclusion, I am pleased to have taught you English."

"It has killed the time."

"Mr. Maxwell will be surprised by your knowledge."

"Señor Fielding, he shall thank you."

I grinned, walked to the side with the telescope, and feigned to be interested with the distant sail. Narrow, indeed, had been my escape! I drew more than one deep breath as I humbugged with the glass. By her deep blush might I suppose she had foreseen what was coming and arrested it – just in time! I felt obliged to her. But, oh, the meanness of so prolonged an act of secrecy! Oh, the treachery of it! I thought, when I reflected on what had passed between us. What had been her motive for not long ago telling me that she had a sweetheart, and was going to Madrid to be married to him? To make me fall in love with her, and to keep me in love with her, so as to assure herself of my constant courtesy and attention, fearing that I would be neither courteous nor attentive if she told me she was engaged to be married?

However, I found out that night when I paced the deck alone, pipe in mouth, that I had mistaken – that, in short. I was *not* in love with her.

This was proved to my satisfaction by my quarter-deck meditations on the subject. First, she was a Catholic; would she have married me, who was a Protestant? No. Would I have surrendered my faith for her hand? Not if that hand had grasped and proffered me the title-deeds of every gold mine in this world. She sung, it is true, in a very heavenly style, but was she not a devil at heart? Did not she offer to stick Yan Bol and the others in the back? Did not she secrete a very ugly, murderous weapon about her fine person? Not for the first time did it occur to me *now* that she was a very likely lady to poniard her husband. One little fit of jealousy, and the rest would briefly work out as a funeral, a handsome young mourning widow, very regular indeed at confession, visited once a week by a man in a cloak, who presently so raises the price of secrecy that by and by she'll have to do for *him*, too.

Another reflection consoled me; in a few years a very great change must happen in the lady Aurora's appearance. The Spanish woman is like the Jewess; she does not improve by keeping. The delicate olive complexion turns into a disagreeable wrinkled yellow; the pretty shading of down on the upper lip thickens into a moustache considerable enough to raise the jealousy of a captain of dragoons; the lofty and elegant carriage decays into a tipsy waddle; the light of the eye is speedily quenched; the white teeth show like the keys of a pianoforte; the rich singing voice may linger, but it will irritate the ear of the husband by its association with noisy quarrels.

These, I say, were reflections which vastly supported my spirits and taught me to understand myself; they proved that my love for the lady went no deeper than an eyelash of hers measured, and before my pipe was out I was heartily congratulating myself on Mr. Gerald Maxwell having come first.

Chapter XXXII.
Mynheer Tulp

I BROUGHT the brig to an anchor in the Small Downs off Sandown Castle toward the close of the month of August, 1815. The weather in the Channel had been thick; I had shipped a couple of fishermen off Plymouth to assist in the navigation of the brig, and from abreast of that port I had groped the whole distance to the Downs with the hand-lead.

It was thick weather when I arrived off Deal; the breeze was a "soldier's wind" for the Channel; I counted five vessels only, and no man-of-war was in sight when I brought up. The Dutch flag flew at our trysail gaff-end, and our decks were bare of artillery from stem to stern; for on entering the Channel I had caused all the guns to be struck into the hold that the little ship, should we be boarded, might present the appearance of a peaceful trader.

On letting go the anchor I sent two letters ashore by a Deal boat; one was for my uncle Captain Round, who I had learnt from the boatmen was well and hearty; the other was in the handwriting of the Señorita Aurora, and addressed to Mr. Gerald Maxwell at Madrid. It was soon after nine in the morning when we brought up; and while the church clocks of Deal were striking eleven my uncle came alongside. He was alone; I had asked him in a mysteriously phrased passage of my letter to come alone; the fellow that rowed him alongside was the decayed waterman who had opened the door to me that night when I visited my uncle after leaving the *Royal Brunswicker*.

My uncle held me by both hands for at least five minutes. The whole expression of his face was a very gape of astonishment. He looked me all over, he looked the brig all over; he panted for words; when he was able to articulate he said, "Bill, I thought you was drowned?"

"You got my letter?"

"Yes, and came off at once."

"I sent you a letter written at sea weeks and weeks ago."

"This is the only letter I have received from you," said he; and, trembling with agitation and excitement, he pulled out the letter that I had sent ashore that morning.

The sailors were watching us, and my uncle, now that he had his voice, shouted; so, taking the dear old fellow by the arm, I carried him into the cabin, where sat the lady Aurora occupied in furbishing up her hat to fit her for going ashore. My uncle started and stared at her. He looked plump and and well kept, with his bottle-green coat, broad brimmed, low crowned hat, and boots like a postillion's of that time. His face was jolly and rosy, despite the blueness of his lips; he seemed, indeed, more weather-stained and sea-going than I, as though it was the uncle and not the nephew who was just returned from three years of the ocean. He stared at the lady Aurora, and whipped his hat off and bent his back in a bow quick with nerve. The lady rose and courtesyed.

"Your wife, Bill?" said he.

"No, a shipwrecked lady. We took her off a rock in the South Pacific."

"Off a rock! Lord love you all! What's next to come?"

"Often have I heard Señor Fielding speak of you, Captain Round," said Miss Aurora.

"Yes, I will believe that of Bill ma'am."

"I am shipwrecked, indeed," she exclaimed with a fine arch smile and flashing look that carried me deep into the heart of the Atlantic and Southern Oceans ere Gerald Maxwell was, or when, if he had been aboard, he'd have seen us sitting very close side by side over a lesson in English; "judge by my gown." She swept it at the knees. "I am not fit to be seen."

"But ye are then, believe me," said my uncle; and he sidled up to me and, rubbing my arm with his elbow, muttered, "handsomest woman I ever saw in my life. Bill; if she ain't the Queen of Spain."

"*Señorita*," said I, addressing her in Spanish, "my uncle and I will talk at this table; let us not disturb you. You and I have no secrets – now."

She smiled and looked grave all in a moment, slightly bowed and resumed her seat and her work. And, indeed, I minded not her presence. Much that I should presently say, much that would presently be spoken by my uncle, must be as unintelligible to her as Welsh or Erse.

We seated ourselves, and I took my uncle by the hand and blessed God for the privilege of beholding him again. I inquired after my aunt; she was well; after my cousin; hale and hearty; married three months since, lived in a small house at Folkestone, whence her young husband traded in a ship of which he was part owner. I asked after Captain Spalding. The *Royal Brunswicker* had passed through the Downs in the previous December; my uncle had heard nothing of her since; he had written to Spalding that I was drowned after having been pressed, and while being conveyed aboard a frigate off Deal. He had claimed my wages and clothes as next of kin, and Spalding had sent him what was due to me and what remained of my togs. I asked how many men of the frigate's boat had perished; he replied only one man was picked up, one of the pressed men, an Irishman.

"That was the fellow," said I, "whose behaviour led to the disaster."

I had many more questions to ask, the tediousness of which I will not bestow upon you. I then entered upon the story of my own adventures from the hour of my leaving his house on that black night of storm and thunder. He stopped me after I had related my gibbet experience to tell me that a tall woman, dressed as a widow, was found about forty yards distant from the gibbet, dead, with her arms round the ironed body of the felon. Miss Aurora looked up at this; she had heard me tell that story of the gibbet and the lightning stroke and the mother. She looked up, I say, muttered, and crossed herself, then went on with her work. I paused to think a little upon the dead mother, then proceeded steadily with my story; when I came to Greaves' narrative of the discovery of the dollar-ship my uncle's eyes grew small in his head with the intentness of his gaze.

He seldom winked; he breathed small and faint until I described the discovery of the dollars and their transhipment, on which he fetched a deep breath and hit the table a sounding blow with his fist. Manifold were the changes of his countenance as I progressed; he lived in every scene I drew; cursed Yan Bol and his crew in the language of Beach Street; started out of his chair to grasp the lady Aurora by the hand on my relating her share in the recovery of the brig. And then he became a strict man of business, his jolly face hardening to the rise and pressure of his old smuggling instincts when I spoke of the chests of dollars in the lazarette and asked him to advise me how, when, and where to secretly convey them ashore.

"Let's have a look at 'em, Bill," said he. The excitement was gone out of him; he was as cool as ever he had been in the most artful and desperate of his midnight jobs. I took him into the lazarette and between us we handled a chest of about three thousand dollars to test its weight. He then said – as quietly as though his talk was of empty casks and "dead marines" – "The money must be got ashore tonight. It mustn't remain aboard after tonight."

"How shall I go to work?"

"Leave that to me."

"Who'll receive the cases, uncle?"

"I will. Bill."

"Sketch me your idea that I may see my way."

"I'll go ashore now," said he, "and make all necessary arrangements. Keep aboard yourself and don't let any of your people leave the brig. Tell them we'll pay 'em off at my house tomorrow. Destroy all your papers – see to that, Bill. The moon's old and nigh wore out – it'll be a dark night, raining and squally, I hope. You'll have a lugger alongside of you when it comes dark. She'll hail you. Her name'll be the *Seamen's Friend*, the name of the man that hails you, Jarvie Files. Trust him up to the hilt, Bill, and leave him to discharge ye. He knows the ropes. Afore midnight them chests, to the bottom dollar, they'll be in my cellars."

"When do I come ashore?"

"Tomorrow. Quite coolly, Bill. Come along with your men and bring 'em to my house, where the money in English gold for paying 'em off'll be ready."

"And what's to become of this brig?"

"How many anchors do ye hold by?"

"One, uncle."

"Moor her, Bill. You've got a snug berth. She'll want a caretaker till that there Mynheer Tulp arrives and settles up. She's his property. And the sooner Tulp arrives the better for all parties."

He was about to make his way out of the lazarette.

"There is the Spanish lady," said I. "Will you take her ashore and find her a home in your house until she's fetched? I'd sooner see her with you than at an inn. She has a tongue. Gratitude will keep her quiet, I hope, but she *might* talk."

"If you're afraid of her, aren't ye afraid of the men?"

"No. The men haven't any settled notions on the subject of the silver cargo. They want to get home, and up at Whitby they may talk if they please. The lad Jimmy will hold his jaw. I've promised to take him into my service. He's a good lad."

Without further speech my uncle got out of the lazarette, and after waiting to see me put the hatch on and secure it, he stepped up to the lady Aurora, and in his homely manner, that nevertheless borrowed a sort of grace from the warmth of his heart, he begged her to make use of his house until she heard from her friends. She thanked him, gazed at me with a short-lived look of confusion, and said:

"Until I hear from Mr. Maxwell, until I receive communications from Madrid, I am very poor. I wish not to part with these rings," said she, looking down upon her hands; "I wish not to remove them; and my earrings," continued she, with a shake of her head, "would not bring me nearly money enough to buy me what I want."

"Leave that to me, ma'am," said my uncle; "name your figure when we get ashore. There's no luggage, I suppose?"

"Nothing that I care to take," she answered. "Captain Round, I will ask you to land me in some secret place, as if I was contraband, and show me how to reach your house by tile back ways. I do not love to be stared at, and many mocking eyes will rest upon me if I appear in this costume in your public streets."

"You shan't meet a soul," answered my uncle, "if it isn't a boatman too bleared with ale to observe more than that you're a woman."

She put on her hat and jacket, then stood a moment looking a slow farewell round her; her eyes met mine, and she turned a shade pale, as though to an emotion to which she could not or would not give expression.

"I'll not say good-bye, Señor Fielding," said she, giving me her hand.

"No; we shall meet again tomorrow, I hope."

The three of us went on deck. My uncle called his boat alongside; Miss Aurora and he entered her, and they shoved off. I leaned upon the rail, watching them as they rowed ashore. The boat made for the beach, a little to the northward of Sandown Castle. There was no play or surf to render the landing inconvenient. My uncle helped the girl out of the boat, and they walked off across the sand hills – those same sand hills which had provided me with my horrible experience of the gibbet.

But the gibbet was gone; the summer sun was shining upon the grassy billows of sand. Afar, on the confines of that hilly waste, were many trees, with a single church steeple among them – the shore sign of the old town of Sandwich. Over the bows ran the white, low terraces of the Ramsgate cliffs, soaring as they rounded out of the bay, and gathering a milkier softness as they rose. Abreast was the yellow line of the Goodwins, and yonder on the quarter stretched Deal Beach, rich with the various colours of many boats hauled high and dry. A row of seaward-facing houses flanked that beach; I could see the corner of the alley where I was gripped by the press-gang, and memories of after-days swarmed into my head.

But there was work to be done; I broke away from my idle musings, and ordered the men to moor ship in obedience to my uncle's instructions. Cable was veered out, and a second anchor let go. I had found a bag of thirty-two guineas and some silver in Greaves' cabin after my poor friend's death. I used this money to settle with the two fishermen, and sent them ashore. I then hailed a galley, and dispatched her to Deal for such a supply of fresh meat and vegetables and ale as would give all hands of us a good dinner and supper, and when the punt was gone I called the crew aft, told them that I'd take them ashore next day, and pay them off in English money at my uncle's house near Sandwich; I also thanked them for their good behaviour during the long passage from the Southern Ocean, and shook each man by the hand as a friend who had served me very honestly at a time when my necessities were great.

The wind shifted during the day, and a number of ships brought up in the Downs. A few small craft dropped anchor near the brig.

I heeded them not, nor the bigger vessels beyond. I feared only the arrival of a man-of-war, and the being boarded by her for men. In the afternoon a fine ship-sloop passed through the Gulls heading west; I watched her with the steadfast eye of a cat, dreading to behold her tall breasts of topsails suddenly shiver to the wind, her loftier canvas vanish, and her anchor fall. She foamed onward, heeling a bright line of copper off the Foreland, and vanished round that giant elbow of chalk with her yards bracing up, and her bowlines tricing out for a "ratch" down Channel.

When the evening came along, the dusk was deep but clear.

There was no wet; the breeze was about south – a steady, warm wind – a six-knot breeze. The scene of Downs was very dark; you would think it black by contrast with the picture it makes by night in these times. Ships then showed no riding lights. Here and there a lantern gleamed from the end of a spritsail yard, from the extremity of a mizzen-boom. The Goodwin Sands were lampless, save in the far north, where burnt the spark first kindled by that worthy Quaker of North Shields, Henry Taylor. The lights of the little town of Ramsgate glowed soft and faint upon the face of the dark heap of cliff afar; the lights along Deal Beach twinkled windily. It was a very proper night for our adventure – dark, and but little sea, and wind enough.

Shortly after six bells – eleven by the clock – I spied a shadow to windward, drawing out of the south. The dusky phantom came along slowly, as though she took a wary look at the several little craft she passed. She shaped herself out upon the darkness presently – a large Deal lugger. When she was under our stern she hailed. I, who had been impatiently awaiting the arrival of this vessel, sprang on to the taffrail and sang out:

"What lugger's that?"

"The *Seamen's Friend*," was the reply.

"Who is the man that answers?" I called.

"Jarvie Files."

"Right y'are!" I cried.

The lugger's helm was put down, and she came alongside. One of my Whitby men was on the forecastle, keeping what we term at sea an "anchor watch." I told him to remain forward.

"There are men enough," said I, "belonging to the lugger to answer my turn."

The others and the Kanaka were in the forecastle asleep. Jimmy was awake in the cabin, where the lamp was alight. Several figures came over the side, and one of them, catching sight of me, said:

"Are you Mr. Fielding?"

"I am."

"I'm from Capt'n Round, sir. The coast'll be dear, I allow; but we'll have to look sharp. Where's the stuff?"

"Follow me," said I.

This Jarvie Files, and, perhaps, five others – men heavily booted, with great shawls round their necks and fur caps drawn down to their eyebrows – tramped after me into the cabin. Lanterns were ready. I showed them the hatch of the lazarette; and, in about half an hour's time, they had cleared out the last case, had stowed it in the lugger alongside, and were hoisting their sail. Their dispatch was wonderful; but they were of a race of men who had been disciplined into an exquisite agility in the art of dishing the revenue by the barbarous severity of the laws against smuggling in that age. I watched the big boat haul her sheet aft and stand away with her head to the eastward. She blended quickly with the obscurity and I lost her. I guessed she was feigning a "ratch" toward the Ostend coast, to dodge any shore-going eye that may have rested upon her, and that presently she would be shifting her helm for Pegwell Bay, where carts waited to convey the silver to my uncle's house.

I went into the cabin when I lost sight of her, lay down, and slept very soundly and dreamt happily. I was too tired to rejoice; otherwise I should have mixed a tumbler of spirits and lighted a pipe, and enjoyed the luxury of a long contemplation of the successful issue of Tulp's expedition.

I awoke in the grey of the dawn, and, going on deck, found promise of a fine day. I searched the shore and beach, down in the bay and about the river, with the brig's telescope, but nothing showed that was to be likened to the lugger of last night. After breakfast, the Whitby men came aft and said they'd be glad to go ashore soon. They wanted to get to Ramsgate, where they might find a coalman bound to their port. I answered that I could not leave the brig until a caretaker arrived, and that there was no use in their going ashore unless I went with them to pay them off at my uncle's. However, half an hour after this a punt, with a big lug, put off from Deal Beach, and blew alongside with five men in her, two of whom came on board and said that they had received instructions from Captain Round to take charge of the vessel while she lay at anchor.

"All right," said I, "you are the men I have been waiting for," and I told the Whitby fellows and the Kanaka to collect their traps and get into the boat. I then took Jimmy into my cabin and gave him several parcels of Greaves' effects to convey to the punt. All that belonged to Greaves I took; I cleared the cabin of nautical instruments, books, chronometers, and the rest, and left nothing but dirt and dust for old Tulp. I then got into the boat with Jimmy, and we headed for the beach.

When Miss Aurora went ashore her gaze had been bent landward; she never once turned to take a farewell look at the old brig that had saved her life. I could not blame her. She had had enough of the little ship. For my part, I could look at nothing else as we rowed to the beach. I had not been out of the brig since I had landed on the island to get the dollars out of the cave. For many long months had the *Black Watch* been my home, the theatre of the most dramatic of all the passages of my life; she had earned me a fortune; she had rescued me from drowning; I could not take a farewell look without affection and regret. She sat very light, and in her faint rolls hove out a little show of grass; but her copper was cleaner than I had supposed it. Her sides were worn and rusty, her rigging slack, her masts grimy, her whole appearance that of a vessel which had encountered and victoriously survived some very fierce and frightful usage in distant seas. I kept my gaze fastened on her till the keel of the punt drove on to the beach.

The sailors and the Kanaka handed their chests over to the landlord of an ale-house for safe keeping; I then gave each man, and drank myself, a pint of beer, after which we trudged off toward my uncle's house. We talked merrily as we went; our hearts were filled with the delights of the scenes and sights of the summer land; our salted nostrils swelled large to the sweetness of the haystacks and the aromas of the little farmyards and orchards we tramped past; no man would smoke, that he might breathe purely.

My uncle awaited us; my aunt gave me such a hug as the Prodigal Son would have got from his mother had his father been out of sight. I asked after Madam Aurora; she had driven to Deal that morning to shop, and, as she had borrowed twenty pounds, her shopping might probably run into some hours. It was one o'clock; a hearty meal had been prepared in the kitchen for the men, and while they ate I dined with my uncle and aunt off a roast leg of pork in the parlor adjacent, where we could hear the fellows' gruff voices and Jimmy's bleating laugh. The chests had been securely landed, Uncle Joe told me, and safely housed in his cellar. The silver made five loads. They asked me to tell the whole story of the discovery of those dollars over again, and my aunt put many questions about the Señorita Aurora, who, she declared, was the finest, most elegant, and genteel lady she had ever seen in her life.

When we and the men had dined, my uncle called them into the parlour and took a receipt from each of them for three hundred and fifty dollars, which he paid down in English gold. They thanked him for his hospitality, begged their humble respects to the lady Aurora, wished me many blessings, and with some hair-pulling and scrapes and bows got out of the room and went their ways. I never saw or heard of those honest fellows again, though I learnt that on this same day, after leaving us, they and the Kanaka took a boat and sailed across to Ramsgate, where, no doubt, they found a north-country collier bound to their parts.

Jimmy had brought Captain Greaves' belongings under his arm and on his back, the others carrying a few of the parcels among them. My uncle and I overhauled the poor fellow's effects, and then sat down to talk over his will, to write a letter to Mynheer Tulp, and to consider how we were to convert what silver belonged to me and to Greaves into British currency.

"First of all, Bill," said my uncle, "we'll knock off a letter to Tulp and send it away. Let him fetch his brig and his money; there'll be more daylight to see by when they're out of the road."

So I took a sheet of paper and addressed a letter to Mynheer Bartholomew Tulp at his house in Amsterdam, his residence being known to me through perusal of Greaves' papers. I stated that the brig *Black Watch* had arrived in the Downs on the previous day, that her voyage had been successful, that the cargo was housed ashore, and that Greaves had died during the passage home; and I begged Mr. Tulp to lose not a moment in visiting me at my uncle's house, that he might receive what belonged to him, for peril lurked in the protracted detention of the brig in the Downs. When this letter was written I dispatched it to Sandwich by Jimmy, that it might be transmitted without delay.

"Tulp will take his dollars at his own risk," said my uncle, blowing out a cloud of smoke; "your own dollars and the silver belonging to Greaves'll have to be negotiated cautiously; it's a lot of money to deal with, and it mustn't be handled in the lump. We'll have to work by degrees through the money changers; find out several of them in London, and deal with 'em one arter the other at intervals. Then we may make it worth the while of the smugglers, some of my own particular friends, to relieve us of a chest or two. My son-in-law'll take some; he's often trading Mediterranean way; but I'm afeared it won't do, Bill, to trouble the banks; we don't want any questions to arise. How it might work out as a matter of law I don't know; safest to look upon these here dollars as run goods and treat 'em accordingly."

I fully agreed with him, and it was settled that the money should be exchanged in the manner he proposed. We then talked of Greaves' will. Indeed, we talked of many more things than I can recollect. Nothing, however, could be done until Mynheer Tulp turned up. Every day I boarded the brig and saw that all was right with the dear little ship; and I remember once that while I stood with the lady Aurora and my uncle on Deal Beach, viewing the vessel and recounting our experiences in her yet again, it occurred to me to buy her, to re-equip her, put a good sailor in command of her, and send her away to make a rich voyage for me. I smiled when I had thus thought; it had been Miss Aurora's notion, and had she consented to marry me I daresay I should have bought the brig. But I said to myself, "No"; the brig is not Tulp's to sell; I must deal with her owner, whose curiosity might prove inconveniently penetrating; I have my money and I'll keep it; and so I dismissed the *Black Watch* as a venture out of my head.

One day – I think it was about a week after I had written to Amsterdam – I returned with my lady Aurora to my uncle's house after a morning's stroll about Deal. I heard voices in the parlour; Miss Aurora went upstairs.

"Who is here?" said I to the old chap who opened the door.

"Mr. Tulp, from Amsterdam, sir," he answered.

On this I knocked upon the door and entered the parlour.

Had I lived with Mynheer Tulp a month I could not have carried in my head a more striking image of the man than my fancy had painted out of Greaves' brief description of him.

He was a little, withered old fellow, a mere trifle of months, I daresay, on this side seventy; nose long and hooked, face hollow and yellow, eyes small, black, and down-looking, though often a leary lift of the lids sent a piercer at the person he talked to; he wore a wig, and was dressed in the fashion of the close of last century. He was the man I had dreamt of – the substance of the phantom I had beheld when I looked at poor Greaves, and wondered whether his dollar-ship was a dream or not.

My uncle was red in the face and was talking loudly when I entered.

"So! Und dis vhas Mr. Fielding?" said Mynheer Tulp standing up and extending his hand. "Veil, I vhas glad to see you."

He uttered even this commonplace slowly and cautiously as though he feared his tongue.

"Now, Bill," cried my uncle, "I want you to show Greaves' bond to Mr. Tulp; for he says you aren't entitled to more than your wages – not even to them as a matter of law, seeing you wasn't shipped by him."

"I tink you vill find dot right," said Mynheer Tulp.

I carried Greaves' bond, as well as his will, in my pocket; I placed the bond or agreement upon the table, and Mynheer Tulp, picking it up, put on a large pair of spectacles and read it through.

"Dis vhas of no use," said he.

"We'll see," said my uncle.

"Understand me, Mr. Fielding," continued the little Dutchman. "I don't mean to say dot you have not acted very veil, und dot you vhas not entitled to a handsome reward, vhich certainly you shall have; but vhen you talk to me of dirty odd tousand dollars – six tousand pounds of English money – " he grinned hideously and shrugged his shoulders.

"What would you consider a handsome reward?" said I.

"You vhas second mate. I learn from your uncle dot your life vhas safed by my brig. Should I sharge you mit safing your life? No. But if I vhas you I should consider der safing of my life as handsome a reward as I had der right to expect for any services afterward performed. But mit you, my good young man, I goes much further. You have navigated the brig safely home mit my money, und I say help yourself, my boy, to five hundred pounds of der dollars before I takes them."

"Before you takes 'em!" cried my uncle. "You'll need every line-of-battle ship that Holland possesses to enable you to catch even a glimpse of the dollars afore all things are settled to my nephew Bill's satisfaction."

"Vhat vhas your name again, sir?"

"Captain Joseph Round."

"You hov der looks of an honest man, Captain Round. You vould not rob me?"

"Not a ha-penny leaves this house," said my uncle, "until Bill here has taken his share according to your skipper's bond, and until he's deducted the money that the captain has left by will, lawfully signed and witnessed."

"I likes to see dot vill," said Mynheer Tulp, speaking always very composedly, and occasionally snapping a look under his eyelids at one or the other of us.

I put the will on the table. He picked it up and read it. When he had read it he again grinned hideously, and said:

"Your name vhas Villiam Fielding?"

"Yes."

"Und you benefit under dis vill to der amount of von tousand pounds?"

"Yaw," said I.

"Und you vitness der vill dot vhas to benefit you? Shentlemen, it vhas not vorth the paper it vhas wrote on;" and he threw the will upon the table.

"It matters not one jot," said I, who, as I had never attached the least significance to the legality of this sailormade will, was in no wise astonished, because I reckoned old Tulp perfectly right. "About forty-two thousand pounds' worth of the thirteen tons of dollars I have brought home for you at the risk of my life I keep, Mynheer. D'ye understand me? I *keep*, I say," and I repeated the sentence thrice, while I approached him by a couple of strides. "Seven thousand are mine; the rest will go to the erection of a church."

"Der money," said Mynheer Tulp without irritation, though his yellow complexion was a shade paler than it had been a little while before, "vhas left to der Church of Englandt?"

"You have read it," said I.

"Now, shentlemen," continued the little Dutchman, "dere vhas a Church of Englandt, certainly; but dere vhas no Church of Englandt dot a man can leaf money to."

"You know a sight too much," shouted my uncle. "The money's in my cellar, and there it stops till you settle."

"Der Church of Englandt," said Mynheer Tulp, "vhas a single body dot has no property. You cannot leaf money to der Church of Englandt. Dot alone makes my poor stepson's vill nooll und void."

"The money remains where it is – " began my uncle.

"Do you allow," I interrupted, "that Captain Greaves has a right to his share?"

"Do I allow it? Do I allow it?"

"You allow it. He could, therefore, do what he likes with his share?"

"Dot vhas right."

"Do you know that he wished a church to be built as a memorial to his mother who was your wife, I believe?"

"Dot vhas very beautiful. But he vhas dead, und dot vill vhas not vorth the ink it took to write out. I vhas next of kin, und I takes my poor stepson's share."

When he had said this, my uncle and I spoke together; and from this moment began an altercation which I should need a volume to embody. Tulp lost his temper; my uncle roared at him; I, too, being furious with the meanness of the wretched little beast, often found myself bawling as though I were in a gale of wind. Tulp's threats flew fast and furious. Uncle Joe snapped his fingers under his long nose, and defied him in a voice hoarse and failing with exertion. I began to see the idleness and the absurdity of all this, and, throwing open the parlour door, I exclaimed:

"Mr. Tulp, get you back to Amsterdam, and there sit and reflect. When you come into our way of thinking, write; and then fetch your money. Go to law, if you please. The Spanish consignees of the dollars will thank you."

The perspiration poured from the little man's face, and he trembled violently. His yellow complexion under the pressure of his temper, which often forced his voice into a shriek, had changed into several dyes of green and sulphur, like that of one in a fit. He stared wildly about him in search of his strange little hat, which, however, he forgot he had already snatched up and was holding.

"You'll have to bear a hand with your decision," cried my uncle, whose face looked almost as queer as Tulp's, with its purple skin and blue lips; "they're beginning to ask questions about the brig, and if you don't send for her soon she'll be *going a-missing*. You know what I mean. The Goodn's are handy, and my nephew ain't going to forfeit his rightful share of the dollars because of *her*. The recovery of this silver is to be more than a salvage job to Bill. There's nigh upon forty thousand pounds belonging to you a-lying in my cellars, but if ye aren't quick in fetching it something may happen to oblige me to send all them chests out of my house, and then it'll be no business of mine to larn what's become of 'em."

The little Dutchman, now perceiving that he held his hat, clapped it on his head and ran out of the room.

We heard no more of him that day; though next morning the old longshoreman who waited upon my uncle said that he had seen the little man pass the house, pause, walk up and down irresolutely, then hurry away in the direction of Sandwich. As I could not get to hear of him at Deal I guessed he lurked in Sandwich, and caused Jimmy to make inquiries, which resulted in the discovery that Mynheer Tulp was stopping at the Fleur de Lys Hotel. Three days after he had visited my uncle he wrote to offer me half a ton of the silver, worth something over three thousand pounds, on condition that my uncle peaceably surrendered the rest of the money to him, and assisted him to convey it to Amsterdam. I answered this by repeating my uncle's threat, that if very shortly he did not agree to my terms the silver would be removed, my uncle would have no knowledge of its whereabouts, and I myself would go abroad.

On the morning following the dispatch of this missive, Miss Aurora received a letter; she read it and uttered a loud shriek, fell off her chair at the breakfast table round which we were seated, and lay upon the floor in a dead swoon. We thought she had died, and our fright was extreme. We picked her up and placed her upon a sofa, and went to work to recover her. Presently her sighs and moans satisfied us that she was not dead. I glanced at the letter she had received; it was in Spanish. I took the liberty of looking a little closely; it was signed by the Señora de la Cueva.

"She has heard from her mother!" I cried.

She rallied presently, and then followed a scene scarcely less exciting in its way than the shindy that had attended the visit of Mynheer Tulp. Miss Aurora read the letter aloud; and as she read she wept, then burst into fits of laughter, sprang about the room, sat again, continued to read, interrupting herself often by clasping her hands, lifting them to the ceiling, raising her streaming eyes, and thanking the Holy Mother of God for this act of mercy in utterance so impassioned that the like of it was never heard on the stage.

My homely uncle, my yet homelier aunt looked on, scarcely knowing whether to shed tears or to laugh. I was very used to her ladyship's performances, but there was something in this exhibition of ecstasy that went far beyond anything I had ever beheld in her.

"I rejoice indeed to learn that the *señora* is safe," said I.

"Oh, it is a miracle! a miracle!" she cried; and then she wept and laughed and carried on as before, reading aloud in Spanish, and lifting up her eyes in gratitude to the Blessed Virgin.

At last she calmed down, and we conversed without the interruption of emotional outbreaks. Her mother gave no particulars of her deliverance. Mr. Maxwell had received Aurora's letter; he was ill in his bed, therefore she, the *señora*, had made her way to London – choosing that port instead of Falmouth, because of the situation of Deal – intending to proceed to Sandwich. But her infirmities had overwhelmed her; the fatigue of the journey had been so great that she was unable to leave her room in London. Her daughter must come to her, and without an instant's delay.

Within three hours of the receipt of this letter my uncle drove the lady Aurora and me over to Deal, where we saw her safely into the London coach. She had said many kind things to me as we drove to Deal, had taken my hand and pressed it while she thanked me for – but what does it matter how and for what this young lady thanked me? She tried to exact many promises; I made none. Before she stepped into the coach she seized my hand, looked at me hard, and her fine eyes swam. Nothing was said; she took her seat; I and my uncle stood apart waiting while the coachman gathered his reins and prepared for the start. The horses' heads were then let go, I raised my hat, the coach drove off, and I saw no more of the Señorita Aurora de la Cueva. I say I saw no more of her; in truth, though I once again heard of her, I never received a single line from her. And possibly I should never have heard of her again but for her sending from Madrid a draft for the money she had borrowed from Uncle Joe. She warmly and gracefully thanked Captain and Mrs. Round for their hospitality, begged them to remember her most gratefully to her valued and valiant friend, their nephew, and then, so far as I was concerned, the curtain fell upon her forever.

Mynheer Bartholomew Tulp lurked through a long week at Sandwich. In that week he sent me four letters and each letter contained a fresh proposal. I sent a single reply: that every proposal must be hugely preposterous unless it went on all-fours with Greaves' will and the agreement with me. He was seen on several occasions in the neighbourhood of the house; once Jimmy perceived him looking in at the gate, and supposed that he meant to call; but the little man made off on finding himself observed.

At last, at the expiration of nine or ten days – and this brought us to a Monday – I received a letter from Mynheer Tulp. We were at dinner at the time; my uncle cried out:

"What does he say. Bill? Willing, perhaps, to spring another hundred pound?"

I read the letter aloud; it was well expressed, in good English. Mynheer said he had thought the matter over, and was prepared to settle with me on my own terms. He admitted that I had a right to the share which van Laar would have received; that Greaves' signature to the will indicated his wishes as to the disposal of his money, which, of course, he would have received as his share of the venture, had he lived. Would I permit him to call upon me?

I immediately dispatched Jimmy with an answer, and in half an hour's time the little Dutchman was seated in my uncle's parlour. He was submissive and, in his way, very apologetic. Yet, though he had come to confirm the terms of his own letter to me, midnight was striking before every point was settled. His rapacity was shark-like. It cost my uncle and me above an hour to make the little man agree to call the value of the dollar four shillings. He disputed long and shrilly over a small share that I claimed for the honest lad Jimmy. He opposed the repayment of the wages of the Whitby men and the Kanaka out of the common stock, as though he believed that my uncle would bear that charge! He was nearly leaving the house on the question of the sum due to Jarvie Files and his men for "running" the dollars. He insisted that my money and Greaves' should bear a proportion of the loss of the three tons of silver stolen by Yan Bol and his crew. He grew furious when my uncle insisted upon charging him for storage and risk, and thrice in *that* discussion arose to go.

But by midnight, as I have said, all was settled. He now asked leave to live in the house until he could remove his money to the brig, in which he proposed to sail to Amsterdam, taking with him for a crew the men of the *Seamen's Friend*. My uncle told him he would be welcome, giving me at the same time a wink of deep disgust at the motive of the old chap's request. It took us several days to count the dollars, and all the while little Bartholomew Tulp sat looking on. What was left as his share, after deductions, I never heard; it came, I believe, near to fifty thousand pounds. When the division was made he went on board the brig; Jarvie Files and his men carried his chests to the *Black Watch* in the dead of night, and when, next morning, I went down to the beach to look for the now familiar figure of the brig riding to her two anchors, her place was empty.

***

This, then, is the story of Greaves' discovery, and of the part I played in it. Of Yan Bol and his men I heard nothing for eighteen months; I then got a letter from Captain Horsley, dated at Whitby. He had touched at Amsterdam Island, found no signs of Yan Bol and his party, then dug in the place I had indicated without finding the silver. There was no look of the earth having been turned up in that place. A gale of wind blew him off the island; then, a fortnight later, he spoke a ship bound to Sydney, New South Wales, and learnt from her that she had picked up a party of seamen sixty leagues eastward of Amsterdam Island; they were six men, three of them in a dying condition for want of water. He had no doubt, and neither had nor have I, that they were Yan Bol and his mates; but what had the wretches done with the three tons of dollars?

Did I, when we had exchanged the large sum of dollars into English money, did I procure the erection and endowment of a church in accordance with the wishes of Michael Greaves? I answer yes; most piously and anxiously did I fulfil my friend's dying wish. Will I tell you the name of the church, and where it is situated? No; I have worshiped in it, but I will not tell you its name and where it is situated, because this book is a confession, and I am informed that if the descendants or inheritors of the Spanish consignees, or the owners of the dollars, learnt that a church had been built out of the money, they could and might advance a claim that would give all concerned in that church on this side great trouble.

One little memorial I erected at my own expense; it long stood in the garden of the house in which I dwelt for many years; need I tell you that it was a memorial to my well-beloved, faithful, deeply-mourned Galloon?

About the Author

WILLIAM CLARK RUSSELL (1844–1911) was born in New York to English parents. Both his mother, Isobel, through her family connection to poet Charles Lloyd, and his father, Henry, a musician and composer best known for writing such stirring anthems as "Life on the Ocean Wave" and "Cheer, Boys, Cheer", had artistic leanings.

Young William himself appears to have had a taste for adventure. It was reported that while at school he and a classmate, one of Charles Dickens's sons, had planned to run away.

William aged 5 years old.

At the age of 13 William became a midshipman in the British Merchant Service and his experience of sea life came from his eight years of service.

Midshipman Russell aged about 17 years old.

After leaving the sea, Russell worked as a stockbroker but decided he wanted to be a writer. His first work, a play, "Fra Angelo" was performed at London's Haymarket Theatre in 1865 but was a flop. He continued with his writing and often used his seafaring experience.

Russell's second seafaring novel, *The Wreck of the Grosvenor*, published in 1877, took two months to write and was sold to a publisher for £50 (the equivalent of the annual salary of a shop worker). The novel was an outstanding success and started a career in writing sea stories.

As an indication of the popularity of Russell's novels, Arthur Conan Doyle mentioned him in one of the Sherlock Holmes's stories, *The Five Orange Pips*, where Dr Watson is described as being "deep in one of Clark Russell's fine sea-stories until the howl of the gale from without seemed to blend with the text, and the splash of the rain to lengthen out into the long swash of the sea waves".

According to John Sutherland, Emeritus Professor of Modern English Literature at University College London, *The Wreck of the Grosvenor* was "the most popular mid-Victorian melodrama of adventure and heroism at sea". It was a bestselling book well into the first half of the twentieth century.

William Clark Russell, successful novelist, aged about 49 years old.

Contemporary Reviews of *List, Ye Landsmen!*

The Graphic, 30 September 1892. This was an illustrated weekly newspaper published in London from 1869 to 1932.

> Mr W. Clark Russell is very much himself, indeed; in his *List, ye Landsmen! – a romance of incident* (3 vols.: Cassell & Co.). It deals with such congenial things and persons as a secret voyage (in the Waterloo year) of the brig *Black Watch*, for the purpose of possessing and running home a Spanish treasure strangely lost, or rather hidden, in a desert island beyond Cape Horn; of the consequent perils and difficulties of the usual young British mate, after the skipper's death, with such shipmates as a mutinous and murderous Dutch crew and a fascinating Spanish lady; of the strange vessels encountered and the wonders of the sea; and altogether of as many adventures as would serve a more economical novelist for half-a-dozen full-sized stories. The tale starts, as is befitting the period, with a press-gang in the fertile hunting-ground of Deal, and hurries the reader along, with an interest which is never for a moment broken, until the young sailor who tells the yarn is left, as he deserves, in possession of an ample share of the dollars, but, happily though, perhaps, to the disappointment of readers of conventional views – not of the lady. There is, indeed, not a single love passage in all three volumes; but Mr. Clark Russell is invariably at his best in proportion as makes fewest sacrifices to the conventionalities. "Miss Aurora," the beautiful Spaniard, is very useful as throwing an extra glamour of romance into the general situation; but we fancy Mr. Clark Russell knows as well as anybody else that feminine interest is not his *forte*, and feels as fully as a great sea novelist of genius must needs feel, how very small is human sentiment, or even human passion, in the more than human presence of the world of waters *List, Ye Landsmen!* is less poetically impressive than several of its predecessors, possibly because the storm-fiend is less than ordinarily conspicuous; but as a "yarn" of days when a voyage might be equivalent to a man's whole life it leaves nothing to be desired.

Clarence and Richmond Examiner, 4 November 1893. Published in Grafton, New South Wales, Australia from 1859 and still published today as the *Daily Examiner.*

> From the moment when William Fielding is captured by a press-gang to his successful landing of the Spanish dollars, some three years later, the reader follows the career of Mr. Clark Russell's latest hero with continual excitement. One reads with growing interest of his being run down in the Downs, of his rescue by a ship's dog, of his agreement to join in the search for the wrecked Spanish ship with its hundred thousand pounds in silver, of the finding of the treasure, the saving of the Spanish lady, of the mutiny and the discomfort of the mutineers, and of his ultimate arrival at Deal; and one wonders whether in *List, ye landsmen!* Mr. Clark Russell has not produced his best romance. It is, in truth, a fine story, redolent of the sea, and giving a quite wonderful sense of reality. The characters are excellent: Jimmy is as good in his way as that other ship's boy, Ransome, in *Kidnapped*; and Galloon the dog, is a continual delight.

Also Available from Solis Press

Solis Press have also published *Wreck of the "Grosvenor"* by William Clark Russell both in paperback and in ebook formats.

The Wreck of the "Grosvenor" tells of the adventures of Edward Royle, the second mate on a sailing ship travelling from England to South America in the nineteenth century.

With a hard-hearted captain and a mutinous crew, it was never going to be an easy voyage. When Royle spots a vessel foundering at sea, the trouble really starts and he is forced to chose between duty and conscience.

The Wreck of the "Grosvenor" is perhaps William Clark Russell's most famous book. John Sutherland, Emeritus Professor of Modern English Literature at University College London described this as "the most popular mid-Victorian melodrama of adventure and heroism at sea".

This new edition from Solis Press of the 1877 bestseller has been completely revised and includes illustrations from the first US publication.

See our website for more information: http://www.solispress.com

Printed in Great Britain
by Amazon.co.uk, Ltd.,
Marston Gate.